T0354507

WINDOW
IN THE WORLD

ROBIN HONE

Order this book online at www.trafford.com
or email orders@trafford.com

Most Trafford titles are also available at major online book retailers.

Printed in the United States of America.

ISBN: 978-1-4669-7369-5 (sc)
ISBN: 978-1-4669-7371-8 (hc)
ISBN: 978-1-4669-7370-1 (e)

Library of Congress Control Number: 2012923926

Trafford rev. 01/15/2013

www.trafford.com

North America & international
toll-free: 1 888 232 4444 (USA & Canada)
phone: 250 383 6864 ♦ fax: 812 355 4082

CONTENTS

PART ONE

CHAPTER ONE

P RESSING HER HANDS TOGETHER, she stared into the dark and prayed as she had been taught, to ask for divine help. First, she prayed for the pain in her legs and feet to stop and she wouldn't hurt anymore, then she asked for sleep. She prayed that she wouldn't be cold anymore and that the hunger gnawing at her insides would go away and she wouldn't feel like she was starving. She *was* starving. She was completely exhausted but sleep would not come. After a time, almost miraculously there seemed to come an answer to her prayer. The pain *did* recede, she didn't shiver from the cold and finally she dozed fitfully.

Having known and overcome severe hardship, hunger and deprivation in her childhood, she thought as an adult she was well prepared for and could easily accept the worst with which this place with the foreign name could assail her. Again, she was wrong. The first few months at the Hidaka-sammyaku school of discipline were worse than anything Fumiko Fuchida could have imagined in her worst nightmares. In addition to the rigorous physical and mental conditioning to survive under adverse and adversarial conditions, the meals were of rice they had to grow themselves and fish they had to catch by hand. Her hair was cropped close, painfully hacked to less than an inch by a sharpened piece of flint for she was not yet allowed access to metal of any kind. She was permitted no possessions other than her rice bowl, a kimono, a belted jacket and pants and a pair of sandals. She didn't even have underwear.

She slept on a thin pad, on a bare floor in an eight-by five-foot room with no windows and no heat. Initially, as the only woman, she had the small room to herself but that gave way to her sharing a room with four other students, all men. She said her name was Fumiko but with her fair skin and crimson hair, she was certainly not Japanese.

The buildings were originally constructed of rough logs; the cracks between filled with a form of adobe. Over the many years that followed, the walls, porches, walkways and patios had been hand-finished, intricately carved and shaped. Dye and enamel were used to adorn the structures. The floors were rubbed smooth by thousands of bare and sandled feet over hundreds of years. In winter when severe cold and blowing snow assailed the tiny community, a hibachi in each room and their own body heat didn't keep them warm but it did keep them from freezing to death.

She and her fellow students learned how to move silently, to blend in with their surroundings and take advantage of the ever-changing shapes of light and darkness. They learned to capture and hold a person's attention with certain hand motions and the sound of their voice speaking softly, the ancient and later resurrected form of hypnotism.

Drugs, potions and ointments made from plants, the elements of the earth, the toxins of animals and reptiles and even those that could be purchased commercially were made into both healing and killing compounds.

Fumiko was always aware of them looking at her, wanting her, lusting after her body but she had no fear of an attack upon her person by any one or all of them together. That was part of the discipline to which *they* were subjected. A nearly—and occasionally completely—naked woman close enough to them to reach out and touch by young men with raging hormones, but forbidden to them thus added to the discipline training. At first she had suspected that this was the *real* reason she was here, just an instructional tool.

Then came the physical combat; how to attack and how to defend. The men were so much stronger, faster, more aggressive, resistant to the kicks, blows, chops and punches she attempted. Even attacking with a weapon such as a lance or a knife, they just took it away from her, bowed politely and handed it back which infuriated her. Whirling rapidly on one foot, arm outstretched and rigid, in precise form she could deliver a perfect spinning back-fist to an opponent's jaw which would momentarily stun him, at best, drop him to his knees for an instant. However, he would be on his feet and on guard again before she could deliver the follow-up blow. Whereas a simple open-hand slap to the face would flatten her to the ground and put her on her back so dazed she couldn't immediately get up. They would politely help her to her feet.

They never hit her or kicked her hard. A leg-sweep cut her feet from under her and landed her on her butt. Her opponent would bow, offer an apology and a hand up and say, "Gomen nasai, Fumiko."

An over-the-shoulder judo throw was pulled up at the last second allowing her to land in a rolling tumble rather than hard and flat on the ground which could have broken her spine. Their kicks and punches were to muscle which hurt, not to bone or joints that could disable and cripple. The young men were not so considerate to each other.

On the lean diet, she lost weight. They gave her small portions of their own meager rations, and she hated them for it. They set a snare and caught a rabbit, cooked it on a spit and gave it to her with rice and soy sauce, cabbage and baby ears of corn. With some understanding but mostly with pity and disgust they all sat and watched her eat the rabbit, ripping the half-raw flesh from the bones with her teeth. She hated them for giving her the food.

Over the next few months, she continued to fight with determination and a reckless disregard for her own safety. Gradually, with the teachings of the Master and help from the other students but mainly because she was bigger than they, she began to achieve some degree of success in hand-to-hand combat. On the few occasions when she actually won, they all gathered around to congratulate her. It only made her mad.

Even with the narrow loincloth-type undergarment they all used, any exaggerated arm or leg movement would pull the kimono apart enough to reveal her breast or her pubic area. That would attract the eyes of the men like a powerful magnet. She began using a narrower loincloth revealing more of her pubic area, and then she wore none at all. If only for an instant, in the middle of a long practiced, memorized and instinctive movement, her opponent's eyes would flick to her thick, rose-colored nipples or the light-colored hair visible between her legs and in that instant his discipline was gone and his training forgotten. In that instant, she struck, bringing the heel of her hand up to slam into his chin, then the hardened edge of her palm crashing down onto the bridge of his nose. She could feel the cartilage break under the blow. The shock and the pain were enough to immobilize, if only for two seconds. Two seconds was enough. It was enough time to follow-through with another spinning kick to the knee or a fist to the sternum; not enough to break but enough to hurt.

Slowly, over the following months, momentarily exposing herself and then striking, she began to win more fights than she lost. The men weren't polite to her anymore and they fought harder against her. She fought back just as hard and she didn't hate them anymore.

Weapons were issued, knives, throwing stars, thin needles and six-foot spears with razor-sharp broadheads twenty-eight inches long, swords and daggers with blades honed to incredible sharpness, and bows and arrows. Surprisingly in this modern world, firearms were not allowed here. They learned the nerve centers in the body that would paralyze, pressure points that would stop the blood flow. They learned how to survive, how to heal, how to dazzle and how to kill.

She gave up displaying her body. Using her sex to gain advantage over them no longer worked for they no longer succumbed to it. It remained, however, a powerful tool in her arsenal of weapons she could use later as was the deadly clear poison with which they all were taught to paint their sharpened fingernails.

The sharpening of the nails was cunning and perfected over centuries. The nails were not cut or filed to a point because it would be too obvious, particularly on a man. They were edged like a knife blade from beneath by hours of slow, careful shaving with a tiny file. Appearing to be normal from all outward appearances, they were poison-covered razor blades.

Along with the change in the curriculum to lessons more serious, the Masters were beginning to teach them how to use mind and imagination to create visions and illusions, and to make them real. Once learned, physical hardships, pain, hunger and cruelties could be ignored. Manifesting the mental illusion of lounging upon a sofa in silks in a warm comfortable room before a blazing fireplace, after a delicious dinner with the finest wine in a warm place, and one could sit and slowly freeze to death while never feeling the cold or being aware of dying.

The key to mastering the mental abilities was the same as the one perfecting their fighting skills. One must believe! Believe that you are stronger and faster and more deadly than your adversary. Believe that you are invincible, and you will be. Believe that you can control your body so that you can walk through fire, that you can ignore hunger and pain, and you can. In the final stage, believe that you are invisible and you won't be seen, believe that you are a phantom and you can walk through walls. It is said that it can be. `

Belief comes from faith and faith must be blind and all accepting. All truths and absolutes must be forgotten. Belief comes from a faith in a power beyond what is known and seen and heard. That it is only real if you can touch it is no longer true. Belief and faith and power are part of the oriental religion taught at Hidaka-sammyaku.

Three days into the final week she used her mind to create the illusion of warmth with no hunger and no pain. She knelt, put her hands together and prayed. It dulled her senses to an attack, but it was better than feeling the cold, the exhaustion, and the ravenous hunger of one naked, freezing, starving and hunted on the steep mountain slopes of Hidaka-sammyaku. If discovered and captured by some the hunters, there would be humiliation and possible expulsion. If found by others, there was the possibility she would be raped, even killed. This was survival of the fittest.

Crawling through and crouching down in the weeds, the bushes and the undergrowth, amid the trees and the spires of jagged rock, hiding by day, moving carefully by night, her body bare and shivering, afraid for her life, striving, fighting to live, her mind and her imagination took her to that warm room with the fireplace, the wonderful meal and the delicious wine. She would use her mind and pretend that she didn't feel the cold, the hunger and the deprivation. She would live within her imagination and pretend that she wasn't naked, dirty and weaponless. She would create illusions, believe in them and make them real. She could be warm, safe, comfortable and not hungry. She knew how to project those illusions. She could hypnotize with her eyes, her voice, and the subtle movements of her hands and her body. She could command and people would obey, she could immobilize and paralyze an adversary long enough to gain a second's advantage.

She knew how to kill in a second. She already knew how to use her sex to get what she wanted from men, now she knew how to use it to attract, to capture and hold, to elicit information and secrets, to put them completely under her control.

Oh! It happened so quickly! One moment she was alone and then he was suddenly there, right in front of her. He was reaching for her as she huddled beneath a bush, hunted, cold, naked and afraid. She didn't think. Her body reacted. Fingers straight and locked, she shoved them up in a lighting-fast jab into his throat that crushed his larynx before he could move or deflect the blow. She had not intended to kill Isoroku, but she did. On his knees, gasping for breath that would not come, agony and terror he tried to whisper, "Fumiko." Then he collapsed and died beside her.

"Isoroku!" she cried, grasping his body, lifting him and cradling him in her bare arms. "Forgive me," she continued, speaking English for the first time in months, momentarily forgetting her fluent Japanese. "I didn't mean . . ." The tears poured from her eyes and she was lost in the tragedy of what she had done. With no reason, in blind panic, she had killed a fellow student, a roommate and a friend because of fear. She had lost her discipline and her focus.

"Oh, God, why did they make me do this?" she cried out in anguish, once again reverting to the Japanese language.

No longer caring what happened to her and with what little remained of her strength, bruised and bleeding from cuts and scrapes, she carried and sometimes dragged Isoroku's body toward the camp at Hidaka-sammyaku, falling often, crawling on her knees, crying over him to confess to her Master what she had done.

From above, higher up on that cold, mist-enshrouded slope there came the sound of heavy footsteps tramping toward her. Bushes and saplings were brushed aside, weeds, grasses were crushed under foot, and a form appeared from out of the dense, wet fog not ten feet from where she lay, clinging to Isoroku's cold body. It was a shape in the form of a huge, powerful man-like creature with a massive bare chest, glowing green eyes and the face of something not human. In her delusions, she thought it said her name, her *true* name.

Starving, exhausted, her throat parched, in the depths of sorrow and anguish, she drifted into delirium and collapsed once again just barely conscious. Her strength was now completely gone along with her will to live. As she lay there dying, she imagined that the man creature she had seen earlier—the naked man-shaped monster with the terrible inhuman face—appeared beside her, towering over her, regarding her with fierce, green glowing eyes. Gently it took them—she and Isoroku—in powerful arms, depositing each over a broad shoulder and carried them away.

She awoke from what had been the strangest dream she ever had. In surprise, she found that she had somehow managed to make her way—with Isoroku's body—all the way to the closed gates of the compound where she once again collapsed and sank into unconsciousness.

At dawn, they discovered them, Isoroku dead and she close to it. Word was dispatched and the news spread quickly to the others scattered over the mountainside. The trial had ended. They abandoned their tactics and gathered quickly to learn the details surround the incident with Fumiko and Isoroku. The contest was over. It wasn't a game anymore.

The next day when she was rested and had eaten a bowl of rice with tender bamboo shoots, mushrooms and pieces of fish, seated on her knees in the main room, dressed in a warm kimono, she tearfully confessed to the Master and all the others standing around her what she had done.

"Dry your eyes, Fumiko. What is done, is done," the Master said. "It is karma. Tears and sorrow will not return Isoroku to life nor will it absolve you of his death. You must accept what is."

"He wasn't going to hurt me. He only wanted to help me. I didn't have to . . . I don't know why I did—"

"Do you *know* that? For certain, Fumiko, do you he wasn't going to hurt you?"

"Yes. Yes. We . . . we liked each other."

"All of you were sent out for five days, pitted against nature and each other to determine who would survive. You reacted as you have been trained to do. You survived."

"But I don't want to survive this way," came her mournful reply. "Yukimasu."

"No, Fumiko. That is not permitted. You will *not* go. You will stay. You will finish your training and learn to live with yourself."

"I cannot!"

"You will!"

"How can I?"

"You will."

"Yes, Master."

"In almost every class since the school began four hundred years ago, someone has died. Often, several have died. We have come to accept this." The Master looked around at the assembled group of rugged, handsome young men. "All of you knew that when you came here and you accepted the danger." Returning his attention to her, he said, "Fumiko, all of us, including me, I am sorry to say, thought you would be the one to fail, to die out there. We thought you the weakest."

"I know that."

"Death is, after all, but a part of living, the final act of being. It is natural and inevitable, something to be understood and accepted. Only the western culture and religions teach a fear of death and a desire to live forever. You live with honor and you die with honor. Sometimes a life must be taken as you move along the way but that changes nothing in the overall scheme of things, not for he who died or the one who cause it. Had it not meant to be, it would not have been."

"Is this true, Master?"

"It is true."

"I understand and I accept."

"Yet something still troubles you, Fumiko."

"Yes."

"Can we help you?"

"I don't know."

"Let us try."

"On my way here, out there in the mountains, I had a vision, a dream of someone, of some*thing* inhuman that appeared out of nowhere. I dreamed it came to help me. I know I was delirious and I imagined it, but it seemed so real."

"Tell me of this inhuman something."

She spread her arms in a helpless gesture. "It . . . it was just, just so big. It looked like a man, a very huge man, but it wasn't a man. It was too big and the face wasn't human. It was like . . . I don't know. Like a monster with huge tusks curving down over the lower jaw."

"And you were greatly afraid of this monster?"

"No, and that's the strangest part. I *wasn't* afraid. Somehow I knew he . . . it . . . wasn't going to hurt me. I thought it . . . he picked me up and carried me. Of course, the creature wasn't really there. It was just in my delirium."

"It may be true that you imagined this. However, there are stories and legends here in Japan, in China, Korea and Manchuria of fictional creatures with the body of a muscular man and the head, hands and feet of a beast, a serpent or a dragon. There were drawings, sketches and paintings in pen and ink and watercolors going back two thousand years depicting such creatures as the artist perceived them. And you are not the first here at Hidaka-sammyaku to relate such a tale of this creature."

"Are you telling me that what I saw was real?" Fumiko was more than dubious.

"Who can say," replied the Master, spreading his hands. "We believe nothing, doubt all things, yet accept everything as possible."

The following day Isoroku's body was cremated on a great log pyre that burned for many hours outside the compound as had so many before him who died in training and were burned in the purifying flames. He was still occasionally spoken of as though momentarily absent or he had gone on to a better place. When they graduated from the only school of its kind in the world, the small group of them stood in their kimonos and received the last words from their Master. The weapons with which they had become expert were given to them and displayed on the ground before each; the long sword, the short sword, the Shuriken, the garrote, the bow and arrows and the lance. They would not take these with them when they left the school for civilization had surpassed such simple implement of war. A Glock or an Uzi rendered the sword and the lance ineffective. A laser-sighted, silenced rifle made the bow and arrow obsolete. It was, then, the skills of the mind and the trained body that would carry them on in the ancient ways of enlightenment, the way of the Ninjutsu, the art of stealth and invisibility.

From their simple beginning as clans of peace-loving farmers nine hundred years ago, hunted by the samurai and forced to defend themselves almost completely without weapons, they learned the skills developed by the Tibetan monks to use an assailant's aggression against him. They never surrendered to the samurai and the feudal warlords who commanded them. Over the years, they improved their tactics until it was said of them that they could enter a room without being seen, kill an enemy and escape without making a sound. Only the discovery of a dead warlord alerted the guards to their past presence.

Over the hundreds of years that followed and into the twenty-first century, the clans continued to develop their skills with weapons in battle and their abilities with light and darkness and their talents to cloud the mind so they could not be seen, heard or touched. While retaining the simple name the clans were commonly called, they become the most feared assassins on the face of the earth.

Ninja!

CHAPTER TWO

T HE TWO UNIFORMED OFFICERS walked slowly with measured strides in perfect military step with each other, their footfalls echoing loudly in the tomb-like stillness of the long colorless hallway lined on both sides with locked, steel-barred doors. The officers' slate-gray uniforms were spotless, the creases in their trousers knife-edged, their buttons polished and shoes buffed to a high gloss reflecting the overhead lights. As deadly as the Black Angel with darkened wings and sightless eyes, the two uniformed men traversed the dimly lit hallway to take a life.

It had always been the same two men over the many years. How long had it been? Five, seven years? Ten years? Few remembered. Always the same two walked down that hallway a short time before dawn. They had come to be known, even among the other guards, as the Angels of Death.

The coldness of winter hanging just beyond the thick, high, cement outer walls was something talked about but not felt in the uninterrupted, unchanging sameness that surrounded those held behind the locked, steel-barred doors. The falling snow spreading its thick, white carpet over the ground was discussed but not seen for there were no windows in the rooms behind those locked, barred doors. It was 5:30 in the morning, Tuesday, December 15, 2006. Ten days before Christmas.

David Savage opened his eyes and lay for a moment on the hard bunk bed looking at the gray ceiling and the single, dim, unshaded but wire mesh-covered light bulb suspended from the ceiling. He had not been asleep. He had been just lying there waiting for them to come, the black angels. Up and down the corridor in identical little rooms with colorless ceilings and wire mesh-security coverings over the light bulbs, eyelids flickered open at the sound of the footsteps, leather soles slapping on the cement. They were men who had been unable to find sleep this dark night knowing that the next time or maybe the next, it would be for them that the angels would come. In the anxiety of the moment, none seemed to notice the subtle differences in the routine.

Thin, almost to being emaciated, with a gaunt face unshaved for the last week and a half—what was the point in shaving?—his eyes red and burning from lack of sleep, David Savage climbed from his bunk, rose to his feet and was standing there waiting when they stopped at his barred door. His shirt and pants of dull, faded blue cotton were wrinkled and soiled from several days without changing. No belt. Shoes with no laces and no coat, jacket or sweater. His cheap wristwatch with the black plastic strap lay on the small table beside his bed along with his other meager possessions. There was a framed photograph of a smiling, attractive woman flanked on either side by a young boy and girl, a couple of books, a lined tablet and pencil, two magazines and his glasses. He wouldn't be needing his glasses now. Wouldn't need his watch, either.

"Is it time already?" he asked. "I thought I had a little more time."

Metal rang faintly against metal as the door slid open along its grooved, well-lubricated track. Wordlessly the two guards entered his little windowless room and wrapped a chain around his waist, securing it with a brass lock. His wrists were put into handcuffs attached to the front of the chain. Another chain and cuffs locked his feet together so that he would be forced to walk in short, shuffling steps. He could not run.

"Why are these necessary?" Savage asked. "You've never done this before." He had never seen a prisoner taken in chains, just handcuffs. Sometimes not even cuffs. He really didn't care, he was just making conversation to cover his fear.

The chains, locks and cuffs were securely fastened and, taking him gently by each arm, the angels fell in on either side as they walked slowly back the way they had come. Their footsteps were not loud or measured this time, but slow and careful to keep pace with their manacled charge.

This was the time for which David Savage had waited, dreaded, and dreamed horrible dreams for four years. Every appeal exhausted, all hope denied, this was the only way left. It was finally over, the minutes, hours, days, and the years of just sitting and waiting to die.

There was a whispered word or two as he passed the other small, windowless rooms.

"So long, guy."

"Spit in their fuckin eye, Savage!" This was a Hells Angel from San Bernardino who had killed two rival bikers with a shotgun.

"I's gonna be right behind ja, white boy. They be com'n for me next, I a reckon. Next month, maybe."

"Don't let 'em give you no fuckin cigarette out there, Savage. It's bad for your fuckin health!" Loud, thunderous, and humorless laughter followed.

"It's a far, far better place you'll be a going than where the hell you are now, Davie."

"Addio, innocenza uomo. Avere Caraggio. Noi incoutrare dentro hell," the Mafia hit man intoned, his arms draped through the bars. He had killed seventeen men before the authorities caught up with him.

Also, there were the silent gestures. A simple uplifted hand from behind the bars, a slight nod and an understudying look from the men who had risen from their beds in the night and who now stood at the barred doors on each side of the hallway watching him being led away for the last time.

They knew him, although most had never even seen him more than once or twice because they were always locked down in their cells on Death Row. But, they had talked to him, long hours of conversation when there was little else to do but talk. There were persistent rumors that they were going to have television sets like the other prisoners, but so far, it hadn't happened. So they talked and they felt a comradeship shared by those few that were damned to know the exact day and time and manner in which they would die. Such knowledge would terrify most, and David Savage was terrified as he walked with his guards along the dimly lit path between the cells of Death Row to the long, narrow courtyard of the Pennsylvania State Prison. There he would be stood trembling and helpless against a cold rock wall with his hands manacled behind his back. He would be blindfolded and there he would be shot to death by a firing squad.

The men and women of the jury of the Superior Court had decided that he was guilty and the State of Pennsylvania was going to kill him. And the most terrifying thing of all was that, unlike the other men on Death Row, David Savage was innocent.

At the end of the corridor, he saw that massive steel door that separated the twenty cells of Death Row from the rest of the prison. It was standing open. He shuffled along, taking baby steps, held by his guards. Somewhere just outside in the courtyard, beyond another steel door, six men were loading their rifles, checking their sights, standing in the snow waiting for him. Five weapons contained live ammunition and one with a blank so that each man could believe that he had not been personally responsible for killing the condemned man. It was an idea originated years ago by some administrative bureaucrat who believed everybody needed an excuse, a way out, a means to avoid responsibility. An idea concocted by a man who had never held a rifle in his hands and therefore knew nothing of the difference between the recoil of a live shell and firing a blank.

In the doorway ahead, under the bright lights of the overhead floods positioned just inside and on the outside of the doorway, stood two more guards. Their uniforms also were clean, pressed and immaculate. Their brass emblems were polished, their faces clean-shaven and their hat-bill pulled low over their eyes.

He was nudged gently through the door and the two new officers took him by each arm to escort him the rest of the way along the hallway away from Death Row. With the chains clanking quietly, he walked between them. The angels remained behind. The massive steel door to Death Row slammed shut.

He had not known that there was a changing of the guard at the entranceway. He, as did the others, always believed that the angels took the condemned man right to the wall. But then, of course, nobody had ever returned to dispute that.

A few steps further on and through another door, he found himself in the main section of the prison with cell doors on each side and up three levels high with cement and steel walkways and stairs providing access to them. Here, he was turned over to yet another pair of guards, these in shirt and trousers without a tie or blouse, and they wore pistols in leather holsters at their side.

Yet another door and another corridor led to still another door to where two more guards waited. They also wore sidearms. Savage was completely confused now. There was definitely something wrong here. When the time came, the man was taken directly to the wall or to the gas chamber and it was all over in just a few minutes. The guards who brought the meals and the ones who wheeled the book cart from the library told them that. No reason for them to lie about it.

He had been brought along so many corridors and through so many doors, he had no idea where he was other than he must be in the main administration part of the facility. But why? Where were they taking him?

It was the clanking of the chains that gave him the idea. The belly chains and the leg irons. They were sometimes referred to as traveling chains. When a capitol prisoner was being moved any distance, like to a court appearance, he was chained this way. That made no sense now. The only place he was traveling to was the courtyard outside and the wall.

Then something else struck him. The walk from Death Row. The two guards. Where was the priest? There was *always* a priest or a minister there to accompany the condemned man to the gas chamber or to The Wall. He would come and they would pray together and then he would walk with them to the place of execution. It *always* happened that way. Where was the priest?

The cold, hard cement floor had long since given way to a carpeted one and the walls were not steel and concrete. There were offices and desks; cubicles partitioned off for privacy. There were dark, blank computer screens and silent telephones, all deserted at this early hour. A sign on the door to which he was being brought said, WARDEN.

Savage was ushered through the door where the prison director, Paula Bennett sat behind her large oak desk, her hands folded on its polished surface. The American flag and the Pennsylvania state flag stood behind her and between them was a large photograph of the Governor of Pennsylvania. One manila file folder lay squarely in the middle of the desktop. Other than a telephone, there was nothing else there. No pens, no paper, no desk pad; nothing to mar the glossy surface. The two guards stopped just inside the room and remained motionless, standing at parade-rest with their hands clasped behind them, one on either side of the door. A tall, immaculately dressed man stood behind the desk beside Bennett watching Savage enter. Although there were two leather chairs in front of the warden's desk, the prisoner was left stranding.

This was to be Warden Bennett's second execution since taking over the prison. After witnessing the first in the gas chamber, she had suffered a nervous breakdown. Still on heavy medication to counteract depression and anxiety, she had only recently returned to work. She was forty-six years old, the same age as the prisoner before her.

Paula Bennett wore a white, long-sleeve blouse with a large bow at the throat. Her suit jacket hung on the back of her chair to appear casual, but there were dark circles around her red eyes, the pupils constricted to pinpoints from the drugs, her face lined and drawn, her nerves on edge. There were streaks of gray in her hair that she no longer attempted to color over. Her hands folded on the desktop were clenched tight to keep them from shaking. She had yet to make her final decision, but time was running out.

Of the methods of execution, lethal injection, the gas chamber and a firing squad, this prisoner had chosen the latter for reasons she couldn't even begin to imagine. Being shot to death was considered by most to be medieval, barbaric, cruel and unusual punishment. Pennsylvania was one of only three states that still provided for capitol punishment in this manner, the other two being Utah and Idaho. Unlike Paula Bennett and all the rest of the ignorant do-gooders out there, the inmates of Death Row were thankful for this. Being stood up and shot to death by men with rifles was bad enough, but at least it was quick. A man could die like a man with some dignity. Being clamped into a chair and choking to death on deadly gas or being strapped down on a table and having poison pumped into your arm was worse than the dying itself. But what the hell did women or politicians know of dignity?

While the stress was painfully apparent on Paula's face, the older man at her side didn't seem to be bothered by anything. His gaze was as detached as was his manner, and his dress was immaculately perfect. His gray vested suit was tailored and very expensive, his long silver-gray hair was beautifully styled, and he wore gold-rimmed glasses, much like those worn by the German SS in all the World War Two movies. He was fifty-five, perhaps sixty but his strong, darkly tanned and handsome face revealed little of his age and the only striking feature about him was the absolute lack of any feeling or life in his gray eyes.

"Prisoner Savage." That's what Bennett had been taught to call the inmates. They weren't misters, they had no given names, they were just prisoners. "Prisoner Savage," she said without looking up from the folder. Her voice was low, almost a whisper. It was fifteen minutes 'til six.

"I know, Warden. Let's just get it over with. Why am I here, anyway?"

"Prisoner Savage," Bennett repeated for the third time, her voice a little louder, a little stronger this time. She touched the closed file folder with an index finger, pushed it a little, poked at it and for the first time looked up and spoke directly to him. "The execution has been postponed. You're going to Philadelphia. Right now."

"What?!" The prisoner was astounded.

"I don't understand it at all. But I have two orders here signed by the Honorable Ralph McAndrews, District Court of Appeals of the Third Judicial District. The first is staying your execution for fifteen days and the second is sending you to the Philadelphia City jail to be held pending a hearing."

"Wh—what?" Savage stammered the word this time. His knees almost buckled. The two guards stepped forward quickly to take him by the arms for support. "What kind of hearing?"

"I . . . ahh . . . don't know," Warden Bennett replied. "It doesn't say. I've been up most of the night trying to verify these orders ever since they arrived here yesterday evening. But as of yet I have been able to get in touch with Judge McAndrews. Yet the documents are official and I can't ignore them." She glanced quickly at the tall figure beside her and then back to Savage. "This is the man who brought the orders. His name is Killingsworth. He says he's your attorney."

"But," Savage protested, virtually hanging in arms of the two guards, "the Supreme Court refused to hear my case. There's nothing left." His voice began to break. During the long years, he had been preparing himself mentally for just this moment so that he could face it like a man, with courage and dignity. So he could stand there against the wall with his hands tied behind his back waiting for the bullets to slam into his chest and take his life without breaking down and slobbering like some despicable coward. He had resigned himself to his fait. It was unavoidable. He would accept it, and that was it.

Suddenly, from out of nowhere came a glimmer of hope, one more tiny chance that he might somehow be free and wouldn't have to die. There would be more waiting, more anticipation, more false hope, more disappointment always accompanied with the incomprehensible, overpowering sense of death at his elbow and in the end, the final result would be the same. He wouldn't be able to stand it again.

"Understand this is just a stay, Prisoner Savage, not a reprieve, so I don't want you to start hoping too much," Bennett said. "But there's always a chance."

"What chance? What are you talking about?" Savage questioned.

Something was very wrong here.

"I don't know any more than what I've told you. You are being transferred to Philadelphia on the chain. Maybe they have found new evidence or something. I just don't know. Good luck, Savage."

The tall lawyer walked slowly around the desk and directly up to Savage, looking at him very closely, cocking his head from side to side as though to view him from several different angles. Almost as though he was viewing an interesting specimen of some kind of unusual animal. His stare was unnerving. Warden

Bennett pulled out a tissue and patted her cheeks and forehead although it was not particularly hot in the room. If anything, it was chilly.

"Shouldn't they be going?" The lawyer asked Warden Bennett.

"Yes. You're right." She signaled the two guards. They continued holding Savage by the arms and walked him back the way he had come through the offices and beside the cubicles. The handsome, gray-haired lawyer strolled along beside them.

Glancing back one final time, Savage saw Bennett open the file folder once again and then hold her head with both hands as she read and reread the Orders from the District Court of Appeals judge.

Before he realized it, they had taken him through the administrative part of the prison and they were going out through the civilian entrance in front to a small courtyard where an armored, barred prison van baring the Great Seal of the State of Pennsylvania on the side was parked close to the door. Only slightly did he feel the sharp sting of the frigid winter air through his thin prison uniform, and completely unnoticed were the deep footprints left in the snow as two guards walked him the few steps to the van. His chains clanked loudly with every movement

As soon as Savage had left with the lawyer, Killingsworth, strolling along after him, Warden Bennett picked up the phone and punched in the number of the home of Tom Moore, the state appointed attorney for the prison, a man whom she didn't particularly like but whose help she desperately needed now. He answered after the third ring, just before it went to the voice mail.

"Tom, there's been a Stay of Execution."

"Savage?"

"Yes."

"You're kidding me." He was already dressed and ready to leave the house. He didn't want to be there and besieged by the media when the man was executed but he needed to be on hand shortly thereafter. There were always legal situations and problems popping up after an execution.

"No, I'm not kidding."

"You should have called me sooner."

"I've been trying to verify the documents."

"Documents? Plural?"

"There's also an order transferring him to Philadelphia."

"Why?"

"For a hearing."

"What kind of hearing?"

"It doesn't say."

"Something's not right here. Who issued the stay?"

"Third Judicial District Court of Appeals. I have the order on my desk."

"I'm on my way. Have you contacted the Governor or the Attorney General?"

"According to Savage's attorney, they have been notified and the orders were served on them."

"Who's the attorney?"

"Killingsworth."

"Put Savage in a holding cell and call the Attorney General at home. Wait a minute, I'll get you his home number."

"Savage is already gone." She was frantic by now. "He's on the chain to Philadelphia."

"What? Call the chain back."

"How?"

"I don't know. Go through the State Police . . . no . . . it's gotta be through the AG's office. The Attorney General has authority over the traveling guard. They've got a radio or a mobile phone in their vehicle. Tell him to get in touch with them. Tell 'em to bring Savage back here immediately and put him in a holding cell. He's not to go to Philadelphia."

CHAPTER THREE

"I HAVE ALWAYS LIKED WESTERN women," he said in perfect English with only the slightest hint of a British accent. That told her he had been toured by an English voice coach or he had been educated in Great Briton when he was young, then spent enough time in America to almost lose the accent. "Because western women are so beautiful. Tall, statuesque and shapely."

"Arigato goziemashita, Tokushima-san," she replied in equally fluent Japanese, bowing her head politely as she spoke. He could not immediately place *her* accent.

Her white, strapless gown revealed smooth, sun-darkened shoulders, deep cleavage and outlined a muscular body with a narrow waist and wide hips while concealing soft-skinned, provocatively curved legs. Her lips were shaded between rose pink and red, there was just a hint of eye shadow, her face as deeply tanned as her shoulders, fingernails long and polished to match the lip-gloss. The earrings she wore were little golden circles of small stones reflecting flashes of blue light when she moved her head. The diamonds were real, flawless and worth a small fortune.

With a faint clicking of chopsticks against fine china plates and black-lacquered bowls and ice tinkling in cut-glass crystal in the background, sushi and rice with stir-fry vegetables and soy sauce, thin sliced Teriyaki beef strips with bean sprouts were all laid out on the elegant table. Although exclusively and traditionally Japanese in cuisine and decor, the furniture was European with regular four-place dining tables and intricately crafted French chairs. At this hour only a few other couples, all Japanese, shared the elegant private dining room and enjoyed the breathtaking view from the fiftieth floor restaurant overlooking the streets and the lights of downtown Tokyo at night. The men wore expensive, tailored suits and the women were fashionably dressed in suits, gowns and dresses purchased at the finest stores in America, France and Japan. There wasn't a kimono to be seen.

Fifty-seven years old, fabulously rich, trim and in excellent health and physical condition, gray just beginning to spread up from the temples into his otherwise jet black hair, Heroshi Tokushima was courteous, polite and considerate in the old Japanese tradition, yet self-confident almost to the point of arrogance. One of the ten richest men in the world, he was accustomed to having anything he wanted, any *woman* he wanted, and he enjoyed the subtle attention he was getting in the company of this beautiful Caucasian redhead in the exclusively Oriental restaurant.

"Another reason I am attracted to western woman, is because they are so independent, not subservient as are most Japanese women. That appeals to me." Receiving no response, he continued. "And your hair, cut as short as it is, is the color of gold in the sunset, not dark like ours." Although he should have known, it did not occur to him that she was wearing a wig. "Your eyes are as blue as the sea. You are young, only twenty-four, I believe."

"Twenty-six," she corrected.

"Ahh, yes. Twenty-six." He knew her true age was not twenty-four but attempted to appeal to a woman's vanity and her eternal desire for youth. The tactic hadn't worked, and he didn't know she, too, was lying about her age. She was twenty-nine. "You must have heard something of me or you would not have accepted my dinner invitation."

"Hai, Tokushima-san. One cannot spend time in Japan without knowing the name of the president and CEO of the second largest electronic manufacturing company in the world. I am honored that you would want to meet me, but I have been wondering why."

"I confess," he replied, changing his approach to one of honesty, and attempted to refill her cup with rice wine heated to exactly the right temperature, "that I was merely curious when I first heard about you. Frankly, what I heard was hard to believe."

"Indeed? What have you heard about me that was so hard to believe?" She appeared slightly amused.

"Each year Japan is becoming more and more modern and Western in its culture. The old ways are not only being abandoned, they are being forgotten. What was for hundreds of years the way of life for the Japanese, the pride of the Samaria, is fast fading into obscurity. There are some here who do not wish that to happen so a school in the Hidaka-sammyaku Mountains which was begun hundreds of years ago to teach the old ways is being funded and maintained. This of course, is being done in secret because not only do some of the classes go on for years, many of the things taught there would be approved by the government, and they can be fatal.

"If it is such a secret, why are you telling me?"

"Partly, in answer to your first question."

She raised her eyebrows slightly.

"I am telling you nothing you don't already know. You were the first western woman to have attended the school at Hidaka-sammyaku and the only woman ever to complete the course."

She hid her startled reaction almost perfectly. Only a slight widening of her eyes gave her away. How could he have known?

"Then I learned this, I was totally intrigued and arranged an introduction. Quite frankly, I'm surprised you accepted on such short notice."

She had regained complete control of herself now but it was too late. He had seen her react to the knowledge she couldn't have even suspected he knew. No one knew. That was part of the contract, the arrangement, the deal. No one was ever to know.

"But I confess, you are certainly not what I expected."

"And what did you expect, Tokushima-san?" The damage was done and she made no attempt to hide her amusement this time.

He laughed lightly, feigning embarrassment. "Someone, ah, let us say, less feminine than you. Certainly not a woman of such incredible beauty."

"You are most complimentary." Again, she bowed her head respectfully.

"There is little in the world and nothing in Japan I do not hear of. Knowledge is a power, often more so than money, and I am in a position to have that power."

"Why would you be interested in Hidaka?"

"I will trust you with a great secret. I am certain it will be safe with you, as yours is with me." He nodded his head slightly and she responded in kind. "I . . . that is . . . my company," he continued, lowering his voice, "contributes financially to support Hidaka, to keep the ancient Japanese traditions and customs alive"

"Traditions and customs?" she asked with a raised eyebrow.

He merely smiled and held out his hands as though to answer, what can I say?

"Ah so desu," she replied with an understanding nod.

"You must know some very important, very influential men to have even been admitted."

"Money off times opens doors."

"It does, but not at Hidaka." He glanced at the faint, thin, slightly curved scar running from the center of her left eyebrow an inch and a half up her forehead. She had lightly covered it with makeup and he would have never noticed it had he not know it was there.

She raised the warm sake to her lips but did not drink. She watched his eyes explore her face, linger on her breasts and shoulders. She displayed no emotion or expression.

"You are well disciplined."

"Thank you."

"I was told that while there, you . . . ah, you had somewhat of an argument, perhaps a romantic quarrel of some kind with your lover. That you . . . I am told . . . you killed him. Could that be true?"

"No."

"No?" You did not have a lover at Hidaka, or you did not kill him?"

She smiled and in English, said, "Mr. Tokushima, as the Americans say, you are fishing."

Also switching language as easily, he replied, "I understand the English metaphor and I assure you I am not, as you call it, fishing. You spent twenty-five months in the Hidaka-sammyaku Mountains under the most severe life and death conditions." He got no response, so he dropped the bomb on her. "There, you were known as Fumiko Fuchida." This got another reaction, but only a very slight one. He went on. "You were the only woman at Hidaka, surrounded by twenty or so handsome, virile men, most of them younger than you, and you claim you did not have a lover among them? I find that hard to believe." He cocked his head slightly partly in question and partly in challenge.

"As you seem to know, Hidaka-sammyaku is a school of discipline. It is also called a survivalist school," she said in reply, giving him no credit for his knowledge. The only serious one outside of the Soviet Union and I couldn't get into that one. I survived."

"Yes, Fumiko, you did. You survived. Do you intend to go on to the next stage? There are many more years of training necessary to achieve perfection of your skills."

She gave him a slight noncommittal shrug of the shoulders.

"May one ask why a person such as you would volunteer for and endure the hardships of Hidaka?"

Again, she shrugged. "I was sent."

"That is all? You were sent?"

"Hai."

"Why would someone send such a beautiful woman to Hidaka and teach you to kill?"

"You'll have to ask him."

During the time in which another couple entered the room and was seated, he picked up a bit of fish with his chopsticks and popped it into his mouth followed by sake. He had a vague idea of who might have gotten her into the school, but he knew it would do no good to ask. If he was right, both the organization and the man behind the organization were wealthy, powerful and had purchased at least two million dollars of specialized electronic equipment form his company over the last two years.

He abruptly changed the subject. Occasionally such a tactic would trigger a definitive reaction that would reveal something of significance. Although he doubted it would with this woman, he had already gotten two involuntary responses from her, slight though they were. "I have a proposition. I would like to hire you, Fumiko, to work for me. I have several western women in my company here in Japan. You would be an asset for us and it would be financially appealing to you."

"Work for you? How? As a geisha?"

"Geisha is an obsolete term. Let us just say I have many American and European customers who would enjoy the companionship of a lovely western woman during their stay in

Tokyo. You would merely entertain them. How you did it would be up to you."

"How much would you pay me?"

"How much do you want?"

"More than you have."

Tokushima raised his head and laughed softly. "Are you really worth that much?"

"Is that why you have invited me to diner? To offer me a job?" She made it sound like an insult. Then he noticed she had moved her food around in the bowl and on the plate but eaten none of it.

"Truthfully, Fumiko, no. I just wanted to see you. Nothing else. I certainly didn't intend to invite you to dinner until I saw you downstairs in the lobby. Your beauty has captured me."

"Arigato, Tokushima-san."

"My name is Heroshi. Will you say it?"

"Yes. Heroshi."

"Should I call you by your western name, your *real* name? In Roman mythology you are goddess of the hunt, identified with the Greek goddess, Artemis."

"Tokushima-san," she said in Japanese, "just what is it you want of me?"

"I would add to your worldly experiences."

"You think I am inexperienced?"

"In some things, perhaps. Yes. There is much I could teach you. Much you could learn about pleasure and fulfillment."

"If that be true, I would learn these things from the man of my secret dreams."

Taken aback, he questioned, "Your secret dreams? And just who is this man?"

"I will know him when I meet him."

"You have not yet met him?"

"I . . . don't think so." It was the first time she had hesitated in her answer as though she was unsure.

"Then I could be he."

"What of your wife?"

"What of her?" He was truly surprised at the question. "She understands."

"In the western world, we believe in fidelity."

"Now, I *know* that isn't true."

"Well, then, Tokushima-san, in *my world,* I do. You should also know in Roman mythology my name also means chastity."

"Is that so?"

"You know it is."

"I honor your beliefs. I would do nothing to bring any dishonor upon them."

"Then I don't understand what it is you want. Certainly not to hire me."

"I thought I was clear. You are a very desirable woman. I would like you to be available to me. Nothing personal, no commitment, just mutual pleasure. You would enjoy it."

"Perhaps, Heroshi, but I'm afraid I am not going to have the chance to find out. I have been called back to the United States and my plane leaves tonight. I was preparing to check out of the hotel when I received your invitation."

"That gives us very little time."

"That gives us *no* time." Having neither eaten a morsel of the meal or drank a drop of the sake, she touched her lips with the napkin which absorbed whatever mist of the Sake that had torched them and, pushing the chair back, got gracefully to her feet. There was an audible gasp of disbelief from the other diners that she had actually stood up while he was still seated.

Ignoring the affront and ignoring the reaction of the other restaurant patrons, he quickly got to his feet and stood in front of her. They were eye to eye for a few seconds. "While I understand some of western culture and I thought I understood western women completely, *you* are a paradox."

"Thank you for a wonderful evening, Tokushima-san. You have made my last day in Japan a most pleasant one."

"I regret that it must end so abruptly."

"All things must end. Maybe we will meet again someday."

"I hope not, beautiful Fumiko," he replied, switching to English once again. "If we did, it would not be my *bed* you would seek."

"Have no fear. You are well protected."

"The world is changing. I'm not sure I understand it anymore." He took her arm carefully, insuring that no other parts of their bodies touched, and escorted her to the elevator where they put on their shoes, then went down to the lobby and to the front doors. Declining his offer to escort her in his limousine, she signaled a cab to take her to her hotel and then to the airport. She wanted no more mention of the survival school referred to as Hidaka on the northern-most island of Hokkaido.

As the cab pulled up he held onto her arm not allowing her to step to the waiting cab. "Don't go, Fumiko. Stay with me. I want you. I will give you anything you desire."

Swiftly as a striking snake she turned, stepped to him, put her left hand on his shoulder and the other behind his head. Wearing three-inch heels, she could look down at him. "I cannot be bought, Heroshi," she said softly as her nails dug deeply into the back of his neck but without breaking the skin. Her breath was hot on his face. She pressed her cheek to his, her lips touching his throat in a gossamer kiss.

Realizing what had happened, the touching of their bodies, for just an instant he stiffened and there was a brief look of terror in his eyes.

"Good-bye, Heroshi." She kissed him quickly on the lips. Then she was in the cab and gone.

"An unusually beautiful woman for an occidental, Tokushima-san," his bodyguard said, stepping forward after the taxi had pulled away. He had remained discreetly in the background but always close enough to prevent a direct attack. They both watched the cab maneuver into the main stream of traffic and disappeared into the distance. "She moves with the grace of a cat."

He was a samurai, from a family with a six hundred-year heritage of the samurai warrior. He was as good with a sword as he was with a knife, a pistol or a rifle. He had been a Japanese Imperial Marine stationed on Okinawa after Japan had taken it back from the Americans. After his discharge from the military, he had continued his martial arts skills and was considered a Master. A powerfully built man with a massive chest and bull neck, he was not greatly intelligent but fiercely loyal. Not handsome, but he was attractive to women as rugged football players appeal to them. He had been occupied with watching her and had not seen the moment of terror in his boss' eyes when the woman kissed him. Nor could he sense the panic or hear the pounding of his heart.

"A cat that has claws," Heroshi managed after regaining control of himself without anybody noticing his moment of loss.

"She really seemed to like you. I think she'll be back." He nodded his head assuredly.

"You think nothing, Wakayama. You know nothing. You see nothing. Why do I keep you? You are worthless!"

"Tokushima-san, I . . . I don't understand. I thought you—"

"You just stood there and let her touch me."

"You . . . I . . . you did not want her to touch you? I thought you wanted her to touch you. I . . . I don't understand."

"Stupid fool! She put her hands on me. I could feel her mouth at my throat and her nails against my neck."

"A most intimate gesture, sir."

"Idiot! Her fingernails were coated with poison. If they had broken my skin I would have been dead in seconds."

"What? Poison, you say? Her . . . but . . . why? How? Gomen nasai, Tokushima-san. I didn't know." Wakayama was aghast.

"No, of course you didn't know. But I did. I walked into the lion's den aware."

"She—"

"She is a most dangerous woman, Wakayama."

"Do you want me to take her, Tokushima-san?"

"No." He smiled as he shook his head and turned back to the front doors of the building. "No, I don't, and quite frankly, I doubt that you could. I would, however, like to know her final destination out of Tokyo. See to it."

It was as though his employer, the man he would give his life to protect, had struck him in the face. He struggled to keep his voice calm and display none of the emotion he felt. "It is done, Tokushima-san."

"I want to know more about the lovely Fumiko. I will tell you her real name. Put our people on it."

"Hai, Tokushima-san." He had offered to kill this woman and Tokushima said he didn't believe he could do it. He couldn't even kill a simple woman? What an insult.

In the elevator with Wakayama, going back to the restaurant where he would finish his meal alone and appear to be in disgrace, he said, "So beautiful she is, and yet so cold and so emotionless. Women are for the single purpose of pleasing men. And she would have pleased me so much, Wakayama."

"Yes, sir," Wakayama answered.

"I wanted to make her laugh, or, at least to make her smile. I wanted her to show me her teeth. It is said, Wakayama, that in the mountains of Hidaka-sammyaku, those who attend the school have their eyeteeth filed down to sharp points. That they can tear out the throat of a man like a savage wolf. It is also said that they no longer have any regard for human life. Not even their own. Those who complete that school have give up their immortal souls to be what they have been trained to be. This may be true." He turned to his bodyguard in an uncommon show of emotion and an appeal for understanding. "But for some reason I can't explain, I feel that the beautiful Fumiko lost her soul a long time before she went to Hidaka." He shook his head sadly. "I would like to be the one to give it back to her."

Wakayama was aghast. "She . . . you say . . . that woman was at Hidaka-sammyaku?"

"Hai."

"Iai! I don't believe it! Oh, Tokushima-san, I'm sorry, I didn't mean to say that. I—"

"It's all right. I didn't believe it either, when I first heard it, but I have now seen her, there is irrefutable proof. I have looked into her eyes. She was there, Wakayama."

"You didn't tell me, Tokushima-san. I would not have let her near you. Why didn't you tell me?"

"I told you why. I want to be the one to give her back her soul."

Outwardly calm and appearing in complete control of himself, inside Tokushima was seething. He had always had his pick of the graduates of Hidaka-sammyaku if he wanted them, and he had had occasion to use their skills once or twice. This beautiful woman Hidaka graduate would have been worth a fortune to him notwithstanding her physical appeal and she should have been available to him. Yet she had refused him! Refused him! Nobody refused him. She would pay for that.

Throughout his very successful business career, he had supported the concept of the Ninja and he admired the feudal samurai with their absolute lack of fear of death, he was not one of them. He would never admit it, not even to himself, but her fingernails at his neck and her mouth at his throat had frightened him more than he had let on. He believed that he controlled life and death but never before had he been so close to the dark angel. She would pay for that, too.

Chapter Four

H E WAS SEATED ON the hard steel bench in the back of the van and secured by the ankle chains attached to the floor by yet another padlock. The two guards sat down opposite him. Both were in their mid-fifties and were facing mandatory retirement in another couple of years. They would try to live on their pension supplemented by social security. Their prospects as well as their future wasn't all that bright.

The doors were slammed closed and locked from the inside. The driver merged from the building carrying a cup of steaming coffee while he chewed on the remains of a donut. He started the engine and massive inner doors of the prison opened to allow the van to move slowly into the sally port. They closed behind and as soon as they were shut, the outside doors opened. The van moved off into the gray light of the early dawn, its wheels slicing cleanly through the fresh snow past the few anti-death penalty protesters dedicated enough to brave the cold. It was 7:00 o'clock in the morning.

They entered Interstate 76 and for almost an hour they rode in silence with Savage feeling every bump in the highway through the hard bench upon which he sat. One of the guards offered him a cigarette but he shook his head. He had not smoked in over three years. He had no money to buy them and there was nobody on the outside to send them to him. The other prisoners who had them would not share. He understood that. Cigarettes were too hard to come by on Death Row.

Another fifteen minutes passed and he felt the van pull off the highway and begin to slow. The guard who had offered him the cigarette stood up, approached him and began removing the chains and handcuffs.

"Are we there already," he asked, rubbing his wrists as the van exited the Interstate and braked to a stop in a rest area. Although he had psyched himself up to die with some degree of dignity and not a sniveling coward on his knees and that was all ruined now, he was still glad to be out of the cell and doing something. It was a welcome break from the methodical routine. He would worry about the next appointment with the firing squad when it came. Right now he was living on borrowed time and he was going to make the best of it.

The other guard opened the rear double doors and the cold air poured in. It was morning and the daylight reflected off the white snow. The dark green of several pine trees peered stoically from beneath their freezing blankets of wet snow. "No," the guard said, jerking his thumb toward the open doors. "We're not there yet. It's another hour to downtown. Just thought maybe you'd like to use the toilet."

"Sure. Thanks. I appreciate it," Savage replied, still rubbing his wrists, glad to be free of the metal restraints. He stepped down out of the van and into the two inches of snow covering the parking area. In the dawning's light and the glare of mercury vapor pole lamps he could see two eighteen wheelers parked at the far end of the lot and one automobile. It was a white Cadillac limousine with darkened windows parked close to the restroom facilities. If he thought something was wrong back at the prison, well, *this,* my man, was outta sight. They take the chains off and let him walk around outside by himself? Yeah, right. In your dreams.

Hugging himself against the frigid air, he had actually taken several steps toward the block building when he suddenly realized that the guards were not behind him. They had not left the van. He was out there by himself. Before he could think further, the driver's door of the Cadillac opened and a chauffeur, uniformed in brown, wearing knee-high boots and leather gloves appeared. He had short-cropped blond hair and a square jaw set in a tanned, almost too handsome face. Walking around the car, he opened the rear door and stood waiting, almost at military attention, his eyes fixed on Savage.

Glancing behind him once more and still not seeing the guards from the van, he waded through the snow and tentatively approached the open door of the limousine. He bent slightly to look in.

"If you would, please, Mr. Savage," said a voice from inside. "There's rather a sharp nip in the air this morning."

He was momentarily startled. It had been *years* since anyone had called him, Mister. It was Suspect Savage, Prisoner Savage, Inmate Savage, Murderer Savage. Never Mister Savage. That word was a symbol of respect, dignity and professional success. All of which had been stripped from him.

Slipping into the car, the door slamming shut behind him, David Savage found himself seated behind the tall, perfectly dressed, bespectacled lawyer with the silver gray hair. It was warm in the car and the seat was soft. That was the limit of his first impression, such had the deprivation of Death Row robbed him of imagination and awareness.

He heard the van start up a short distance away, turned to look through the window and saw it pull out of the lot and back onto the Interstate. "What . . . what's going on here?"

"You are, ahh . . . I think, escaping, is the term, Mr. Savage," the lawyer replied with amusement in his voice, a slight smile on his lips that did not reach to the cold, gray eyes behind the gold-rimmed glasses.

"I don't understand," Savage said. "Who are you? The warden said you're my lawyer, but I don't know you. Why are you doing this?"

The engine of the Cadillac started and the car backed away from the block building. Turning sharply it sped off in the same direction the prison van had been going.

"Patients, please," the lawyer said, raising his hand. "All will be explained to you. Sit back and enjoy the ride. I trust it is more comfortable than the vehicle you just left. These are yours, I believe." He handed Savage his glasses.

"Thank you," Savage replied, putting them on. The prescription needed to be updated but he could see much better with them on than without.

"I have a proposition to offer you. It is one in which I believe you may well be interested. I represent an organization which has been looking for someone like you for some long time now, several years in fact, and as of this moment we are prepared to offer you a job."

"Are you really a lawyer?"

"Oh, yes, I am. And a very good one, too, if I might say so myself."

"A job? What kind of a job? I don't understand any of this, Mr . . . . I'm sorry, I don't remember your name."

"Everything will be explained. Just don't be impatient. We're going to go on a little trip and you are going to meet a very special, very important man. After you have talked to him and he has presented this proposition to you, you will fully understand. Should you decide, at that time, not to accept the position, other arrangements will have to be made. Am I making myself clear to you?"

"No. I haven't any idea what you're talking about. I don't know what's happening here. Who are you, anyway? The CIA?"

Killingsworth laughed and then reclined in the soft, crushed velour seats. "The CIA. Oh, that's wonderful, Mr. Savage. My goodness, you have such a sense of humor. The CIA. No, Mr. Savage, I'm not the CIA." Then his mood changed abruptly and he began speaking as though addressing a child or a subordinate of severely limited intelligence. "We have arranged your escape from prison and from the execution squad you were to face rather cleverly, I think. I am indebted to Warden Bennett. She was a political appointee, you know. Not very bright. I'm not at all certain this would have worked with any other prison warden.

"Nonetheless," the lawyer rushed on, "in return for your release from prison, you are in our debt. In other words, Mr. Savage, from this moment on, we own you. You will do anything and everything you are told to do immediately, without question and you will do it to the best of your ability. Is that clear?"

"I understand what you are saying, yes."

"Should what I have just proposed not be satisfactory or acceptable to you, the prison van which brought you here will be waiting at the next rest stop twenty miles away. You will be returned to it, the chains will be put back on you and you will be taken back to Death Row where tomorrow morning, or the morning after that, you will be shot to death in the courtyard. You have approximately fifteen minutes to think about it."

"And if I decide to go along with you on—"

"One step at a time, Mr. Savage. Make a decision first, then we'll go on to the next part."

"I've got snow in my shoes."

"A minor problem, all things considered."

"I would be incredibly stupid not to take advantage of your offer," Savage remarked.

"Are you incredibly stupid, Mr. Savage?"

"And I certainly have nothing to lose. I was supposed to be dead an hour ago."

"Quite true. Do you accept?"

"Yes."

"Very reasonable of you, Mr. Savage. Now bear in mind that there might be a great deal more to lose, more than you can possibly imagine. I say this not to frighten you but to make you understand that your escape is not without a price tag, and that price might be even more severe."

"And what if I go back and I tell them about you, about this arranged escape?"

"Really, Mr. Savage. Tell them what? Who would listen? Even if they did, nobody would believe you. The three men in that van, all long-time and reliable state employees, will testify that absolutely nothing unusual happened on the trip. You were taken to Philadelphia where they knew nothing about your intended arrival. You were brought back to the prison where you would go to your cell until the execution order would be carried out as planned."

"What about the stay, the Order to take me to Philadelphia?"

"Ahh, yes. The stay of execution. The order. Unfortunately, Mr. Savage, the Honorable Judge McAndrews, the man who issued and signed those documents, died of a heart attack about, ohh . . ." the lawyer consulted his gold Rolex watch, "about six o'clock yesterday afternoon. That was about an hour after he signed the documents—he had been in failing health for some time, you know—so nobody will ever know what he had in mind or why he issued that stay and ordered that you be taken to Philadelphia. And he had absolutely no reason or authority to do either, I might add."

"I see," Savage said with resignation. "It's not binding, is it."

"No, it isn't."

"And Warden Bennett?"

"Mrs. Bennett has developed a well documented drug abuse problem. Anti-depressive stimulants to bring her up and barbiturates to control anxiety and calm her down. So far she has been able to balance the two carefully, but should she mistakenly combine them or take the wrong one . . ." Spreading his manicured hands, he let the sentence trail off.

"So they will find out that I'm missing."

"Of course. In a day or so, maybe three if we're lucky."

"Then I don't have much of a choice, do I."

"Very good. You have made the right decision, I assure you."

The limousine passed the rest stop with the prison van sitting in the parking lot. Two of the uniformed guards were tromping through the snow to the restroom while the third remained unseen in the van. The limousine turned north off of the Interstate at the next exit and headed for Reading. Thirty minutes later, followed closely by a gray, four-door sedan with all blackwall tires, the Cadillac pulled into the Carl A. Spaatz airport located within the sweeping bend of the Schuylkill River and stopped at a private terminal at the far end of runway number three. The chauffeur emerged, opened the rear door and Mr. Killingsworth stepped out, motioning for Savage to slide across the seat and follow, emerging once again into the cold, ankle-deep snow and slush. The dim sunlight filtered through dense, black, low-hanging clouds, revealed a snow-bordered runway with a Twin Lear roaring, ready for takeoff along the freshly plowed strip. It had begun to snow lightly.

The lawyer led the way, walking carefully along the asphalt runway and up the four steps to the plane. He held his trousers up with both hands so that his cuffs would not get wet, looking a little like, Savage thought, a sissy walking through rain puddles trying to keep his socks dry. The high-booted chauffeur put a gloved hand on Savage's shoulder to firmly guide him up the stairs to the open door of the aircraft, and then into the warm interior. This accomplished, he turned and began walking back to the limousine.

The gray sedan with the blackwall tires stopped beside the Cadillac and two men emerged, both wearing hats and trench coats. One of them intercepting the chauffeur and a short conversation followed. Then they both walked to and entered the plane while the other man got behind the wheel of the Cadillac and drove it away.

Savage was shivering when finally placed into a seat in the opulent interior of the plane, his seat belt fastened for him by the chauffeur who's suntan appeared to have suddenly faded. Then in what seemed to be only seconds, the jet leaped skyward, its engines winding to a pitch almost beyond the range of human hearing.

The pilot must have already had his flight instructions with an additional order of haste, for the Lear was in an almost vertical power climb that pressed Savage back into the seat and held him there until the aircraft leveled off at 40,000 feet and approached Mach one in its Westerly flight.

The interior of the jet was paneled in dark, dull red Mahogany veneer and four deep cushioned leather chairs were bolted securely to the floor around a circular table in the center of the plane. Small lamps were attached to end tables beside each chair and there were round holes in each of the tables to accommodate cocktail glasses. Two more sets of chairs and side tables at the far end of the cabin were occupied by the uniformed chauffeur and a rugged looking man in a khaki safari jacket with matching trousers under the discarded trench coat. His six foot two, two hundred-pound frame was crammed into the seat and held there by the seat belt. He made no attempt to hide the Israeli made Uzi on his lap, and his sharp, deep blue eyes never left David Savage. He was the man from the gray sedan.

Another man in a tailored sky-blue uniform with gold wings stitched above the left breast pocket brought a tray containing bottles of liquor, a pot of coffee, some juice, glasses and ice which he offered to his passengers. They all accepted them with a polite nod and ignored completely that there was no drink for David Savage.

Killingsworth occupied his time alternately with a book in his lap and papers he took from an attaché that had somehow appeared on one of the empty seats. The high octane, ice-filled drink was in his left hand. "Do you know the classics, Mr. Savage?" he asked, glancing up from the book. They had been in the air for a little over an hour.

"Some."

"I thought this appropriate to our situation. May I read?"

He shrugged. "Sure."

"A great while ago," he quoted from the book, "the world began, with hey, ho, the wind and the rain—but that's all one, our play is done, and we'll strive to please you every day." He looked up from the book. "What do you think?"

"It's Shakespeare. But I don't know which one."

"Guess."

"I don't know."

"Twelfth Night."

"Oh, yes. Now I remember. Or Do What You Will," he said, glancing at the man beside him.

"Very good, Mr. Savage. I'm impressed."

"Don't be. I've had a lot of time to read."

"I'm sure. What's the highest mountain in the world?"

"Everest."

"Why don't people say Sahara Desert?"

"What?"

"Please pay attention. What is wrong with saying Sahara Desert?"

"Everybody says Sahara desert."

"But it isn't right. Why?"

"Sahara means desert. You'd be saying desert, desert."

"Very good. Now, name the four horsemen of the Apocalypse."

"Why?"

"Because I asked you to."

"Is this a test?"

"Yes."

"What do I get if I pass?"

"Your freedom."

"Ah . . . conquest, war, death and . . . ah, famine."

"Excellent. Your mind and memory seem to be functioning well. Who was Alos?"

"Could I please have some coffee?"

Mildly surprised that Savage would ask, the attorney signaled for the pilot to bring another cup.

When the coffee had been served, Jerry Comfort walked slowly back to the cockpit, dropped the tray and brushed his hands together several times as though to rid himself of any trace of the serving tray. No drink for the man in the prison uniform. Killingsworth had said that. Don't even look at him. He isn't here. You never saw him. Then, bring the man a cup of coffee. He shook his head in disgust.

Captain Jerry Comfort was an airplane pilot, not a goddamn waiter. He flew jets, he didn't wait tables. His eyes and his hands had guided Mach three fighters in combat against the best the enemy could put up against him and his guns and rockets had blasted them from the skies. Lieutenant Colonel Jerry Comfort had been decorated for bravery by the United States Air Force Commanding General himself. He, too, could have worn a General's star had he just waited a few more years.

Private pilot, aircraft captain Jerry comfort settled into the left-hand seat and wondered if maybe he should have stayed in for the star instead of taking the $200,000 a year salary that lured him away from the Air Force. His wife certainly didn't think so. And he had two boys in collage that were costing a fortune. Generals didn't serve drinks to arrogant lawyers or chauffeurs and ignore mousy little guys in prison suits. What about that guy with the Uzi? He had hired gun written all over him. What would the

FAA say if they knew he was transporting prisoners and men with machine guns? Revoke his license, that's what they would do.

David Savage was afraid again, afraid this time because he didn't know what was happening to him. This could be another of those awful nightmares he had so often while on Death Row, dreams of freedom in sleep that became nightmares when he awoke and found himself still in his cell waiting to die. What was different? A dramatic escape. A lawyer who was going to save him, a jet plane in the sky, a man in uniform serving drinks to his passengers?

He sipped his coffee and felt himself begin to warm up. It was good coffee. Not like the stuff they served at the prison. He closed his eyes. It could have been only an hour or it could have been ten hours in the air before the jet began to descend. He couldn't tell. He had lost all track of time in the strange surroundings. The aircraft windows were curtained so he could not see out and couldn't tell if it was daylight or dark. He had tried talking to the lawyer, Killingsworth, several times during the trip, asking where they were going, who they would see, what was happening. He never got an answer. Once he had agreed to be a willing participant in his own escape, the lawyer had ignored his questions and with the exception of the memory quiz, had ignored him completely. Then he appeared to doze for most of the trip. After a time, Savage too, exhausted from his days without sleep, dozed in the comfortable cushioned seat.

The sleek jet began its descent faster than it had climbed, screaming down through the clouds in almost free fall that left David's stomach up in his throat and his fingerprints imbedded in the seat armrests.

A red warning light suddenly began to flash on Jerry Comfort's instrument panel and a buzzer, not unlike that of an alarm clock or a missile-lock alert, went on and off, on and off, in the cockpit. The plane shuddered and began fishtailing, the rear end whipping back and forth in the air.

Captain Comfort didn't need the light or the alarm to tell him what was wrong. Instinctively he keyed his mic and called in his situation. "Palmdale Tower, this is Papa Zulu One Nine, we have right engine flameout. I replete, we have right engine shutdown. I'm attempting a midair restart. We are at four thousand feet in final approach. Palmdale, do you copy?"

"We copy you, Papa Zulu One Nine."

"Palomar base, do *you* copy?"

"Palomar base, copy," the radio said in his earphones. "Can you do anything for them, Palmdale Tower?"

"Your field is almost thirty miles from us, Palomar. I don't think we could never get there in time to do anything but I'm going to launch helicopter Rescue One now. Papa Zulu One Nine, you copy that?"

Jerry Comfort fought the controls, trying to hold the heavy jet in its glide path to the runway. "Give me full flaps and up trim on the rear stabilizers," he shouted at his copilot, a man ten years his junior but with the same rank. Aircraft captain. "We gotta bring that right wing up. We're dropping like a rock. We're gonna roll in a minute."

"I know!" the copilot replied, working frantically.

"Initiate restart procedure!"

In the passenger compartment David Savage felt the tremors in the aircraft, he felt the seat beneath him rise as the right wing dropped and the plane began to dip. His companion seated opposite him was instantly alert, sitting suddenly upright in his set. The uniformed chauffeur at the far end of the cabin was white-faced and gripping his seat with both hands.

Another red light and the buzzing sound increased in the cockpit as the left engine sputtered and died. The plane was now without power, two thousand feet in the air and a mile from the end of the runway.

"Palmdale Tower, we now have left engine shutdown. We're gliding. Palomar base, do you copy?"

"Palomar copy. We're working on it."

"Papa, Zulu One Nine, this is Palmdale Tower. Full flaps, drop your gear, drag your tail and try to bring the nose up to stall. You can pancake it in."

"I'm doing that already, goddamn it!" Captain Comfort shouted. "I didn't fly an F-14 all those years to crash this thing now!"

"We seem to be experiencing some technical difficulties, gentlemen," Killingsworth said in a quiet, emotionless voice as he pulled his seatbelt tighter. "I suggest we all relax and brace ourselves for a rough landing. It's probably just a crosswind or something like that. Nothing to worry about, I assure you."

"Flaps are full, gear is down, stabilizers are all the way up, nose up and the ground is coming up awfully fast," Jerry Comfort said into his mic. "And we're not gonna stall. If I can land this thing, I'm going to burn out the brakes bringing us to an abrupt stop. Palomar, you better have some fire equipment standing by when we come in."

"Copy, Papa Zulu One Nine. What's your estimate of touchdown?"

Looking out the window, he said, "About fifty seconds."

David Savage had been aboard enough airplanes to know that there definitely *was* something to about which to worry. Something was terribly wrong. He tried to reach over and pull the curtains away from the window next to his seat but Killingsworth slapped his arm down. "There's nothing to see out there, Mr. Savage. We'll be down shortly. Just be calm."

"We're falling!" Savage shouted.

"Just your imagination. There's nothing wrong."

Like a fast elevator the Lear jet dropped from the sky, hit the runway hard and bounced back into the air. Savage was slammed down into his seat and then thrown against the lap belt as the plane hit and bounced again. Tires screamed on the pavement as the jet again grabbed for the ground, finally settling its great weight onto the cement. Smoke began to pour from the wheels as Jerry Comfort applied the brakes, attempting to bring the hurtling craft to a stop before they went off the runway and into the sand at the far end.

There was a loud pop, like a distant gunshot, and the right side of the plane dropped. A different sound, that of tearing, grinding, twisting metal came from the landing gear digging into the ground after the tire blew out. The plane lurched to the right, swinging around in a half circle to the edge of the runway where the left wheel dropped off the cement surface and into the soft sand. Savage and Killingsworth were thrown forward against their seatbelts as the plane ground to a jarring stop.

"It appears as though we have arrived, Mr. Savage," Killingsworth said, apparently completely unruffled. "Shall we deplane? You may follow me."

He unfastened his seatbelt and walked casually to the door which was being opened by the chauffeur, very pale and still shaking from the experience. He stepped back as the lawyer approached, stopped and stood waiting for the steps to be lowered. The man with the automatic weapon joined him and stood close by the door as soon as it was swung open. He, too, seemed a little pale but otherwise unaffected by the ordeal.

In the cockpit, Captain Comfort breathed a sigh of relief and dropped his hands from the yoke into his lap. His copilot just sat there rigid and said, "Damn!" Foul smelling black smoke was billowing up from the burning tire.

A fire engine roared up and screeched to a stop close to the plane. Several men with fire extinguishers applied foam to the burning wheel and signaled that there was no danger. Close behind the fire truck was a jeep occupied by four men, all armed with automatic rifles and side arms. Last came a twin to the white Cadillac limousine that had taken them to the airport in Reading. A man in a colorful tropical shirt and light trousers exited the driver's door of the limo, leaving it open and immediately climbing into the jeep while the four, dressed in tan uniforms and boots, spread out and scanned the area for any sign of trouble.

The booted chauffeur stepped ahead to open the rear door of the limousine. Killingsworth entered the car and immediately flattened himself against the seat, his hands lying casually in his lap. Savage was ushered in behind him by the man in the safari jacket who then slipped into the front seat of the vehicle beside the chauffeur. The limo pulled away from the runway followed closely by the jeep.

The weather was very warm, the sky slightly overcast with the sun barely above the eastern horizon. It was early morning and there was no sign of snow anywhere. Rolling hills covered with brown, dry grass, stunted and strange looking trees, small green and brown bushes and a lot of large rocks made up the landscape surrounding the airfield. Located in a long, wide, natural valley with foothills on either side, there was a view of only the very tops of mountains in the distance. The ridge of the valley was bare with no vegetation at all. The dryness indicated perhaps the edge of a desert.

The blacktop road that began at the landing strip and ran straight off between the buildings began to wind its way through the hills and low mountains into an adjoining valley where it ended at the great circular drive in front of an estate that was their final destination.

The house was huge, three stories, white and Eastern Colonial in design with spacious and beautifully maintained grounds around it. Flowers of almost every color and description grew in expertly arranged beds. Small shrugs, budding bushes and dark green trees were all surrounded by lush grass expertly trimmed and manicured. A grove of fruit trees stood to the left of the house but Savage couldn't determine the type, and to the rear more trees spread off into the distance. The air was not nearly as dry.

The automobile stopped in front of the house, the chauffeur opened the door and the passengers took the short walk up three steps between fluted columns to the porch and approached a massive walnut door over two inches thick which had been carved from one solid piece of wood. It was hung by huge brass hinges.

Inside, Savage was allowed only a glimpse of the interior of the house as the attorney rushed him through the large living room, past a curved, grand staircase, across thick carpeting, by dark polished wood and expensive furniture, oil paintings in intricately carved wooden frames and a grandfather's clock ticking loudly. The time was 8:20. A hallway led to and ended at a room in the back of the house. The door to this room also appeared to be walnut, but when it was pulled open and then slammed shut again behind them, the ring of solid steel belied the thin veneer of decorative wood. It was a sound Savage knew well.

Only a second's glance at the large windowless room lined from floor to ceiling with shelves of books was cut short by a row of three bright track-lights mounted on the ceiling that shown directly in his face. He tried to raise his hands and shield his eyes from the glare but they were pushed down by the lawyer's cold hands.

"Mr. Damarjiane, this is Doctor David Savage," Killingsworth said as he held David by the elbow and guided him to a large desk in the center of the room, "the man you asked me to bring." There was more respect in Killingsworth's voice than David had heard in any of his conversations before.

"Doctor Savage," came a voice from the darkness behind the lights. "How do you do? I am the Director of the Palomar Foundation. It is a privately funded organization dedicated to science and humanity. It was I who . . . ah . . . arranged for your release from prison and had you brought here to help us in our work."

The voice was deep and rasping and there was heavy breathing, signs of advanced age and some respiratory problems, probably pulmonary emphysema. The Death Row inmates had little else to do with their time so they played a game with each new resident of the Row. They would disguise their voices, create sounds and symptoms and make the new guy guess. After a while they would tell him. Then they would move on to something new. Like a person who is blind, his ears told him a great many things the average person never heard.

"I've read several of your books. Very good escape fiction."

"Thank you, Mr. Ah . . . Damar . . ."

"The Philadelphia City jail authorities had no knowledge of your intended arrival so the fact that you did not arrive is of no immediate significance. The warden is in possession of what she believes to be a legitimate document transferring you and relieving her of responsibility for you. Given her state of mind, there would be no conceivable reason for her to pursue it. With her many and varied duties of running the prison and all of the problems that involves, I would presume that she has already put you out of her mind. By the time the actual fact that you have escaped emerges, you will be totally beyond the reach of either law enforcement or the criminal justice system. That much I promise you. You will never have to return to confinement or face a firing squad again if you elect to join us and accept the employment I offer you."

Something in the voice betrayed to Savage's prison-trained ears just a hint of hesitation, something he wasn't saying, perhaps disappointment and some reservations with the unshaven, slender man in the ill-fitting prison uniform fidgeting in the spotlight. His dark brown hair was thinning, short in regulation prison style and hanging limp and damp. The most disturbing thing about him would be the lack of luster in his eyes. Prison had done its job well. There was no life behind those once penetrating deep brown eyes. There was no ambition, no future, no life. Just a hint of fear, and nothing else.

"Then I am free?" Savage asked, a flicker in the brown eyes, just the tiniest of a flicker of interest.

"Are any of us truly free, Doctor? Free of obligations, duties and responsibilities to home, family, and business, earning a living, the struggle to survive? No, true freedom is an illusion, one for which we ever search but never find. But from the prison, yes, you are free."

"What about the guards? The ones who left me at the rest area. They'll know I escaped."

"Mr. Killingsworth?" the man behind the lights inquired.

"The two guards and the driver were quickly approaching retirement age. All three were divorced, living in apartments with few if any ties to their communities, and very little faith left in the state retirement system. Their assignment to the Traveling Guard or The Chain, as it is called, destroyed whatever personal life they might have had and furthered their disenchantment with their future. I would surmise that they will immediately put in for early retirement and just vanish without ever being missed, with enough money to live very comfortably the remainder of their lives. Oh, yes, very comfortably indeed."

"The press. What about the news media? They are always there to cover an execution," Savage insisted.

"Do not be concerned, Doctor. That, too, has been taken care of."

"How?"

"You do not need to know that."

Through the bright lights shining in his eyes, the table lamps in several locations throughout the room helping to penetrate the glare, Savage could just make out the large desk covered with papers and books scattered over it, and he glimpsed a figure behind it. From the bulk, he appeared to be a very big man, fat or just large. Light sparkled on diamond-studded cufflinks at his wrists. Attempting to see his host more clearly, he raised his hand again to shield his eyes, but once again, the lawyer prevented it.

"I got you out of prison," Damarjiane continued, "and all I require in return is your assistance. Mr. Killingsworth will show you around and introduce you to the staff, and then we'll go on from there."

"But I don't understand," Savage said. "Are you part of the government? How could you get me out of prison and promise me that I'd never have to go back? What do you want of me?"

"After you've had a look around, Doctor, we'll talk again. I just wanted to meet you and introduce myself. That's all for now. Mr. Killingsworth, would you see that he gets cleaned up a bit?"

"Of course, Sir." Killingsworth's hand was on his arm.

"Wait," Savage insisted. "Where am I? This certainly isn't Pennsylvania."

"You are in southern California, Doctor. That's all you need to know for the moment." A second later he was led subserviently from the room. Ringing steel signaled the closing of the heavy door behind him.

CHAPTER FIVE

A T A LITTLE AFTER 11:00 AM, the jumbo 747 taxied to the terminal at San Francisco International Airport and the scream of the four huge Rolls Royce engines began to wind down. After flying for almost fourteen hours, the passengers were stiff, irritable and suffering severe jet lag. As though to add to the discomfort, it was overcast and raining lightly in the Bay City. It was cold. "The coldest winter I ever spent was summer in San Francisco." Although it was attributed to him, Mark Twain never said it.

The thick, pressure-sealing door was opened from inside. The passengers leaving the plane and filing into the concourse with their carry-on luggage wouldn't be subject to the adverse weather or the outside noise because of the covered, insulated walkway extending out to connect the terminal with the plane. That was some help. A few of the older, well-seasoned flyers remembered the times when the door would open, a metal staircase on wheels was pushed up to the doorway and everybody would walk down and troop across the blacktop between the lines painted on the blacktop in whatever weather conditions existed.

In first class and with no luggage, dressed in a dark blue pants suit over a pale blue blouse and wearing comfortable flats, Diana was the first person to exit the aircraft. "Thank you for flying with us," the stewardess said as she passed. Diana did not respond or even acknowledge the stewardess who would say the same thing again some three hundred times before the last passenger had left.

At Customs, she presented her passport and State Department security clearance. With nothing to declare and no suitcases to search, the customs agent glanced through her nearly empty purse, looked at her and cleared her in less time than it took her to walk through the airport and get a cab outside. There were a lot of glances and some outright stares from men and even a few from women as Diana made her way to the exit. Some thought she was a movie star although they couldn't place her. Others believed her to be a cover girl model, but they couldn't remember on which magazine they had seen her picture. All agreed that she was a strikingly beautiful woman with a figure that put meaning to the word, lust.

The awning kept the rain off of the sidewalk and the pedestrians who were milling around and waiting for transportation. A yellow cab pulled forward and she stood waiting for the door to be opened for her. Before the cab driver could close the door behind her, a tall, muscular man in a conservative business suit appeared seemingly from nowhere, pushed by the cabby and climbed into the seat beside her.

When the door was slammed shut, he settled back and said, "You look like shit, Diana. You've lost a lot of weight and there are lines in your face."

"Thank you. You look pretty good yourself," she replied.

"Welcome home."

"Thanks, again."

"Rough?"

"You can't even begin to imagine, DeShane."

"It might surprise you, but maybe I can. They're all waiting for you."

"I figured."

"Qualatron terminal," he instructed the driver. "About three quarters of the way to the far end of the airport."

"Oh, wow! That's it? Half a mile?" the cabby objected. "What do I get, a 30¢ trip?"

"If you get us there today, there might be a tip."

"Yeah, sure. That's what they all say."

"Just drive."

"I'm driving. I'm driving, already." The windshield wipers slapped back and forth across the glass.

DeShane leaned forward, turned and took Diana by the shoulders forcing her to look at him. "Are you all right?"

"I'm starving. Can we stop and get something to eat?"

"As soon as we get home. You sure you're okay?"

"Just how much do you know, DeShane?"

"More than I should."

"Then, yeah, I'm all right."

"It's going to be a touch-and-go when we get home."

"Why?"

"We are going to have a guest."

"What does *that* mean?" She took his hands from her shoulders and they both sat back in the seat to stare through the windshield.

"Just that. We're going to have a guest. You're not going to like it, but it's what the boss ordered."

"When?"

"I don't know. He might be there already."

Ten minutes later the cabby was instructed to leave the stop-and-go airport traffic and drive through the open chain link gate of a private terminal and cross the asphalt to the edge of the landing area marked with wide strips of yellow paint.

"There," DeShane said, pointing to a twin Lear with the passenger door open. "Pull up there."

"Got'cha."

"Take a drive into town," DeShane continued, handing the cab driver a $100.00 bill. Taking her hand, he assisted Diana out of the cab while continuing his instructions to the cabby. "Log it that way on your trip sheet. We were never here."

"Shit! Who the hell are you people, anyway?" He looked down at the bill and back up at the man who had given it to him. "CIA or something?"

"Russian Secret Police," DeShane replied matter-of-factly.

"Yeah? I didn't know they had them anymore."

"They don't. We're really KGB."

"Sure you are. Is this real?" He held out the $100 bill."

"It is."

He shook his head as he shoved the bill into his pocket and stomped on the accelerator, spinning the tires on the wet tarmac and heading back through the gate to the main terminal. Hell, they might really be KGB, the cabby thought. So what did he care. A hundred bucks for a half-mile trip. Son of a bitch.

The Lear was racing down the runway under full thrust and climbing into the wet sky before the cab cruised into metropolitan San Francisco with a female passenger going to the Sir Francis Drake Hotel.

CHAPTER SIX

T HE CHAUFFEUR WITH THE shiny boots, his hat tucked neatly under his arm, watched the two men step into the hallway from the boss' bombproof private office. It was a room he had never been in despite his four years of service here and he resented the pale little runt of a man now following along meekly behind that lawyer, Killingsworth. He really hated Killingsworth.

Through the partially open door of a small office adjacent to the steel chamber, the man in the safari jacket stood in the semidarkness also watching as Savage was led back through the house and up the wide, grand staircase to the second floor. Although he couldn't see him from where he was, he was also aware of the chauffeur's presence in the living room.

At the top of the staircase, Savage was led along a wide, well-lighted hallway to a three-room apartment half way down the hall. The trip was almost a blur for him as he was urged on hastily by the lawyer and then left in the apartment with the door locked behind him.

The living room was large and furnished with an eight-foot sofa, massive coffee table, end tables with lamps, an armchair, console TV and a stereo with CD player. Thick beige carpet and floor to ceiling drapes behind which were French doors leading to a small balcony. Although not large, there was a complete kitchen separated from the living room by a breakfast bar, small dining table with three chairs around it. An empty bookcase took up much of the inside wall beside the door and there was a computer terminal and monitor on a large desk.

Equally hazy and dream-like was the next hour, then the lawyer returned. Killingsworth said, "there have been amazing advances in computer science and formation access during the last five years, Doctor. You will be taught how to use the terminal on the desk there and how to draw information from sources never before available. They call it, surfing the web. I think you will be impressed."

He was shown through the bedroom to an adjoining bathroom and told to undress where he stepped into a luxurious shower, his first in several days. While in the shower, his prison clothes disappeared and in their place ws a robe and slippers. A barber came to his room, shaved him and cut his hair in a more conventional and civilian style, then a tailor measured him for clothes and shoes. Although it was still morning, a meal of roast beef, potatoes and vegetables was set on his dinette table and he was bid eat while still in the long, white robe monogrammed with his initials over the left breast. Hot, spicy, succulent and covered with rich brown gravy, the dinner overwhelmed him with its taste and the dark, red wine served in a cut glass goblet beside his gild-edged plate seemed the best he had ever savored.

It must be that he really *had* been killed in that cold, snow-covered prison courtyard, and this was only a fleeting second-in-time before death took him to that deep, dark, silent forever with no awakening dawn. That or he was still in his cell having one more desperate dream of freedom before they came to get him. None of this could be real.

The plates and glasses were cleared away and then there was a knock on his door. Killingsworth entered immediately and walked to his table. "You may watch television if you like, Doctor," he said, indicating a large set on the far side of the room. "You probably have a lot to catch up on. Then I would suggest you get some more sleep. You look rather haggard. A mild sedative was put into your food. You will shortly begins to feel drowsy."

"You drugged me?"

"Yes. But only to permit you to rest. Your last few days have been very harrowing, your current surroundings strange, your future a mystery. Given all that, you might have trouble relaxing."

"That's one heluvan understatement."

"It is requested that you do not attempt to leave this room. The surroundings are unfamiliar to you and you might injure yourself. For your protection, the door will be locked from the outside. At least *that* should be familiar to you. I will see you in the morning after breakfast."

As abruptly as he had entered, Killingsworth turned and left without waiting for a reply while Savage stared at the closed door.

The locked door meant another prison cell, but looking around the room again, he would take this prison cell over the one he had just left anytime. He thought for a moment about turning on the television set, but he was not ready for any more startling news of rocket ship trips to Mars or maybe transplanted brains. He went to the bedroom, closed the heavy drapes and crawled naked into the bed between fresh, ironed and starched sheets. There was a massive headboard upon which sat a clock radio. He noticed neither. He was asleep in seconds, exhausted, and the sedative along with the rich food took him to a state of complete unconsciousness.

There were no dreams or nightmares during the night, just an incessant, annoying female voice saying something about butter, margarine and the cost of both. There was a lot of light flooding the room.

He opened his eyes and looked up at the clock radio blasting out its commercial for the fat-free spread in the yellow tub. It was morning, the drapes were open as was the window and a slight breeze flittered through the room. Underwear, shirt, trousers, socks and shoes were laid out at the foot of the bed. The robe which he had dropped to the floor last night when he scrambled into the bed was folded neatly beside the other things.

The strong smell of fresh-brewed coffee came to him and he grabbed the robe. Breakfast had been set out on the dinette table along with a tall, silver pot from which the fragrant aroma came. "Now this isn't half bad," he said aloud as he sat down and began to eat hungrily. "Maybe this is heaven and I'm going to spend all eternity just sitting here eating." He chuckled at his silly idea, drank more coffee and finished the eggs, toast, bacon and fried potatoes.

The sound of the lock turning on his door tore his attention away from the table. Killingsworth entered, walked to the table, sat and poured himself a cup of coffee as though he did this every morning of his life. Wearing a blue pinstripe suit and light blue tie, freshly shaved, manicured and hair in perfect place, he looked more like he was about to enter a courtroom than conduct a guided tour.

"You slept for almost twenty-four hours, Doctor. I trust you are sufficiently rested," he said between sips of coffee.

"I feel better than I have in a long time."

"Good. Get dressed. We have much to do today. I'm going to take you on a tour and part of what I am about to show you is a very closely guarded secret. You could not even begin to imagine the amount of money that has already gone into this project, nor could you conceive of the results we've achieved. Do hurry. Come with me and I'll show you the price of your freedom."

Back in the bathroom, he found an electric razor but running his hand over his chin, he decided he didn't need to us it so close was the shave he had gotten the day before. The presence of the razor indicated that he would probably not be getting anymore professional grooming.

"What happened out there, with the airplane?" he called out from the bedroom as he dressed. "We almost crashed."

"Engine failure, I would imagine. It happens sometimes. Nothing important." He took another sip of coffee.

"Oh, yeah? Well, I've done quite a bit of flying myself and I can tell you—"

"You fly regularly in a four million dollar private jet aircraft, do you, Doctor Savage?"

Savage emerged from the bedroom buttoning his shirt. "I didn't say I—"

"Now, please pay attention to what I'm telling you, Doctor," Killingsworth continued, interrupting and ignoring his attempted reply. "It's important."

Tucking in his shirt and buckling his belt, David remained silent as the lawyer went on. "You are about to be shown the heart of the project and the reason for you're being here. I caution you to remain silent and listen until you comprehend it all. It is really quite utterly fantastic. Now, will you please come with me." He refilled his coffee cup and took it with him, leaving the saucer on the table.

Putting on his socks and shoes, he quickly followed the lawyer out of the room, back down the huge, curved staircase, through the house and out the back door. Here a brick sidewalk curved through the flowerbeds, the neatly trimmed bushes and shade trees, around a patio continuing two stone benches surrounded by a horseshoe-shaped hedge six feet high. Another stone bench was set beside where the sidewalk split and Killingsworth led the

way along the left path to a gravel road running past a number
of buildings. A bisecting road led off into the distance and many
of the buildings along it looked like greenhouses. They entered
a large stucco building with a tile roof and double sliding doors.
There were more bushes and shrubs around it and two gardeners
worked close by.

Inside the building there was a pickup truck, a tractor, a wagon,
two power lawnmowers, a golf cart, wheelbarrows, coiled garden
hoses, rakes, sickles, clippers and hoes hanging on hooks. Near the
back of the building was an eight by ten-foot metal utility cabinet.
Killingsworth took a key from his pocket, opened the door and
motioned for Savage to enter. The cabinet was empty.

The lawyer pulled the doors closed and a light came on
overhead. "077477, Killingsworth," he said aloud. "Please look
up there, Doctor." He pointed to what appeared to be a piece of
round glass near the ceiling. "That's a TV camera."

The floor suddenly began to drop. Savage was startled.

"This is an elevator. It will take us down approximately sixty
feet to an elaborate complex of rooms and passageways below.
There are living quarters, a dining room, a complete hospital,
medical offices, work-out rooms, showers, just about anything
you can imagine that people will need and want to live. There
are two very sophisticated electronics labs in which a number
of sophisticated and highly classified electronic gadgets have
originated."

The elevator stopped, the door opened and they emerged in a
small eight by eight-foot room with a massive steel door in front of
them. "Tungsten steel, two feet thick," Killingsworth continued,
rapping his knuckles on the door. "You can't blast it open and
it would take twenty hours to burn through it with a torch. If
someone *did* try to burn through it, the C-4 in the walls would
blow and sixty feet of reinforced concrete would come down to
plug the shaft."

"You work for the government?" Savage asked, amazed by what he was being told.

"No, we are an independent contractor. The world demands. We supply. A short time ago we were working on a computer concept now known as Virtual Reality, but somebody beat us to it and we had to abandon it. Industrial espionage is big business these days, Doctor, so security is tight and expensive."

There was a deep hum and the huge steel door began to move out and open. "Everything is operated from inside. There is absolutely no way anybody could come in here uninvited. I am one of only a very few who has unlimited access to this facility. All of the equipment we have down here has been brought one piece at a time. The original designer was more concerned with security than access.

"The protection and security facilities are becoming even more elaborate," Killingsworth continued his explanations, "with this new discovery. It will be even more difficult to get in here as soon as the new identification systems are installed. But now, we only face armed men who have been instructed to kill, and they are paid enough money to insure that they will.

"Now, before we enter, Doctor, please understand that once inside, if there is even the slightest hint that you might reveal anything or do anything to jeopardize the project, you will be terminated immediately. It is important that you understand this."

"Terminated? You mean I'll be killed?"

"Yes," replied the lawyer. "You will just disappear."

"You can do that?"

"Yes, we can do that," Killingsworth said again. "Do you understand?"

"Yes," Savage replied in a weak voice.

"I did not intend to frighten you, Doctor. It is just that you need to know the rules by which you are playing." There was just the edge of contempt in the lawyer's words for the frail figure before him.

The door completed its swing open and Killingsworth ushered his charge into a hallway and through another door—a regular one this time—into a small L-shaped anteroom. As they entered, an armed security guard confronted them from behind three inches of bulletproof glass. He picked up the phone, spoke, then motioned for them to continue.

At the end of the short section of the L past the guard station were two more doors, one at the end of the hallway, the other on the left side a few feet before the end. Both doors were out of sight of the guard. One appeared to be a normal wooden door with a round, brass doorknob. The other looked to be solid steel and there was a place to insert a key but no handle.

"That leads to the lab," Killingsworth said, pointing to the steel door. "The other is to the living quarters. A number of people have access to that area. Only a very few may enter here." He took a key ring from his pocket, selected one and inserted it into the slot. "There are only four keys to this door," he told Savage, "and the lock is changed several times a year at random. The walls and ceiling are steel reinforced concrete and the contractor has assured us that it might well withstand a nuclear explosion."

Behind the metal door was a huge room crammed with electronic equipment. On the floor, mounted on stands, situated on tables and benches were computer screens, keyboards, instruments with fluctuating needles, pulsating lights, panels with rows of switches, dials, knobs and buttons. Cables, some an inch thick, were secured to the walls and bolted to the floor. The room was bathed in fluorescent light from dozens of overhead fixtures.

A short, heavy-set man with thick glasses, wearing a white short-sleeve shirt and bow tie turned toward them as they entered. One other man in a long white lab coat sat at a console on the far side of the room glanced up and then back down to his work.

"Is this him?" the man with the bow tie asked Killingsworth. Disappointment was written across his face.

"I'm afraid so," the lawyer responded with his usual lack of interest.

Bow Tie took off his glasses, stuffed them into his shirt pocket and stood with hands on hips looking at Savage. "I was very pleased when Mr. Damarjiane informed us that you would be joining us here on the project, Doctor Savage. Ahhh . . . I followed your trial in the papers, you know. I'm not sure . . . ahhh—"

"Yes, he is quite a disappointment, isn't he," Killingsworth said. "I wasn't sure I should even have brought him."

"Well, since he's here . . . We'll see."

"Show him around, Professor. Find out if he can grasp any of this."

"All right. Doctor Savage, please come with me."

"Professor?" Savage questioned.

"One of Mr. Killingsworth's little jokes. My name is John Boucree, Ph.D. Electrical engineering."

"Doctor Boucree." Savage nodded slightly and followed him through the tables, benches and equipment.

"We have fifteen people actually on the staff here now," Boucree explained. "And we're bringing in one or two more every week. Brilliant individuals. You might even know some of them. Most are working in the lab next door. In addition, there are about twenty or thirty more on the estate who are connected to the project in one way or another but don't know any specifics about it. That doesn't include the gardeners, maintenance and janitorial people, of course. You will get to know everybody as time goes by and some will probably already know you, by reputation anyhow, as one of the world's foremost geologists. And you wrote some pretty good papers on conservation too, as I recall."

"Thank you," Savage replied with some hesitation. "I had no idea that I was that well known."

"Well, if your scientific accomplishments didn't make your name a household word, that trial certainly did. I'd like to ask you about that sometime if you wouldn't mind discussing it."

"Well, I—"

"It took a great deal of determination and courage to do what you did and although I don't approve of it, I assure you, Doctor, I can't help but to admire you."

"But I didn't—"

"And now this is the center of our project here, Dr. Savage." The smile on Boucree's face revealed his pride as he extended his hand toward a large steel frame with wires, hoses and tubes leading to and from it. These were attached to various pieces of machinery and apparatus in the room.

It resembled a polished metal doorframe four feet wide and seven feet high set directly into a brick and rock wall. Inside the frame was a forest scene in such beautiful detail and colors in dark and light greens and browns that Savage first took it to be real until he remembered that he was far below the ground. Although the scene was somewhat miniaturized, the motion of the leaves on the trees, the movement of the grass and weeds in the breeze was clearly visible and very lifelike even at a distance, as though he were looking through a large, thick-glass window.

"You've perfected three-dimensional television!" Savage exclaimed, taking a step closer and squinting at the screen. "It's fantastic. And such a large screen. I had no idea things were so far advanced. Just look at that detail. It looks as though you could just walk right in there."

"Television?" Boucree seemed puzzled and the smile left his face for a moment. "Why, no, Doctor, that's not television. Didn't Mr. Damarjiane explain?"

"No. He didn't tell me anything about it."

"He didn't? Well, then—" The smile returned to Boucree's lips at the opportunity to talk about his work. He had had no such opportunity in recent years and now rushed at the chance. "Just let *me* explain."

John Boucree had spent most of his twenty-five professional years in electronics working for North American Aviation in the research department trying to improve flight and navigational circuits in fighter planes. He was gifted and innovative, daring and unconventional which led to discovery after discovery and helped to put North American at the top of the list in electronic design and functional computer controlled flight.

His immediate superior, a woman also gifted in electronics but ambitions and unscrupulous, had stolen one of his most advanced designs, claiming it to be her own and had ridden to a vice presidency on the innovation. When Boucree protested and threatened to sue, he was gently but swiftly forced to retire with the threat that he could be fired and his pension might be subject to revocation if he continued to be vocal about the improved circuit design. The word of a corporate vice president would be taken over his in any lawsuit he might choose to file. Beaten and frustrated, he took his pension and left the company.

Angry, bitter and helpless, branded a liar and a troublemaker, unable to find another job in the electronics field, he began drinking heavily and using cocaine in ever-increasing amounts. He eventually ended up in the hospital where his condition was misdiagnosed as a liver ailment, he was given the wrong medication and he almost died. To the first of his good fortune, for a change, one of Mr. Damarjiane's men discovered him by accident while he was still on the critical list and recognized his name. Money was made available and Boucree woke up in a private sanatorium where he was detoxified, restored to health and offered a job at a good salary with veiled promises of enough power to take revenge on the vice president bitch who had destroyed his career. With little choice, he accepted and went to work for the Palomar Foundation. The woman vice president who had been the cause of his problems died in a car accident less than a year later.

"This," Dr. Boucree explained, indicating the scene within the frame, "is the result of our experimenting with light and concentrated energy fields. I won't go into the technical makeup of the project. You probably wouldn't understand it anyway. You don't have the science for it. I hardly understand it myself, it's so complicated. But very simply, we theorized that by using a magnetic field and certain power boosters, we could defy a heretofore firm law of physics and shoot a pulsed laser beam at a speed faster than the normal speed of light, 186,000 miles per second.

"For what purpose," Savage asked.

"Space travel, of course. The distances between stars are so great that it would take ten, twenty, thirty years, traveling at the speed of light, just to reach another solar system. To cross the galaxy would take thousands of years unless we could prove Einstein wrong and travel faster than light. And what we wanted to travel faster than light was light itself. So, we set up a magnetic energy field inside that frame you see there, a field which was so powerful it began to drag pieces of equipment off the tables. Something like a black hole. That's why everything is bolted down. We used four lasers, two reds, a green and a yellow, all produced independently but focused on the same spot in the center of the field. You can just make out the beams projected onto the field from right up there." He pointed out the four laser guns.

"We hoped the magnetic field would increase the speed of the light beams, throw the combined beams into the fourth dimension and actually bend time and space. That would give the beams unlimited range, limitless power and, of course, unlimited speed, and remember, speed is what we were looking for. If we could move a laser beam which is just light, *faster* than light, then we could move anything faster than light. When the beams first struck the energy field, however, they seemed to join and blend then to spread. The scene you see before you suddenly appeared.

"We had no idea what we had created, what it was or what it could do. We tested it for solidity and we found that an object can pass right through the frame into whatever is beyond. It actually goes into and becomes a part of that forest scene there."

"Wait a minute," Savage objected, pointing to the screen. "Are you trying to tell me that this is some kind of matter transmitter or something you've invented? That a solid object can be put through that screen and it will actually be sent from here to some other place around the world?"

"Oh, no, Doctor, that's not what I'm telling you at all," Boucree replied, dry-washing his hands in front of him like a TV cartoon villain and obviously enjoying himself as he continued to explain. "Because that scene you're looking at isn't *on* this world. We don't know where it is, but it certainly isn't on earth. We've established that. It might not even be in our galaxy.

"But part of your observation is correct. It is a transmitter. Somehow, we have created a window, an opening through time or space or distance and who knows what else, maybe even into the subatomic structure of the universe itself, to some other microscopic universe, some place, some planet, some world somewhere out there." He pointed a finger first to the ceiling, then to the image in the frame. "And this is our window in the world."

"I don't believe it."

"Believe it, Doctor."

"It's utterly fantastic."

"Yes, isn't it."

"I still don't believe it."

"You have but to look. It's there in front of you."

"How does it work?"

"We don't know. It just does. We've tried recreating it. We have another lab set up next door, just down the hall, with the exact same equipment, a dozen electronics experts working on it with the best computer equipment and software we can buy, but so far we can't get it to work. So, this is the only one he have right now."

"It staggers the mind."

"Yes, it does. We couldn't believe it at first and it took awhile to realize what we had discovered, or created, if you will. The potential of it is beyond imagination. There are days and nights there. Things grow there, it rains, the wind blows and we think we've seen things scurrying through the grass."

"You mean living things? Are you saying that there is life there? Animal life? Human life?"

"Animal life most certainly, and as for the rest, we'll know soon enough, won't we Doctor." Boucree seemed to think his remark was understood and he turned toward where the lawyer stood watching them. Behind him was the sound of the huge vault door began to open.

"There has been a slight change of plan, Professor," Killingsworth said a few moments later, stepping into the room.

"Change of plan? What change of plan?"

"Patients, Professor."

Savage watched as the sound of the vault door opening subsided and the door to the lab opened admitting a young woman wearing a white blouse and very short shorts. She had reddish-blonde hair cut short, skin deeply tanned and even with no makeup, she was the most beautiful woman David Savage had ever seen. Her breasts were well developed, she had wide hips, beautifully shaped legs and a muscular body. He openly stared at her, much to the lawyer's amusement.

"Why is she here, Killingsworth?" Boucree asked.

"Having now met him, do you believe that Dr. Savage is currently up to his task?"

"I was told that David Savage was going to be the man who . . ." Boucree's eyes scanned Savage from head to foot. "Well, he isn't exactly the—"

"Precisely. She's here to render an expert opinion."

"All right. I see. Well?" Boucree looked at the young woman.

"That's him?" she asked. It was a toss-up whether there was more contempt in her voice or in the look she gave him.

"That's him, my dear," Killingsworth responded. "This is Doctor David Savage, in the flesh."

"You're telling me that he's—"

"Yes."

"He wouldn't last a day," she said.

"Do you concur, Professor?"

"A day might be long enough," Boucree responded, guardedly.

"No it wouldn't and you know it."

"Well, yes, all right. How long then?"

"How long do you need?" the lawyer asked the young woman in shorts.

"Six months."

"Out of the question. Two at the most."

"Three," she countered.

"Can you do it in three?"

"I can do something in three months."

"I'll present it to Mr. Damarjiane. If he approves, that will give you three more months. Professor," Killingsworth went on, turning to Boucree, "you have three months to set up the second window. Can you do it?"

"I don't know."

Agitated and annoyed that everyone was talking about and around him but excluding him completely, Savage asked, "Just what is it that I'm supposed to be doing around here, anyway?"

"They didn't tell you?" Diana's surprise was genuine.

"Tell me what?"

"My instructions were to bring him here." Killingsworth held up both hands, palms out. "Nothing more."

"I assumed he knew," Boucree said, shrugging his shoulders.

"If you didn't know, why did you agree?" Diana asked Savage, focusing her eyes on him.

"Agree to what?"

"What you are going to do."

"Just what am I doing to do?"

"You don't know?"

"Know what?"

"You are going to be the first human being to go through the Window to the other world."

CHAPTER SEVEN

"I'M GONNA DO WHAT!?" Savage shouted the question.

"You're the guinea pig, Dr. Savage," Diana said. "You go through the Window there and if you don't explode and you don't instantly drop dead or start foaming at the mouth, we'll have some idea whether people can survive on that world, wherever it is."

"You're outta you fuckin mind, lady, if you think I'm gonna—"

"Guinea pig is a very harsh term, Diana," Killingsworth remarked, looking down at her. "Must you be so tactless?"

"Diplomacy is your business, not mine," she shot back at him.

"Even so, a little tact—"

"Hey! Remember me?" Savage shouted. Prison had changed him. Those years of association with the lowest, most brutal class of human animal had influenced his language, his attitude, and his outlook on everything. "Don't fuckin talk around me. I'm right here."

His language did indeed shock most of the people there, but they concealed it well. "I'm sorry, Doctor. We had planned,"

Boucree said, felling his anger rise as he glared at Diana, "to give you some time and let you familiarize yourself with the project before explaining your specific role in it. Lead up to it gradually, so to speak. Cultivate your interest; stimulate your curiosity, hopefully leading you as an explorer to make the suggestion of going through the Window, yourself. Hitting you in the face with it like this on your first day here was not the idea, I assure you."

"Okay. I apologize for the language. I'm just not used to being around . . ." he almost said people . . . "women. But this, this is—"

Diana appeared to be somewhat angry herself, but also partly amused as she listened to Boucree's explanation.

"It's all rather academic now, isn't it," Killingsworth remarked, he too with a look of disgust at Diana. "Get on with it. You have three months." He then turned and walked to the door where he stood waiting for the project director to continue his explanation to Savage.

"As far as we have been able to determine," John Boucree said quickly, attempting to overcome and compensate for the shock Diana had intentionally given him for some unknown reason, "it is a primitive, rugged world which will require all of your experience, knowledge and the physical conditioning and survival skills Diana can teach you."

"*She* can teach me?" Savage questioned, looking back at the woman. "What the hell are you talking about?"

"In addition, your mental condition, your attitude must be changed to one of initiative and aggressiveness rather than, forgive me, Doctor, the one of submission and subservience which you now seem to have, and you will need to brush up on your geology and meteorology if you are to send back accurate reports of the conditions there. Absolutely everything you could possibly require will be provided, but we must begin at once. As you have just been informed, you are now scheduled to go through the Window in three months."

"Is it safe? I mean, ahhh . . . can a person actually go through there and survive?"

"We think so, Doctor," Boucree explained patiently. "We have made exhaustive tests, put through several experimental animals including a large dog and they all seem to have made it without harmful effects. A human shouldn't experience any additional problems, we believe."

Not yet recovered from the surprising revelation and intent upon what Boucree was saying, Savage did not see the look of hate and contempt Diana gave the project director when he mentioned the dog. From across the room, Killingsworth saw it and he smiled. The dog had been his idea.

"We have taken atmospheric readings," Dr. Boucree continued, drawing Savage's attention back to the Window, "and we've verified the air content as breathable, slightly oxygen rich by Earth standards. You might experience a mild euphoria initially, but it will pass quickly. If you will look closely there at the bottom of the frame, you can see some of our instruments on the ground in the grass. There are a couple of strange gases we can't identify but it appears that a man can survive there. The barometer shows thirty-point-two, which is pretty normal. Humidity is at seventy-six percent." He looked directly and intently at Savage. "But you'll let us know for sure, won't you, Doctor."

"I'm not gonna do this."

"But . . . but, that's why you are here. Your background, your experiences, your education is perfect for it. You can report back everything we need to know to live there. You will be the pathfinder, the trailblazer, the vanguard to a whole new world. Not since Leif Ericson discovered North America has a man had the opportunity you have, Doctor Savage. Should you actually survive, think of the contribution to civilization and mankind."

"Should I survive? *Should?* What are you giving me for a life expectancy, Doctor Boucree?"

"We have no specific figures to—"

"Forty-eight hours," Diana said. "A week, absolute max."

"Not a chance," Savage responded.

From near the door Killingsworth stood with his arms folded, leaning casually against the wall. He said, "You are living on borrowed time as it is, Doctor. We are offering you three months plus two days or a week. Take it. You know the alternative." He pointed his index finger and dropped his thumb on it. Bang, his lips said silently.

"And just what is it that I'm supposed to be doing in this three months?"

"Getting back into shape, Doctor," Killingsworth said, launching himself forward and walking to the small group. "Diana will teach you, train you, get you ready for the jump into the new world. Perhaps it will help. Perhaps it won't. I would prefer sending you through right now, just to see what would happen. I believe the professor would agree with me. He's waited a long time. But the final decision is not up to either of us."

"I think, first," Diana said, "Dr. Savage needs a complete physical examination. He appears to be undernourished, in ill health and physically deficient. He will need strict conditioning and a balanced diet."

"I will leave him in your care," Killingsworth said.

"This way, Dr. Savage," Diana offer, putting her hand on his bony shoulder and then quickly jerking it away as though she had touched something hot or repulsive. Killingsworth was leaving through another door that led to a different part of the underground complex.

"Come in anytime," Boucree called out, "there's a lot more to tell you about the project and what we hope to do with it."

Diana led him through the door by which they had entered the lab but this time they turned left, away from the vault door. Savage found himself in a well lighted, wide and carpeted hallway with wood paneled walls and an acoustic ceiling. Along the corridor there were ordinary wood doors leading off both sides.

Had he not been shown, he would not have believed that he was some sixty feet underground.

"I don't understand how someone could allow themselves to get into such terrible physical shape," Diana said as they walked side by side. "Have you been ill?"

"That's as good an explanation as any, I guess."

"Serious?"

"Yes. There for awhile I thought it was terminal."

"And you are now recovering?"

"Recovering."

"Cancer?"

"Something worse."

"What could be worse than cancer?"

Savage didn't answer.

The medical facility to which the young woman took him was as modern and complete as any hospital with every machine and device known to medical science, and the physical examination he received was given by a competent and professional young MD. Diana didn't introduce him to the doctor nor did she offer to leave the room when he was asked to strip to his shorts, ignoring completely that he was obviously embarrassed by her presence in the examining room.

It was more his sunken chest, his thin limbs and his lack of build rather than his nakedness that made him so self-conscious. Although the prison food was plentiful and nutritious, the death sentence had a profound effect on his appetite and he ate little. His once rugged and muscular body, conditioned by the wooded, mountainous and frozen terrain he covered in his quest for new oil and mineral deposits, quickly deteriorated during his years on Death Row. Atrophy was the result of his confinement to a single cell with almost no physical exercise, leaving little but a skin covered skeleton with hollow eyes, bad teeth and pale lips. In the presence of this lovely woman, the first live women he had seen in over four years—other than Warden Bennett—he wanted very much to feel like a man.

"He'll need the right food and a good exercise program," Dr. Worthington said to Diana, "to build up his body, and an atmosphere as free of anxiety as possible. His blood pressure's pretty high." He made a number of notes in a folder he held.

PROJECT WINDOW

```
SAVAGE  Dr.DAVID L.

   Age:  46
Weight:  145 pounds
Height:  6 feet ½ inch
  Eyes:  brown
```

"How long have you worn glasses, Doctor?" the physician asked, turning back to Savage.

"Off and on for the last fifteen or so years."

"More on that off lately, I would guess. I would also suspect the beginning of glaucoma although I can't be sure without a test. I'll arrange for an examination by an ophthalmologist tomorrow morning to confirm my findings and then have you fitted for contacts so you can see. Unless you would prefer to wear glasses."

"That's just great," Savage replied, trying not to think about going blind because of glaucoma.

Misunderstanding the reply, the physician continued. "Will you be all right until tomorrow?"

"Oh, I have glasses. I just didn't bring them with me today."

Diana had gotten bored with watching the examination, wandered around the medical office for a few minutes looking at things that didn't interest her and then left. She returned almost an hour later just as the doctor was finishing. "He's all yours."

"He said he has been seriously ill. Any chance of a relapse?"

"Ill?" Worthington looked at Savage. "He didn't say anything about being ill."

"That's not what I asked you."

"Ah, no. I don't believe there is any danger of a relapse."

"Good. I think we should start with a few simple calisthenics and then some jogging. I think he can handle that. Later we can increase it to weights, the universal gym and some serious running. It'll be a good start for somebody in his condition." Diana made no attempt to hide her feelings about him or the disdain for the job she had been given. She spoke neither to him nor to the doctor, more to herself or some nonexistent third person. Then with only a slight glance at David Savage she continued, "Follow me."

If she noticed the shake of his head and the disgusted look the medical doctor gave her because of her attitude, she ignored that too and walked from the room with the same air of detached boredom for which Killingsworth was known.

Savage put on his clothes, nodded to the doctor and walked from the room. He found her waiting for him in the hallway outside, leaning against one of the walls appearing to examine her fingernails. Without a word she led him further down the corridor to a fully equipped exercise room, gave him a gray sweat suit to replace his clothes, then again stood and watched as he undressed to his underwear and put on the sweats.

"Are you ready, Barney?"

"Barney?" he questioned, turning his head to look at her out of the corner of his eye.

"Like Barney the scrivener," she said. "It's a short story by Dickens. You may have heard of it. It's about a little wimp who sat at a tall desk in a dark room with only a candle for light and scribbled all day with pen and ink. It seems to fit you."

"Yes, I've read it. Is that really what you see when you look at me?"

"It doesn't matter what I see. I have a job to do and so do you. So let's get at it."

"Why are you being so spiteful?

"You're right, Doctor, and I'm wrong. I apologize. I was not told until just this morning that you would need extensive physical conditioning and it was my responsibility to provide it. Even then, I wasn't appraised that you had been ill or the extent of your . . . deterioration. It throws everything off schedule. My first reaction was resentment, my second was the time it would take to get you into shape, but I had no right to either of those. Again, I apologize."

"Okay. Forget it. I'm a mess. I know it. Anything you can do to help will be appreciated. But believe it or not, I was in pretty good physical shape at one time."

"Yes, time. That's what does it. Time."

"So, time will catch up with you, too. What are you, twenty-four, twenty-five?"

"That's not important."

"No, I suppose not now. But in another fifteen or twenty years—"

"Let's begin with a few simple exercises," she interrupted. "They will loosen you up."

"Lead on. I'll follow. If I can."

Together they did a few sit-ups, a few push-ups, some deep-knee bends and then she put him on a treadmill. She trotted beside him on the moving belt, her deeply tanned body moving in effortless strides while he pounded along beside her in short, clumsy steps. Five minutes of running was all he could endure and he stumbled off the treadmill gasping for breath.

"You are in about the worst physical shape I've seen in a long time," she commented, turning the machine off. "Good thing you don't smoke cigarettes. You'd be in a coughing fit right now."

"Yeah, well, I did smoke for quite awhile. Finally gave 'em up. Just couldn't afford them anymore." He tried to laugh at his joke but it caught in his throat and he drew in deep, labored breaths, almost ready to break into the coughing fit she had mentioned.

"Take a break for a few minutes and then we'll do it again. We're just reactivating your muscles now, not attempting to build them up. That will come later. You might be a little sore later on."

"I'm a little sore right now."

"Nothing like you're going to be."

"Can I look forward to that?"

Not sure how to respond, she said nothing, just sat with her back to the wall and watched him. His eyes were closed, his chin almost on his chest and his jogging suit soaked with perspiration. He looked half-dead.

"On second thought," she said after a few minutes, "I think that's enough for the first time. There's a steam room and showers through that door over there," she said, pointing with one finger. "Go take some steam and then a shower. It will help you breathe better and get rid of some of the poisons in your body. We'll begin again tomorrow morning. When we get into the weights, it's going to be a lot harder."

Without replying he climbed to his feet and shuffled to the door she had indicated. The steam room was to his left with hooks and hangers on each side of the door. A rack held a number of thick, white towels all neatly folded. Struggling out of his sweat suit and underwear, he took one of the towels, wrapped it around his body and pulled the door open.

Large enough for a dozen people, with wooden benches on three sides, the room was already hot and full of steam. Dropping onto one of the benches, he inhaled slowly and deeply, feeling the heat and the moisture reach his lungs and penetrate his body. It had been years since he had been in a sauna and it was pure luxury for him. With his eyes closed, breathing in the steam, feeling the heat on his body and the perspiration pour from him, he felt himself relax completely for the first time in longer than he could remember, and he slumped against the wall losing all track of time.

"Doctor? Hey, Doctor Savage?" He was half-asleep and the voice cut deeply into his quiet, tired contentment. "Better go hit the showers, Doc. You've been in here quite a while."

"What?" Savage looked up through the misty steam, trying to focus on a shape in front of him.

"You're going to turn into a lobster if you stay here much longer."

"Oh, yeah, sure," Savage said, climbing to his feet. He was able to better focus now and he could see the man who had been on the plane, the one with the Uzi. Mr. Safari Jacket who now wore only a towel around his waist and no Uzi.

"Hey, you okay, Doc?"

"Just a little tired. I'm used to sitting a lot in a small room without too much to do."

"Sure. I can identify with that. Done a bunch of it myself. Name's DeShane. Can I give you a hand?"

"No, I'm fine. Thanks. The shower will help."

"Yeah, it does. Start out real hot and then get it as cold as you can stand it. I do this almost every day after a workout. Man, it's great. I haven't felt better in years."

"Nice to make your acquaintance, Mr. DeShane." Savage looked at the young man before him, his hairy chest rippling with muscles, biceps bulging, his entire body appearing to be as solid as stone. That's what I used to be, he thought to himself as he staggered toward the showers and let the water pour over him, slowly adjusting it from hot to cold. Within just a few minutes, DeShane had joined him in the shower.

"Feels good, huh, Doc?"

"Yes, it sure does. You didn't stay in there very long."

"No time, Doc. Busy as hell, you know. Just grab a few minutes here and there whenever I can."

"You were on the plane with me."

"Yes, I was."

"Who the hell are you, anyway?"

"Told you. Name's DeShane. I work here, just like you."

"All right. *What* are you?"

"Security. Just one of the uniforms. You'll see us all over the place around here."

"Sure."

After they dried off and were dressed in clean clothes laid out on the bench outside the steam room by a person or persons unseen, DeShane led the way through the underground halls to the steel connecting door, then up to Savage's room on the second floor of the stately mansion.

"Until you get to know your way around here a little, I thought maybe you wouldn't mind some company. It's pretty easy to get lost down here in all of those passageways," DeShane said. "Took me awhile to get used to it." He turned away, leaving Savage at his door.

"Yeah, ah, thanks," Savage replied. "Ahh . . . you want to come in for awhile?"

"Nope. Got other things I gotta do. See you later, Doc."

Entering the apartment and glancing around briefly, Savage thought seriously about a drink, a real stiff one of aged Scotch and just a dash of soda, his first in several years. However, a quick search revealed that there was no alcohol anywhere in his rooms. Even the remainder of the wine he had with the meal was gone.

Settling for a glass of orange juice, he sat on the couch and looked out through the large picture window onto the back yard with its sidewalks, hedges, and groves of trees and flowerbeds profuse with color. The grass along the sidewalks and around the blower beds was neatly edged and there wasn't a weed in sight.

Still attempting to ponder and understand this unbelievable turn of events in his life, this place, the lawyer and Mr. Damarjiane, the beautiful Diana and that security guard, DeShane, and exhausted from the workout he closed his eyes and fell asleep on the couch.

It was a little after noon and there was a knock on his door. The knob turned and lunch was brought to him and spread on the dinette table. Another knock and DeShane entered carrying a large brief case that he sat on the floor beside the table.

"Brought you some stuff," he said, taking a seat across from Savage. "VCR tapes and some books on survival and weapons, some text books, stuff like that. Since you're cooped up here for awhile, it will give you something to occupy your time. If you get bored, you can watch regular TV. There will be somebody in later to update you on the computer and show you some of the new programs."

"Do you have to keep that door locked?"

"Yeah, I'm afraid so, at night anyway. That's the orders. If you need anything, all you have to do is pick up the phone and ask. It'll be brought to you."

"How long do I stay locked up?"

"I don't know, Doc. but I would guess not very long. Just a security precaution, you understand. You're pretty valuable to the people around here, so I'm told."

"What's the chance of getting a drink?"

"A drink? You mean booze?"

"Yeah."

"None. The physician says your system can't handle it right now."

"Why?"

"Don't know."

"Don't know or won't say?"

"Take your pick."

"Is there something else wrong with me that I don't know about?"

"Ask the doc, Doc."

"You're a big help."

"I try."

"You're *very* trying. Tell me about the plane."

"What about it?"

"Double engine failure in the final approach? I wonder what the odds are on that."

"It's being looked into, Doc. That's all I can tell you at the moment."

There was another knock at the door but nobody entered. Savage looked at DeShane who just shrugged. Getting to his feet, David Savage crossed the room and opened the door.

"Am I interrupting anything?" Dr. Boucree asked. "Just thought I would drop in for a few minutes."

"I was just leaving," DeShane said, climbing from the chair.

Seeing the littered table, Boucree hesitated. "I didn't realize I had caught you in the middle of lunch. I can come back."

"No, really, it's all right. Ahh, Mr. DeShane, you don't have to leave, you know."

"No place for the hired help, Doc. I'll have something sent up for you, Dr. Boucree. Excuse me."

"Well, thank you, DeShane. If Dr. Savage doesn't mind, I think I *will* join him for lunch."

"Are there guards on my door out there?" Savage asked after DeShane had left.

"Oh, yes. There are guards everywhere. Quite comforting, actually. You should have seen how tight security was when I worked for North American."

"Comforting to you, perhaps."

"Doctor, I don't think you realize yet just how important this project is, what it can mean to the world, to humanity. It is more revolutionary than the discovery of electricity, air travel, space flight, atomic power. We are on the threshold of the most fantastic advancement in the history of man."

"If you can figure out how it works."

"Well, yes, we will, Dr. Savage. We will."

"And you don't think somebody else somewhere in the world is working on the same thing right now?"

"How could they? Nobody could conceive of such a thing. I told you we discovered it completely by accident. You couldn't get half a dozen scientists in the entire world to admit that such a thing was even possible. Had you not seen it, would you believe it?"

"I've seen it and I'm still not sure I believe it."

"So you stated. Have I made my point, Doctor?"

Still another knock on the door and lunch was brought in and placed on the table for Boucree. Both men sat and ate.

"Why me, Boucree? Why did they pick me?"

"I really don't know, Dr. Savage. Mr. Damarjiane makes all the final decisions. However, I presume that you were the best man for the job. That's the way he picks people."

"Who is this Mr. Damarjiane, anyway? I've never heard of him."

"Well, I can tell you this. He's a great man. He's interested in science and saving humanity. And he has the money and the power to do it."

"Saving humanity? I didn't know humanity needed saving."

"I'm talking too much. You need to be asking him these questions."

"Now you're sounding like DeShane. Can you at least tell me who *he* is?"

"DeShane? He's the Chief of Security here. Reports directly to Mr. Damarjiane, I understand."

"He told me he was just one of the guards."

"Well, if that's what he told you, he must have had a reason. Please don't say anything. I . . . I have a tendency to talk too much."

"What about that lawyer, Killingsworth? Who's he?"

"Please, Dr. Savage. Please. No more questions. I just can't help you."

"Sure, Professor, I understand. Enjoy your lunch."

—*—

For an hour he and Diana did stretching, loosening up and isometric exercises while his huge breakfast had an opportunity to digest. It quickly became apparent that she was superbly trained, that she had knowledge and skills completely unknown to the body builders and physical fitness addicts the "pumping iron" gyms made millions on.

"In addition to physical conditioning," she said, "there are mental exercises. Lessons to be learned in both."

"Such as?"

"The ability to control things around you."

"Such as?"

She told him to hold his right arm out straight in front of him, hand extended, palm up. He did. She placed an ordinary ballpoint pen in his hand and sat watching him. After a short time she asked, "Is it heavy?"

"What?"

"The pen."

"The pen? No, of course it isn't."

"It will become heavy."

"It will?"

"Yes. Very heavy. Look at me. Look at my eyes. The pen will become heavy. Your hand will begin to tremble. The pen will be so heavy you cannot continue to hold it up. Do you feel it?"

"No."

"Do not look away. Look at my eyes."

"You have beautiful eyes."

"Don't speak. Look at my eyes. Listen to my voice. Your hand is beginning to drop. Hold it up."

"I am."

"Be silent and look at my eyes, David. Look, David. My eyes are the deep blue color of the sea. Soft, warm, caressing. The temperate waters wash gently over you, bathing you in luxury. The blue is spreading. Everything is blue. You see nothing but my eyes. You hear nothing but the sound of my voice. Listen to my voice, David. The pen is so heavy. Your arm is dropping. The pen is so heavy, you can't hold it up. The pen is so heavy you can't hold it."

Perspiration began to break out on his forehead and trickled down his face. "No. No, it isn't heavy."

"Quiet. Concentrate, David. Hold the pen up. Hold it up. It is coming down. Hold your hand up. Hold it up."

"I . . . I am."

Her voice was a low, soft, almost musical purr resonating with ever-increasing intensity, but with no more volume. It was like no voice he had ever heard before. "Look at me, David. Look deep into my eyes. You can't look away. Listen to my voice. The pen is so heavy.

"Look at your hand. It is almost to the floor. You can't hold it up. The pen is so heavy. Now!" she shouted sharply. "Look at your hand."

Savage tore his eyes from hers and looked down at his hand. She was right. His fingers were almost touching the floor.

"You . . . you hypnotized me," he said in amazement, raising his hand and clutching the pen in his palm. It weighed nothing. "In less than a minute. That's not possible."

"Forty seconds," she corrected. "You were difficult. It usually takes less."

He just shook his head and tried to speak but couldn't. Finally, he managed, "How did you do that?"

"As you said, hypnotism. A simple trick. It sometimes helps to gain a momentary advantage."

"A trick?"

"Yes. A trick."

"Forty seconds?"

"Yes."

"And I really wasn't difficult, was I?"

"No, Doctor, you were not."

"I'm very impressed, Diana. And more than just a little intimidated."

"Don't be. Now that you have experienced it, I couldn't do it to you again."

"Well, I'm not so sure. Where in the world did you learn to do something like that?"

"We need to start working on your muscles, now. In the beginning, the build-up will be slow, but each day you will improve. Let's begin on the treadmill."

"You didn't answer my question."

"No, I didn't."

After a thirty-minute workout in the gym leaving him panting and hurting, he spent fifteen minutes in the steam room and then took a cold shower. As before, his clothes were laid out on a bench when he finished the shower.

Wearing a different blouse, pale blue slacks and her hair still damp from the shower, Diana declined to give him a tour of the underground complex. "Killingsworth is the tour guide here, not me."

"Do I get the impression you don't like him very much?"

"Get any impression you like, Doctor."

She took him up the elevator and back to his room where more textbooks, newspapers and VCR tapes had been delivered. A light rain had begun to fall making everything gloomy.

"This tape was recently released," Diana said, putting it into the VCR. "I think you'll find it very interesting."

The majority of the hour-long program was on the 1990 volcanic eruption of Mt. Saint Helens in Western Washington State and some revolutionary theories that were presented. Photographs showed a valley a hundred feet deep and two hundred feet wide cut through solid granite and a small stream running through the center. The narrator of the film claimed that the valley was made when the mountain exploded, that the huge chasm was cut in less than an hour. A comparison was made to the Grand Canyon in Arizona and the suggestion was made that maybe the Grand Canyon hadn't taken millions of years to form, but may have taken only a few days or weeks. The accepted geological explanation of water cutting away an inch or two every thousand years could be wrong based on the Mount St. Helens discovery.

Another series of pictures showed a sheer cliff sixty feet high with the layers of strata clearly visible. The claim this time was that it had been formed in one day by the thousands of tons of ash, dust, rock and lava falling there.

The program turned out to have been made by a religious group attempting to verify the biblical claim that the earth was created in six days. It failed, but the swift creation of the valley and the cliff could not be ignored. Photographs before and after the explosion verified that they had indeed been made in a matter of hours or days, certainly not years or centuries.

She watched the tape with him and snapped off the TV when it was finished. "Well, what do you think?" she asked.

"Fascinating," he replied.

"Does it question established geological explanations?"

"Well, yes and no. When Krakatoa blew in 1883, the whole island vanished in a single afternoon. They made a movie of it with Frank Sanatra. It was called The Devil at Six o'clock or something like that. Then, in 1902, Mt. Pelee erupted and destroyed the city of St. Pierre, killing some 30,000 people because they couldn't escape fast enough. So, we've always known things can happen quickly. The valleys and cliffs below St. Helens just add to our knowledge and gives us more answers to difficult questions."

"So you're telling me the Grand Canyon could have been formed in a month or a year?"

"There's an easy way to find out."

"How?"

"Weathering. The eroding effects of wind, rain, running water, flying sand, freezing and thawing, earth tremors, anything that causes physical change. If the canyon *was* formed in a short time, the walls would be uniformly affected from top to bottom. If it wasn't, they won't."

"I assume this has been done."

"Yes."

"Was the Mt. Pelee eruption unique in history?"

"Is this a quiz?"

"Yes."

"All right. No. It was not unique in history. Vesuvius buried Pompeii in 79 AD killing everyone there. It was called a glowing cloud eruption. As with Pelee, the toxic gasses from Vesuvius traveled down the mountain at something like 70 miles an hour. In a Hawaiian phase volcanic eruption, the flowing lava can move faster than a horse can run."

"I'm impressed, Doctor."

"Don't be, Miss . . ." He spread his hands in a helpless gesture. ". . . Diana. Any first year geology student could have told you that."

"Really?" She stood up and marched to the door.

"What did I say?"

She opened the door, stomped through and slammed it behind her. He heard the lock turn.

He had intended to invite her to stay for lunch with him, hoping to get to know her better. But somehow, he had only succeeded in making her mad. Tomorrow's workout in the gym just might be a killer.

Lunch was brought to him by the silent waiter and he turned on the worldwide news in an attempt to catch up on the events of the past five years. He was particularly fascinated by the collapse of the Soviet Union, the war with Iraq and the government sponsored, socialized medical plan the current president was attempting to foist off on the public at their own expense. It had been tried in other countries before and it never worked. Why did this president think it would work here?

There was no news of his escape or that he was missing form prison. No news was good news, but it had only been two days and he was an entire continent away. Maybe a mysterious prison break on the other side of the country wasn't news here. Switching off the TV, he tentatively picked up the phone. Immediately a male voice responded. "Yes, Dr. Savage."

"Oh, ahhh . . . would it be possible to get some out of state newspapers, particular Philadelphia?"

"I'll check, Doctor."

"Also, could I speak to the physician who examined me when I got here yesterday? I don't remember his name but—"

There was a click and a hum, the sound of him being put on hold, and then another barely discernible click. Another man came on the line. "Doctor Savage, I'm glad you called. I'd like to go over your test results with you."

"Yes, well, I've got a couple of questions about—"

"I'll be waiting in my office. I'm free right now and the ophthalmologist is here. Why don't you come on down."

"Well, I'm not so sure I can do that just—"

There was a quick knock at his door, the lock clicked and DeShane entered. "On second thought," Savage said, "yes, I guess I can. Thank you, Doctor."

"Need a guide dog, Doc?" the security chief said, standing beside the open door. He was wearing a tan shirt and trousers with the cuffs bloused over high, lace-up boots. He had a raincoat over one arm.

"You know, Mr. DeShane," savage said, hanging up the phone. "You're a little scary."

"Just part of the job, Doc. He was grinning, obviously enjoying himself.

"You were listening in on the phone, weren't you."

"That's part of the job, too. But actually, no, I wasn't. Somebody else was. I was just told to come get you."

"Know where I want to go?"

"No, but I'm sure you'll tell me."

"All right, Mr. DeShane. Let's go."

"Go where?"

"To see my doctor, of course."

"Of course. Grab an umbrella. It's gotten pretty nasty out there. A Southern California downpour. Rare as fuzz on a frog."

Once again he traversed the hallway, down the curved staircase to the main floor and then through the back door into a pouring rain. The gravel road was filled with puddles. Savage followed Mr. Safari Jacket, the man he now knew as DeShane into the shed, through the vault door, down the hallway and on into the medical office.

"Tell me something, DeShane," Savage said, while they were still in the elevator. "Do you always travel around the country in airplanes with a machine gun?"

"Sometimes. It's part of the job I do, Doc."

"Are we in some kind of danger?"

"None that I know of."

"I've been told this isn't connected with the government in any way."

"Good grief, no! Can you imagine what a mess this place would be if the government got their fingers into it?"

"Then why all the security?"

"Money, Doc. This outfit's got it and whenever there's a lot of money around, there's somebody always trying to get their hands on it one way or another."

"Oh," was Savage's only reply. DeShane obviously wasn't going to tell him anything.

The security chief courteously opened the door and Savage entered. The physician was waiting, dressed appropriately in a white hip-length coat and tan trousers. The only thing missing was the stethoscope hanging around his neck.

"I'll wait outside," DeShane Said.

"Let's talk in my office," the doctor said and led the way to a comfortable room containing a desk, table, several chairs, bookcases full of hard-bound volumes, white oak paneling on the walls and floor-to-ceiling drapes behind the desk as though there was a window behind them.

"How do you stand it?" Savage asked, settling himself in one of the chairs before the desk. "Down here, underground all the time. You never see the sun. It must be like a dungeon." Or like a cell on Death Row, he didn't say out loud.

"I worked in a hospital in New York before I came here. The building covered a square city block and was forty-two stories high. My office, on the rare occasions I could spend some time in it and if I could remember where it was, was about the size of a broom closet. I never saw the sun there, either. I decided to bag it, go into private practice and have a life outside of the hospital."

"Sounds reasonable."

"Do you have any idea how many doctors there are in New York City? All of them competing for patients to pay for their offices, staff, equipment, malpractice insurance, attorney on retainer, ads in the Yellow Pages, instruments, drugs, bandages? No? Well, I didn't either.

"I didn't know how many patients were on Medicare and how much paperwork it took to get reimbursed or how many clerks it would take to get all of that paperwork done. I didn't know how many patients paid with bad checks or how many just didn't pay at all. I didn't know how much medical malpractice insurance was or how many lawyers there were out there just itching to sue a doctor. I got so discouraged I thought about looking for a job as a gas station attendant in Taos, New Mexico.

"One Friday afternoon Mr. Killingsworth came strolling into my office right past my receptionist, my medical secretary and the woman who was supposed to be the buffer for all outside traffic, introduced himself in front of my desk and ask me if I would consider leaving New York. Before I could answer, he casually dropped a certified check in front of me and when I looked at the amount, I almost went into cardiac arrest. So, here I am and I've never regretted it for a minute."

"I'm sorry, Doctor. I didn't intend to pry."

"You didn't." He picked up what appeared to be a TV remote and pushed one of the buttons. The drapes behind his desk opened to reveal a large window showing a view of the back yard and walkway by which he and DeShane had entered the underground complex. The falling rain was very apparent.

Savage stared and half rose from his chair.

"How—"

"Pretty impressive, isn't it," Dr. Worthington said. "Makes you think you're on the surface." He leaned back in his chair and rapped his knuckles on the window. "Closed circuit TV. Five by six foot screen, only two inches thick and as you can see the clarity is amazing. It was developed right here at Palomar. They are making small versions now as computer monitors but the big ones should begin coming out next year and you will begin to see an ever-increasing amount of sub-surface apartments and offices appearing in the major cities. They can put the camera anywhere. Instead of seeing sidewalks and people, you could see the ocean or mountains in the distance. Any scene you want."

"Amazing."

"Yes. Now," he opened a file on his desk and looked at it, "you have a severe case of gastroenteritis, Dr. Savage," the physical informed him. "That's an infection of the stomach and intestine linings. We can cure it easily with antibiotics, but I don't know how bad the damage is without some more tests and some x-rays. That damage might lead to other problems."

"You mean like stomach cancer?"

"No, you don't have cancer but it's going to take a combination of drugs and strict diet to stop what is happening in your body. You have neglected yourself for a long time and now, I'm afraid, you are paying the price for it."

"Am I going to die?"

"We all die. As a scientist, you know that. The only question is, when. What I think you are really asking is, will I die next month or next year. The answer is, no."

"Thank you for that, Doctor."

"Certainly. Take two of these and call me in the morning."

Savage laughed at the cliché.

"I know who you are, Doctor Savage. I'm glad you're with us."

There was an instant of fear. "Who I am?"

"You were sort of an Indiana Jones character to most of us in the professional field with twenty years of schooling and new on the job. Of course, the Doc Savage paperbacks didn't hurt your name recognition any, either, I might add. But you, Doctor, you were a *real* Indiana Jones, not just a movie character. You were out there, the rifle slung over your shoulder, that stupid grin on your face in the news photos with the hat just like Harrison Ford wore. I always wondered if they got that hat idea from you. You should sue for infringement on a trademark. Anyway, there you were finding oil fields, diamond mines and mineral deposits, doing things we about which we could only read and dream. All you needed was newsreel footage with your foot propped up on a trophy kill, something with horns or claws."

"Was I *that* bad?"

"No." There was actual admiration in the physician's voice. "You were that *good*. Of course, there were the adventure books you wrote. I can just imagine you sitting out there somewhere near a campfire writing your stories with a pencil stub although you were probably dictating into a cell phone or sitting in an office using a computer."

"Believe it or not, most of them *were* written in the field on my exploration trips. Gave me something to do when I couldn't sleep at night and I finished my last paperback."

"I read Alaskan Plateau twice. The Amazon Treasure was another one I couldn't put down. Did all of that stuff really happen?"

Savage grinned. "About half of it. The rest was pure imagination."

"Even so, do you know how many kids you inspired to become geologists because of those stories? Your characters were so real and their adventures so believable that it was like it was really happening. You were right up there with Clive Cussler."

"Thank you, Doctor Worthington. I'm flattered."

Worthington folded his hands and became very serious as he looked across the desk at his patient. "We were so shocked when we first heard the news on television about the accusations, your arrest and then we were shocked again when you were found guilty and sent to prison to be executed. I don't know how you got out and I don't want to know, but I'm very happy you did."

"Then there won't be any mention of me being here?"

"There's no mention of anybody or anything aside from the current project. Everything is on a need to know basis and security is tight."

"So I've heard."

Worthington chuckled, propped his elbows on the desk and clasped his hands together in front of him. "I used to have a girlfriend in town but with one or two of DeShane's men always there keeping me under constant observation, no relationship was possible aside from a one night stand now and then. Finally, I just gave up. I'll make enough money in the next five years to go back into private practice debt free and pretty well fixed. Then I can have a normal life."

Savage was incredulous. "You were followed into town on a date?"

The doctor nodded. "It's all a part of this place. I understand it now. I'm going to turn you over to your ophthalmologist. His name is Daniel Gunville. He needs to give you complete eye exam and fit you for the contacts."

"You have your own ophthalmologist?"

"We have our own everything. It's been a real pleasure, Doctor." He stood and held out his hand.

"For me, too." He grasped the physicians hand in what he hoped was a firm grip.

The office door opened and a man stepped in. He was balding, fifty or fifty-five, wore glasses and had on a sports jacket and brown slacks. Short with narrow shoulders, thick waist, hands with long delicate fingers and neatly trimmed nails. "Doctor Savage," he said, "it is a pleasure to meet you. I'm going to give you x-ray vision."

"If he could do that," remarked Dr. Worthington, "he would have done it for himself."

"Why not? I'd love to look through Diana's clothes. Now, why don't you come with me and we'll get your vision in shape."

"One more thing, Dr. Savage," the physician said. "Your cook will be given instructions about your meals. Please adhere strictly."

"My cook? I have a cook? Just for me?"

"Yes, you have a cook and no, not just for you. There are several people here who require special diets, including Mr. Damarjiane. Diana will handle your medication. I don't really approve of that but I follow orders, too. Now, I have a number of other people I must see today, so if you will excuse me."

"Wait a minute. You're saying that woman is going to handle my medication and you don't approve of it? Don't I have anything to say about—"

"No, I'm afraid not."

"But I—"

"That's the way it is here, Dr. Savage. Now, you really need to see about your eyes. If you will go with Dr. Gunville."

"Right in there, please." He led Savage to a smaller office containing a chair and the other equipment used in vision and eye examinations.

"I'll have a pair of glasses ready for you later this afternoon," the ophthalmologist was saying half an hour later as Savage sat in the examination chair. Several instruments had been used on him during the exam, some large and mounted on a stand which was wheeled before him, others attached to the chair itself. "And several pairs of soft contact lenses tomorrow."

"You can do it that fast?"

"Oh, yes."

"What about the glaucoma?"

"You don't have glaucoma, Dr. Savage, but I'm afraid you *do* have a much more serious problem concerning the optic nerves. Normally I'm not so blunt with a patient but I was told to give it to you just like it is. And since you are a physician yourself—"

"My doctorate is in Geology," Savage corrected.

"Oh, I see. I'm sorry, I had just assumed . . . I'm sorry. Tell me, have you had moments of vision blackout where you can't see anything?"

"Well, once or twice. But it lasted only a few seconds."

"Yes. Normally AF and TIA are diagnosed almost exclusively in older patients. Younger patients with these conditions may have a history of diseases that could bring it on. Have you ever had Rubella?"

"German measles? No. What's AF?"

"Amaurosis Fugax. It's a painless, monocular loss of vision. There are drugs that can arrest it but they must be given over an extended period of time."

"And if they are not?"

"I'm sure you know the optic nerve cells, like the brain, do not regenerate."

"You didn't answer my question."

"Over a period of time, untreated, the periods of vision loss will increase from seconds to hours. Finally, well, the result will be permanent loss of vision."

"I'll be blind."

The ophthalmologist hesitated for several seconds and then said quietly, barely above a whisper, "Probably. Yes."

"How long?"

"There's absolutely no way to tell for sure."

"Educated guess."

"Doctor Savage, I—"

"I need to know."

"Six months, a year at the outside. Look, Doctor Savage, I feel terrible about this. I wish there was some way I could offer you some hope, the use of the drugs over an extended period. It has been done successfully in some rare cases. But I'm told there is no time for that, so—" He let the sentence trail off with a shrug of his shoulders and both hands held in the air.

"Thank you for being frank, Doctor. I appreciate it."

"Look, I'm going to start the treatment anyway. There's always a chance."

He left the doctor and the medical facility and stepped into the hallway. He was going blind. He had an intestinal infection. He was going to be sent to another world where he might die instantly. They were going to discover that he had escaped from prison and everybody's looking for him. What else could possibly happen to him?

What would Killingsworth or Mr. Damarjiane do when they found out about his eyes? Cancel his part in the project and send him back to prison? What need would they have for a blind explorer, a geologist who couldn't even *find* a rock much less identify it?

"Everything okay, Doc?" DeShane asked as he stepped through the doorway into the hall.

"Sure. Fine."

"You don't sound fine."

"Do you know where the gym is?"

"Sure. Why?"

"I just need to work off some anxieties, a distraction. You ever hear of runner's euphoria?"

"Been there."

"Show me that treadmill."

Ten minutes later, still in his clothes and leather shoes, he was really working up a sweat, his feet pounding loudly on the moving surface. Under his arms and the back of his shirt showed the wetness. DeShane stood a short distance away watching him.

"Just what the hell do you think you're doing?" Diana yelled the question at him from the doorway across the room, her hands on her hips and a scowl on her face. She had taken only a step inside before stopping to shout at him.

"What's it look like?" he replied without looking up or turning the machine off.

"Get—off—of—there!" she commanded.

"Look, lady," he finally turned toward her and saw the anger and determination on her face.

"No, *you* look, Savage," she countered. "I've been put in charge of your physical conditioning. I didn't want it but I've got it so I say when, where and how much. Understood?"

"I know what I'm doing."

"Do you?" she questioned, walking to him with determined strides and tossing him a towel to wipe his perspiring face. She reached out and flipped the switch, turning the machine off. "Body building training is an exact science. You use your muscles, strain them, abuse them and even damage them slightly. They repair themselves a little better and a little stronger than before. But you must allow for that repair. That's why in weight training you do it every other day or every third day, to give those parts of your body time to repair themselves."

"I know that."

"Sure you do. Right now you're setting yourself up for a heart attack. Now please go back to your room, rest and do what you are told." She turned on the security chief. "And you, DeShane, don't you *ever* let this happen again."

"I don't take orders from you, Diana. And I don't get all hot and bothered every time you wiggle your ass either, so back off."

A look of absolute fury spread across her face and her eyes blazed. Without realizing it she bent her knees slightly and raised her hands in front of her, fingers tightly together. "One of these days, DeShane, you're going to go too far."

"You try any of that Ninja shit on me, lady, and you're gonna get hurt."

She laughed at him.

"Look, Diana, the Doc just got hit big-time with something real bad. He had some frustrations to work off. That's all. I've been there. So have you. Just let it go."

"You're right, DeShane." Her face and entire body relaxed. "I don't want to fight you." She turned to Savage. "I'm sorry, Doctor. There's just a lot going on here that you don't know about."

"Maybe you should tell me."

"Maybe I will, but for now, will you please go back to your room? DeShane?"

"This way, Doc. Diana, it's been a pleasure, as usual."

As they walked along the hallway toward the vault door and the elevator, Savage asked, "Would you tell me what the hell just happened back there?"

"Oh, a slight disagreement between a couple members of the staff. High stress environment. Stuff like that. Happens all the time, but it shouldn't have happened with a guest. That's you. Think nothing of it."

"Slight disagreement?"

"That's all it was."

"How did you know I received some bad news?"

"You came out of the doctor's office looking like somebody just ran over your dog so bad news ain't too hard to figure."

"What was that reference to Ninjas in there?"

"Ninjas? Why, hell, Doc, I never even heard of 'em. Why would I say something about Ninjas?"

"Why indeed, Mr. DeShane. Why indeed."

Chapter Eight

GIVING SAVAGE AND DESHANE time to leave, Diana made her way along the passageway, through the vault door and up the elevator alone. She did not feel the rain pouring down on her, soaking her clothes and trickling into her shoes as she walked slowly along the path to the house. She felt nothing. What was wrong with her? Why was she so angry? Why had she challenged DeShane? He was a very macho man, tough, confident and well trained. She couldn't fight him. She didn't know how to fight him. She only knew how to kill him.

Up the grand staircase, her wet, muddy shoes leaving prints in the thick carpet that would have to be steam-cleaned out, she stomped her way to her apartment. What had changed? What had happened to her absolute control over herself? What was different? Ha! What *wasn't* different? But *right now,* what was different?

Savage. He was the only thing different right now. He was the only thing that had changed in the last few days. Finding out if a human being could live for any period of time in the world beyond the Window didn't require the guinea pig to be in good physical condition. It only required that it be alive and breathing.

So why the training? Why the conditioning? The answer was obvious.

She entered her apartment and went directly to the bathroom where she stripped off her wet clothes, dropping them to the floor in a soggy pile, and then turned on the shower. Just before she stepped in, she glanced at herself in the large mirror over the double sink counter. She would let her hair grow longer. Long enough to frame her face and drape over her shoulders. Highlight the red tint, cover the blond. It would glow like a magnificent sunset.

Steam began to pour from the shower. She stepped in and let the hot water stream over her. No. She would cut her hair even shorter. Long hair would get in the way. She had scissors. She could do it in just a few minutes.

David Savage. That subservient, mousy little wimp she had been ordered to make into a man was different. Now DeShane, *he* was a man. A little young perhaps, but he certainly had the physical equipment. Why had not anything worked with DeShane? One kiss. That was it. One kiss and it hadn't meant anything. He knew where to touch her, *how* to touch her. But there was no response. There was Marc, but there wasn't anything there either. She was dead inside.

Stepping from the shower, Diana dried herself off with a thick fluffy white towel. Without putting on underwear, she belted a satin robe round her and walked barefoot into the spacious living room of her third floor apartment. She stared without seeing at the beautifully carved wood doors covering the screen of the large console TV occupying one corner of the room.

David Savage. David. She had used his first name to put him in the trance. It was necessary. One had to be close, there had to be feeling, affection, sincerity and emotion for it to work, to draw them in, to gain control. She liked saying his name. David. Part of the closeness. But she wasn't supposed to like it. She had gotten too close.

No, David Savage wasn't going to be another Isoroku. It would be an unavoidable accident. Tragic. She knew enough ways to kill so that nobody would ever suspect. They would just have to get another guinea pig to shove through the window. She would kill him, too.

—*—

The following morning when Diana entered his room, Savage was waiting, dressed in his sweats, his breakfast of steak and eggs uneaten on the table. He had not shaved and his eyes were once again red from lack of sleep. Glancing from him to the table and back again, Diana said, "Dr. Savage, please eat your breakfast. I'll come back in half an hour."

"I'm not hungry."

"I don't care whether you're hungry or not. Eat it! I've got damn little to work with now. At least give me some help."

She spun around and slammed out the door.

Exactly half an hour later she was back wearing an abbreviated halter barely containing her ample breasts and the brief white shorts which left little to the imagination. In her hand, she had a plastic container about four inches square and an inch thick. She appeared to be in a much better mood. Although they had gotten cold, he had nevertheless eaten most of the steak and eggs on his plate, Diana saw. "Once again I find myself apologizing for my behavior, Dr. Savage. Chalk it up to PMS for lack of something better."

"PMS? That's a term I haven't heard in a long time."

"Would you prefer that I was just in a rotten mood?"

"That I can identify with. I've been there a lot."

"Starting now," she said as she began to empty the container and lay the contents out on the dinette table, "I will be giving you a vitamin B-12 shot every morning along with steroids. They will help you gain weight and build up body tissue." She placed two disposable hypodermic needles side-by-side on the table. "And this is Valium, one of the Benzodiazepine drugs used to control anxiety. These are sleeping pills that you will take every night until you begin to sleep naturally. She laid out a small handful of capsules and tables beside the needles.

"I want you to know I don't approve of this one bit," she continued, "especially the Valium and the steroids. The right food, exercise, self-discipline all work much better with no side effects. But there is a time factor involved and—"

"Yeah, I know about the time factor, probably better than you. For whatever it's worth, I don't like needles. Will the drugs work?"

"Yes, they'll work."

"Let's get on with it then, shall we?"

"Anything you care to tell me?" she probed gently.

Looking over his glasses at her, he replied, "No, but thanks for asking."

Yesterday's rain had been reduced to a slight drizzle but it was still overcast and chilly. He managed to last a little over half an hour before he collapsed at the end of the treadmill sucking in loud gasping breaths. Twenty sit-ups, five push-ups, deep knee bends, and a few exercises he had never heard of before left every muscle in his body hurting. He almost crawled into the steam room where DeShane sat waiting for him.

"Great time, huh, Doc?"

"Oh yeah, just great."

"I dropped off another load of books and tapes in your room. Some of the best stuff out."

"You gonna be there to go over it with me?"

"Me? You kidding. I can't even pronounce half the words in the titles. I wouldn't be any good to you. I'll see if Diana can find some time. In addition, they're getting a computer tech to come in and teach you some real fancy advanced stuff on your PC. They've installed a bunch of new programs, too."

This morning, in addition to underwear, a pair of jeans, a plaid long-sleeve shirt and a jean jacket were laid out for him. It had been years since he had worn real blue jeans. Beneath the bench was a pair of new high top hiking boots. "Thought you might like to start breaking 'em in, Doc." DeShane offered.

As they walked along the corridor to the vault door, Savage asked, "Why'd you tell me you were just one of the guards when you're the head of security?"

"Somebody blabbed, huh? Well, just one of the guards is less intimidating. You'd ask me why."

"So I'm asking?"

"Diana's idea."

"Is she running this place?"

"Sometimes one gets that impression."

"So, why?"

"You, Mr. Damarjiane, Mr. Killingsworth and a couple other VIP's are my personal responsibility, in addition to the entire security of this place. They're paying me a bundle to see that it's done right. You don't get any more special treatment than the others, Doc. Well, not much, anyway."

They went through the steel door and up the elevator to the surface. The drizzle had almost completely stopped.

"Who are the other VIP's you personally protect?"

"You don't need to know that, Doc."

"Do you kill people, Mr. DeShane?"

"What? Now, why would you ask me a question like that?"

"Why else are you here? You, your guards and all the security. You're all not carrying guns just to look authoritative."

"I already told you why I'm here, Doc. Money."

"Not to mention the project they're working on here."

"Don't know anything about any project, Doc."

"You're telling me you really don't know what they're doing down there?"

They entered the house and walked into the living room adjacent to the grand staircase. "Yep. I'm telling you I don't know. Now, would you look at that? Gonna be a beauty, isn't it."

Savage turned to see a tall bushy blue spruce pine almost touching the ceiling of the living. Three men were busy stringing lights, hanging delicate glass ornaments and tinsel. "I had almost forgotten about Christmas."

"Not much of a celebration where you came from, huh?"

"You know about that?"

"I don't know anything." He held up his hands, palms out. "Diana said you had been sick so I figured you'd been in a hospital or something."

"Why don't I believe you?"

"They put on quite a bash here. You'll like it. Go on up. I'll see you later, Doc."

Savage was pleased that DeShane had sent him on alone and had not taken him to the door. Maybe the lock wouldn't be turned for awhile and he could actually stick his head out and look up and down the hall if he felt like it.

Still very much aware of his aching muscles, he dropped onto the couch and began looking through some of the books and magazines DeShane had left stacked on the coffee table. There were books published on Colt Firearms, *1836-1960 by James E. Serven*; Smith and Wesson, *The Illustrated Reference of Cartridge Dimensions; Book of the Springfield* by E. C. Crossman, *Ruger—The Second Decade*, by John C. Dougan, and several other well-known firearms companies. Mostly they were self-serving advertisements for their products, but they were well written, the information was accurate and the photographs, drawings and graphs impressive. *Shooter's Digest, Firearms Assembly and Disassembly* in hardback and several magazine copies of *Guns Illustrated* and *Rifle* overwhelmed him with more information than he could immediately absorb. Although familiar enough with firearms in general, he had no idea that there were so many different types of weapons available on the marked, both public and private.

They published muzzle velocity in feet per second, foot-pounds, recoil, hitting power, killing power, weight, handling ability, advantageous features, magazine capacity, scope sights, laser sights, lighted sights, adjustable sights, rounds per second, the type of steel in the recoil spring, on and on and on in endless descriptions of what each weapon could do. Some of the videos showed weapons being fired. Hand guns, rifles, semiautomatic shoulder weapons, fully automatic machine guns from the hand-held Uzi to monsters with revolving barrels firing twenty rounds a second. There was a Ruger, two-shot .44 derringer small enough to fit in the palm of your hand and powerful enough to knock down a charging Brahma bull (probably break your wrist and dislocate your elbow in the process).

Almost completely absorbed in the publications laid out on the low coffee table in front of him, a knock on the door interrupted his studies. Lunch was brought and served by two uniformed waiters. They put it on the kitchenette table behind him. Trout almondine, parsley potatoes, glazed baby carrots, a small garden salad and dinner roles with butter, all laid out o his dinette table with linen napkin, real silver and find china. A goblet of milk and a tall glass of water were placed beside his plate. He put the books aside and took his seat before the meal.

Some lunch! He had attended celebrity dinners that were not this good. They really were trying to fatten him up. Now, if he only had somebody with which to share it.

Half way through the meal there was a knock at the door but nobody immediately burst through as had been the case in the past. Somebody was actually waiting for him to answer the door. He crossed the room and opened it.

"DeShane happened to mention that you wanted to see me," Diana said. She was wearing tight jeans and a long-sleeve shirt almost like his, and this time she had on lipstick.

"Well, no, actually, I just wanted somebody to go over this . . . he said he didn't understand it and suggested that you might . . . I don't want to interrupt you or anything. Please, come in."

"I wasn't doing anything, anyway." She stepped into the room and he closed the door behind her.

"Can I say you look very good in jeans, or would I get in trouble for it? It seems like I've been off on the wrong foot with you ever since I got here. And I don't know why."

"Thank you, Dr. Savage. The compliment is accepted and the problems isn't yours."

"That was quite a lunch I had. You should have been here to share it."

"Dr. Savage, I don't want to have lunch with you or have dinner with you or cocktails later on. Our relationship is purely professional. Is that quite clear?"

He took the verbal slap in the face quite well, all things considered. But, then, he was beginning to get used to it. "Yes, ma'am. Maybe you should just leave."

"Why?" The laugh was quick but it was there. "Do you think I'm afraid of you?"

"No, but I might be afraid of *you.*"

She almost said it but caught herself in time. Putting him on guard would be a stupid move. Rather to lull him into a comfortable sense of security and safety in her presence. "I would be happy to go over the material with you, Doctor. We can research it together. Finish your lunch."

She began looking through the material as he ate the rest of the fancy lunch. The remainder of the afternoon went quickly with them pouring over books and VCR tapes on Geology, Forestry, Meteorology, Archaeology and some of the weapons books and magazines DeShane had left. There were books and tapes on chemistry and biology, both difficult for him since he had no background in them. She asked significant and probing questions about specific subjects and he got the distinct impression that she was learning with him, not just testing. She knew a great deal about the natural sciences and firearms, more than a layman did and certainly more than most women.

"It's been enjoyable, Doctor," she said, standing up and arching her back with both hands on her hip. "Maybe we can do this again. See you in the morning." She marched to the door and left. His eyes were glued to the sway of her hips as she walked.

"Damn! I need a drink," he said out loud. He went to the kitchen, opened the refrigerator, and poured a small glass of orange juice. "No vodka, but it's better than nothing."

In the early evening, he happened to be looking through the French doors leading to a small balcony outside his room when he saw Diana in the courtyard below. She was with a man and they were sitting very close together on a stone bench surrounded by shrubs and tall hedges, completely hidden from every part of the house except his window. She was holding his hands, pressing them into her lap and they papered to be talking intently to each other. She shook her head, pulled one hand free, reached up and touched his cheek. Short blond hair and a too-handsome face. It was the chauffeur without his high boots.

A loud knock on his door tore his attention momentarily away from the scene below. He didn't want to answer it. He wanted to know what was going on below with Diana and Marc. The loud knock sounded again. Annoyed he went to the door and opened it. Dr. Gunville stood there waiting to deliver the contact lenses along with a regular pair of glasses and a large bottle of antibiotics from the physician."

"Did I come at a bad time?" Gunville asked, seeing the expression on Savage's face.

"No. No. Please come in."

"We didn't get around to discussing style with you," the ophthalmologist said, "so I picked frames for strength and comfort rather than looks. I hope you don't find them unsatisfactory."

"I'm sure they will be fine, Doctor."

"Why won't we sit at the table." The eye specialist put the glasses on Savage's face, took them off, did a bit of minor adjusting, replaced them and stepped back. "How's that?"

Nothing was fuzzy or blurred and he could see at a distance as well as close up. "I'm really impressed," Savage said. He went to the window and looked out but the bench was vacant and there was no one in sight.

"You can wear the contacts for up to forty-eight hours if necessary, but I would suggest taking them out every night if you can. Just throw them away. I'll keep you supplied."

"I'm having a problem believing that an ophthalmologist would have enough to do around here to keep you busy."

"You'd be surprised, Doctor."

"I'm sure I would. Thank you again."

The food arrived at 6:30. Dinner salad, meat loaf, mashed potatoes with gravy and a vegetable in generous proportions, a pitcher of milk and the glass of wine. He took the sleeping pill first and then started on the salad. At least they weren't surreptitiously drugging his food anymore. They just gave him the drug right up front.

He finished eating. Left the dishes on the table and started for the bedroom when there was another loud knock. A door-to-door salesman, no doubt. "Come on in," he yelled, not even bothering to go to the door. "Everybody else does."

The door opened slowly and a young woman with a pixy haircut, pink blouse and white slacks stepped in. She didn't look much older than a teenager. "Hi," she said, tentatively. "I'm Marci."

"Okay. Hi, Marci."

"The computer tech?" It should have been a statement but she made it a question. She held out her hands, palms up in mystery. "I'm here to teach you how to get into the World Wide Web?" Another question. She had small breasts and narrow hips but was still very feminine and attractive.

Savage shook his head. "I'm sorry, ah . . . Marci. I don't know what you're talking about."

"Your computer. Access? How to hook into MCI, AOL, ATT International? So you can access what you need. I'm here to teach you how. They said you didn't know much about computers. I couldn't really believe that. *Everybody* knows about computers."

"It's really not a good time, Marci."

"Oh, I'm sorry. It's just that—"

"Look, I really do know something about computers."

"Well, I knew you did, but the programs in this one are pretty complicated. You don't know about them."

"I don't?"

"With the model you have and the software, you can access just about anything. I'm here to teach you how. Grab a chair." She walked to the computer on his desk and turned it on.

Although reluctant, he dragged a kitchen chair in beside the one in front of the computer terminal and sat watching as her fingers danced over the keys.

"Okay, we're going to make your name your access code. That puts you on line. This is your mouse. Now, what do you want to look at?" She typed in DAVIE as his password.

"I don't know. What choices do I have?"

"Oh, Davie, sweetie, you're putting me on, aren't you."

"Davie, sweetie?"

"Well, he said your name is Davie . . . Dave."

"Who said my name was Dave?"

"The man who hired me. Isn't that right? Dave? Did I say something wrong? They told me to be nice to you."

"No, nothing's wrong. Okay. Put me . . . ah . . . put me on line."

"Okay. Give me a subject."

"Ahh, astronomy."

"Okay, watch." She typed in the word, astronomy and then clicked, search. A list of sub-subjects appeared. There were twenty of them with a choice to view twenty more. She scrolled down the list.

"Nothing new there," he said. "Let's try star patterns,"

"Okay, watch." She typed in the words star patterns and got the same results.

"Take the first one, the Andromeda galaxy," Savage said.

A pattern of white dots appeared on the screen. "That's pretty easy," Marci said.

"I'm sorry, Marci. I've done all of this."

"Well, that's it." She turned from the screen and looked at him, studying his face. "Why am I doing this? Teaching you this stuff?"

"I don't know. Why are you?"

She took a deep breath. "The man who hired me, his name was Mr. Killingsworth told me to. It's what I do. I know computers. I even got to show Dr. Boucree a few things."

"You know Dr. Boucree?"

"No. I spent a couple days with him on the computer, and then he . . . well . . . that was the end of it. You know. I did a couple of sessions with Mr. DeShane. But you're cute, Dave. For an older man, that is. You're not like Dr. Boucree or Mr. Killingsworth. You seem nice."

"And you're a very pretty girl, Marci. Would you spend the night with me here?"

If she was shocked, she didn't show it. As cute as she was, maybe she was used to being propositioned. "Hey, Davie, sweetie, I just do computers. If I like a guy, well you know, nobody is going to . . . well, you know . . . you're a fast learner, Davie. You're going to be real good on the computer. A few more lessons and you'll have it down pat. Maybe tomorrow we can—"

"No, not tomorrow, unfortunately. Tomorrow either Diana or DeShane, one of them, or maybe both, are going to be here telling me—"

"Mr. DeShane? Diana? You mean that woman who . . . Why would *she* be here with you?" Marcie studied his face closely. Suddenly her hands flew to her mouth. "David? Oh, my god. You're David Savage. Doctor Savage, I'm so sorry. I didn't know. I wouldn't have been such a smart ass."

"It's all right, Marci." He laughed. "How do you know about me?"

"How do I know? Are you kidding?" she asked as she turned back to the computer and her fingers typed words in the SEARCH box. "Dr. Boucree mentioned you several times when I was working with him, so did Mr. DeShane." Then, on the screen was a picture of him as he had looked almost eleven years ago, the Indiana Jones hat on his head and a rifle slung on his shoulder. There was a whole page of information about him.

"Well, I'll be damned," he exclaimed, scanning the information quickly. "Where did you get all of this?"

"Geology department, UCLA library."

"That's really in the UCLA library?"

"Yes."

"Well, if I get stuck in this computer thing, how do I get in touch with you?"

"You should ask Mr. Killingsworth about that."

"Okay, I apologize for that remark about spending the night."

"Oh, Dr. Savage, I'm flattered." There was a mischievous grin on her face. "And I live in Newhall. I'm in the book. Keep it in mind."

"I will."

"I've programmed the computer for voice. You don't have to do anything. Just talk to it."

"Talk to it?"

"Yeah. Talk to it. Like, you start, you know. I'll change your password. Davie just doesn't sound right now that I know who you are. So, anyway, you tell the computer you're Dr. Savage and you ask it a question. And you get an answer either on the screen on in voice." She went into *settings, change password,* and typed in Doctor Savage.

"Whose voice?"

"I don't know. They're all different. What difference does it make, anyway?"

"I'd feel silly talking to a machine."

"Then use the keyboard."

"This will work?"

"Yes."

"Okay. This is Dr. Savage. I'd like the current price of Gulf Oil Stock."

"No, no," Marci corrected. "Do it just like you would if you were typing it out. You've got to go through the menu. Tell it, stock market first, then when you get the sub menu you do stock, the company name and today. Then request the price."

Savage did as he was instructed and within seconds was rewarded with a reply. "Good day, Dr. Savage," a man's voice responded from the twin speakers in the top of the monitor. "The current price on the New York Stock Exchange for Gulf Oil Corporation stock is $55.25 a share. Up 3 cents from yesterday. Do you want it on the NASDAC also?" At the same time, the words appeared on the computer screen.

"Amazing."

"You can leave the computer on all the time and whenever you identify yourself, you can access. Or, you can turn it off and then back on line by voice or keyboard. It's a really advanced system."

"I can see that."

"The software won't be available to the public for another four or five years."

"Yeah?"

"It was developed right here at Palomar by Dr. Archibald."

"Who?"

"Sara Archibald. MIT?" Marci spread her hands if frustration.

"I guess I'm a little out of touch.

"Boy, you must be. You don't know Sara Archibald. But, s'a-right." She looked at the watch on her wrist. "I gotta go, Doc Savage. Bye."

She was out of the chair, through the door and gone in a whirlwind of youthful energy.

He spent a few more minutes on the computer but the sleeping pill had begun to take effect and his eyelids began to droop. In the bedroom he removed his clothes and crawled under the covers with thoughts of Marci and her slender figure drifting through his mind.

—*—

The next day was the same, a big breakfast, Diana giving him the shots in his upper arm, stretching and loosening up exercises, treadmill, pushups, sit-ups, deep knee bends, hand, shoulder exercises, steam room shower and the question and answer session taking two hours. He would have to spend twice that much time studying in anticipation of her questions the following day. Once an expert in his field with a Doctorate in natural science, a BA in English and an Associate's Degree in half a dozen other subjects, Diana treated him as though he was a college freshman just learning his profession again, coaching and tutoring him in the basic fundamentals.

In the afternoons when he wasn't studying and he was finally almost up-to-date on the world news, he took to watching movies on the cable channels with his new contacts in an attempt to distract his thoughts of blindness and helplessness in a world of darkness. As an adventurer and explorer, he had tramped the jungles, the deserts and the mountains of a dozen countries in the world, seeing natural wonders that most people never even dream of, and he got paid for it; paid very well for it. Now he sat in anticipation of a white cane or a guide dog leading him around by a leather strap in his hand. Better to be dead than that.

He spent two hours on the computer continually amazed by the amount of information he could call up on the screen. It made textbooks almost obsolete. Almost by accident, he discovered he could call up copies of newspapers from any major city in the world. He checked several Pennsylvania papers looking for any mention of him or his escape from prison. He found nothing.

He took the sleeping pill with diner and soon began to feel drowsy. There was nothing from Mr. Damarjiane about his eyes. Surely he had been told by now. Nothing from Diana or DeShane, either. Maybe they didn't know. No reason to tell them. Everything here seemed to be compartmentalized and nobody except Mr. Damarjiane and Mr. Killingsworth appeared to have the complete picture.

Before he went to bed he walked softly across the room and gingerly tried the door. Locked.

As he looked in the mirror to shave the next morning, he had to admit that the pills had helped. He slept well, his eyes were not red anymore and even the thought of going blind didn't seem as devastating as it had the day before. There was no drug hangover people had told him always went with sleeping pills. Maybe it was something new he had never heard of. There were probably a lot of new thing out there he had never heard of.

Breakfast, shots, exercises, steam, shower and study. The mornings were all the same. He thought about casually mentioning to Diana that he had seen her down in the courtyard from the window, but he didn't. She was slightly less hostile and sarcastic now, and he didn't want to give her any reason to start in on him again.

Dinner was late and he began to wonder since everything around here seemed to run with military precision. He was about to pick up the phone and call when there was a loud rapping on his door. Nobody had ever knocked on his door. They just walked in. He went over to answer it.

DeShane stood there in slacks and a sports coat. "Come on, Doc. You're gonna join us, aren't you?"

"Join you for what?"

"The festivities, Doc. You mean nobody told you?"

"Told me what?"

"It's Christmas Eve, Doc. The Christmas party. Mr. Damarjiane always puts on a big feed and party for everybody."

"I'm invited?"

"Of course. Everybody's invited. And I'm your date." He held out his hands.

"Wonderful," Savage replied flatly. "Just let me change clothes."

During the time he had been here, his wardrobe had steadily grown. He had dress shirts, slacks, sports jackets, suits, even a tux. There were jogging clothes, shorts, jeans, casual shirts and shoes, boots and sneakers. The dresser drawers were filled with underwear and socks.

"How formal is this," he asked from the bedroom.

"Semi. Wear whatever you want."

"They're not taking any pictures, are they?"

"You kidding, Doc? Not a chance. Cameras are strictly verboten here."

"That's good."

Downstairs in the formal dining room adjacent to the living room, the huge oval table was laden with food. The chairs had been removed and the beautiful wood sliding doors to the living room containing the decorated tree were open allowing people to move freely between the two rooms. A man in a short, red jacket was carving turkey and roast beef on a butcher block while a white-jacketed bartender behind a portable bar near the adjoining doorway was doing a brisk business pouring drinks to those standing three deep before him.

Twenty or thirty people moving between the rooms, some carrying food, others with just a glass in their hand, were all well dressed in suits, dinner jackets and floor-length dresses. There were no uniforms or lab coats here. Some had a sprig of holly or mistletoe on a coat lapel or blouse collar and a few wore pointed party hats and threw confetti in the air.

"Looks more like New Years Eve than Christmas," Savage remarked over the familiar notes of Jingle Bells and Dashing Through The Snow with Bing Crosby crooning White Christmas pouring from unseen speakers just loud enough to hear but low enough to allow normal conversation. He had chosen a dark blue suit with a red tie. It was the first time he had worn a suit since his last court appearance.

"Well, a party is a party," DeShane replied, leaning closer so he could be heard. "It's been a long, hard year. They'll use any excuse to celebrate."

Savage saw Dr. Boucree and recognized several of the security guards now in civilian clothes. Both the physician and his ophthalmologist were there, going easy on the alcohol but taking advantage of the layout of food.

"Good to see you, Dr. Savage," Gunville said. "How are the contacts doing?"

"Perfect. I'm so used to them now I don't even need the glasses."

"Great, but hang on to them just the same. You never know when you'll have to use them."

Savage was surprised to see several of the Mexican and Asian gardeners present, clean and neatly dressed, eating and drinking with the scientists and technicians. The only unusual sight, the only thing that made it different from the dozens of Christmas parties he had attend when he was a renown guest of noteworthy people, was the presence of two uniformed guards wearing side arms and with M-16's slung over their shoulder while trying to remain discreet and out of sight on each side of both rooms.

Diana was in the living room standing by the Christmas tree. She wore a very expensive, powder blue tailored pants suit and heels, the bottom of the coat coming down well below her hips and concealing their curves. A Pink blouse and earrings that sparkled in the light. She was closely engaged in conversation with Mr. Too Handsome Face.

"Isn't that the chauffeur that was on the plane with us?" Savage asked DeShane, trying to be casual about it.

"Marc? Yep. That's him. Pretty much of a flake if you ask me."

"Diana seems interested."

"Yeah. Well, no accounting for tastes. He's what the Hollywood types would describe as a hunk. Pumping iron and flexing his biceps. All muscle and no brains. But I'll tell you what, as much as I hate to give him credit for anything, he sure knows cars. He can tear an engine apart and put it back together again better and faster than anybody I ever saw. Wish I could get him to work on my car."

"So ask him."

"Naa. He doesn't much care for me. He'd probably put the pistons in backwards. Like the women, I just kind'a stand back and admire from a distance."

"Him?"

"Sure."

"You're putting me on."

"You're right, I am. Let's go grab some chow. The boss says you can have a couple of drinks tonight. If they don't kill you, it's back to prohibition tomorrow."

"Doesn't look like Diana is drinking."

"No, she doesn't, and she doesn't have much use for those of us who do. Desecration of the temple, and all that, you know."

"Huh?"

"You mean she hasn't given you that 'the body is a temple' speech yet?"

"No."

"Stick around, you'll get it. We all have. Grab a plate. You want turkey or roast beef?"

"All right, everybody!" Dr. Boucree's voice rang out over the soft Christmas carols. He was wearing a green leisure suit from the late 1970's with a sprig of holly pinned to the lapel. "Come on in here around the tree. Mr. Killingsworth couldn't make it tonight. He's still back in Washington buying us some more politicians. They're having a sale on them this week." He laughed loudly and several joined him. "But he's gonna try to make it for New Years Eve." He paused to let the laughter did down.

"Mr. Damarjiane sends his regrets for not being here with us and he hopes you all enjoy everything. But you know the boss. Last I heard he was down in South America negotiating to purchase Argentina."

More laughter.

"But seriously, folks, there's something here for everybody and I speak for both Mr. Damarjiane and Mr. Killingsworth in hoping you all have a very merry Christmas. Eat, drink and make merry and if you can't make Mary, there's always the girl you came with. Ha. Ha. Ha."

"DeShane, tell me he didn't say that." Savage took his first drink of Scotch and soda in more years than there were drops of soda in the liquor. When that bartender made a drink, he really *made* one.

"Yep, he said that. And the next one will be about the guys in the bar who were sitting around drinking and feeling rosy until Rosy got mad and went home."

"I heard those at the Rotary Club in Houston twenty years ago."

"Yeah, and we've heard them every year since he's been here. He ain't too original but he's funny and it's Christmas Eve. So lay back and enjoy it, Doc."

". . . rosy until Rosy got mad and went home," Boucree was saying.

"He *did* say it."

"I told you he would."

"And now I think some of you know," Boucree was serious now, "and most are at least aware of Dr. David Savage who has just recently joined us here on the project. If you want a weather report, he's probably one of the best meteorologists in the world. We tried to get Professor Clarence E. Koeppe of San Diego State University but he died back in 1968 and even Mr. Killingsworth can't figure out how to raise the dead."

Laughter again.

"But he's working on it!" Boucree shouted and the laughter increased.

"So, everybody say hello to Dr. Savage. He's right over there." Boucree extended his arm and pointed his finger directly at Savage who smiled and did a little half-wave with his free hand. "Doctor Savage is a world renowned geologist and explorer, he's written several books, and he's working for us now."

"Sounds like he's been at the sauce for a while," Savage said out of the side of his mouth.

"Nope. The professor doesn't drink. Used to be a lush, I understand, so he can't touch it. Straight Ginger Ale. How's the Scotch?"

"They must have changed the recipe in the last few years. It doesn't seem to taste as good as it used to." He took another shallow sip. "It's pretty good Scotch, though. Maybe I'm just not used to it."

"Then, let's eat. Probably be better for you anyway."

"You don't drink either?"

"Me? Hell yes. Like a fish, but now I'm on duty. I'll do my drinking when the party's over."

"What's that in your glass?"

"Ginger ale."

"You're drinking ginger ale, too?"

"Yep."

"Do we get tomorrow off?"

"Everybody but you. It'll be hangover'sville in the morning for just about everybody, but not for you. Christmas or not, it's business as usual. Sorry, Doc."

"Great." He looked around at everybody having a good time, talking, laughing, eating, drinking, ripping colored paper off of boxed presents, the few women being surrounded by men vying for their attentions. And the women loving it.

"I don't see Diana and what's his name, Marc. Did they leave or something?"

"Doc, ain't no offense and don't take this personal, but just forget it. You aren't going to get to first base with that woman. Whatever it is she needs—and I wish to hell I know what it was—Marc is evidently providing it."

"Yeah?"

"Yeah."

"What makes you think so?"

"Well . . ." DeShane appeared to be embarrassed. "Last year . . . at the Christmas party, the mistletoe over the door, you know, I kissed her."

"You did?"

"Yeah."

"Did she kiss back?"

"Yeah."

"And?"

"It was like kissing my brother."

Savage exploded with laughter and several heads turned toward him in curiosity.

"Don't laugh," DeShane responded, "my brother doesn't kiss all that well. Enjoy Christmas Eve, Doc."

"Dr. Savage," said a young man wearing thick glasses. He had dark hair and wore a sports coat without a tie. He held out his hand. "Glad you could make it."

Savage grasped the hand and DeShane whispered in his ear, "Dr. Phil Dendron."

"Thank you, Dr. Dendron."

"Phil, please. Money is my vice, not vanity." Seeing the vacant look in Savage's eyes, he went on quickly, "I'm one of Dr. Boucree's assistants."

"Oh, yes. Of course." Savage tried a quick recovery, finally remembering the man in the lab coat the first day he had seen the window.

"Don't worry about it. I've worked with some of these people for two years and I can't remember who the hell they are. We get so tied up in our work and that's all that matters, you know."

"Sure, Phil. Wait a minute. Is this a put-on?"

"No," Phil replied, laughing. "I'm surprised you picked up on it so fast. And yes, my middle initial is O."

"I don't believe it. Phil O. Dendron?"

"It gets worse. My sister's name is Rhoda."

"Now I *know* you're kidding."

"Nope. It's real."

Savage just shook his head.

"Hey," Dendron said, "I went to college with a Russian guy named Ivor. His first name was Herb."

It took Savage a few seconds this time. "No. Herbivore?"

"Swear to God," Dendron replied, chuckling as he held his right hand in the air. "We really had a lot of fun with it. Only problem is what to name our kids, if we ever have any. What *do* I have is a lot of admiration for what *you're* going to do. I wish I had the guts to do it."

"Thank you," Savage said as Phil wandered off. He turned to DeShane. "Philodendron?"

"We get all kinds."

"Still, he seems like a very sincere young man. Good sense of humor. I like him."

"Everybody here is likable in his own way. Mr. K has assembled quite a team."

"I still don't believe Herb Ivor."

"Me neither," DeShane answered. "I think he made it up."

"Yeah?"

"Except I knew a girl in the second year of high school named Misty Woods."

"Yeah, I believe that. I knew one named Candy Bar."

"They had to hate their parents."

"I'd agree to that."

Their plates piled high with food, they found a place on one of the couches in the living room where they sat, cut, forked, and ate. The beef, spiced ham, potato salad with garlic and onion, vegetables sautéed in butter and Balsamic vinegar, tender yet still crisp, the black Russian caviar on thin wafers, the onion, garlic and avocado dip for the celery and carrot sticks, French cognac, vintage wine, it all was exquisite. After all the years of prison food, sufficient and nutritious to keep him alive long enough so he could be killed, the Christmas Eve meal was extravagant.

Dr. Worthington, the physician from New York stopped for a few words as did two of the lab technicians, but for the most part everybody stayed at a distance. "I don't know hardly anybody here and since I'm to be the sacrificial lamb, everybody's embarrassed around me. So if you don't mind, I'm going to call it a day."

"Why would they be embarrassed because of you?"

"Well, I'm sure they've all been told about my part in the Window project and they—"

"Hold it, Doc. I don't want to know about any projects. Keep 'em zipped, okay?" He ran his fingertips over his lips.

"But you're the Chief of Security. You *have* to know what going on."

"No, I don't. If I get taken, I won't be able to tell them anything."

"What do you mean, taken?"

"Grabbed. Snatched. You know, kidnapped."

"You're kidding me."

"No, I'm not. The stuff they got here is worth big bucks. I mean *BIG* bucks. That's why security is so tight. Somebody puts the snatch on me because I'm the head of security and they get nothing. Nada. Capish?"

"Capirsi a vicenda."

"Hey! You speak Italian?"

"Some. I used to know a guy in the Mafia."

"You did? In the Mafia? No shit?"

"Yeah, no shit. Lived right next to him for several years."

"You get more interesting all the time, Doc. You're going to have to tell me about that one sometime. We'll be opening presents later. Mr. Damarjiane always gets something for everybody. And there's a gift exchange."

"If there's something for me, bring it up tomorrow, will you. Tell them I was tired or something. I don't feel very festive and I don't want to spoil the party."

"Auh, come on, Doc. Don't be like that. It's Christmas."

"Yeah, I know, but I'm the new kid on the block here. Give me some time."

"Okay, sure. I understand. Just hang around for the Christmas stories, okay?"

"Christmas stories?"

"Sure. Every year somebody tells a favorite Christmas story. Something personal, something they just made up or something they saw in a movie. It's kinda interesting."

"I don't think so."

"Come on, Doc, it's Christmas. Tell me a story."

"No, thanks."

"Just me, then. You don't have to tell them."

"You got one, DeShane? A Christmas story?"

"Me? Naaa. I'm just a man with a gun doing a job. You, though, you gotta have a story. Family? You got kids somewhere?"

The look he got told DeShane to back off. "Sorry, Doc."

Finishing his food and depositing his plate and utensils in the tub at the far end of the table, he excused himself and made his way back to his room amid a few smiles and nods as he left. Climbing the stairs, he listened to the sounds of the music and the party below. His first Christmas Eve party in years, and he wasn't even interested. He wondered where Diana and Marc had gone. Maybe he would ask her tomorrow. No, that would just antagonize her. Leave it alone.

He took his sleeping pill and dropped onto the couch to flip through a dozen channels of Christmas celebrations on TV. He caught White Christmas at the part where Danny Kaye was conspiring to set old Bing up with Rosemary Clooney and just left it on the channel until the sleeping pill began to take effect. The question from DeShane started him to wondering what his ex-wife and kids were going on this Christmas Eve and if he would ever get to see them again. Carrying a torch for her was a worthless emotion but he still had hope that his kids might eventually understand and accept him regardless of what they had been told about him. If he was so important to the project, maybe Killingsworth could arrange that, too. He would bring it up at the first opportunity. He fell asleep on the couch while the celebration continued downstairs and it began to snow in Vermont.

Christmas morning just after he finished breakfast, Diana was at his door in shorts and a halter. "Don't you ever get cold?" he asked, looking at all the exposed flesh.

Ignoring the question, she said, "I'm glad you left early to get some sleep. An all night party wouldn't have done you any good." She gave him the B-12 shot and the steroids.

"I'm surprised you noticed," Savage replied as they headed out the door and down the stairs. "You seemed a little preoccupied."

"I didn't notice," she shot back. "DeShane told me. And what what's that supposed to mean?"

"Nothing. Just making conversation."

"Save your breath. You'll need it. It's going to be a tough morning."

"Aren't they all."

"You haven't seen anything, yet."

"Did Marc tell you we came in on the plane together?"

"Marc? No. Marc and I don't discuss business."

He almost asked what they *did* talk about, but that would have been a mistake, so he said nothing as they went out the back door, along the path and took the elevator to the exercise room I the underground complex. She put him through another grueling session of physical exertion. This was Christmas Day and here he was going sit-ups and pounding along on a treadmill amid admonishments and bored looks from a beautiful, sexy woman displaying a lot of leg and he couldn't get close to her. Some Christmas. Bet nobody even got him a present.

Shower, steam, dressed in jeans again and escorted back to his room by Diana where he had lunch alone and sat on the couch with almost every muscle in his body hurting. If this was what Diana was intending to do, she was sure doing a good job of it.

And that was another interesting thing. Christmas Day. What was Diana doing playing drill instructor with him in the exercise room? Why wasn't she out celebrating with everybody else? Or with Marc?

A little after one in the afternoon, there was a knock on his door and DeShane entered. He held out a small rectangular box wrapped in Christmas paper and tied with a bow. "Merry Christmas, Doc," he said. "From Mr. Killingsworth."

"Really?"

DeShane just shrugged.

Tearing off the paper and opening the box, he saw a key. He looked up questioningly at DeShane.

"It's the key to your door, Doc. It means you don't have to be locked up anymore. It's kinda symbolic, you know. Kr. K, well, he's got kinda strange sense of humor."

"Yeah." Savage tossed the key into the air and caught it in the palm of his hand. "Thanks, DeShane."

"Thank Killingsworth. There are some more gifts for you under the tree. You can open them whenever you feel like it. One of them's from me. One from Doc Boucree 'n a couple from the staff. They really didn't know what to get you so the gifts are petty generic and mostly symbolic. See you around, Doc." The door closed and the security chief was gone. There was no click of the lock closing this time.

He put on his shoes, smiled as he opened the door and went downstairs to the first floor. The remains of the party had been cleared, the chairs returned to the dining table and the ribbons, bows and paper picked up from the floor. Kneeling beside the tree, he examined the dozen or so packages under it. The tag on a long, thin parcel was addressed to Doc Savage. He tore it open. Inside was a dark red necktie with a green Christmas tree in the center. Laughing, he remarked, "A tie. Just what I always wanted." There was a card with it. Opening it, he read; Got this for Christmas 2 years ago and never knew what to do with it. Now I do. Thanks, Doc. DeShane.

He chuckled again and then became serious. Bad move, guy, he said to himself. It was a funny note. The package should have been opened and the note read at the party to everyone's amusement. That's what DeShane had intended but by walking out and leaving, he had ruined the moment.

In the next present he opened, he found an appointment book and day-by-day planner with attached pen. "Something else I really need." Another box contained a beautiful and obviously expensive digital watch. A card enclosed said simply, Merry Christmas. Damarjiane.

"Now *that's* interesting. And it's something I *can* use."

Dr. Boucree's package contained a gift set of after-shave and cologne. Savage could use that. There was a bottle of good brandy. He could use that, too. A brown sweater vest. Not a bad Christmas, considering his last six.

—*—

The next five days were the same, Diana there in the morning, shots, and exercises until he dropped and then sit and ache all afternoon. Had it not been for the news programs on the TV, he would have not even know what day it was. Declining to attend the New Years Eve party, he intended staying in his room, just flipping through the text and weapons books half-heartedly and watching old movies. A phone call from Dr. Boucree changed that.

"What do you mean you're not coming?" His question was both intimidating and accusatory. "You're the main character in the project. You are the most important person here. It is you we are all relying on to test the work we've been doing. Like a test pilot in a new airplane. Everybody expects you. Doctor, you can't disappoint us."

"I just didn't think I'd be missed."

"This is the beginning of a new year, the most important year in the history of the human race since the discovery of fire. I've stacked up the wood and you are the man with the matches. We'll see you down here shortly."

He hung up the phone and then picked it up again. "Yes, Dr. Savage?" the voice replied instantly.

"Will you ask Mr. DeShane to come up, please?"

"Yes, Doctor."

"Ahh, is Diana going to be at the party?"

"I wouldn't know, sir."

"Of course. Thanks." He hung up the phone again.

A few minutes later when he was finishing putting on his tie and slipping into his jacket, the security chief entered after a quick knock. He wore an open necked shirt under a dark brown sports jacket with gold buttons on the sleeves. The coat was tailored to conceal the 9-millimeter, sixteen shot automatic in a shoulder holster under his left arm.

"Hold my hand, DeShane. I don't what to do this."

"Relax, Doc. You'll enjoy it."

"Christmas was a disaster."

"No, it wasn't. Doc Boucree has talked to his people and I've talked to mine. It's going to be a lot friendlier this time. I guarantee it. Diana will be there and Marc the hunk is strangely absent. Seems as though he had to take the car in for service."

"On New Year's Eve? You're kidding."

"Hey, Mr. Damarjiane wants his car in good shape all the time. When it's time for service, it's time for service. Old Markee, he might be gone for hours."

"DeShane, you're too much."

"Me? No, Doc, I don't have that kind of clout. Doc Boucree is the one who sent him out."

"Boucree? What's *he* up to?"

"You'll find out."

"What's *that* supposed to mean?"

"Sorry, Doc. Nothing I can talk about."

"All right. Let's go do it."

"Like the tie?"

"No, DeShane. I didn't."

"Neither did I. You gonna wear it?"

"No, but next Christmas I'll give it to somebody else."

"How do you think I got it?"

"And how about *this*?" He pulled up his sleeve to show the watch.

"Christmas present?"

"Yep."

"Impressive."

"Gotta bottle of good booze, too."

"You open it yet?"

"No."

"Good."

Down the semicircular grand staircase, several of the lab crew waited at the bottom and raised their glasses to him as he descended. "Happy New Year, Dr. Savage," an attractive brunette shouted. Savage vaguely remembered her as a laser technician he had met briefly at the Christmas party. "May they all be as good as this one." She was happily plastered.

Almost all of the scientists, technicians and security personnel on the project were men. That woman holding out her glass in salute had to be awfully good in her profession to be here. Mr. Damarjiane considered only one thing when he hired people. Ability.

As with Christmas, the Mexican and Asian maintenance people and gardeners were present. Marcie, the cute computer tech waved at him from across the food table

A man beside the brunette thrust a glass toward him. "French champagne, Doctor. Only the best here. Happy New Year."

Stopping on the last step, he replied to them, "Thank you," and accepted the offered glass of wine he really didn't want. "Happy New Year to all of you."

"You're the center of attention, Doc," DeShane whispered in his ear. Enjoy it."

"I'll get you for this," Savage snarled back.

"Not me, Doc. Look."

Moving easily and gracefully through the small crowd collecting at the bottom of the staircase, smiling and nodding as they stepped aside quickly at his approach, Mr. Killingsworth in formal attire with a black tie, champagne glass in hand, addressed himself to Savage. "To a most successful and prosperous new year,

Doctor. Mr. Damarjiane sends his regrets. He was unavoidably detained."

The lawyer's unusual congenial attitude and his salute would have been would have been enough to surprise Savage, but there on his arm and wearing an elegant, exorbitantly expensive silver Dior gown and three-inch heels with ankle straps, a dark green, fiery emerald necklace encircling her throat, Diana raised her glass to him also. On her wrist was a matching emerald bracelet. "Happy New Year, Doctor." She said it more warmly that she had ever spoken to him before.

"Counselor," he replied, raising his glass. "Madam Teacher." Again, he hoisted the glass and for lack of anything else to say, he began to quote the silly phrase Boucree had used at the Christmas party. "Let us eat and drink . . ."

". . . for tomorrow we shall die," Killingsworth finished it for him. "Isaiah 22, verse 13, I believe. How appropriate, Doctor, wouldn't you say?"

"It is? I mean . . . I didn't—"

"All that champagne is going to get warm if you don't start drinking it folks," Dr. Boucree spoke up loudly. "And there's a lot of food here. Let's get at it."

DeShane said softly to Savage, "Sorry, Doc. Bad idea. But let's make the best of it."

They stepped down from the stairs and began mixing with the others. "Did you know that the eat, drink for tomorrow you die thing came from the Bible?" Savage asked DeShane. "It's just hard for me to believe Killingsworth quoting the Scriptures."

"Everybody's heard it, Doc, and no, I didn't know it came from the bible. But don't sell Mr. Killingsworth short. You may not like him but I've never met anybody smarter."

"No day off tomorrow again, huh?" Savage changed the subject.

"Not my rules, Doc. I'll get you out of here. Trust me."

"Yeah, sure."

"An hour, that's all. Everybody knows you're in training. They won't think anything about you leaving early. Eat some chow and do a little glad-handing. You've done that before. You'll be out of here before ten. I guarantee it. You'll be snug in your bed by eleven."

"Oh, yeah?"

"Would I lie to you?"

"Yes."

"Doc!" DeShane looked reproachful.

"DeShane, tell me something. What's Diana doing here hanging onto lawyer Killings-worth? And where did all the flash come from?"

"The flash?"

"The jewelry. Those things have got to be worth more than most people earn in a lifetime."

"I know what flash is, Doc. I just didn't know *you* did. You really don't want to do this?"

"No. Is it necessary?"

"Just an appearance. And, hey, I'm sorry, Doc."

"About what?"

"You're a little more of a savvy guy than they told me you were. Wave good-bye and you're out of here. Nobody will say anything. Probably most won't even miss you after a couple more drinks. It's going to be a long day tomorrow."

"You never answered my question."

"You noticed." DeShane grinned. "Find your own way up."

"Sure. Happy New Year, Mr. DeShane. May it be better for all of us."

Back in his room, he swallowed the sleeping pill, took off his jacket and tie and turned on the TV for the Ten o'clock World News Tonight looking for any word of his escape from jail. It was hard to believe that after fifteen days they still didn't know he was gone. Mr. Killingsworth must have really muddied up the waters back in Pennsylvania.

CHAPTER NINE

THE BED WAS ALWAYS made when he returned from the exercises, and the linen was changed every day. His rooms were cleaned, his meals served to him and the dishes cleared away, and the barber returned to cut his hair, keeping it short, neat and stylish. Had it not been for the rigorous training sessions, he would have thought of himself a pampered guest.

In mid January he was given another complete physical. "You'll have these every two weeks for a while now," Doctor Worthington said. "With the vitamins, the steroids, the high protein diet and the way Diana is pushing you, I want to monitor you very closely. The antibiotics are working well and you are definitely improving."

"That's good to know."

By the end of January the workouts in the gym were all morning long, alternating the severe, muscle-punishing exercises with dumbbells, barbells and a Universal Weight Machine every third day so that every muscle in his body was used and then given time to repair itself and grow stronger. The five minutes on the treadmill became ten, then twenty, and then thirty. He ran until he was ready to collapse, then went to the steam room and the shower.

What Diana did after the exercise period, he never knew. Maybe she waited until after he had gone and then used the steam room and showers herself in private, unwilling to expose that beautiful, muscular body to anyone, especially him. DeShane was almost always there to, either in the steam room with him or lounging just outside waiting for him to emerge. On a few occasions, he used the gym equipment and did the same exercises beside Savage. It was obvious from her attitude that Diana didn't want him there, so the two of them exercised together rarely.

In the afternoons, Diana took him back to the exercise room again and onto mats that had been laid on the floor. She introduced him to simple forms of judo and Eastern Oriental mediations where he was required to sit absolutely sill for long periods of time to cleanse his mind as the steam and water cleansed his body. Or so she told him. He became consciously aware of his breathing, the air going in and out of his lungs, the beating of his heart, how it would speed up and down with exercise and relaxation, of the blood coursing through his body. Then she began to teach him the advanced forms of self-defense.

"In Japanese, the word karate means the empty hand," she told him. "It comes from an ancient form of self-defense developed by the monks of Tibet during the reign of Genghis Khan in about 1180 AD. The monks were pacifists and forbidden by their religion from striking any sort of aggressive or offensive blow to another person. As a result, many of them were slaughtered by the Mongol hoards sweeping through Asia at that time.

"But by using balance and leverage, they could use an enemy's force and blows against them and thereby defend themselves without aggression. They called it Dz'iuet. In time, it was developed into a more aggressive form of combat called Kung Fu. The Japanese learned it and they called it jutitsu from which came the more advanced form of Ninjutsu, the art of stealth or the way of invisibility. It is said that these men could remain absolutely motionless for long periods of time and use the darkness so well that they would actually be invisible. The final step was the combination of Kung Fu and lethal Karate. Those that became proficient at it became a group of elite assassins called Ninja."

"How do you know all of this?"

"It's history." She shrugged.

"Not any kind of history I ever learned. But I do know the word, Ninja. DeShane used it once, referring to you."

"I don't know what you are talking about."

"I don't either. I was just asking."

"Let's finish the training, shall we, Dr. Savage? I have other things to do."

"Sure."

It was the longest single conversation he had had with her so far. Up until that point she was still aloof and answering his questions in a word or two, or sometimes not at all. It began to appear, however, that she was slowly becoming even less hostile toward him, less sarcastic and her condescending, 'I'm better than you' attitude was giving way to one of distant, polite tolerance. There was even a time or two when he imagined that she took a genuine interest in him, and he certainly had a genuine interest in her.

DeShane occasionally accompanied him back to his room and stopped in for a glass of orange juice or some of the fruit punch in his refrigerator, but generally he was left alone. He began to recognize some people by name when he saw them in the underground hallway or occasionally on the path behind the house. They still had not given him access to the underground without being in somebody's company. "You have no reason to be down there alone," he was told when he asked Diana about it.

"It sounds like I'm not trusted," he replied.

"Trust has nothing to do with it, Doctor," and that was the end of the conversation.

Mr. Damarjiane lived on the third floor of the house on the rare occasions when he was there, and that floor was off limits to almost everybody. There were no stairs leading to it that he knew of and the only access was by an elevator operated by a code punched into a keypad. He was reasonably certain that Killingsworth lived up there too, and had a suspicion that Diana might also, but he had never seen her enter or leave the elevator. There were other rooms on the same floor as his but he had not observed any other occupants. DeShane's guards were everywhere and they weren't going to stand by and allow him to search through somebody else's rooms.

The size of his meals continued to be large and appetizing, and he was gaining weight rapidly. The exercises and conditioning insured that the weight was muscle and flesh, not fat. He ate so many steaks at dinner that he was actually becoming tired of them.

"When am I going to get to go outside and look around by myself?" he asked DeShane.

"I don't know, Doc. When they say you can, I guess."

"You don't have any influence?"

"Nope. I take orders just like you do."

"What about Diana?"

"Give it a try. She carries a lot more weight around here than I do."

"Really?"

"Really."

"Think it'll do any good?"

"No, but you can always ask."

"Do you live here, in the house or on the grounds somewhere?"

"Me?" He laughed. "In the house? Hell, no. I've got a broom closet of an office down on the main floor, but I sure don't live here."

"Where *do* you live?"

"No need for you to know that, Doc. Drink your orange juice."

"Tell me about Mr. Damarjiane and this foundation or whatever it is that we're working for."

"Can't, Doc. I guess they'll tell you when you need to know."

"Who do you report to, take orders from?"

"Mr. Killingsworth."

"Oh. I was told you worked directly for Mr. Damarjiane."

"Never met the man."

"So what else do you do besides follow me around?"

"Can't tell you that, either. Just don't ask so many questions, Doc. I can't answer them. Oh, and by the way, Mr. Killingsworth asked me to give this to you." He withdrew a legal-size envelope from his inside jacket pocket.

"What is it?"

DeShane shrugged his shoulders. "Open it and see. Catch you later."

Frustrated and exhausted after the security chief left, he had dinner and went to bed early, not even caring to watch the news on TV or open the envelope.

At breakfast the next morning following his shower, Savage opened the envelope DeShane had left for him. It contained two newspaper articles. The first was dated, December 30.

HARRISBURG, PENNSYLVANIA. The attorney General's office has finally confirmed the disappearance and probable escape of Doctor David Savage from the state penitentiary. Doctor Savage was convicted in 1999 of capital murder and was sentenced to die by firing squad on December 15 this year, but the execution never took place for reasons the Attorney General has yet to explain. The warden, Paula Bennett, has been unavailable for comment.

Doctor Savage was allegedly taken by prison van to the Philadelphia city jail on the evening of December 15 but officials there say he never arrived. The two prison guards and the driver who escorted him to Philadelphia have been on Christmas vacation and haven't been available for comment. A statewide manhunt is underway.

With his heart pounding and fingers shaking, he picked up the second clipping dated January 20.

ALLENTOWN, PENNSYLVANIA. Among the four bodies removed from the remains of a devastating skid row hotel fire that broke out early yesterday morning was that of a man believed to be escaped convict David Savage. Tentatively identified by dental work and the shattered remains of a pair of prison issue eyeglasses, authorities are reasonably certain that Dr. Savage perished in the blaze. The statewide manhunt has been called off. Fire department arson investigators believe the fire in the sixty-five year old building was started by an Oriental couple using an open charcoal stove for heat. Filling the small room with deadly carbon monoxide fumes, the couple were overcome and somehow knocked over the stove sending flames racing through . . .

The newspaper column was neatly trimmed off at that point. With a slight laugh, he looked up from the articles and said aloud, "Well, I'll be damned."

—*—

"When am I going to get out of this place," he asked Diana when she entered his room. "I've been here over a month now and I've never been anywhere except the back yard and down there in the catacombs. I was introduced to Dr. Boucree, shown a scene I still don't believe, and I haven't been allowed in there since. I haven't seen the sun except through my windows and I'm tired of living in a cave."

"Funny you should mention that today, Dr. Savage. You're scheduled to be given a complete tour this morning to familiarize yourself with the estate. You've gained over fifteen pounds and your muscles are beginning to firm up nicely so going on a tour will not be a hardship for you.

"How long am I to be guarded?"

"What do you mean, guarded?"

"DeShane. He doesn't just *happen* to be around all the time. It's planned. Do you think I'm going to try to run away or something?"

"Mr. DeShane is your bodyguard, Doctor." She was very formal with him and always polite in her form of address. "He has been assigned to protect you and to do it as unobtrusively as possible. We thought that by being a friend and companion, another man to talk to, you would feel more comfortable with him."

"Bodyguard? Why the hell do I need a bodyguard?"

"You probably don't, but after that business with the plane, we don't want to take any chances. You're very important to this project."

"So there *was* something wrong with the plane. I *knew* it! It was sabotaged."

"I wouldn't have any idea about that, Doctor. I'm just your training instructor. I don't know anything about airplanes or sabotage."

"Okay. I don't believe you for a minute, but we'll leave it at that for the time being. What about my suggestion to go outside? Were you told to agree to it as soon as I asked about it?"

After a moment of silence, he continued. "You were, weren't you."

"You know what, Savage, you're not as dumb as you look. Yes, I was instructed to take you outside as soon as you asked to go. Your first assertive action. Satisfied?"

"For now. So tell me, where do you get your instructions? From Mr. Killingsworth?"

"Where I get my instructions is none of your business. If you want to go outside, then let's go."

"Okay, sorry. Lead on."

They went down the circular staircase and out the front door of the mansion. It was a rare, rainless, sunlit January afternoon. The porch, steps and sidewalks were swept clean, the lawn and winter flowers were green and in bloom and the cone-shaped trees emitted a scent of pine that permeated the air. Everything was clean and fresh.

Alone the wide, circular inlaid rock driveway, tall Rhododendrons and Bougainvillea were climbing and entwining on tall trellises, there were dwarf Maples cut and shaped into Bonsai trees, redwood treasures, and flowers everywhere.

"Flowers in January?" he questioned.

"There are varieties of flowers that bloom at all times of the year and will grow just about anywhere."

They walked across the lawn to the north side of the house where there was a row of huge glass greenhouses stretching for several hundred yards.

"Are they what I think they are?" he asked. "I noticed them before."

"Yes. This is an orchid ranch. The Foundation sells orchids all over the world."

"I thought all the orchids came from Hawaii."

"A lot do, and some come from Asia, but the Palomar Foundation is one of the major distributors of orchids in the United States which is the principal consumer. It's a cover; it's the front so nobody will now what really goes on here."

"From the size of those greenhouses, I would imagine that they do pretty good. I bought an orchid for my wife once, and it wasn't cheap,"

"You're married? They didn't tell me."

"Well, actually, we're divorced. Why? Is it importunate?"

"No, not at all. Forget it."

The thundering roar of the Lear jet dropping from the sky toward the landing strip a mile away suddenly shattered the quiet. They both looked up at the sound but the plane was out of view beyond the house. He thought about asking Diana if there had been any other incidents regarding the aircraft but decided against it. She wouldn't tell him even if she knew.

They walked along a well-maintained gravel road to the first greenhouse where Diana opened the door. "Interested?" she asked.

"All right."

Inside the heat and humidity hit him immediately and he was reminded of a South American rain forest. There were hundreds of plants in neat, straight rows with vines running along horizontal trellises. Some vines were laden with flowers while others were bare. About half a dozen men and women, all oriental, were moving around in the big room engaged in various tasks to maintain and harvest the flowers.

"These vines can grow up to a hundred feet long," Diana explained, "but they are normally kept trimmed to about fifteen feet. Each vine can grow up to thirty flowers. All in this house are the same variety. The other greenhouses have different varieties, different colors, shapes and fragrances. The blooms are harvested, packaged, and shipped all over the world."

"You know quite a bit about this."

"On occasion I act as an agent for the orchid company when I don't want anybody to know what I'm really doing."

"And what are you really doing?"

"Rehabilitating you, Doctor."

"You are quite an amazing woman, Diana."

"Now let's don't start hurling insults, Doctor," she replied with a slight smile.

Savage was amazed. She had actually made a joke.

"Shall we continue on or do you like this heat and humidity?"

"I've seen enough," he said.

Back along the gravel road, they reached the path in the back of the house used to get to the elevator and the underground complex. Along the path, he stepped into the horseshoe enclosure of bushes that concealed the stone bench.

"What are we going here?" she asked.

"Just something I wanted to see. Do you mind?"

She raised her eyebrows but didn't respond so he entered the enclosure and stopped at the bench where he stood looking at it for a moment.

"Just what is the significance of all this?" she asked.

He sat down on the bench and turned to look over his shoulder. "That's my window up there."

"So?"

"Well, from up there it just looked like a good place for a . . . a rendezvous if you didn't want to be seen."

"Seen by whom?"

"Anybody."

"You don't make a lot of sense sometimes, Doctor Savage," she said in an offhand manner but she glanced up at his window with some concern. "You wanted to see the place. Now's your chance."

They went along the walkway to where it forked at the stone bench but this time they turned away from the shed with the elevator. There was a large orange grove and another of avocado trees, each covering several acres. The ground had been turned and leveled adjacent to the stand of avocado trees indicating they intended to expand the grove.

"Do you like avocados, Doctor?"

"Not much."

"It's a money-making crop. In some places one avocado will retail for over $3.00."

"Not from me, it won't. It's a slimy green thing and civilized people don't eat them."

Diana laughed.

Forty minutes later, they had left the maintained grounds of the estate and were running along a narrow path that meandered up into and around the low foothills. The orchid greenhouses and the huge forests of carefully maintained, evenly spaced avocado trees were left behind as they climbed higher.

"Running is the best physical conditioning there is," she said, jogging along effortlessly beside him. "It exercises almost every muscle in the body. Better than working with weights, better than aerobics and better than all of those exercises you see on TV."

"If you say so," he managed, breathing heavily. "I used to do it back when jogging first became fashionable. Had the jogging suit and the shoes. Up in the morning, ran a couple of miles or so before breakfast. Everybody was doing it."

"Why'd you stop?" The question was serious and innocent.

"Well, things got a little confining after awhile." He shouldn't have said it. It was juvenile, but he was beginning to enjoy the irony and the double meanings in the statements he made, knowing that she didn't understand them. It helped to offset the coldness he felt from her. "I'd sure hate to see all of this place on foot," he commented, a little embarrassed and quickly changing the subject.

"That would take some time," she replied. "The Palomar Foundation owns almost twenty square miles around here."

"Twenty miles! That's a lot of ground."

"Yes, it is."

"And just exactly where is *here*?"

"What do you mean, where is here?"

"I mean, just exactly where the hell are we? I know we're somewhere in Southern California. I recognize the terrain and the Joshua trees, species Yucca brevifolia, if I remember correctly."

"Are you trying to say you don't know where you are?" She sounded disbelieving.

"Yes, that's what I'm trying to say. Hey! Can we stop for a minute?"

"Another quarter of a mile, then we'll stop, and as to your question, we're just north of a town called Saugus in the Angels National Forest. Thirty miles south of here is Los Angeles. I'm really surprised that you don't know where you are."

"Well, there've been a lot of surprises lately, not the least of which is you."

"Oh?"

She *had* been a surprise for David Savage. She was very frustrating for him, too, to be this close to such an attractive young woman after those years in the isolation cell on death row. Other than masturbation in the early morning hours when he reasoned everyone else to be asleep, he had almost forgotten what sex was like. In that segregated cell, he was not even privileged to share the homosexual experiences other prison inmates used to satisfy their desires. He had learned to control the mental and physical urges and to disregard them, much like he imagined a priest would do, and used his mind to create images of himself standing against the stone wall and being shot to death reduced the unwanted bulge in his pants and dispelled the memories of warm, pleasant nights in bed with a woman. But with Diana close to him so much of the time, in shorts with her beautiful, smooth, soft and sexy legs exposed, the curves of her hips and the bounce of her breasts as she ran with him, he was on the verge of attempting rape if necessary, except that he knew she would beat him to a pulp if he tried it.

"Why am I such a surprise?" she asked, slowing her pace slightly.

"Well, given my situation, I just didn't figure—"

The quiet sound of an electric motor behind them interrupted his reply and they both stopped, turned and saw Mr. Killingsworth riding slowly along behind them on a golf cart with a sunshade overhead. He wore his usual white shirt, vested suit and highly polished black shoes.

"Mr. Damarjiane would like to see you, Dr. Savage," he said as he brought the cart to a halt behind them. "Get in and I'll take you back to the house, now."

With a shrug and a glance at Diana, Savage settled onto the seat beside the sliver-haired lawyer and then almost shouted a protest as the cart turned back leaving her standing there alone.

"My instructions were to bring you, Doctor," Killingsworth replied. "Not both of you."

"Well, did he specifically say that you were to leave her out here to walk back?"

"The question is rather academic now, don't you think?" Killingsworth drove on toward the big house.

"Why right now?"

"He just got back and I don't believe he will be here long. This is only one of the enterprises in which he is involved, and he travels extensively all over the world. He needs to see you now."

The golf cart purred along the path carrying them over the gentle ridges and into the shallow valleys, through the dry brush and the wide expanses of hard, dry, barren ground, finally into the orchards behind the house and the grass and green shrubs irrigated by the automatic sprinkler system simulating daily rainfall. The contrast was eye catching. Where the round, four-inch, pop-up Rainbird sprinklers poured out their morning cascade of water, everything was lush and growing. Beyond was drab and dead even with the winter rains.

Savage opened his mouth several times during the trip to voice an opinion, a reiteration of his previous protest about leaving Diana out there alone, but he thought better of it. Finally, he said, "I got the newspaper clippings," then felt stupid for saying it. Obviously, he had received them with DeShane as the mailman.

"I thought they might amuse you."

"I guess thanks are in order. How in the world did you arrange it?"

"Arrange what, Doctor?" Killingsworth had a completely innocent look on his face.

"Nothing," he replied and remained silent until the lawyer parked the cart in the shed beside other vehicles and led him along the familiar path to the house and then to Mr. Damarjiane's office. The steel core door opened and David Savage was again ushered into the office of the Director of the Palomar Foundation. The only difference this time was that there was now a comfortable chair placed before the desk. The blinding overhead spotlights were on again, preventing all but a vague, shadowed image of the man behind the desk.

"Please be seated, Doctor," Mr. Damarjiane said in his whispered voice. "I understand that you are adapting well."

Savage settled in the seat aware that the lawyer remained standing somewhere just behind him, probably with folded arms and a look of condescending boredom.

"Adapting well? I don't know," Savage replied. "I guess so."

"You're looking much improved since you first arrived. The medical reports are encouraging."

"Thank you."

"What do you think of Project Window?"

"It's the most fantastic thing I've ever seen and having seen it, it's still hard to believe."

"And your part in it?"

"That came as quite a shock."

"Yes. I was advised of the manner in which you learned of your purpose here. Diana can be a bit . . . ahh, blunt at times, but she means well."

"Why do you call it a window? It's more of a doorway."

"That's quite true, it *is* a doorway. But, you see, when we first created it we were unaware that it was a physical threshold to another place. We thought it was just a portal of observation and referred to it as the window. Later, when we discovered the capability of egress, we had been calling it a window for so long it seemed inappropriate to change and start calling it a door.

"I see."

"I'm sure you've been wondering why you were selected for this project," Mr. Damarjiane continued.

"Sure, I have. But, then, I don't have much to lose if it fails, do I."

"But you have a lot to gain, Doctor. And it's not going to fail."

"I'm glad to hear that."

"You were not selected at random for this project as you may think you were, just because you were in state prison, on Death Row and this might be a suicide mission."

Savage winced visibly at the word, suicide.

"Someone less well known, someone who had committed a less spectacular crime would have been much easier to free." Mr. Damarjiane raised his hand in anticipation of a protest. "But do not be concerned. I do not believe for one moment that this is a suicide mission. No. It will succeed. You have the education and the knowledge I need to insure that it does. In addition to your extensive information on the subjects needed to do the job, you are an intelligent, innovative man with an aggressiveness necessary to your mission. At least, you were at one time. You were concerned with the environment and with ecology. I need that as opposed to someone who has no real interest in nature.

You will be able to provide me with the facts I need in evaluating what we have found.

"And what we have found, Doctor, is a whole new world, as you have seen. We are going to explore that new world and the time is short. Things here are much worse now than when you were sent into prison. You have been isolated and may not have kept up with world conditions."

"Such as?"

"First, there are too many people in the world. There are not enough jobs, not enough houses, and not enough food to sustain them. Birth control is being ignored or opposed by organized superstitions. Wages and prices have escalated beyond imagination. In Germany at the end of World War II, it took a wheelbarrow full of Marks to buy a few potatoes. It's not that bad here, yet, but it will be. Lower class people have been imported into this country by the shipload and they are dragging it down to their level. The governments of the world have grown so big and powerful that they are concerned with those whom they govern only to insure that they continue to govern. The era of the expanding economy is gone. We have no place left in which to expand.

"Casting about for new areas of influence, something that hasn't been done before, something by which the sheep may be led, the politicians have hit upon what they call the homeless and the disadvantaged. Worthless derelicts are upgraded to be called inoffensively, street people. Drunks, winos and narcotics addicts are now referred to in vague medical terms as chemically dependent and drinking alcohol has been made into a disease. Misfits, sexual perverts, freaks and dissidents, the elderly and the terminal ill are not allowed to die off as nature intended them to. Instead, they are supported by the government at the expense of the working people. Welfare costs exceed their budgetary limits every year and that money could very well be used for other, more productive projects.

"For the first half million years of man's life on this planet, less than a billion people were produced, lived and died. This coming year, the year 2007, there will be six billion people on the earth. In one more generation there will be close to twelve billion, then twenty-four billion. Even with disease, wars, natural deaths and self-destruction the death rate is far below the births. The earth can't support that many people. Right now, today, Dr. Savage, one out of every twenty people who ever lived on this planet is alive, procreating, and trying to double the population again. The carrying capacity of the earth has been reached and very soon, the die-back factor will set in. You are familiar with those terms?"

"Yes, of course. The carrying capacity is the life one piece of ground can support and the die-back factor is self-destruction when the population exceeds it."

"Some say AIDS is a created virus intentionally introduced to kill black people and homosexuals. Do you believe that?"

"I hadn't heard that, but, no, I don't believe it. I believe it began as a simian virus first discovered in the late eighteen hundreds."

"That is correct, Doctor. But there are people who believe otherwise."

"Some people will believe anything. They believe in flying saucers, little green men from Mars, ghosts, vampires and an electronic doorway to another world through which one can step and span the galaxy."

The old man chuckled at Savage's irony. "Yes. But you have *seen* the doorway, haven't you, Doctor."

"I've seen something I can't explain."

"Imagine if you can, sir, that we have already developed space flight and every hour on the hour, twenty-four hours a day, 365 days a year, spaceships open their doors, extend their ramps and take on a thousand people. That's a lot of weight. It would take a lotta fuel to lift them and fly them off the earth and out to the stars. Those space ships would transport almost nine million people a year. The whole city of Los Angeles, gone! Next year, New York. Gone.

Yet it wouldn't even make a dent in the population explosion threatening to inundate us in human bodies.

"We are up to our ankles in pollution and garbage and people producing more people to make more pollution and more garbage and more people. Shortly we will be up to our knees in it, then to our waist, our shoulders and shortly thereafter, we will be drowning in it. Man is doomed by his own mindless, uncontrolled procreativity and nobody seems to know how to stop it!

"Until now.

"With the discovery of the Window, I can save the human race, Doctor, or at least a good part of it, that portion that *should* be saved. We have found the way and you are going to be a vital part of it. Your reports of the new world will be of the utmost value to us in determining man's ability to survive there. In a very real way, you are the most important person on this project. I want you to understand that."

There was a note of desperation in Damarjiane's voice as he spoke and Savage detected it.

"I have told you these things because we need your sincerity and your loyalty in addition to your scientific skills. Work hard, do well and your rewards will be immeasurable."

"Rewards? What rewards? Am I getting paid for this? I mean, am I on salary?"

"Paid? Do you wish to be paid?"

"Well, sure. If I'm going to work for you, I think I should be paid. Shouldn't I?"

"And what will you do with the money?"

"Well, ahh . . . I haven't really thought about it, but, I guess, when I get back here, I'll need to buy a house, some property; I'll need something to live on. Maybe I should send something for child support. You know, to take care of my kids. I haven't exactly been the best provider the last few years."

"Your children are doing fine, Doctor. They are in no immediate need."

"You know about my family? You've checked?"

"Yes."

"Oh, okay. Well, that's good to know. Can you tell me about them?"

"I don't believe this is the time for that."

"When then?"

"Later."

"I'd like to know about my kids."

"And you shall. Trust me."

"All right, so, what am I gonna be paid?"

"I've already paid out almost a million dollars finding you, securing your freedom and bringing you here, Dr. Savage. How much more do you want?"

"I cost you *that* much?"

"Give or take a decimal point."

"All right, I'm impressed. Now tell me about that airplane that brought us here. It *was* sabotaged, wasn't it. Was it *me* they were trying to kill? Why?"

"There has been no evidence of sabotage, Doctor. Moreover, as for someone trying to do away with you, I very much doubt it. With the exception of security personnel and the members of the research team, nobody knows who you are or that you are even here."

"Then why all the security guards around this place?"

"The project we have undertaken is revolutionary as you have seen. I have told you my intentions, to save the human race. However, just suppose, for the sake of argument, I intended to market it commercially. Think of what it would be worth. The figure is incomprehensible. But more than that, think of the repercussions of a proliferation of these machines.

"Imagine, if you can, Doctor, the corporations, the businesses, entire industries that would become obsolete overnight because of the Window. Airplanes, trains, buses, automobiles, ships, all forms of transportation both private and commercial which we now have, and all of the companies that support them; oil companies, manufacturing companies, fuel, tires, plastic, glass, all would be completely out of business in a year.

"Communications companies, communications equipment, the mail and package services would vanish. Why call or write when you can instantly go to the person you wish to deal with and talk to him direct, face-to-face? Half the people in the world would suddenly have no job. An assassination team or an entire army could march into the presidential palace and take over the country. Governments would fall. Think of it, Dr. Savage. The implications are staggering.

"What would you pay, what would you do to prevent the Window from being manufactured if you had the power? If you were the CEO of General Motors, AT&T or American Airlines, what would you do? If you were the President of the United States or Prime Minister of Great Britain and half of your country's population was going to be unemployed tomorrow, what would you do? Destroy the Window? Steal it? Kill a few people to stop it? Kill a *lot* of people? World wars have been started over a lot less."

"Yes," Savage said, contemplating the disaster to the employment market the Window would make if it was offered commercially. "Yes, I see. I never really thought about all of that before, but you're right. It would be a disaster. But you said you're not going to sell it so how could anybody know about it?"

"Perhaps they don't, yet. Something of this magnitude, however, cannot be kept secret for very long. A word here, a story there, somebody told somebody else about a rumor they overheard. A hint, an innuendo, a guess. The word gets around. Believe me, I know. I've been there before. This isn't the first revolutionary discovery I've made. I can't keep everybody confined here nor can

I keep them from talking regardless of the security or how much I pay them. I can only hope to limit what they have to talk about.

"Industrial espionage, businesses spying on other businesses, has become so profitable and sophisticated that the CIA and the FBI could take lessons from industrial espionage agents. And I can assure you, Doctor, you have never before in your life met a more desperate and ruthless man than one CEO trying to protect his company from the competition.

"I'm tired now. It has been a long trip and I didn't intend to make a speech, so if you will excuse me—"

"What about my eyes?" he blurted out. "Surely you've been told about my eyes."

"Yes, I've been told about your eyes. It was an unforeseen element, Doctor. But then, we would have had no way of knowing about it since even you didn't know about it. Nonetheless, I see that it should make no difference. There will be sufficient time."

"Then my part in this won't be cancelled? I won't be sent back to prison?"

"Great heavens, no. Is that what has been worrying you. Your sight?"

"Yes! It—"

"While I have been speaking of the plight of millions, your only concern is how long you will be able to see." There was a deep sigh.

"Well, ahh . . . Mr. Damarjiane, I—" Savage suddenly felt humiliated.

"Be assured, Doctor, your job remains secure. Now, good day."

Killingsworth's hand fell on his shoulder and he got slowly to his feet. He had really muffed it this time and he tried desperately to think of something to say, anything to salvage something of the meeting. He found himself outside the metal-encased office before anything came to his mind and he was met by DeShane who accompanied him upstairs to his room. He did not notice the lawyer re-enter Mr. Damarjiane's steel office.

DeShane, wearing a tan military style shirt with the tail out and down over his trousers—probably to conceal a gun on his hip, Savage thought—poured himself a cup of coffee from the pot on the counter while Savage slumped in a kitchen chair to think about what Mr. Damarjiane had said.

"How'd the interview go with the Big Man, Doc?"

"The big man? Oh, you mean Mr. Damarjiane. All right, I guess. Maybe I just don't understand much of what's going on around here. And he sure put me in my place. Made an absolute selfish fool out of me."

"Yeah, he does that a lot, I hear. Give it time, Doc. They'll tell you everything you need to know. Meanwhile if you want, feel free to bounce the stuff off of me. I'm a good listener if you need one."

"Thanks, DeShane, but I really don't know what to say right now. I've got a lot to think about."

"Yeah, I'm sure."

"But right now I've got a question. Why is Mr. Damarjiane in that steel box?"

"The metal office? Well, I just know what I hear, you know."

"Okay, what did you hear?"

"A bunch of years ago somebody tried to blow him up in his office with a bomb. He's been paranoid about it ever since. So he made his office bomb-proof."

"They could plant a bomb somewhere else."

DeShane raised his hands. "I'm no shrink, Doc, so don't ask me to make any sense of it. It's just one of the boss' little quirks."

"Sure."

There was a long silence in which Savage could think of nothing else to say.

"Being in the joint still bothers you, don't it."

The question was like a razor-sharp sword stabbing through his body. He was so startled that he couldn't speak for a moment.

He stared at DeShane like he was some kind of an alien. Then he managed, "I though nobody knew about that. They weren't supposed to tell anybody. Who told you?"

"Nobody told me, Doc, but I can recognize prison duds when I see them, that first day when we put you on the plane back there in snowy Pennsylvania." He cocked his head slightly and nodded knowingly. "And then there is the world-famous Doctor David Savage whom I'm now suddenly responsible for, a man who came here looking like death warmed over. So I thought maybe I'd better took into it. That was *some* trial, Doc. I even went and read one of your books."

"Well, I'm glad you know. I'm not much good at playing games. And yes, it bothers the hell out of me."

"Don't let it. It's all behind you now and a lot of good men have done some hard time. You paid your debt and it's over. Hell, I did some time at the Graybar hotel myself. That's where Mr. Killingsworth found me. Bought my way out."

"You?"

"Yeah. You want some coffee?"

"How long were you in for?"

DeShane was quiet for a minute looking down at the floor as if trying to make a decision. When he looked up to meet Savage's eyes, he said softly, "Life."

"Life? Jesus, what the hell did you do . . . never mind, I don't want to know."

"Other than Mr. Killingsworth and Mr. Damarjiane, I guess, you are the only other person who knows. I think. Hadn't a been for them, I'd be rotting in jail for the rest of my days, so you can understand how strongly my loyalty is to those two men."

"Thanks, DeShane. It helps."

"Anytime, Doc."

So DeShane was an ex-con, too. Do'n life. So what the hell did he do? Good bet it wasn't something like kidnapping or train robbery. Professor Boucree was a reformed drunk. How did he get to be a drunk? Probably something morn' he just liked the taste of the stuff he was drinking. Damarjiane certainly wasn't the old man's real name and maybe he's not even in his right mind. Who the hell is he? And what about the beautiful Diana? She's sure a lot more that she pretends to be. How many secrets is she hiding?

His mind returned to the conversation in the steel office of the Director of the Palomar Foundation. Mr. Damarjiane was going to save the human race from suicidal extinction and Savage was going to be a part of it. A few weeks ago, he couldn't even save himself. Now he was going to rescue all of humanity. Or maybe all of it was just bullshit, a smoke screen, and Mr. Damarjiane really did intend to sell the Window to the highest bidder.

"DeShane," Savage said finally. "Is all of this for real?"

"What do you mean?"

"Well, you know, the Window, Damarjiane and everything."

"I don't know anything about any windows, Doc. Like I told you, I've never met Mr. Damarjiane. Mr. Killingsworth hired me and put me on as chief of the security staff here and then I was assigned to you, personally, in addition, of course, to keeping the troops in line. Beyond that, I don't know much of anything."

"And you wouldn't tell me if you did."

"Hey, Doctor Savage, I've already told you more than I should."

"But aren't you even curious about what goes on here, down there in those underground labs?"

"Doc, I was a Staff Sergeant in the Marines when President Reagan sent us in and we took Granada, and we did one heluva job there. After that, there just wasn't much going on. When my enlistment was up, I got out and went looking for employment. But there weren't any jobs in civilian life for a combat Marine without a college degree, so I became a mercenary fighting in border wars and overthrowing one-horse governments all over the world for anybody who would pay me. But there's always that chance that you're going to get your ass shot off, or get caught."

"You were a mercenary?"

"Yep. Worked for a guy named Elliott for awhile, made a lotta money and spent most of it. Then I got caught. Most of the company was killed and for a while I wished I had been, too but they took me alive and made an example out of me. Wasn't much of a trial, not like yours anyway. They charged me with terrorism, gave me the max, locked me up and threw the key away. So a couple a years later Mr. Killingsworth shows up, contacts me inside, says he can get me out and offers me this job for more money than I can believe. I'm gonna turn it down? Hell, no. I took it, right then, and I don't ask no questions. It ain't any of my business, anyway. So I'd advise you to do the same. This a pretty damn good outfit to work for."

"Where were you? If it's any of my business."

"You really want to know?"

"Yes."

"South Africa. Most of the company was German and Afrikaners, couple of Frenchys. I was the only American."

"Wow! Where did they send you after you got caught?"

"Pretoria prison, just outside of Johannesburg."

"Wow!" Savage said again.

"And I'll tell you something else, Doc. The joint over there isn't nothing like what they are here. You don't get no mail and you don't get no visitors. There ain't no radio or TV. The guards are brutal, the food is rotten and I mean that literally. If you try to escape, they shoot you and the rest of the cons there will kill you for your bowl of soup and piece of bread. The first day you're there, the guards take you out and show you this great big pit outside the wire. That's where they bury the dead cons. Plant 'em in the daytime and the animals come along and dig 'em up at night. The mortality rate is pushing forty percent."

"Wow!" Savage said a third time.

"You're a real nice guy, Doc and we seem to have something in common. Part of my job is to protect you, Dr. Boucree and the others. Another part of my job is to report anything and everything you say and do to Mr. Killingsworth, so keep that in mind. And just between you and me, I don't think he likes you very much."

"Why do you say that?"

"Hell, he doesn't like anybody very much. Why should you be different?"

"Thanks, DeShane."

"For what? I didn't say anything. And we never had this conversation." He took a sip of his coffee and looked over the cup with hooded eyes at David Savage. He had come to genuinely like the mousy little guy and he waited patiently to have his turn at him.

CHAPTER TEN

A NOTHER WEEK CAME AND went. Running outside along the paths winding through the low hills and the calisthenics in the back yard, weather permitting. Weight training in the underground gym and dinner in his room. Occasionally DeShane would join him and they would have dinner together. When in the security chief's company, he could have his dinner in the small underground dining room where the lab techs and security personnel ate. Although the food he was served in his room was better and more nutritional, he preferred the dining room to eating along, and he was finally beginning to become acquainted with the members of the staff.

The guards worked in three shifts and the men and women in Window Lab Two who were trying to create the second Window worked in two shifts. Only during the hours between midnight and six in the morning was the subterranean complex quite.

Seven more days passed and Savage was busy during the daylight hours. The physical training was very demanding and the refresher courses on everything including microbiology were even more taxing. However, at night, alone in his room, his diner served to him by the silent, uniformed waiter, he would begin to think about the Window and the new world on the other side. He would be exhausted from the day's activities but more often than not, sleep would evade him and without the sleeping pills, he would lay awake late into the night, his mind swirling from subject to subject.

He was not afraid of death, only the anticipation of it. That old saw, a coward dies a thousand deaths, a brave man dies but once might be true on the field of battle, but prison had a way of taking everything out of you, including courage. Brave man, coward, it didn't make much difference on Death Row. It was difficult to be gallant when you *knew* absolutely that you were going to die shortly and there wasn't anything you could do about it except sit and wait for it to come. It is truly amazing what you can learn to live with over the years when you have no choice in the matter. Now he was a fugitive but he wasn't afraid of being caught. If Mr. Damarjiane could get him out of prison, he could certainly prevent his recapture. So, with this sudden, new found freedom, maybe it was life he was afraid of. Or maybe it was Diana.

She was almost always there now, spending six to eight hours a day with him, often in shorts and halter, in a jogging suit that looked a lot better on her than it did on him, or just in slacks and a blouse. Whether leaning over him at his breakfast table with her warm breath on his neck, her face close to his cheek, or her hand touching his arm or his shoulder as he did his exercises, her fingers were soft and pleasing when she touched him. Later they became terrifying weapons in their hand-to-hand combat when she jabbed his midsection or delivered a painful chop to the bridge of his nose. Her eyes were warm, exciting and always searching when she talked about the project or quizzed him on his scientific knowledge. Then they were cold and hard in combat, flashing out their warning of danger, danger!

It was a hard Southern California rain that kept them indoors all day using the underground exercise room and then later running through the downpour to his second floor room continuing with the physical sciences. Diana was seated opposite him at the dinette table stacked with books, pamphlets and lined tablets, asking questions from a Physical Geology book.

"The average rate of erosion in the US is two point four inches per thousand years," she quoted from the book. "By measuring the amount of erosion which has taken place in a given area, the number of years that the land has been eroding can be accurately measured and the age of the land mass established with a high degree of accuracy. So how do you account for the six point five inch erosion rate in the Colorado River?"

"Particle size," he replied from his position on the couch, a half-empty coffee cup on the table before him. "The maximum size particle that can be moved by a river is proportional to the square of the velocity. Doubling the velocity increased by four times the size of the particle that can be moved. The formula is $D = pi$ squared times V."

"Good. How does that relate to the new discoveries at Mt. Saint Helens?"

"It doesn't. Diana, why won't you talk to me?"

"What do you mean? I'm talking to you now." She laid the book aside with a puzzled look on her face.

"I mean about other things. Yourself, for instance. We've been together for almost two months now and you always seem so cold and businesslike about everything. When I first came here, I wasn't much of anything. Maybe that's why you didn't like me. But I'm improving, aren't I?"

"You have improved admirably, David." It was only the second or third time she had used his first name. "You've gained over twenty pounds and it's solid muscle, not fat; you are physically stronger and more confident and you are learning self-defense tactics at a very rapid pace. I'm proud of you."

"So why don't you like me?"

Surprised and apparently a little amused, she said, "I don't dislike you. You are a part of my job. That's all. And I want to keep it that way, on a strictly professional basis."

"Not like with Marc, huh?"

"What do you mean by that?"

"Nothing." He could feel his face flush. What a goddamn stupid thing to bring up. "I shouldn't have said anything."

"No, go ahead. I'm interested. What about Marc?"

"No, really, I—"

"You started it. Finish it."

"All right. Remember when I told you I could see that stone bench from my window? Well, what I saw was you and Marc." He was into it now and there was no way to stop. "At the Christmas party the two of you looked pretty close."

She started to laugh and then caught herself. "Not that it's any of your business, Dr. Savage, but there's nothing at all between Marc and me. My god, he's almost three years younger than I am. He's just a friend, almost like my kid brother."

"Some kid brother," he responded flatly. "That's not what I hear."

"So just tell me what you hear."

"Nothing. Look Diana, I shouldn't even have brought this up in the first place. You said it. It's none of my business."

"Well, I'm glad you did. It's interesting. Oh, the rumors that fly around. Yes, Marc *is* like a kid brother to me. He tells me things, things he can't talk about to anybody else."

"Like what?"

"That's none of your business."

"You're right. I'm sorry. I'm way outta line here. Let's change the subject."

For reasons he could not even begin to imagine, she would not let it drop. "This goes no further, agreed?"

"Sure."

"Marc is afraid of flying and his duties require him to accompany Mr. Damarjiane and Killingsworth on the plane. It terrifies Marc but he can't say anything because he'd lose his job. I just try to reassure him, help him cope with that fear, that's all. I'm just somebody to talk to who will listen."

"Why would he talk to you? And more important, why would you want to listen?"

"I have a degree in psychology."

"Really? What?"

"Masters."

"You have a Masters? Why didn't you go on for your Ph.D.?"

"No point. And you should be more concerned with yourself and not Marc. And certainly not me.

"So, what about myself?"

"Your physical and mental conditioning and the job you have to do. That's what."

"Is that all?"

"David." She hesitated and then plunged right on in. "I know about your eyes. Your physician told me. Mr. Damarjiane is very concerned about it, that you won't be able to accomplish what you need to."

"He told you that?"

"Killingsworth mentioned it." Again, she hesitated. "Did you know that there is an operation that could possibly save your sight?"

"No. There are some drugs. I'm taking them now but I don't think there's enough time for them to do any good. But I didn't know about any operation."

"Well, there is, but it would set everything back even further than your physical conditioning. Damarjiane isn't willing to wait."

"So? Nobody expects me to survive, anyway. I'm a guinea pig. Isn't that what you called me?"

"Yes, that's what I said. I was told initially that you were brought here for the sole purpose of finding out if a person could go through the Window and live on the new world for any period of time. Your physical condition and educational background had nothing to do with it. Either you lived or you died. It would determine whether or not the new world could be explored, and if humans could live there."

"Yeah, that's pretty much the impression I got. If I lived, somebody else, somebody skilled and already trained for survival would be sent through the Window after me to do the *real* exploring of the planet, and then report back to Mr. Damarjiane."

"That was the plan."

"But something changed."

"Yes. Something changed."

"What?"

"You. You're what changed."

"Would you care to explain that?"

"No, I wouldn't."

"Come on. You brought it up."

"No."

"You told me about Marc. I'm not going to blab everything you say to anybody."

"Aren't you loyal to Mr. Damarjiane?"

"Sure, to a point. But that doesn't include betraying a personal confidence."

"I wonder."

"You've got to trust somebody, Diana."

She laughed but without humor. "I've heard *that* before."

"Yeah, I'm sure you have."

"All right." She seemed to reach a decision. "Up to a point."

"I'll accept that."

"You came here with a title and Boucree seemed to be impressed with you. I was ordered to recondition you but nobody would tell me anything about you. So I went to the library in LA and looked you up. Doctor David Savage, Ph.D. in Geology, Masters in Astronomy with a BA in Meteorology, Minor in Archaeology, AA in Literature; an explorer, author, a lecturer, and a millionaire. You're famous throughout half the world."

"Yeah, I was really something for awhile there, I guess. That all?"

"Is there more?"

"Where'd you get that stuff?"

"World Book Encyclopedia." She seemed pleased with herself. "You got almost a whole column. There's even a little picture of you with your Indiana Jones hat on."

"Ha! Indiana Jones. I heard that before. Anything else? Newspaper accounts, maybe?"

"I wasn't *that* interested. The World Book article was printed several years ago. Then you just sort of dropped out of sight. I'm only speculating now, you understand, but considering your physical condition and that you have been sick, it's possible that you contracted some catastrophic disease and almost died and have been in a sanitarium. You are only now just recovering. On the other hand, maybe the illness is just in remission and is actually terminal. That's why you are being trained, isn't it. You are going through the Window and since you're already dying, it doesn't make any difference whether you live or not."

"I'm not dying, Diana."

"Really?"

"Really, and nobody has told me much of anything about what I'm going to be doing."

"I don't believe you."

"I'm sorry you don't. But what difference does it make, anyway?"

"What difference? They are forcing me to train you to do this; just hoping your eyes will last long enough. Hoping *you* will last enough."

"Then, I don't see—" Suddenly it hit him and he was momentarily speechless with the significance of it. "I think I must *already* be blind," he finally managed. "I really didn't know. If I don't make it, somebody else will explore the world. Believe me, Diana, this isn't a job for you."

"Oh, isn't it?" There was a hard edge to her voice. "I've studied and trained for this since the Window first come into being, over three years ago. I've endured conditions and hardships you can't even begin to imagine and I have an opportunity to explore a world no human being has ever before seen. And nobody is going to take it away from me."

Savage nodded his head in continued understanding. "And now you are being forced to physically condition me to survive on that world. Knowing my fields of expertise, my qualifications, you believe I am going to replace you as the first explorer of this world beyond the Window."

"Yes!" she spat at him. "But *that* isn't going to happen."

"Well, now I understand where all your hostility and resentment comes from. I wish you had told me." He got up from the table, stuffed his hands into his pockets, and took a few steps into the living room. Stopping, he turned back and looked at her. "Diana, when I was first brought here, I had no idea why. When Boucree showed me the Window, explained what it was and then you said I would be the guinea pig, I believed it. I had no reason not to. But if there were any plans for me to be the initial explorer and to replace you, I didn't know anything about them."

"I don't believe you."

"Believe anything you want. I'm telling you the truth."

"Then, just what *did* Damarjiane tell you?"

"About the Window? Nothing. He just talked about the security problems. What might happen if people found out about it. What he has planned for the new world. He told me that we can save humanity. Just us, here. We can save all of humanity."

"Save humanity? That's what he said?"

"Yeah, that's part of what he said."

"And you believed him." She, too, stood up from the table and began to pace across the living room and back again.

"Why shouldn't I?" he asked.

"Humanity. Damarjiane could care less about humanity."

"What makes you say that?"

"He's willing to sacrifice you, isn't he?"

"Not much of a sacrifice."

"You seem to think very little of yourself, Doctor. Is that false modesty?"

Savage just shrugged and looked away. After a few moments, he turned back to her and said, "I have the feeling that you're still not telling me all of it."

It was Diana's turn to shrug.

"Dr. Boucree seems satisfied with what we're doing. And Mr. Killingsworth—"

"Killingsworth!" she spat, whirling to face him. "That trained seal! That perverted, egotistical—" She clamped her teeth together and began to pace again.

Savage smiled slight. "Do I get the impression that you don't like him?"

"No."

"Something personal?"

"It's none of your business."

"You're right. It isn't. I'm sorry."

"All right. I'll tell you. Killingsworth likes young girls, *very* young girls, and he has—" She stopped herself again and continued to pace, aggravated and obviously resentful.

"And as a woman, that offends you?"

"It should offend everybody. But that's not the issue here. You asked me to tell you the rest of it, so I'll tell you about the Palomar Foundation, Damarjiane and his so-called interests in humanity." She suddenly changed the subject and turned to face him. "Let me ask you something. Do you believe in God?"

"About as much as the next man, I guess."

"Which means you probably don't. But *I* do. God put everything in order. Everything is arranged as it should be. You are a child of the universe, no less than the trees and the stars: you have a right to be here."

He continued for her, ". . . and whether or not it is clear to you, no doubt the universe is unfolding as it should. Therefore, be at peace with God, whatever you conceive Him to be."

"Once again, I'm impressed, Doctor. I don't know one other person in this world who could quote Desiderata, picking it up where I stopped."

"I'm sorry, Diana, I read a lot. But I don't see what you're leading to."

"The new world. God didn't intend this to happen. Look, back then, when we were still living in caves and little huts in Africa, what if some being, some man from Mars or somewhere, came to Earth and just took over everything."

"You think that's what's going to happen?"

"Damarjiane is a businessman. If this new world we've discovered is habitable, he'll send people by the hundreds, by the thousands but only people he approves of, people just like himself. Nazi thugs and power-mad industrialists, and of course the slave laborers to do the work. He will build factories, dig oil wells and mines to strip the new world clean just as he and men like him have done here on Earth. He talks about pollution but he doesn't tell you that he and the other industrialists are responsible for it. His nuclear power plants are contaminating the rivers and the oceans, his oil is fouling the beaches and killing marine life—"

"You sound just like I did some years ago, Diana," Savage interrupted, "but a lot more bitter."

"It said in your bio that you were a conservationist and a member of the Sierra Club at one time," she continued, "and I've wondered why you're involved in this. You must know that there are people who have never even seen a forest, much less walked through one, those who have never breathed clean air, swam in a clean river or seen wide-open spaces.

"I was almost sixteen before I knew flowers grew in places other than in pots on window ledges, before I saw more than two trees together in the same place. Grass was just something rich people had in their front yard behind high fences I wasn't allowed near.

"Nature, the natural environment should be available for everybody to enjoy and if the new world is safe to live in, it should be for *all* people regardless of their political views or social standing. It should provide life for people, pleasure, freedom, clean air and water and blue skies free of pollution, but Mr. Damarjiane doesn't care about that. He's a misanthropic industrialist who wants a whole new world to destroy."

"I don't believe that."

"Believe it!"

"If all he wanted was more money or power, he could sell the idea of the Window. He could name his own price. He could be the richest, most powerful man in the world."

"You still don't get it, do you. He doesn't like this world the way it is. He wants to change it so that it conforms to his ideas of what it should be. However, as rich as he is or could be, he still can't do it. Men have tried to do that throughout history and none have succeeded. Alexander the Great, Charlemagne, King Richard with his crusades, Hitler, they all tried. But no one man can ever hope to have that much power on Earth. So Damarjiane's going to create his own world and be the absolute master of an entire planet of millions of people. He wants to be God. People who don't measure up to his standards, those who aren't just exactly the way he believes they should be and people who won't worship him on *his* world won't get to go."

Diana was passionate in what she said and it reminded him of Damarjiane's 'drowning in garbage' speech. "I don't think he could ever have that much influence."

"He's got you, hasn't he? You believe everything he says, even though he intends to send you there knowing you will go blind without medical help, that you might die the instant you arrive there."

"So what do you propose? Sabotage the project?"

"I wish I could."

"You really mean that?"

"Yes, I do."

"How? Quit? Destroy the Window? How could you stop it?"

Her anger had turned her face red and she was shaking with emotion as he stood before him, her hands balled into tight fists.

He walked quickly to her and reached out to put his hands on her shoulders, to console her. "Diana, I think you're over-reacting. I—"

She pushed him back roughly with both hands against his chest. "Get away from me!" she yelled sharply, her eyes blazing. "Don't you ever touch me again or you'll get hurt!" She turned abruptly and left the room, slamming the door behind her.

"What did I say?" he called after her, but she was already gone.

He did not see her for the remainder of the day and DeShane showed up at his door near dinnertime looking worried.

"Troubles, Doc?"

"What makes you ask that?"

"Well, first of all, Diana. Saw her go storming out of the house a while go and she asked one of my guys if he had seen Marc. What the hell happened between you two? I thought you were finally beginning to get along."

"Nothing. Just me and my big mouth."

"Well, at least she isn't going to have time with loverboy for consoling. He'll be gone first thing in the morning, for about a week with Mr. Damarjiane."

"Why is *he* going with him instead of you?"

"Priorities."

"Yours or his?"

"You're kidding."

"Okay."

"Marc can handle himself all right."

Where are they going?"

"Can't tell you, Doc?"

"On the plane?"

"That I *can* tell you. Yes, and why do you want to know?"

"DeShane, you ever know anybody that was afraid of heights, afraid of flying?"

"Sure. Acrophobia. I heard of it. Why?"

"Acrophobia is a fear of heights. I'm talking about flying."

"Okay, flying. So what?"

"Well, if old Marc has a fear of flying, wouldn't it be hard on him and wouldn't he want somebody to talk to about it? Somebody like maybe a shrink?"

"A shrink? Are you kidding, Doc? Where'd you ever come up with a nutty idea like that?"

"Nutty idea like what? If I remember correctly, I wasn't the only one scared to death when we landed here that first day with no power and falling like a rock."

"Doc, before he got the job here, old Markie was a skydiver. He's also into hang-gliding on his days off. Does that sound like he's afraid of flying? You know what, though, you're right. He *did* look pretty scared that day and he didn't want to make the flight at all. I had to practically threaten him to get him on that plane. I wonder why?"

Savage was also wondering. Why had Diana told him that story? Did she believe it or had she just made it up to conceal something? But why hide it from him? He was as mystified as DeShane appeared to be.

"You know something you're not telling me, Doc?"

"What? Me? No. No. I was just making conversation."

"If you say so. You okay?"

"Yeah. I'm just going to stand here and kick myself for awhile. Wanna help?"

"No. I do it on a regular basis, myself. There's something I gotta check into right now so I'll pass this time. Take a rain check."

After the security chief had gone, he walked to the window and looked out through the rain at the stone bench on the ground below where he had seen Marc and Diana. This wasn't helping any. He needed to get his mind off of the disturbing events having just occurred and the possibility that Diana had intentionally lied to him to cover for Marc. If that was the case, maybe she really did have some deep feelings for him.

He walked to the phone and picked it up.

"Yes, Dr. Savage?"

"Would you ask Mr. DeShane to come back and see me?"

"He's tied up at the moment, Doctor. Can it wait? I can send somebody else."

"No. That's all right. No hurry."

He switched on the TV and flipped through forty channels without finding anything of interest. He finally settled for the news on CNN. There were Riots in Ireland, England, France, the Middle East, Detroit, Seattle and Miami; there were burnings, there was looting, killing, political leaders promising pie in the sky and something for nothing. The world was tearing itself apart. Maybe Mr. Damarjiane was right. Humanity needed saving from itself.

An hour later there was a knock on his door. "What's up, Doc?" DeShane asked as soon as Savage let him in.

"I'd like to have dinner in the underground dining room tonight. I need some company. Will you take me?"

"Sure. There's also a bar down there. Did you know that?"

"No."

"Even got a dance floor if you can find somebody to dance with. I figured Diana wouldn't tell you about that."

"And I'd like to have another talk with Dr. Boucree. Can you set it up?"

"Don't see why not." He walked to the phone and punched in three numbers. "Hey, Doc, it's DeShane. Doc Savage would like to pay a call. Okay?"

"You're invited," the security chief said after a short silence and replacing the phone. "Grab a jacket. Got your umbrella? It's coming down out there."

"I noticed."

They went through the house, along the path through the rain and into the shed. Before entering the elevator they shook off their umbrellas and folded them. Stepping into the elevator, DeShane looked up at the camera and called out six numbers. After a moment, the car began to descend. "When you're ready to come home, just pick up any phone and punch in 911. You'll get security. I'll come and get you."

"911? Cute."

"I thought so."

"Anyway I can get an outside line?"

"Who do you want to call?"

Savage shook his head sadly. "Nobody. I'm just asking."

"Okay. Yeah. There's a way, Doc."

"Any limitations as to where I can go down here? I mean, is there an off limits area or something?"

"For you? Not that I know of, but don't try to kick open any locked doors."

"Thanks, DeShane."

The elevator door opened. "This is as far as I go. Don't get lost."

The elevator went back up and Savage walked to the lab door he had passed so many times on the way to the gym with Diana. He opened it and entered the L-shaped room with the guard behind thick glass. As before, the guard picked up the phone, spoke, and then motioned him to continue and enter through the door beyond the guard's view.

While waiting for Dr. Boucree to notice that he was there, he took off his water resistant, down-filled jacket and hung it up along with his umbrella just inside the door. His shoes were wet and he hoped he wasn't tracking in mud from the road that might cause a problem in the dust-free room. Turning around he looked, fascinated, for a time at the scene through the frame and tried to imagine what it was going to be like stepping through there into a world where no man had ever been.

"I'm sorry, Doctor," Boucree said. "I didn't hear you come in."

"Just trying to learn a little more about this thing, Professor," Savage explained using Killingsworth's title for Boucree. "It's still so unbelievable."

There were two other people in the room and they regarded Savage curiously for a few moments and then went back to whatever it was they were doing

"Well, come over here and I'll show you something." He took Savage by the arm and led him to a complex control board with a thick, plastic cover locked down over it. Beneath, among the dials and switches were four knobs graduated from one to nine. "You will notice that everything is locked down so nobody can touch anything."

"Yes, I see that."

"These two controls here with the meters above them regulate the power going to the magnetic field within the frame." He shoved a finger at two large black knobs with white arrows pointing to the number seven in the circular series of numbers around them. "These four control the lasers." Once more, he indicated with his finger.

"When we first set this up, rather than to attempt to focus and align the lasers manually, by hand, we mounted them on movable platforms," he explained, "and ran it through the computer system so that we could make adjustments down to one thousandth of a degree and then we brought the beams together. After the scene in the frame appeared, we worked with it and tested it for months and then decided to realign the lasers to see what would happen.

"Using the computer, we moved the top, right laser, that green one up there," he pointed upward, "two one thousandths of a degree and the whole scene in the frame changed. I don't know what happened but suddenly there was something like a swirling white blizzard and all the air in the room was being sucked into the frame. It was incredibly cold and we were almost asphyxiated. The whole thing lasted less than two seconds and then the computer realigned the beam, bringing the forest scene back. We don't know if the Window was suddenly opened into the vacuum of intergalactic space or on another planet with a lower atmospheric pressure. Whatever it was, we finally realized, we understood that it was a physical hole, a window, a doorway, whatever you want to call it, into somewhere else. Somewhere extraterrestrial. What if we moved it so that it opened on the surface of a star? We and this whole complex, maybe the entire state, would be incinerated in a microsecond. We've been afraid to move anything since. That's why everything is locked until we can figure out just how the Window was created and how we can duplicate it."

"You have no way of telling what you're looking at, what it is or where it might be?"

"No, but we've only been at it a little over three years, not including the time it took to set up the equipment and install the power. That's really a pretty short time for a scientific experiment as complicated and complex as this one is."

"Impressive."

"Once we recreated the Window, we'll have to learn how to focus and align it, to move it from place to place, from world to world, galaxy to galaxy, and not open it on the surface of a sun or in the depths of outer space. Develop a guidebook or instruction manual so we can position the Window exactly where we want it. That in itself could take another dozen years.

"And therein lies another of your tasks and responsibilities. As an astronomer familiar with star patterns, once you look at the night sky from the new world, you may be able to provide us with an idea of where you are in the galaxy and that will give us a starting point, a point of reference, if you will."

"Actually, I'm a geologist, not an astronomer."

"I know that, but I also know you have an extensive background in astronomy."

"Well, some. You still don't know how it works?" He changed the subject away from himself.

"No. Like so many major discoveries, it was an accident. The right things in the right place at the right time, the right circumstances. If the equipment ever failed, if the scene within that frame ever disappeared, it might take months or years to find it again and bring it back. More likely, we would *never* find it. We just wouldn't know how or where to begin. That's why everything is checked over a dozen times a day, why this place is so heavily guarded and why everyone is so thoroughly screened. We simply *can't* let the system go down, even for an instant. If the system *did* go down, it would all be gone. We have our own power, our own generators with backup generators and batteries to back up the generators. We have a UPS unit that will sustain the power for almost a full minute until the generators kick in."

"I presume you are not talking about the delivery service."

"What? Oh, the UPS unit." He chuckled. "Uninterrupted Power Source."

"The cost must be staggering."

"I presume it is but that is not my problem. My problem, well, *our* problem is to understand how it works and once we understand how and why it works, we can build bigger Windows. Interstellar and intergalactic travel will be possible without spaceships or long periods of time to get there. It will be instantaneous and we'll know what's there before we go. We can build Windows at the other end so there can be travel both ways. Each individual household could eventually have its own Window. A man could live on the fourth planet of Alpha Centarui and commute to work on the planet Mars in less time that it now takes to walk across the street.

"Soldiers of a peace-keeping-force could march through the Window from its base in the Andromeda galaxy to anywhere in the universe, assuming that there would never be another tyrant or another war among mankind. The possibilities are endless, Dr. Savage."

"And just how long is it going to take to accomplish all of these wonderful things?"

Dr. Boucree smiled. "Good question. With another miraculous discovery or two, maybe five or ten years. Without it, maybe twenty, thirty, fifty; who knows."

"But it will happen eventually."

"Oh, yes, it *will* happen. We're on the threshold of a whole new age in electronic science."

"How's it coming in the other lab with the duplicate Window?"

Boucree's smile faded slightly. "It's not. There's nothing, so far. However, we're not discouraged. There are so many variables, you know."

"Such as?"

"Well, even without going into the makeup of the energy field itself, the laser beams are, well, look for yourself. As you know, the world laser stands for Light Amplification by Stimulated Emission of Radiation. The photons of light drop, line up and are emitted in a straight line. We're using green and red light, but you can have blue lasers, yellow lasers, about anything you want, but they're all different. Since we don't know exactly what caused the Window to appear in the first place, we don't know what we're looking for.

So, it's a trial and error process. Like I said, it will take time, but we'll find it.

"Thanks, Professor. You've made it all seem worthwhile."

"Oh, it is, I assure you, Doctor. The world will never be the same again."

Momentarily overcome by the vast implications of the project in which he was an intricate part, he put aside his resentment of confinement and the death sentence he had lived with for those long years. His biological urges and his feelings for Diana were subordinated in favor of the greater good and survival of mankind. Not since the Manhattan Project had there been such a giant step forward in science.

"Is it all right if I have a look at the other lab?"

"Oh, of course. I'll call them and say that you're coming. It's right through that door over there."

"Why do you have to call them?"

"Everything is so strictly controlled that . . . well, we don't know if the body heat or the electrical energy output of one additional person in the room might affect something. So we compensate for everything."

"I see."

He waited until Dr. Boucree had completed his call and nodded to him, then went to the second Window lab where the same electronic equipment had been set up. Four men in long, white coats were working with it. As he entered, one came toward him with his hand extended. "Dr. Savage, I'm Phil Dendron, Dr. Boucree's chief assistant. We met the first day you got there and then again at the Christmas Eve party, but I doubt that you remember."

"How could I forget?"

"Understandable." He grinned. "Can I show you what we're doing?"

"Please. I see that the Window is out in the middle of the floor here, not up against a wall like in the other lab."

"Well, theirs *was* in the middle of the floor. They built the wall later to protect the equipment. The generators and all the power leads supplying the field are behind the wall as is the mirror. You can see here how it is all set up. Once we realized what we had created, we were afraid to touch anything so we just walled it off. The next thing we realized was that we didn't have a clue *what* we had created or how to do it again. That's when this lab was set up."

"You're in charge here?"

"No, Dr. Boucree is, but he can't be in two places at once."

"Why the mirror?"

"As you know, our original intention was just to accelerate a laser beam faster than the speed of light by the use of energy fields. The beam would bounce off the mirror behind the Window and be projected out through a hole in the ceiling." He pointed to the three inch opening in one corner of the room. "That hole is lined with an inch of Tungsten steel and goes up at a forty-five degree angle opening in the hedges ten feet above the ground. Since we had no idea what would happen if we were successful in moving a laser beam faster than light, we weren't taking any chances. Even air traffic was restricted from this area when the laser was first turned on."

"So, what happened?"

"The laser beams didn't hit the mirror. They never even penetrated the energy field. They just sort-of merged together with the magnetic field somehow and they created the Window."

"And you haven't been able to duplicate it."

"No, and our beams here are passing through the field but they aren't moving faster than light, either. We have instruments to measure it."

"What happens to the beam going out through that hole?"

"Oh, nothing. It dissipates; just turns into ordinary light about a hundred feet up.

"Disappointing."

"Yes, so far. But we did it once. We'll do it again. We check everything we do here with the one in the other lab, and as long as that one is up and running, we'll duplicate it. Look here." He showed Savage a complex control panel containing dozens of gauges, dials and indicators. "We are altering the power input to the magnetic field one ten thousandth of a watt, one ten thousandth of an amp at a time, maintaining the ohms at a constant, doing the same with the lasers. We keep a close watch on the atmospheric pressure and—"

"Wait a minute. Atmospheric pressure?"

"Sure. You open a door real fast in a room and the curtains at the window on the other side of the room will move because you've sucked in a bunch of air and changed the pressure, maybe only by ounces or grams per square centimeter, but you've changed it. Maybe somebody opened the lab door at the precise moment the lasers hit the field and the pressure fluctuated. We don't know. The thing is so revolutionary, so far beyond our present-day science, anything is possible so we have to explore everything. Like, for example, maybe the exact conditions it took to created the Window are different than those now necessary just to maintain it."

"Boy, you're way over my head. Sounds impossible."

"We plod along."

"I've sure got a lot of admiration for you people."

"No. We're just technicians. You're the one to be admired, Dr. Savage. I guess I'm a little bit jealous, too. The first man to set foot on an alien world."

"Well, not exactly, Phil. Neil Armstrong beat me to it quite a few years ago."

"Yeah, but that was just the moon."

"It was still an alien world."

"But nothing like what's on the other side of the Window."

"You're right. Now, show me what you're doing."

For the next hour, Dendron took him step-by-step through the tiny changes in the intensity of the energy field, through the alternations in the laser beams, the careful recording of the movement of the photons, the comparisons with the Window in lab one. None of it meant anything to Savage. He was so far out of his element he felt like an aborigine in a loincloth dropped off in downtown New York by an itinerant cab driver who couldn't speak English.

There was no separate exit from the second lab so he was forced to re-enter the first and leave via the L-shaped room. He did not see Boucree and the other two men who only glanced at him as he passed through, pausing only long enough to put on his jacket and pick up his umbrella. In the hallway outside, a uniformed guard holding an M-16 snapped sharply to attention and said, "Good evening, Doctor."

"You weren't here when I came in."

"I was just down the hall, but I saw you," the guard replied.

"Oh." He looked at the automatic rifle in the guard's hands and asked, "Do you really think you might need that?"

"Never can tell when a scientist will go berserk and try to wreck the place. I hear it happens all the time."

With a start, Savage responded, "You're kidding!"

The guard grinned. "Yes, Doctor, I'm kidding. We're here to *protect* you, not shoot you."

"That's comforting." With a slight, polite node of his head, he walked slowly along the wide, bright corridor to the door and the elevator that would take him to the surface. With the complexities and possibilities of the Window swirling around in his mind, he completely forgot about his intention of eating in the underground dining room with members of the staff.

There was a phone attached to the wall beside the door and he picked it up, punched in 911 with a slight smile, and waited.

"Yes, Dr. Savage?"

"How did you know it was me?"

"TV camera, on the ceiling to your right."

He turned and looked up. There it was, pointing straight at him.

"I'd like to go up now," he said into the phone.

"Yes, sir. Would you like an escort on the surface?"

"No. I think I can find my way to the house. But thanks, anyway."

"Please hang up the phone, Doctor."

"Oh, sure."

The massive vault-like door swung outward and he stepped into the elevator as the chunk of steel began to close. His mind wandering, he exited the elevator in the shed and walked out onto the gravel road finding that it was now night and the rain had stopped. A short distance away along the gravel road was the walkway to the house.

Despite what he had just seen and had been told, his thoughts had turned to the beautiful woman who was becoming more and more a part of his life. There was so much anger within her, so much hostility and resentment for which he could not account. She was young, beautiful, physically fit, and obviously well educated. That was much more than most women had. Perhaps it was her affair with Marc turning sour. Notwithstanding her insistence that he was just a friend and someone to talk to, DeShane had hinted at a much deeper involvement between them, a physical relation Savage wanted, even more than he wanted his continued freedom.

Question. Would he be willing to return to prison for one night in bed with her?

Yes.

No! Definitely not. What nonsense. What was happening to his mind? Why couldn't he think clearly? Why did he mentally strip her clothes off every time he saw her and imagine her naked before him?

There were other women. They all had the same equipment. If he went to Killingsworth or Mr. Damarjiane, maybe even DeShane, and just said honestly and flat-out that he really needed a piece of ass—it had been a long time—they were men, they would understand. Arrangements would be made. He wouldn't have to sleep alone every night.

But was a night of sex what he really wanted from Diana?"

Yes.

No. What he wanted was what he had had with his wife, the woman he married and had lived with for almost ten years amid his long absences and the trips to all parts of the world. His kids were a part of both of them, the result of their love for each other, a physical manifestation of their desire and passion, the children whom were not being raised by another man married to their mother.

Every ten feet along the pathway there were low intensity lights raised six inches above the ground and placed to illuminate the walk. Artistically concealed in the flowers, shrubs and ferns, they were almost invisible in the daylight but provided a gentle glow at night to light up the way.

His hands thrust in his trouser pockets, his mind bouncing from his wife and family to Diana and the Window, and the new world on top of it all, he didn't notice that the pathway lights were out and how dark it was. He turned to the right and took just two steps when his leg slammed into something, catching him just below the knee. There was a blow to his back, directly between the shoulders and he was propelled forward, stumbling and falling over whatever was in his path. Somehow, he managed to jerk one hand out of his pocket and thrust his arm forward in an attempt to regain his balance. That one single act saved his life.

Tumbling hard over the obstacle in his path, his left arm slammed into the curved stone bench just ahead and his head hit his extended forearm. Had he not had that hand and arm outstretched, the front of his skull would have been crushed against the stone bench.

The surveillance microphones picked up his cry of pain when his arm hit the bench and the infrared monitors recorded his heat image slumping toward the ground. In the security command center, emergency radio signals were sent and two security guards were there with guns drawn in less than twenty seconds. DeShane exploded out of his office and hit the back door of the house on a dead run, his gun in hand. In the bright glow of the flashlights held by the two security guards, he skidded to a stop and saw Savage draped over a wheelbarrow which had been left in the middle of the walkway. His arm and head resting on the bench.

"Christ! Are you all right, Doc?" he asked, replacing the weapon in his shoulder holster and kneeling beside Savage.

"I think I broke my arm."

"Get the doctor out of the pit," DeShane ordered.

"Already done, Chief," one of the security guards replied. "He's on his way up as we speak."

"Dr. Savage, can you stand up?"

"Yeah, DeShane, I can stand up. Just give me a hand, will you?"

"Sit on the bench here. Your physician will be here in a minute."

"God. Damn! My arm hurts."

"He'll take care of it, Doc."

"Hey, Chief! There's something here you gotta see," the tall, blond security guard said to DeShane. He put his pistol back in its holster, told Savage to sit still, and turned his flashlight on to one of the raised sidewalk lights. "Go look at the lights."

"What am I gonna find?" DeShane asked.

"Somebody unscrewed it. That one down there, too. This portion of the walk was blacker than the inside of a cat."

"So the Doc wouldn't see the wheelbarrow in the middle of the walk. That's what you're saying?"

"Looks like."

"DeShane," Savage called, having overheard what the security guard said. "Somebody pushed me. I tripped over the wheelbarrow, but somebody hit me hard from behind and shoved me over it."

"You sure?"

"Yes, I'm sure."

"Neat accident. You fall over a wheelbarrow, hit your head and die. Okay. Works for me." He turned to the blond security guard. "Flynt, we got twenty-four hour coverage on the Doc, but I want it doubled. Two men on him every minute. He goes to the bathroom, I want somebody there handing him the TP. And I want video and sound. You got it?"

"Yes, sir. We may have bring in some more people."

"Then do it!"

"Yes, sir."

"DeShane, I need some privacy," Savage protested.

Ignoring him, the security chief continued his instructions to Flynt. "I want to know where everybody was the last two hours, if anybody saw anyone out here. You know the drill."

"Got it, boss."

The physician appeared out of the darkness wearing a light ski jacket over his lab coat, dropping his bag onto the ground and gingerly took Savage's arm in his hands. "Slip your coat off. I need some light here," he said. Immediately a security guard put the powerful beam of a flashlight on them.

"Ouch!" Savage responded to the probing fingers of the physician. "That hurts!"

"You're lucky, Doctor. There's nothing broken, but you're going to have quite a bruise there. I'd like to take a couple of x-rays just in case there's a hairline fracture. Might not hurt to immobilize that arm for a day or so, too."

"Mr. DeShane?" Killingsworth questioned, approaching the small group quickly. He had on an expensive ankle-length robe over his shirt and trousers, and was without a tie. "I saw the commotion from my window."

"Just an accident, Mr. K."

"Are you all right, Doctor?" the lawyer asked Savage. There seemed to be genuine concern in the lawyer's voice.

"Tripped and fell," he replied, taking his cue from DeShane.

"Could I talk to you later, sir?"

"I think you better, Mr. DeShane," Killingsworth replied, turned abruptly and started back for the house.

Two hours later Savage was alone in his second floor room with a sling on his arm and a large dark blue bruise rapidly turning to black. Even with the painkiller he had been given, the arm pained him greatly.

There was a gentle rapping at the door and DeShane entered with a bottle in his hand. He went to the kitchen, put ice in two glasses, poured, and offered one to Savage. They sat at the small kitchen table facing each other.

The Scotch burned as it went down but it tasted better than it had at the holiday parties. "Got anything yet," he asked.

"Too soon," DeShane replied. "But it was no accident. You piss somebody off lately?"

"Not that I'm aware of. Come on, you've got to have *something*!"

"Don't put me on the spot, Doc."

"Hey, it's my life we're talking about here."

"Okay, I can tell you this much. When you got to the surface, we were tracking you. The infrared camera picked up your assailant's approach and that's why we were already moving when you went down. Wasn't supposed to be anybody else there, and if it had still been raining we wouldn't have picked up anything on the I. R. Lucky break for us. Nobody came up the elevator after you so everybody underground is cleared."

"What about up here?"

"A couple of conflicting stories and a couple of no-alibis, but nothing concrete."

"Tell me."

"Can't. Gotta run it by Mr. K first."

Savage grumbled and took another drink of Scotch. "Everybody else getting the same surveillance you're putting on me?"

"Yep, and they don't like it any more'n you do. Sleep well, Doc." He took the bottle with him.

Shortly after DeShane left, there was a knock at his door. The white-jacketed man pushing his four-wheeled cart entered and dinner was served. In the wonderment of the Window and the excitement of the accident, he had completely forgotten about eating. However, others were there to take care of that.

The painkiller and the Scotch began to take effect and by the time he finished eating, he could hardly keep his eyes open. He had actually nodded off a couple times, awakening with the fork in his hand and food in front of him. He took another bite, chewed and nodded off again. After only a couple of seconded he opened his eyes. Enough of this. Forget everything, he told himself. Just get some sleep. And forget Diana. She was like one of the guards or like Warden Bennett at the prison. An authoritative figure. Inaccessible.

—*—

The alarm woke him and he crawled out of bed favoring his injured arm. The ugly bruise was an inch wide and over two inches long but the skin was not broken, the bone not damaged so he would heal quickly. Slipping naked into the bathroom he showered and stood looking at himself in the mirror as he shaved. Even without the contacts or his glasses, his eyes were clear and his face had taken on a fuller look. There were no dark circles under his eyes now and his cheeks were not so sunken. He raised his good arm and wiggled his fingers, watching the tendons move

just beneath the skin of his wrist. He made a tight fist and saw
the muscles expand in his forearm. He looked at his chest and
saw the firmness of his flesh where before there had been only
depressions between his ribs. The hair on his chest seemed to be
getting thicker; it was getting gray too, but it was there.

He lashed out with a closed fist toward the mirror, stopping
an inch before the glass. He stepped back and made several more
boxing punches that reflected in the mirror. Things were getting
better. The next time somebody tried to kill him, he would be
prepared.

Just after breakfast, there was a knock at the door and Diana
entered. Instead of her usual shorts and halter, she wore jeans and
a blouse. She stood looking at him in his jogging suit, his left arm
in the sling. "Killingsworth told me you had an accident."

"Tripped over a wheelbarrow somebody left outside on the
walk."

"Just your arm? Nothing else damaged?"

"You sound disappointed."

"I take offense to that remark, Doctor."

"I'm sorry, Diana. Have some coffee. I'll be all right."

She sat at the table with him and poured from the silver pot
in the middle of the table. "We're starting a new phase in your
training today," she said, her eyes intently searching his face. "But
it can be postponed."

"No."

She reached across the table and picked up his coffee cup, held
it to her nose and sniffed. "A little early for brandy, isn't it, Doctor?
Where'd you get it?"

"There was a little bit left over from last night."

"Who brought it?"

"The tooth fairy."

"I see," she replied with a disgusted look on her face, but
she pressed on. "Today, Mr. DeShane is going to start teaching

you marksmanship. You've read the books; you know what the weapons can do. Now, you just need to know how to do it."

"I know about guns," Savage replied. "I've carried a gun for a long time."

"Indeed? Well, we are gonna just have to assume you know nothing about them and start with the basics. Step-by-step. You are going to be an expert with every kind of weapon there is before you go through the Window."

"Why?"

"Because we have no idea what you will find there and you have to survive until you can make a report. That's what this is all about."

"So, I'm going to be prepared to kill anything I see?"

"No, not at all. Only to protect yourself if it becomes necessary. Come on, we're going to the pistol range first."

"Where's that?"

"In the complex down the hall from the labs."

"You're really going to trust me with a gun?"

"That's a stupid question, David. Come on."

Down the grand staircase, out of the house and long the walk to where the wheelbarrow had been left. Two oriental gardeners were snipping dead leaves off of plants and pulling an occasional weed they found. Savage stopped and looked around not knowing what he was looking for. There was no sign anywhere that anything unusual had happened here.

They went through the vault door and down into the subterranean hallways. "I want you to do some calisthenics that won't bother your arm and about half an hour on the treadmill. Take a shower and I'll meet you here in about an hour and a quarter."

"All right." It was the first time she had not done the exercises with him. That was strange. Stranger still was the fact that she made no inquiry into his accident, no question about any injury and generally had no interest in the incident at all. At least, that's the way it appeared.

When he dried off from the shower, his jogging suit was gone and jeans, a denim shirt and a new pair of boots replaced it. So he had to break in another pair of boots. Wonderful.

She was waiting for him in the gym and led him further down the hallway than he had been before. If she noticed that he no longer had his arm in the sling, she gave no indication of it. A door almost to the end of the corridor led to a complete, modern and well-equipped shooting range with movable targets and individual shooting stalls. It was to a stall at the far end wide enough to accommodate several people that she took him. On the counter were a dozen weapons, pistols, rifles and machine guns.

"You are just going to be firing for familiarity today," she said, handing him an S&W Model 66 .357, loaded but with the cylinder open. "See what you can do with this before DeShane gets here."

"No noise suppressors?" he asked, looking around for ear covers.

"You won't have any in the field. You need to be accustomed to the loud bang."

He closed the cylinder, spun it checking for a high primer, and took a two-handed stance. Before he could draw a bead on the target she asked, "Don't you think you should take the safety off, first?"

Slowly lowering the weapon, he turned to look at her. "You're putting me on, right?"

"What do you mean?" she replied in feigned innocence.

"Are you going to stand there and tell me you don't know there isn't a safety on a revolver?"

She just shrugged.

"Suddenly, I'm beginning to be concerned about you."

"David, I know about guns. I don't like them but I know about them. Can't you take a little humor?"

"Sorry."

"Next, I want you to try this." She pointed to an old military .45 automatic on the counter in front of him.

Again he lowered his weapon and looked at the .45. It resembled almost exactly the one he had carried for so many years, only newer. It also brought painfully to mind what had happened to his old .45. "Why? It has no effective range and damn little accuracy."

"True. But the hitting power is fantastic and like the old M-1 rifle, you can throw it in the mud, run over it with a truck and it'll still fire when you need it."

"You really *do* know a lot about guns—"

"For a woman?" She finished the sentence for him.

"No, that's not what I was going to say." Of course, it was.

"Wasn't it?"

"Well, I'll admit I've been wondering why you are the one training me in unarmed combat. I'd a thought they'd have a Green Beret or a Marine drill instructor, somebody like that."

"You have a problem with me?" There was that anger flashing again.

"No, not at all. I think you're terrific. I just asked, okay? Don't get mad again."

"I'm not mad," she snapped.

"This a private fight or can anybody just jump in?" DeShane asked, walking up behind them.

"I'm not sure," Savage replied.

"You gonna stick around, Diana?" DeShane asked.

"No," she replied. "You go ahead and watch him. I've got other things to do this morning. See that he doesn't shoot himself in the foot." She turned and walked away without looking back.

"She's in a worse mood than usual," DeShane said, watching the sway of her hips as she went through the door to the outside hallway. "She must like you."

"Hardly," Savage replied, raising the pistol toward the target once again. "Thanks for speaking up when you did. She was about ready to let go at me again."

"At least she talks to you, Doc. She doesn't even know the rest of us are alive. If it wasn't for the sarcasm, she'd never say anything to us. But she's quite a girl, isn't she."

"Yeah, I'd agree with that. But why do *you* think so?"

"Well, with a face and figure like that, she's really something even without her other abilities and accomplishments. Did you know she has a Masters in Psychology? She's a terrific athlete, a black belt in karate and she's a crack shot with just about any weapon. She's really into that Oriental mediation stuff, too. Claims it gives her inner powers, whatever *that* means. She went to some kinda special school in Japan and I think it kinda screwed her head up."

"Ninjas?"

"Don't know nothing about any Ninjas, Doc."

Standing with his feet spread, the pistol in both hands, arms extended, Savage fired six shots, slowly, using double action. The six holes in the target were scattered unevenly around the center of the target.

"Been awhile," he said, opening the cylinder and extracting the empty shells.

DeShane removed the pistol from under his jacket, sighted in, took a breath, let half of it out, and cranked off eight rounds as fast as he could squeeze the trigger. He almost cut the center out of the target, so tight was the group. "Just showing off, Doc," he said, putting the gun away. "Try the Glock this time. It's got a real smooth trigger pull, but it's not as heavy so it will have more of a recoil. Remember to compensate."

His first shot was almost dead center but the gun kicked higher than he had anticipated and when he came down on the target for the second shot, it went high.

"Told you," DeShane said. "Go ahead, crank off the rest of the clip and we'll get to the fully automatics."

"How long have you known her?" Savage was very envious of the husky young ex-mercenary with the broad shoulders and a rugged face.

"Who, Diana? She was here when I got here. We got along pretty well at first but, Doc, I gotta tell you, she's just impossible to get along with for very long. What a little hellcat. And then when they took her dog, well, boy, let me tell you, she really came goddamn unglued."

"Dog? Somebody took her dog?"

"Yeah. She had this big shepherd that went everywhere with her. The two of them were almost inseparable. She used to sit around and talk to that dog just like it was a person. She claimed it was attack-trained, but it was sure friendly. Word was with everybody that she though more of that dog than she did of any people. Then one day Doc. Boucree and Mr. Killingsworth took the dog into the lab and it never came out. I've never seen it since."

"What happened to it?"

"Don't know. I guess they cut it up or something. None of us have ever been inside the lab and my men have orders to shoot anybody who tries to get in there without authorization. But I'm sure you know that."

"Yeah, I was told."

"Hell, even I couldn't get in there without authorization."

"Did you know about me? That I was coming here, I mean?"

"Oh, sure. We had a description and pictures of you a month or so before you got here."

A month! They knew a month beforehand that he was coming here.

"Funny thing, you know, that Mr. K would order a man shot just for going in there. Must be something pretty important."

Maybe it was longer than a month. Maybe Mr. Damarjiane and the Palomar Foundation had planned this for years while he languished in prison.

"But that's the way it goes. I don't ask any questions. Anyway, after the doggy disappearing act, that's when she took up with Marc and wouldn't have anything do with me or any of us. She'd just stick her nose in the air and walk right by like we weren't even there. But don't get me wrong, Doc. She's a really nice girl. Maybe it's because she grew up an orphan, never knew her parents, and that's why she's so bitter about everything. The children's home she was raised in was a real dump of a place, I guess, and she never had anything. Hey! Good shooting, Doc!"

Seething with the information he had just gotten from DeShane about how long they had know about him in prison, he took out his anger on the target before him. Reloading the Glock, he put six shots in the center of the target equal to DeShane's group. He listened to the security chief talk about Diana but the words didn't immediately register with him.

"So, anyway, that's where Mr. K found her, in that orphanage. He was the attorney for the place, or something like that. I don't know. She was, maybe, fifteen or sixteen at the time. A real looker, I guess, even then. So, he got her out of the orphanage, bought her clothes, put her through school and then college. He really took care of her. Probably the only nice thing he ever did in his whole life. And I never said that."

"Killingsworth did that?" Savage was suddenly very interested.

"Yeah. He did."

"That doesn't sound like Killingsworth. What did he do, adopt her or something?" Savage was calmer now as he sighted in on the target.

"Adopt her? Are you kidding, Doc?" DeShane questioned in disbelief. "He married her. Diana Killingsworth. She's his wife. You didn't know?"

Savage's next bullet struck the floor almost twenty feet in front of the silhouette target.

CHAPTER ELEVEN

IT TOOK ONLY TWO days for Diana to confirm the attitude change in David Savage. He had become cold, withdrawn and had hardly spoken to her. The first afternoon following the physical training and marksmanship lessons she went to his room a usual to continue tutoring him but he said he was tired and didn't want to do it. He was polite but definitely gave her the impression he didn't want her there. She thought that reasonable because she had been pushing him even harder later, both physically and mentally.

The second afternoon she had to enter his room without invitation. He simply wouldn't answer the door, and once she was inside, he stayed at the computer ignoring her completely. After waiting for almost fifteen minutes and saying his name a couple times with no acknowledgement, she left. That evening Killingsworth informed her that her pupil had requested someone else to continue his training, but the request had been refused.

"What did you do this time, Diana," he asked as they shared dinner in their elegant third floor apartment.

"Nothing," she replied.

"Well, try to regain his confidence and cooperation. Time is getting short."

She flung her napkin onto the table and barked at her husband. "Why should I? I didn't what to do this in the first place."

"You know why," he replied calmly.

The truth was that she was deeply disappointed that David Savage suddenly didn't want her around and she needed to find out the reason. Despite her outward attitude toward him, she found herself becoming more and more interested in the man, enjoying his company and their conversations, and she no longer looked upon him as just a subject to train. Her feelings about him bothered her. It painfully reminded her of a very handsome young man in the Northern province of Japan who's named she could no longer say.

"Why don't you just ask him?

"Sure, Damian. Ask him. Like, gee, David, why don't you like me anymore?" She got to her feet and went to the French doors, opened them and stepped out onto the small balcony.

"My, my, my," Killingsworth remarked, looking at her back as she leaned her elbows on the railing. "Do I detect a display of actual emotion?"

"Would you really like to see some emotion?" She was becoming angrier by the moment. "Christ, Damian, the way you push me at every man. You—"

"Diana," he replied, "I haven't pushed you at anybody. I just don't interfere."

"You mean you don't care. That's unnatural. Your wife is out sleeping with other men and you don't care."

"As I have told you before, what you do is your own business. I have never understood the attitude most men have that as soon as they sleep with or marry a woman, nobody else can touch her. They proudly show off her pretty face or nice legs, but when it comes to her talents in the bedroom, they suddenly become selfish and possessive. Makes no sense to me."

"That's because you're a pervert. Any girl over fourteen is of no interest to you. You're disgusting."

With a dismissing shrug Killingsworth went back to finish his dinner, then turned on the TV to catch the late news.

—*—

Three more weeks went by and David Savage's body filled out and hardened even more from the physical conditioning and the expert training he received from Diana Killingsworth. He gained another ten pounds and fought with knifes and clubs, he fought barehanded with Diana, DeShane, the security guards and anybody who would train with him. He fought so viciously it was often necessary for one of the younger, stronger, more physically agile security men to fight back desperately more than once to hurt him badly in self-protection while fending off one of his more violent attacks. He fought like a wounded animal with no regard for who got hurt or how badly. He suffered cuts, many bruises, bloody noses, split lips and even a dislocated jaw. Still, he fought viciously, asking no quarter and giving none, and now it was becoming almost impossible to defeat him

He spent hours in meditation, sitting cross-legged on the floor in his apartment cleansing and purifying his mind as Diana had taught him. He spent more hours learning to move with no sound and without being seen, the way of invisibility, the art of stealth. The physician spent more and more time patching up his abrasions and reminding him of his age and his physical limitations. DeShane continued with the shooting lessons but began avoiding him socially, remaining close, but just out of sight. The nocturnal visits to his room for a cup of coffee or a chat had ceased.

Having completely mastered it, he put in hours at the computer that provided him with access to information libraries around the world. A specially designed program re-created the twelve major constellations of the zodiac, Ursa Major, the Southern Cross, Hercules, Pegasus and Capricorns as seen from both the southern and northern hemispheres and displayed them in ten different views of how they would look from different parts of the galaxy. It was too much for him to try to memorize, even if he had been able to give it his undivided attention, so he had everything printed out.

After his conversation with DeShane at the shooting range, he had cut himself off from everyone, particularly Diana. Although she still spent considerable time with him, he kept his distance, maintaining the relationship on a strict business-like basis as she had been doing, and while he still admired her beautiful body, he no longer allowed himself the luxury of anticipating what it would be like to make love to her. She was another man's wife.

He considered calling Marci on the pretext of a problem with the computer and then attempting to entice her to spend the night with him. Nobody would object. She probably wouldn't either. She might even do it willingly.

No. That wouldn't do. He had to face the problem squarely and deal with it. It was more than a physical desire. He had fallen in love with Diana Killingsworth.

"You're doing great, David," she said as they ran side-by-side up a steep grade north of the big house. "Remember to breathe through your nose, not your mouth."

"I know."

The last week had been better. He was talking to her again. The wall he had so suddenly built between them had begun to crumble and when they sat close together in front of the computer screen researching exotic plants or mineral deposits, she could touch his arm or hand and he wouldn't pull away. She didn't *want* to touch him, but she kept doing it and chastised herself each time she did.

She wore slacks and a blouse, or a full jogging suit when she came to his room in the afternoons. She must preferred shorts and a brief halter; actually she would have rather worn nothing at all, but there were always men around with their bedroom eyes and leering, suggestive glances, restrained desires to put their hands on her and . . .

The path snaked its way along the deserted countryside through twenty miles of rough terrain, winding up and down hills, across blistering sands of the canyon floors, along rock-strewn ravines and into the foothills around water-starved scrub bushes with thorns an inch long. Desert flowers born of the winter rains had already begun to fade and die as spring everywhere else became summer in Southern California.

"A month ago, you'd have fallen flat on your face after a couple of miles on this course," Diana said. "Now you've covered more than six and you aren't even berthing hard."

"I owe it all to you, teach," he said.

"Let's stop for awhile," she said a short time later and quickly dropped to the ground to sit by the trail hugging her knees, her back against a huge bolder. He walked back to her and started to side beside her when she suddenly rolled onto her side, braced her arms on the boulder, and lashed out at him with both feet in a vicious duple kick that could have broken both of his knees if it had connected.

He saw it coming, straightened quickly, sidestepped, spun on one foot, and sent a kick of his own to the back of her thigh while her legs were straight out. The force of the blow jarred her. "You never quit, do you," he said, quickly dropping into a fighting stance, waiting for a reply.

"You've got to survive," she said. "You've got to be ready for anything. Be prepared every minute, every second. Never let your guard down. You have no idea what you'll be faced with there."

"I'll be ready."

She relaxed and lay there on the ground looking up at him. "What's happened to you, David? These past few weeks you've been so cold, so distant. Some of DeShane's men have said that when you fight it's like you are trying to kill somebody."

"The way you aimed that kick, you must be pretty sure of me," he said, ignoring her question. "Or were you really trying to put me out of commission for good?"

"Why would I want to do that?"

"Jealousy. Revenge. I don't know. You were supposed to be the explorer of the new world beyond the Window. I was just the guinea pig to see if I would live, you could survive there. But I think that's all changed now, hasn't it."

"That's the most ridiculous . . . no, no it isn't." A flush of anger touched her face. "I trained hard for this. You can't believe what I went through to go through the Window. Now, all of a sudden, I'm not qualified."

"Who says you're not?"

"It's pretty obvious. David Savage, Geologist, the world-renowned explorer, fresh out of the hospital or an alcoholic ward or where ever the hell you've been. And I have to nursemaid you back to health, educate you, train you, and make you fit to embark on the greatest adventure, the most profound discovery since fire. God! How I hate you!"

"Somebody tried to kill me last month. They just about succeeded. Was it you?"

"I don't know what you are talking about."

"You don't know anything about the wheelbarrow left in the path and somebody shoving me over it onto a stone bench?"

"So *that's* what your accident was all about. No, I didn't have anything to do with it."

"Why don't I believe you?"

"I really don't care what you believe." She rolled over, sprang to her feet, stumbled, and bent to grab the back of her leg. She flopped back to the ground and lay back on her stomach. "Damn. I have a cramp in my leg where you kicked me. See if you can massage it out."

"You're kidding."

"Please."

He knelt beside her, his hands on her leg, his fingers searching for the constricted muscles. Skin as soft as velvet and as smooth as silk greeted his touch. Warm, firm flesh under his hands and the sight of her curved, sexy legs ignited a fire within him.

"Higher up," she ordered, the anger still showing in her face but concealed from him and covered in her voice.

His fingertips were almost touching her white shorts and he could see the swell of flesh, the rise of her buttocks profoundly visible beneath the tight fabric hat accentuated rather than hid the deep valley between her firm cheeks. His hand found no evidence of a cramping muscle. Her white panties were just visible under her shorts, hugging the curves and crevices barely beyond his fingers.

Her body stiffened under his touch and her lips were drawn into a hard line across her teeth as she rolled over to look up at him. "If I had wanted to kill you, Savage, I wouldn't do it at night from ambush. Even as good as you think you are now, I could easily kill you in a fight."

"I don't want to fight with you, Diana."

"I know," she said, sitting up with fire in her eyes. "You'd rather put your hands all over me and have sex with me. I was curious to see what you'd do when you touched my legs. If you had put your hands on my butt, I've broken your goddamn neck."

The hate and disgust in her voice hit him like a slap in the face and he winced from it. She got to her knees and then to her feet so she could look him straight in the eyes, savoring the moment and the blow she had struck. Then something in his eyes changed and there was a look she had never seen before. Her verbal victory over him seemed to suddenly wane.

"Yes, you're absolutely right, Mrs. Killingsworth," he said through lips that hardly moved as he struggled to maintain his calm. He stared back into her eyes. "I wanted to touch you. I wanted to make love to you. I've wanted you since the first time I saw you. You should be used to that, men wanting you.

"But you've been wrong about almost everything else. I haven't been in a hospital or an alcoholic ward. Since you looked me up on the Computer Internet and found my biography, I'm surprised that you didn't know that I just spent the last five years of my life on Death Row in the Pennsylvania State Prison, in complete isolation. You were the first woman I'd seen in five years. So don't be too damned impressed with yourself."

He turned and ran back down the path toward the big house, oblivious of the miles before him. His outward appearance of calm and unconcern was gone now, the anger, embarrassment and humiliation boiled inside him and he drove himself to an even faster pace, his legs churning, his chest heaving, the tears pouring from his eyes.

She had hurt him in an area where he had no defense and he ran to find the exhaustion that would numb his mind of the pain. The fact that just three months ago, he would have sat and whimpered, afraid to speak, afraid to challenge her did not occur to him nor would it have lessened the pain he felt if he had.

Approaching the house, his tears now dry, Savage caught Killingsworth just coming out the back door. "I want to see Mr. Damarjiane," he demanded.

"Quite impossible, Doctor. He's not here."

"I know better than that. I heard his plane come in last night."

Seemingly unconcerned that he had been caught in a lie, the lawyer said, "Mr. Damarjiane is otherwise disposed at the moment."

"You arrange it, you little bastard, or I'll tear your head off and shove it up your ass."

"And be shot the instant you attempted to touch me? Really, Savage, that's not very intelligent of you."

"I thought I was pretty important around here."

"Not *that* important, I assure you. And also be aware that my parentage is not in question, so please refrain from the petty insults."

"What?"

"I will inquire, Dr. Savage. You may wait here."

Savaged followed him into the house and stood beside him as he picked up the phone. Looking at Savage with utter contempt, he spoke into the phone. "Dr. Savage is demanding to see you, sir. He appears somewhat angry and distraught. I believe he has become delusional and dangerous. He should be put in restraints."

Killingsworth listened for a few moments ant then glanced at Savage with a look of surprise in his eyes. He replaced the phone and said, "Go right in, Doctor. You know the way."

"No, this time you go in first. I don't what you behind me."

"Really, Savage. You're almost amusing at times."

He proceeded David to Mr. Damarjiane's door where there was now an armed guard standing at parade-rest. He studied both men carefully for several moments before letting them pass.

The metal door slammed shut behind him and he marched up to the big desk, shielding his eyes from the overhead lights. "I want to know how long you knew about me before you brought me here!" he shouted. "And turn out those goddamn lights!"

"There's no need to shout at me, Dr. Savage," Damarjiane replied as the spotlights blinked off. "Please be seated. I've been waiting for you to start asking questions."

"Well? I'm asking," Savage replied as he remained standing, looking down at Damarjiane who leaned back in his high leather chair, an open book on his lap. Seeing the man clearly for the first time, David Savage was shocked. Gaunt, with sunken cheeks, a pointed nose and dark liver spots on his face, pouches under each eye and a slight, frail frame weighing no more than a hundred forty or fifty pounds, the man was wearing a suit and tie that looked to be many years old. He had a full head of white hair but his dark brown eyes seemed to have no life left in them. With his bloodless lips, the Palomar Director looked old. Very old, tired and sick.

"You've reached the point of, who gives a shit? Yes? Good. That's the next step in your training. I wanted aggressiveness," he continued with a slight smile, placing the book face down on the desk. "It would appear that's what I'm getting."

"So?"

"So, to answer your question, one of my investigators discovered you about six or eight months ago and you appeared to be everything we needed. Unfortunately for you, getting you released took some time and considerable expense. Although you were not guilty of the crime for which you were convicted and sentenced to death, the process of obtaining your freedom was complicated; as I am sure you can appreciate."

The fire suddenly left Savage's eyes and his shoulders slumped. He opened his mouth to speak but he was barely able to mumble, "What did you say?"

"Say about what, Doctor?"

"You . . . you said I was innocent." He fumbled for the chair and collapsed into it.

"Yes. It seems as though you had some powerful enemies, Doctor, and evidence was manufactured to convict you. They did a pretty neat job of it, too. Once convicted and all the appeals denied, only a gubernatorial pardon could have saved you from execution. And I assure you, bribing a governor is next to impossible with things the way they are these days."

But . . . but if you knew I was innocent, why didn't you just present the evidence to the court, or to the governor's office. There wouldn't be any need for bribes."

"Quite impossible, Doctor. I have no evidence, only knowledge. It's all very complicated and very involved so I did the next best thing. As you might recall from our first meeting, considerable money was required to arrange the last delays that kept you alive until I could obtain your release by this somewhat dubious means, but the fact remains that you *are* free and that's the important thing, is it not? All in all, I have a considerable amount invested in you right now."

"Then, I can eventually be acquitted? My name will be cleared?"

"No. That cannot happen. But you won't be here, anyway. Once through the Window, you will be completely inaccessible to the authorities."

"They could come through after me."

"Hardly a possibility, Doctor."

"Or waiting for me when I come back."

"Also an impossibility. No, I assure you, you are safe and free and will remain so. I promised you would never return to prison and I keep my promises. And I expect you to keep yours."

"But why all the training? You already had Diana trained and ready to go."

"Who told you that?"

"Never mind who told me,"

"As you wish. It's of no importance."

"Well?"

"She was never intended to be the explorer."

"Why?" Another surprise for Savage.

"Insufficient technical knowledge among other things. She just couldn't do the job. I needed a man. It's as simple as that."

"She knows almost as much as I do and she's a lot more physically able. But that's not the reason, is it."

"That is indeed part of it, but you're quite right, of course. Most women absorb information like a sponge. They can be taught to do almost anything. Program them, tell them what to do and they will carry it out to perfection. That's why girls do so much better in school than boys. But *don't* try to teach them to think. If they encounter a situation for which they haven't been programmed, they don't know what to do. Most women simply cannot make decisions, and even when they do, they are usually wrong. The old saw about it being a woman's privilege to change her mind was just another way of saying she couldn't make a decision.

"This exploration of the new world we have discovered will require someone who will constantly be faced with the unknown, with circumstances and events for which we could not possibly plan, and who will be required to make reasonable, intelligent and logical decisions instantly with no help from anyone. Diana just isn't capable of that.

"But it might interest you to know that she will be the next one to go through the Window to the new world if you survive. I have to know if people can reproduce in this alien environ-ment. That's why she is training you, so you two will learn to get along together, to get to know each other and be ready to produce children on the new world. "You'll have six months there and if you survive, she will follow you."

"She's a married woman."

"In name only," Mr. Damarjiane replied, seemingly unaware that Savage had only recently learned of her marital status. "Mr. Killingsworth has already given his permission, not that it was altogether necessary for our purposes. And it might interest you to know that you are the only person Diana has been able to get along with since she's been here."

"You call our relationship getting along? She may well have been the one who tried to kill me."

"I've considered that and Mr. DeShane is looking into it very closely."

"So if I live, Diana comes through, I fuck her brains out and try to get her pregnant to see if people can breed there. Is that it?"

"Very crude, Doctor, but essentially, yes."

"And what if she doesn't want to go along with that?"

"Physical needs and desires will take care of it. And there will be no need for you to have her consent."

"Oh, are we talking rape here?"

Damarjiane was beginning to lose his calm demeanor along with his patience. "Dr. Savage, females are here to provide comfort and pleasure for men and to perpetuate the species. Nothing more. Part of your job on the new world is to determine if the species can be perpetuated there. Is that clear?"

"You sure do have a low opinion of women."

"On the contrary, Doctor, I hold women in the very highest esteem—in their place."

"I see. That makes me wonder," David said, "what you *really* intend to do with this new world if Diana and I survive."

"You really *have* been asking questions, haven't you."

"I'd like to know."

"I presume that she has been giving you that equal opportunity stuff and alluding to environment polluting factories and industrial plants. Oil wells spewing up gushers all over the landscape. Yes, I know pretty much what she believes and talks about. That's another reason she is not qualified to go first. But just listen and I'll tell you something.

"I don't intend to set up factories to pollute and destroy the environment. Even if I did, it would take hundreds of years, and by then, using the Window, we would have found more worlds. I'm not interested in making another fortune. I've got more now than I could ever spend. I'm an old man with a limited number of years left and I want to go to the new world myself and live out my remaining years there in peace and tranquility where there is no crime, no wars, no government and damn few people.

"There are those here—and Diana is one of them—who believe that the opportunity to go to the new world should be open to everyone who wants to go. Draw lots, take a number, stand in line, everybody can go. You've probably been told that I won't allow that. Yes! Absolutely! I *won't* allow that!

"I want healthy, rugged, productive people who can live and prosper in a wild, unexplored land, who can make a living and a home for themselves, raise a family, to coexist with any inhabitants we might find there, or fight and conquer them if necessary.

"I won't have a bunch of sickly misfits or a group of cripples or the feeble minded. I don't want the ordinary man off the street who is so lazy he won't survive a week without government support of some kind.

"The world is going mad, Doctor, and that madness is spreading at an alarming rate. The planet Earth is beyond saving. Most people have become spoiled, spineless, narcissistic and corrupt and they won't make it on the new world. But the people I send there *will* make it; they *must* survive, so that I can survive there."

"Diana was right. You *do* intend to abandon the Earth."

"The Earth, yes, humanity, no. I never said I was going to save the Earth but I *will* save mankind, and someday man will rule the stars, the men I choose. That's the truth, Savage. Now, good afternoon."

CHAPTER TWELVE

A NOTHER WEEK PASSED, SEVEN long days and nights during which he slept fitfully, awakening often to pace the floor in his robe. Damarjiane knew he was innocent and he had been wrongfully sentenced to death. Maybe others knew it too and there was a chance he could be cleared and get to see his kids again. If his felony conviction was overturned, nobody could keep him from seeing his kids.

Diana had not appeared at his door in the morning nor was she there to supervise his training. It was just as well after the fool he had made of himself out on the running path. He exercised by himself, continuing the training as she had taught him. He weighed 170 pounds now and could run ten miles carrying a rifle and twenty-pound backpack. He needed to move that up to a forty-pound pack as soon as possible.

Tired from the day's exercises but no longer exhausted by them, his eyes red and burned from hours in front of the computer screen, he lay in his bed and tried to sleep, but he couldn't stop his thoughts. He couldn't turn his mind off and sleep. He tossed and turned and finally got up to walk around his apartment until almost dawn.

In addition to the shocking statement Damarjiane had made about his innocence, Diana was ever present in his mind. Her face, the sound of her voice, the way she walked, and that brief wonders moment when he had his hands on her legs. Forcing himself to concentrate on something else only worked for a short time and he found himself dwelling on her again.

Escorted to the underground complex by DeShane, he lunched with Dr. Boucree who talked at length about his career in electronics.

"I've been meaning to ask," Savage said as they sat over the remains of lunch in the huge underground cafeteria, "about your description of the new world. You've said it is primitive and rugged, Diana has said that it will take all the skills she and DeShane can teach me just to survive."

"Yes?"

"From that tiny scene in the Window, how do you know all of that? You could be looking at the neglected portion of somebody's back yard in east overshoe, New Jersey, or a national park, a stand of trees somewhere in some farmer's field. What makes you think you've discovered a wild, primitive planet ready for colonization?"

"Your observations and conclusions are quite correct, Dr. Savage. We *don't* know. We have only made an educated guess based on the data we have. That is one of the main reasons you are going through the Window, to find out.

"Personally, I don't believe it is some farmer's back yard or a grove of trees next to his corn field in God-knows-where-but-I-don't, Alabama or wherever, and I eventually want to go through the Window too, if the experiment with the first couple—you and Diana—is successful. It will require only a few more months of waiting to be absolutely sure, and then we will have our wonderful new world."

"I guess you know, too," Savage said, "that part of this experiment, as you call it, is to find out if children can be produced and if they can survive there. Diana and I are just the white rats in this experiment."

"Oh, far from it, Doctor," Boucree replied. "White rats, as you put it," he chuckled quietly to himself, "are available by the millions. If survival and procreation were all that we sought, we could have them lined up at the door begging for an opportunity with money in hand to be the first, the second, or just any number. Shove them through the window and see what happens. Oh, no, Savage, you and Diana possess unique skills highlighted by your psychological profiles and your physical attraction to each other. A child born of your union is an almost certainty. And that child will be gifted far beyond the normal."

"Wait a minute. You're saying that Diana is attracted to me? Boucree, you're out of your tree." He got up and started to walk away.

"Am I, really?" Boucree laughed softly again, watching Savage stomp out of the room. "Everybody can see it but you."

Diana was nowhere to be seen, presumably staying in her apartment on the third floor of the bit house, the one she shared with her husband. It was a huge, three-bedroom affair with a living room, kitchen and den, catering to the extravagant demands of the lawyer.

DeShane paid a surprise visit to his room in the evening, pouring himself a cup of coffee and taking a flask from his inside coat pocket. The aroma of cognac soon blended with that of the coffee. Sitting on a chair backwards, he regarded Savage sternly. "That wasn't very bright, Doc," he said, after taking a sip of the coffee.

"What wasn't?"

"I heard about the confrontation between you and Mr. K. the other day. You could get killed that way."

DeShane held out his hand, fingers spread and wiggled it back and forth. "Well, DeShane, right then, I really didn't much give a damn."

"Maybe you should. There are a bunch of us around here who really like you and wouldn't want to be put into a position of divided loyalties. You get my meaning?"

"Yeah. I guess it *was* pretty dumb."

"And there's a few of us who would have loved to say the same thing to Killingsworth." He grinned, got to his feet, and handed Savage the remains of a cup of coffee laced with liquor. "See you around, Doc."

"Hey, DeShane," Savage called out as the security chief reached the door. The liquor-laced coffee smelled so good. "You got a first name?"

"Yeah," he replied. "I do." He opened the door and left.

Savage laughed and looked at the closed door. He walked across the room and looked out the window. He took a sip of DeShane's coffee. It tasted as good as it smelled. He enjoyed the quiet and the view for several minutes.

The phone rang. He walked to it and picked it up.

"Can you come down to my office for a few minutes?" DeShane asked. "Something I want to show you."

"Sure."

"Down the hall past the boss' office, last door on the right."

"On my way."

Wondering what DeShane had in mind, he left his apartment and walked downstairs. A short distance from Mr. Damarjiane's wood veneer-covered steel door was the security office. Savage knocked softly and the door was opened immediately.

Inside the small room cluttered with filing cabinets, boxes, chairs and a desk, along one wall was a row of television monitors, two of which showed his living room and bedroom. Watching his gaze fix on those two screens, DeShane Said, "I told you, Doc. Don't get mad."

"Is this what you wanted to show me?"

"No, but I guess it's best you know. Don't do anything in your place you don't want recorded on videotape. Come over here." He indicated his desk that was pushed up against the wall. "Take a look."

On the desktop were two large, clear plastic bags inside of each Savage could see white objects. One was flat and thin, about the size of a coffee cup saucer and looked like a stopper for the kitchen sink. The other was round like a tennis ball. They appeared to be connected with a piece of thread about six inches long.

"Both you and Captain Comfort kept harping on sabotage when your plane almost crashed and you were so insistent I thought I'd look into it if nothing more just to shut you up. Comfort said the flameout was as if they had suddenly run out of gas but the gages still showed a little over an eighth of a tank. I had 'em open the wings up and rip the fuel tanks out. Didn't make Mr. K very happy, I can tell you. Cost a bunch of money. Found these inside both main tanks." He pointed to the objects in the plastic bags.

"What are they?"

"They're made of polyvinyl chloride. You know, like PVC pipe you use in plumbing. Strong, won't rust and lasts forever. There are only a few solvents that will break it down and make it dissolve."

"So?"

"So the flat disk there is weighted with a brass nut glued to the top of it. It's connected to the round disk by that thread. The round one is full'a little air pockets and floats; the flat one doesn't because of the weight. As the fuel dropped in the gas tanks, the flat disk attached to the buoyant one drifts closer and closer to the opening leading to the fuel line. When the fuel drops to six inches from the bottom, the disk is sucked in and covers the fuel line opening. All of a sudden, you're out of gas. The engines quit. Flameout! In final approach it could be deadly."

"So the plane *was* sabotaged."

"Yep. By somebody who understands rate of fuel consumption and just about where the plane would be when the supply was cut off."

"But if we crashed, there would be an investigation. That thing," he pointed to the bags on the desk, "would be discovered."

"Nope. A final approach crash with six inches of fuel in each tank and the whole thing would probably explode and burn. Evidence destroyed. However, if no crash . . . well, who's going to split a wing open and rip out the fuel tank to look inside? Just little old me. And I told you PVC will break down and dissolved in time. One of the things that will dissolve it is kerosene also known as jet fuel. Let it sit there in that stuff for forty-eight to fifty-six hours and there's nothing left of it. Just a couple of brass nuts and a thread. Evidence destroyed."

"So who did it?" Savage sank into the extra chair beside the desk.

"Don't know yet, but I'm working on it."

"How long have you known?"

"The day after you got here."

"Was he—they—after me?"

"Don't know that either, but—"

"Yeah, I know. You're working on it. Thanks, DeShane. It's nice to know I'm not paranoid."

"You and Jerry Comfort, both. He was there when I had the tanks ripped open."

"Who else knows?"

"Just Captain Comfort, me, one mechanic who opened the tanks for us. Now you. And Mr. K, of course."

"You told him?"

"He's my boss, remember? He signs my paychecks."

"So what now?"

"I've got some leads. I'll let you know. But keep it under your hat, will you? I'm not supposed to be telling you this stuff."

"I never saw anything. I've never been in this room."

"You keep your eyes and ears open, Doc. And I'm going to be hanging around you like an old girlfriend."

"Thanks again, DeShane."

"Goes with the territory."

Savage turned to leave.

"Hey, Doc, it ain't any of my business and I don't want any details, but, you getting yourself together?"

"Yeah. Thanks for asking."

"A couple of my guys said they were afraid they were going to have to really hurt you the way you went after them. You musta really had something to work off."

"Yeah."

"You get it worked off?"

"Yeah."

—*—

He knocked, waited and knocked again, louder this time. There was another wait and a louder knock. He was actually nervous. He hadn't been nervous in more years than he could remember. Finally, from behind the polished walnut door the sound of a lock being turned was heard. The door opened.

"Can I come in?"

"Why?"

"I'd like a few minutes of your time."

"I see you're wearing your storm trooper uniform. Starched khakis, boots, holstered pistol. What happened to the sports coat and slacks?"

"I'm comfortable in this."

"Yeah, I'll bet you are. What do you want, DeShane?" Diana asked, her hand still on the door as though ready to slam it shut in his face.

"A couple'a words."

"About what?"

"Ask me in and I'll tell you. Unless, of course, your husband might get jealous."

"Funny," she replied with a sneer, but walked away from the door and let him enter. She was barefoot, wearing tight jeans and a blouse tied together in front to expose a bare midriff. No bra.

"You know, Diana," he said, closing the door behind him, "you really do have a nice ass."

She spun around and snarled at him. "Get out of here, DeShane."

"Nice set of tits, too. That's what all the guys say. You must be one heluva lay."

"You sonofa—" She tensed, took a step toward him moving into an attack crouch and then suddenly stopped, looking him straight in the eye. She cocked her head and straightened up. "No. You can be crude sometimes but you don't talk that way. Why did you say that?" She continued staring at him. "You're trying to intentionally provoke me, make me mad. Why?"

"Why?"

"You're up to something. Why would you come here and deliberately try to start a fight? You're trying to make me mad."

"Okay. You're right. I am. I wanted you so pissed off you'd be momentarily out of control and maybe answer some questions for me."

"Like what?"

"Like what's going on between you and the Doc?"

"The Doc? You mean Savage?" She was genuinely surprised. "That's easy. Nothing."

"Something happened, Diana. You've got his head all fucked up. He's a mess. I came up here to find out what you did to him and to ask you to leave him alone."

"DeShane, you amaze me." She turned and walked to the huge L-shaped sectional couch and dropped onto it, the momentary anger completely gone. "What do you care?" She sprawled out, extending her legs and crossing her ankles.

In front of the couch was a massive ornate coffee table in oak, end tables also of oak with tall lamps on each. In addition, there was overhead indirect lighting, a floor-to-ceiling window looking out over a half acre of flowers which, when in full bloom, provided a kaleidoscope of color.

"He's my responsibility. Like you are. That's why I want to know what happened."

"It's none of your business."

"Probably not." He walked to her and stood looking down at her. "But I need to know."

"Why?"

"I don't know what's going on down there in that gopher hole and I don't want to know, but the Doc's got something to do with it and he's having a problem handling it. On top of all that, there's you. You're a sexy broad, Diana, and you know it. Every guy that sees you wants to get into your pants. You know that, too. But the Doc, he's different."

"What do you mean, different?"

"You did something to him."

"I didn't do anything to him."

"He's in love with you, Diana."

The statement caught her by surprise. "What . . . why do you say such a stupid thing like that?"

"It's obvious as hell. It's written all over his face every time he sees you."

"Love? He's just—"

"Horny? Yeah, probably, that too. But it goes a lot deeper with him." He reached down, grabbed her ankles and swept her feet from the couch forcing her to sit up and look at him. "He's a different kind a guy."

"Yeah, I know. I read about him."

"Yeah?"

"I thought he had been sick. But he was in prison."

"Yeah."

"You knew?"

"Yes."

"He's a criminal."

"In a manner of speaking, a lot of us are."

"Care to explain that?"

"No."

After a moment of consideration, she decided to partially answer his question. "He's taking the job I was supposed to have. I trained for it, it was promised to me and now he's taking it. I hated him. I wanted to hurt him so I set him up and he walked right into it."

"How?"

"I'm not very proud of it now." She dropped her eyes.

DeShane sat down beside her and just looked at her until she was again able to meet his gaze. "I thought he was just another wolf on the make. All that stuff about him in the library, the jaunty pictures with the rifle, the arrogant expression on his face; he was like John Wayne on safari with admirers hanging around. I . . . I didn't know he had been in prison."

"Does it make a difference?"

"It might. Do you know what he did?"

"Ask him."

"I'm asking you."

"He was convicted of murder and sentenced to death. He was going to be shot by a firing squad."

"Murder?" Another shock for Diana. "Him? Who did he kill?"

"A United States Congressman."

"You're kidding."

"Nope."

"I don't believe it."

"A jury did."

"Then why is he . . . how did he get here?"

"Ask your husband."

"You think he tells me anything?"

"Pillow talk."

"Ha. Ha." There was no humor but a lot of sarcasm in the two short words.

"Look, Diana, I don't know what this job is you are talking about but I don't think the Doc had anything to do with taking it away from you. Maybe the boss or Mr. K, they are the ones running things here. Go talk to him. Patch it up."

"How?"

"You're asking me? How do you feel about him? The Doc."

"I . . ." She shook her head slowly. "I really don't know, DeShane. I thought I hated him. Now, I'm ashamed to tell you what I did to him and I'm afraid of what I feel about him."

"So you *do* feel something. What?"

"I told you, I don't know."

"I don't get it."

"What?"

"Killingsworth. And now, Savage."

"I'm attracted to older men, all right? I always have been. A lot of women are."

"That's not what I meant. If you're attracted to him, why are you always bust'n his balls?"

"To keep him away, I guess. So I *won't* get involved. So I won't get hurt."

"I thought you *were* involved, with Marc."

"Not you too!" She looked at him and rolled her eyes, amused. "What is this with Marc?"

"Everybody thinks you two are an item."

"Baloney. Marc's got a problem. I'm just trying to help him with it."

"His fear of flying?"

"What?" The surprise showed on her face. "How did you know that?"

"The Doc told me."

"The bastard!" She pressed her lips together in a firm, hard line. "I told him that in confidence."

"Don't have a fit, Diana. It's probably a good thing he did." DeShane went on to tell her about Marc's membership in the parachute club, his skydiving and hang-gliding, that he was still doing it whenever he got a few days off.

"I don't believe it."

"There are times when I don't like you very much, Mrs. K, but I wouldn't lie to you. It's true."

"Then why—"

"Yeah. Why indeed. You offer him a little therapy to take his mind off his problem? Maybe he suggested it, hinted at it? Patients often become physically attracted to their doctor, and vice versa. A couple hours in the rack with you could cure all his fears."

"God, you're gross."

"Tell me it hasn't come up."

"It hasn't and I wouldn't do it."

"Does he know that?"

"I don't know and I don't care. Now, would you please leave."

"What are you going to do about the Doc?"

"I don't know, DeShane. I really don't."

"Well, do something, Diana. You've got the degree in brainwashing. Do something right, maybe do something wrong, but do *something*!"

"Sure. Give me a hint."

"Okay, I'll give you a hint. Christmas Eve, at the party when you were crawling all over old Marc—"

"Oh, spare me, DeShane."

"I was talking to the Doc about the Christmas stories Doc Boucree puts us through every year. Everybody's got a Christmas story."

"So?"

"He told me one. I think you ought to hear it. Might give you a little insight into his personality."

"Why should I care?"

"I don't know, Diana. Why the hell should you? Maybe you got a Christmas story of your own to tell? Huh?"

She immediately thought of December at the camp in Hidaka-sammyaku. The Japanese did not celebrate or even recognize Christmas. "No," she replied. "But go ahead, tell me the story. You've wasted some of my time already. What's a little more?"

"You got an appointment to keep?"

"You came here. I didn't invite you. Are you going to tell me or not?"

"Okay, I'll tell you. The Doc said it was a whole bunch of years ago, back when he was a lot younger and still going to college. He was working his way through school, taking jobs here and there to make enough money, and a few times, he even had to work on Christmas Eve.

"He said he was coming home to his apartment on the bus pretty late one night, it was cold as hell and there was a lot of snow on the ground and a thick mist everywhere. His feet hurt from walking all day and he was feeling depressed because the few friends he had were out enjoying themselves or home with their families. He had to change buses downtown for another long trip to the south side of town where he lived.

"As the bus came down the hill, across Seventh Street, he saw a bright starburst out there just hanging in the mist. A huge, glowing star with rays of light streaming up from it into the night. It was just a Christmas decoration on the side of a department store building, a neon starburst going up sixty or seventy feet, and through the mist he thought it was one of the most beautiful things he'd ever seen.

"He got off the bus early and walked the last five blocks to where he'd catch the next one for home, and he saw that there were thousands and thousands of tiny white lights strung in the trees that lined the downtown streets. Through the mist, they were all hazy and twinkling, and it was so quiet he could hear his own footsteps.

"Somewhere in the distance he could hear the Christmas song, Silver Bells, and he suddenly realized that he didn't feel so depressed anymore, his feet didn't hurt as much and it was probably because of the mist that his eyes and cheeks were wet.

"Everybody's got a Christmas story,' the Doc said to me. 'Guess this one's mine. Good night, DeShane,' he said, and just walked away."

Diana was quiet as she listened to the story, trying to imagine David Savage walking along that street all alone, seeing the lights and hearing the music. It was certainly not the image she had gotten of him from the news bulletins and the encyclopedia.

"So, whaduyu think?

"I don't know, DeShane. I really don't."

"And you better do a little rethinking about old Marky, too. He ain't quite as dumb or as naïve as he pretends."

"Yeah, so it would seem."

DeShane got up to leave. "Hey, Diana, thanks," he said and started for the door.

"For what?"

"For listening."

"I've been meaning to ask for awhile, you got a first name, DeShane?"

"You know, it's funny, but the Doc asked me that same question just the other day."

"So what did you tell him?"

"I told him I did. Good night, Diana."

She sat with her chin in her hands after the door close behind DeShane. For the first time in longer than she could remember she wasn't sure what to do. Maybe talk to her husband. She didn't want to, but Damian had an amazing ability to analyze a situation and come up with a solution. If not that, there was only one other thing to do.

CHAPTER THIRTEEN

A LMOST TWO WEEKS PASSED and Diana was still absent. Nobody would tell him anything about her. Both Killingsworth and DeShane were gone. Finally, during lunch, Dr. Boucree let it slip that she had flown to Los Angeles in the Lear with Mark the chauffeur, having commandeered the plane and pilots as though they were hers to command. When she returned and quietly entered the house late at night, everybody pretended not to notice. Nor did they speculate on the explosive scene she must have had with her husband for taking the plane and tying it up for two weeks. What she did in LA was anybody's guess except Mark, the aircraft captain, Jerry Comfort and his copilot, and none of them were talking, not to Savage, anyway.

In the evenings while she was gone, a frustrated David Savage dug through old magazines and studied the awards and plaques on the walls of the big house. They were presented to the Palomar Foundation for humanitarian works, efforts to preserve various wild species, movements to protect the environment and numerous charitable contributions. The magazines also told of criminal and civil law suits filed against many of Mr. Damarjiane's companies for unfair labor practices, destruction of public lands and pollution of the air and water around factory sights. There was one black-and-white picture of a field of oil well towers spread across an Oklahoma landscape with a caption beneath saying something about taking land from the Indians. Newspaper articles both praising and condemning the foundation appeared in the most conservative of publications as well as the most liberal. One article mentioned a company named Jade Pharmaceuticals going suddenly and unexpectedly out of business. He was more confused than ever now, attempting to separate truth from lie, to be sure of what he was doing. He had to believe in the project if he was going to risk his life for it.

Most interesting was not what he had found but what he *didn't* find. Although there was an occasional reference to Mr. Killingsworth as the foundations' attorney, there was no mention anywhere of Mr. Damarjiane by name or reference. It was as though the man didn't exist.

With his computer on-line, he typed in Damarjiane's name and clicked, SEARCH. A minute passed. It was late and he should be getting ready for bed. He took another sip of the brandy-laced coffee, a cup every evening now since DeShane had given him the first one. As he reached out to cancel the search, ten headings appeared on the screen. There was a golf pro named Nicole Damarjiane, there was a Linda and a Beth, a company named Gould and Damarjiane, a real estate agent named Jacquelyn Damarjiane and a boat with that name. Out of curiosity, he clicked onto the boat and the picture of a three-masted sailing ship appeared on the screen. Below it was an artist's painting of the same vessel with full sales racing magnificently through a rough sea with spray flying from the bow. The ocean was dark blue with high foam-flaked waves and the sky was overcast with threats of rain. Although it was daylight, there was no sign of the sun or any light through the dark clouds. It was a powerful picture. In both the photograph and the painting, the ships name could be plainly seen cut deeply into a long wooden plaque mounted on the forward gunwale. D A M A R J I A N E

The frigate was built at the shipyard in Portsmouth, England and commissioned in 1850, but was of Jamaican registry, sailing out of Port Royal near Kingston. It was listed at 5,000 tons and mounted twenty-one guns. The width, length, cargo capacity and speed at full sail were also listed, but little else. In 1923, it was overhauled; the canons were removed, it was completely refitted as a luxury vessel and became an American ship with a registry out of Boston harbor. There was nothing more under that title.

Savage typed in the name again and hit SEARCH. He sat back in the chair to wait and let his mind once again turn to the beautiful Diana. Now that she was back, he felt he had to somehow attempt to see her, talk to her, apologize for his outburst o the running path that day when he lost his temper, if she would listen to him at all. Time was running out. There were only a few days left until he would step through the Window. If she was to follow and become his companion on the new world, he didn't want her to come hating or resenting him as she did her husband. Or worse, perhaps now, she would refuse to come at all, having Mark to fulfill her needs.

His thoughts were interrupted by a soft knock o his door. "It's open," he called out.

"I don't know exactly how to begin," she said as she stood uncertainly in the doorway. "But I need to talk to you."

"Diana!" He scrambled to his feet, almost spilling the coffee. "Come in. I . . . I was just thinking about you."

"There are some things I need to say, David," she continued, still standing in the doorway, "but I didn't know whether you would let me in or throw me out."

"I was just about to bust out of this place and come looking for you when I heard you were back." He put the coffee cup carefully on the desk beside the computer.

"Big fight with Damian about the plane," she said, entering the room and closing the door behind her. "And I got the pilot in trouble, but it was a nice vacation away from here. I enjoyed it."

"Good company?"

"I suppose you're referring to Mark."

"Sorry, none of my business." He held up both hands, palms out.

"Yes, it is, and yes, I asked him to come with me. No, he was not good company. There were some things I needed to get straightened out. When we landed, I just left him at the airport. That sure wasn't the way he wanted it but that's the way it was. It's the truth, David. You can ask Jerry."

"Jerry?"

"Jerry Comfort, the pilot."

"You were with him?"

"Almost the whole time. I couldn't get rid of him. I checked into a hotel and he and his copilot took the room right next to me. They kept me out of trouble until DeShane showed up."

"DeShane?" Savage's eyebrows arched. "He was there, too?"

"Yes. A couple of days after I got there. Jerry must have called him. He told you prefer a woman in a dress rather than pants and this is one of the few casual dresses I have."

"You look lovely," Savage replied, impressed by the soft blue color and the hemline just above her knees. She wore matching heels and a single strand of pearls. Her hair had grown out and the rich auburn tresses touched her shoulders.

"I want to apologize to you for what happened, for the things I said—"

"There's no need. I'm the one who should apologize."

"There *is* a need," she interrupted. "And please don't stop me. You don't know how hard this is for me." She hesitated, almost afraid to look at him. Taking a few steps away from the door and turning to face him at the computer, she continued, "and there's so much I have to say."

"All right. I'm listening."

"It went further with Mark than I intended it to, but I have needs and desires but my husband doesn't want anything to do with me. And evidently neither did you."

"Diana, you're—"

"Let me finish." She held up one hand in a symbol to stop. "I really thought Mark had a fear of flying and I was helping him overcome it. It was just a line and I fell for it. You'd think I would know better. I got to know him before I left. Damian was always shoving me at one man or another. I let Mark hold me, kiss me, touch me but it never went any further than that. I swear to you, it didn't.

"Then when I got back from Japan I was told about training you and then Mark came on to me about his phobia and asked for my help. That evening you saw us together on the bench behind the house he said he loved me and wanted me to run away with him. I told him, no, but at that point I was so confused and angry, everything hitting me at once, I took my frustration out on you. I'm sorry."

He started to say something but she held her hand up again to silence him. "I took him to LA with me and on the plane I confronted him with everything. After initial feeble denials, he finally admitted that he had lied about the flying phobia to have a reason to be with me. I told him to get lost. He became very angry. It was pretty ugly."

"He might have hurt you. He's a pretty big guy."

"I just wish he would have tried. Look, David, I didn't know about your past, about you being in prison until you told me. DeShane has filled me in on some of the details. He said you murdered somebody, a Congressman, but I don't believe it. You couldn't kill anybody. And that's funny, you know. That's what DeShane and I have been trying to teach you all this time, how to kill. I asked Damian about it when I got back but he wouldn't tell me anything. He just screamed and yelled about the cost of the plane and the pilot."

"I'll tell you if you really want to know."

"No, not now. Maybe later. There's something else I have to say. Will you listen?"

"Of course." He climbed from the chair, took her by the hand and led her to the couch where they sat side by side, looking at each other.

"You were just somebody I was ordered to train to take my job, and I resented you for it. And then, after you had been here for awhile, Damian told me I'm going to follow you through the Window and live with you on the new world as your mate. To find out if we could have children there. I *really* resented that.

"After that scene on the trail where I behaved so badly, DeShane came to see me and . . . I just ran away rather than face you again. I intend to stay in LA, maybe find a boyfriend and never come back here. But I just couldn't get rid of Jerry Comfort and his copilot. Every time I came on to a man in a bar or a restaurant, started talking to him, tried to pick him up, Jerry came walking up, stuck out his hand and introduced himself as my father." She laughed nervously. "And that ended that.

"David, almost all of the men I have known in my life were only interested in how long it would take to get my clothes off and me into bed. But you didn't make any advances toward me although I could tell from the way you looked at me that you wanted me. You undressed me with your eyes and looked at my body, and I hated it. Then you told me about the prison your confinement in isolation and I knew how much you respected me, how much control you have over your emotions."

"It's unimportant, now," he said, taking her by the shoulders and turning her to face him.

"It *is* important, David," she replied, covering his hands with hers. "I wasn't aware that you know about Damian and me, that we were married, and I didn't want you to know. Oh, I didn't care at first. You were such a mousy, undernourished and insignificant person. Barney. That's how I thought of you. I even said that to you. But you worked so hard and improved so much. You're quite a man now, David Savage.

"We spent so much time together; I began to care for you. Oh, I tried to fight it and I was intentionally mean to you so I wouldn't get involved. I even took up with Mark again after I told him I wouldn't leave my husband. But it didn't work. I couldn't get you out of my mind. You never knew but I watched you almost every minute and I went to sleep at night thinking about you.

"Mark was really never more to me than just a friend although I thought for a while maybe he could be a lover. He certainly had the body for it. But I have an image in my mind of someone or some*thing,* half man, half monster who rescued me, saved my life, someone I'll never find because he doesn't really exist and it didn't really happen. A man in my secret dreams. I made him up when I was half delirious and starving in the Hidaka-sammyaku Mountains."

"Maybe you *will* find him someday, Diana."

"Only in my dreams."

"I have dreams, too."

"Of me?"

"Yes." He pulled her to him.

"Let me finish what I have to say first," she whispered. "You need to know all of it."

"No, I don't."

"I was pregnant when Damian found me," she went on, "just fifteen years old and pregnant by a boy whose name I can't even remember now. I discovered when I was thirteen that I could get privileges, attention, even presents just by lifting my skirt a little. I didn't have to know anything, do anything, be anything, just smile and show my legs. I got a lot of attention and I got laid a lot, but when it was over, they talked behind my back about what an easy piece I was. That was all I was. Not a girl, not a person. Just a piece.

"But Damian married me. Thirty-five years older and knowing what I was, aware that he could have had me just for the taking, he made it legal. Suddenly I was a respectable married woman with a husband, not just a knocked-up, teenage orphan whore about to produce another bastard." The self-resentment in her voice almost made him pull back, but he steadfastly refused move away from her or register any emotion.

"She died two weeks after she was born. In her crib. I was sixteen then and I tried to commit suicide so I could die with her. Damian stopped me. He made me live and I owe him for that, what he did for me, my education, my clothes, the jewelry, all of it. Maybe that's why I've stayed with him all these years. But then after Isoroku, everything changed. I changed."

"Who's Isoroku?" Savage asked.

Diana ignored him. "We have separate beds, you know. We don't sleep together. We haven't for years. I undress in front of him and he doesn't even look at me. I'm too old for him now but we still get along all right because I'm the only one who will argue and fight with him. Everybody else is so damn afraid of him they won't say anything. He respects people who will stand up to him. He'll try to destroy them, but he respects them while he's doing it. I heard about your confrontation and what you said to him. DeShane told me. You know what I think?"

"Do you know what I think, Mrs. Killingsworth? I think you talk too much."

His hands pulled her to him and she did not resist when his lips sought hers, silencing her with the kiss. Her arms went around his neck, she closed her eyes as her mouth opened to his, feeling him, tasting him, wanting him.

"It's been years for me, too, David," she managed to murmur. "So many years since I've let a man touch me. But I want you to touch me, and that scares me. I'm afraid of you."

"Don't be afraid. I won't hurt you." He felt the rise of her breasts pressing against him and the heat of her body through his clothes. His hands were on her back holding her to him.

"I still don't know how I feel about you but I made the decision to come back here, to attempt to talk to you and tell you the truth. I . . . I'm not untouchable, David."

"I love you, Diana."

"Oh, David, don't say that. Just say you care about me. That's all I want to hear."

"It's true. I know what I feel."

"You said it, yourself. I'm the first woman you've seen in five years. Of course, you're attracted, physically, sexually, but you're not being fair to yourself. Give it some time. Meet some other women. Maybe you will find out it is me you love. And maybe you won't."

"Do you *really* want me to go out and romance another woman, assuming I could get out of here and do it?"

"Maybe you should, David. You need to know."

"I love you, Diana," he repeated.

She pulled away and turned her back to him. "I don't even know what love is. I've never loved anybody in my life."

He gently turned her around to face him. "Then just what *do* you feel for me?"

"I don't know. I'm still confused about it."

"We have time."

"Not much. And there are some things I have to know."

"What?"

"Tell me why you killed that man, that Congressman."

"You know about that, too?"

"Yes. Why?"

"I didn't. I was framed."

"I want to believe that, David."

"Mr. Damarjiane knows it. So does your husband. Ask him."

"How do they know?"

"I don't know. But Damarjiane told me he knew I was innocent."

"Tell me about your wife."

"What?"

"Your wife. Tell me about her."

"Why?"

"Because I want to know."

"She filed for divorce the day after I was convicted. She got married again a few months later."

"Do you have any children?"

"Diana . . . this is really hard for me to talk about."

"How long were you married?"

"Diana . . ."

"Did she come to your trial?"

"No."

"Do you still love her?"

"I love you."

"Kiss me again, David."

He hesitated. "There's a camera in here. They're recording everything that happens in this room."

"I don't care. Let 'em watch." She put her arms around his neck.

"Well, I care. Give me a minute." He pulled free of her and walked quickly to the phone and picked it up.

"Yes, Dr. Savage?"

"Will you turn the camera off in my apartment for awhile?"

"I'm sorry, Doctor, I can't do that."

"Then get me DeShane."

"Chief DeShane is off station at the moment, sir."

"Put me through to Mr. Killingsworth."

"Sir. Doctor. Mr. Killingsworth is . . . ahh . . . he's aware of the . . . ahh . . . the current situation with you and Mrs.

Killingsworth and he . . . ahh . . . he's ordered that the scene be taped, sir."

"You're kidding."

"No, sir."

"Shit!"

"Sir, I'll turn my monitor off, but I can't stop the tape. I'm sorry."

"Not even in the bedroom?"

"No, sir."

"Thank you for telling me." He hung up the phone and turned to Diana. "Everything is being taped. Your husband is going to know."

"He won't care. I don't either."

She came into his embrace and he felt the warmth and softness of her flesh pressing against him as he kissed her. He held her tight, savoring, tasting her mouth, feeling himself becoming aroused. He slid his hands down her back and grasped her hips, pulling her to the rising bulge in his pants.

"I'm sorry, David," she said breathlessly, feeling his hardness through her dress. "I've got to get out of here. This is going too fast."

"Diana."

"Please."

"Okay. I understand. I just . . . got carried away. Thanks for coming. See you tomorrow." He let her go and walked her to the door where he kissed her good-bye, feeling his heart pounding as she hurried down the hallway to the stairs.

—*—

Stupid! Stupid! Stupid!

She said the word over and over as she traversed the hall, stepped into the elevator and punched in the code to her floor. The doors closed and the car began to rise.

She needed to know what she felt for David Savage. That's why she went to his room, to talk to him, to find out. What did she do? She asked him about his wife. Brilliant. Stupid!

Other than the handsome Tokushima, the mature, sophisticated Japanese corporate executive who had put the move on her in Tokyo, Savage was the only man since she was a teenager who had turned her on.

Why didn't she just tell him? If this thing worked, she was going to be living with him and sleeping with him anyway. It was what Killingsworth and Mr. Damarjiane wanted to see, if they were sexually compatible. And to be honest, she wanted it, too. So why was she acting like a shy schoolgirl? She was no stranger to sex. Go back. Tell him. No, not with the cameras there. She wasn't going to put on a show for anybody. Stag films for the boys in the security force to watch and enjoy, seeing her naked, seeing her get laid. No she couldn't do that.

She slammed the door of her apartment so hard the wall shook. What to do. Did she love David Savage or did she just want to sleep with him? What to do.

They could take the plane, go to LA. She had plenty of money. Get an apartment there somewhere near the beach. No. Damarjiane would never let him leave. What to do.

Late the following morning she appeared in David's room wearing the same dress and shoes.

"Good morning," he said. "No exercises today?"

She didn't reply and appeared very nervous.

"Did Killingsworth say anything about last night?" he asked.

"No," she replied and began pacing back and forth across the room.

"Has he seen the tapes?"

"I don't know."

"Diana, what is it?"

"He left early this morning."

"So?"

"Come on." She grabbed his hand and almost pulled him from the table toward the door. With quick steps, she led him along the hall, down the stairs and to the elevator where she punched in the code. As the car began to move upward, she squeezed his hand but didn't look at him.

"Diana?" he questioned.

"There are no cameras in *my* apartment."

The exit from the elevator and the walk along the thickly carpeted hallway of the third floor was much slower and more calm, as though some major hurtle had been passed. She opened the door and brought him in, walking straight to the bedroom where she released his hand and stepped away.

The luxurious apartment with its couches, chairs, table lamps, framed paintings and huge windows overlooking the grounds, the bedroom with two double beds, nightstands and shaded lamps were a blur to him, registering only in his subconscious.

Kicking off her shoes, she reached behind her, unzipped the dress, and let it fall to the floor in a single fluid motion. She wore only a bra and panties beneath.

"Since I don't have love to give you, I'll give you what I do have."

Diana."

"I made up my mind last night."

"This isn't the way I wanted it to happen."

"Don't you want me?"

"Yes. I do. But this is a part of love, of caring. Without the emotion, the feeling, it's just . . . just—"

"Sex?"

Suddenly she was in his arms, her mouth on his and his arms were around her. She pushed her lower body toward him and kissed him deep and hard, exploring his moth with her tongue.

"Do what you wanted to do out there on the trail," she whispered, pulling her lips away just far enough to speak. "Put your hands on me."

He felt the fabric of her panties and tried frantically to pull them down.

For in just an instant, in his mind, he was on the running path again, looking down at her laying on the ground before him, showing her legs and the gentle, provocative contours beneath those white shorts.

The panties came off, sliding down along her legs and she stepped out of them. "Take my bra off," she said, raising up the front of his jogging suit and pulling it over his head.

With the bra still in his hands, she stepped away from him. "Look at me," she whispered.

Her nipples were firm and protruding, her breasts jutting out from her muscular body without the slightest bit of sag. The fine, silky triangle of reddish gold did little to conceal the valley between her legs and his eyes were drawn to it. His heart was pounding and his breath quickened.

"I want to lay down," she whispered, falling back onto the bed. He went down with her and she grabbed his hair with both hands, dragging him lower so that his head was below her waist. Leaning back and pushing her hips forward, raising her legs, she pulled his face down between them, feeling his mouth against her hot, throbbing, wet opening. The room was filled with the scent of her. His fingertips explored the velvet smooth, satin softness of her behind, touching, feeling and making her thrust again and again saying in a deep, throaty voice filled with passion, "Oh, yes. Do it! Do it! Put your tongue in me. Taste me. Yes, yes, do it!"

Reluctant to take his hands from her even for a moment, he grabbed at the waistband of his sweat pants and dragged them down. Then off came his shorts.

"Do you like it?" she asked, but he could not answer so tightly was she holding his face between her legs.

She continued moving her hips up and down and in a circular motion, moving his mouth up to the tiny bud near the top of her crevice. The surround hair caressed his face. He lunged forwarded, climbing up between her outspread legs until he was poised over her ready to penetrate deep into her body.

"Slowly, David. Enter me slowly. It's been so long. I'm afraid it will hurt."

A hard nipple was thrust between his lips as he began to push into her. The heat, the softness, the tightness were all incredible and he used every ounce of his self-control to keep from ramming it in. She wrapped her legs round him and drew him deeper and deeper into her. She felt the softness, the hardness, the warmth and the throbbing, the motion and they rhythm of his body. She matched the rhythm, thrusting when he did, taking everything he could give her.

"Oh, God, I love it. I love it. I love it," she moaned in rhythm with the thrusts.

"Do you love me, Diana?"

"David. Oh, David."

"Say it, Diana." He raised his head just enough to look at her face and into her eyes. "Say it."

She looked back at him through blurred vision. "David."

"Say it. Say it."

"No."

"Say it, Diana."

"I'm afraid."

"Say it."

"I love you, David."

"Again."

"I love you."

"Again."

Oh, God, David, I love you. I love you."

He kissed her hard on the mouth and she felt it coming. Pulling her lips away from his and putting her face against his neck to muffle her voice as the waves of ecstasy swept over her, she felt him erupt inside her, the heat pouring throughout her entire body. She bit him on the neck just under his ear, her teeth drawing the taste of blood and stifling the scream of her climax.

A second later, an hour, a year later, momentarily rested but still wanting more, still inside her, he grasped her breasts with both hands and greedily sucked her nipples, alternating from one to the other.

"Can you come again?" she asked, her fingernails raking his back and the flesh of his butt. "It felt so good."

"I don't know," he replied, trying to smile. His face was flushed and his eyes glassy. "I've never had anything like this before."

"Let's see if I can make you." She tightened up, pressed and clamped him more firmly with her legs.

Later when he sat on the edge of the bed with his back to her preparing to go to the bathroom, she gasped. "Oh, David. God! Did I do that?"

"What?" he asked in surprise.

"Your back."

"What about it?"

She looked at her hands and to her fingernails. There was blood on them. "I'm sorry, David. I didn't . . ."

"Will you please tell me what you're talking about?"

"Your back is bleeding. I . . . I scratched you."

"I didn't feel anything."

"David, I clawed the hell out of you. Come on. We need to do something about it." She crawled out of the bed and led him by the hand into the bathroom. "I've got some medicated cream with a local anesthetic in it," she said, turning on the light and rummaging through the medicine cabinet.

"But it doesn't hurt," he protested.

"Look," she instructed, turning him so he could look over his shoulder and see his back reflected in the large bathroom mirror.

"Christ!" he exclaimed, seeing long, red gashes in his skin and his back covered with blood.

"I'm sorry. I didn't do it on purpose."

"Yes, you did." He took her by the shoulders. "And you'll just have to believe me, I didn't feel it. But I'm flattered. No woman has ever done anything like this to me. Maybe I did something right. Huh?"

Both were standing naked in the bright bathroom light as she gently swabbed his back with water-soaked cotton to get the blood off and then with vitamin E healing cream. He watched her in the mirror, unable to take his eyes from her lovely body.

"Haven't you had enough?" she asked, laughing, as she watched him look at her.

"I could never have enough of you, Diana. I devour you with my eyes."

"You've already devoured me with your mouth. And I loved it."

"Say it, Diana."

"David." She looked away and raised her hands silently in a gesture of helplessness.

"Say it."

"No."

"You said it before."

"We were in bed. You were in me. I wanted it. You did it. I liked it. I like you. Tomorrow, maybe we can do it again."

"You're a hard woman, Diana."

"And don't you forget it."

"And you love me."

"Oh, you're impossible."

"I don't think so," he replied, "not considering where we're going. Now *that's* impossible."

"But we're not going right now."

"No, not right now."

"And you're not going alone."

"Just for a short while. Now say it for me. Even though you don't mean it. Say it."

"I love you."

"Again."

"I love you."

"You know, if you keep saying that, you might just start believing it."

"Good luck." She turned and started to walk from the bathroom to get dressed. He stopped her with a hand on her shoulder. "I love you," he said. "Now go put some clothes on before I rape you."

"Just try," she replied, laughing. "Oh, please try."

"You mean you could do it again?"

"Wanna find out?"

"I'm sorry, Diana, I don't think I—"

"I'm teasing you, David. Don't take things so seriously. You've given me more than any man has in years. I might even be able to love you. I know I want to sleep with you and live with you. Is that enough?"

"Yes, Diana, that's enough. For now."

Coming into his arms, she asked, "Oh, David, how did we get into this?"

"Damned if I know. I'm going to go run for awhile. I need the high."

"Haven't you had a high already?"

"Oh, God, yes. Higher than I've ever been. Maybe what I should have said was, I need something to bring me down. Back to earth."

"I'm going to take a shower. Get out of here, Savage. I'll find you."

Chapter Fourteen

A T 7:00 AM THE next morning when breakfast was brought in by his personal waiter, the tray contained plates and food for two, the silent man pretending that nothing was different or out of the ordinary. He poured two cups of coffee, laid out the dishes and served the eggs, bacon, hash browns, buttered toast and orange juice. Savage looked at him questioningly but before he could give voice to his curiosity Diana came through door dressed in her usual shorts and halter.

"Good morning, David," she said, very business-like and impersonal.

"I was wondering what happened to you," he replied as she sat down and began to eat. What he *really* wanted to ask was, where were you all afternoon and last night.

"I was moving," she answered.

"Moving?"

"To the underground complex. There are apartments there used by the staff. I've moved into one of them."

"Why?"

She gave him a scathing look.

"Oh. Okay. Won't your husband object?"

"If that was meant to be sarcastic, the attempt was wasted."

"No. I didn't mean it that way at all. I just—"

"All right. No, he won't object."

"I don't imagine those rooms are as luxurious as your third floor suite."

She laughed but there was little humor in it. "You should have seen the last place I lived."

"Yeah. Me, too."

"Touché."

"We run today?"

"We do."

He sat for a moment watching her casually eat at his table as though she had been doing it for years. Seeing him staring at her, she asked, "What?"

"Yesterday wasn't just a dream, was it? I mean, I didn't just imagine it."

"If it was a dream, we both had the same one."

"You're just setting there calmly eating and I'm about ready to drag you into the bedroom, camera or no camera."

"I'm sure you've been told that I'm a very cold, emotionless person. You're seeing some evidence of that, now."

"I think what I'm seeing is a very good act."

"Believe whatever you want."

They finished breakfast and as they left the table, David noticed the computer screen. In the center, there were three sentences pursuant to his second search.

In 1936, the frigate DAMARJIANE was purchased by Tidewater Oil Company of Los Angeles, California to be used as a cruise ship for company executives.

In 1966, ownership was transferred to the Palomar Foundation but there is no indication of a recorded sale or a specific price.

The DAMARJIANE's current harbor is unknown.

"What is it?" Diana asked as he leaned over the computer screen.

"Just something I've been checking into. Give me a minute and then we'll go." He typed in the SEARCH box, Tidewater_ Oil_Company.

"Damarjiane is a ship? I don't get it," Diana said, looking at the screen.

"I don't either." He told her of his unsuccessful attempt to locate something, anything on the director of the Palomar Foundation. "A person with as much money and power as Damarjiane can't be the invisible man. But that seems to be the case."

"So, what's it all mean?"

A full page of information appeared on the screen. The top of the page began:

Tidewater Oil Company of California, a wholly owned subsidiary of Getty Oil. Founder and Chairman of the Board of Getty Oil and President of Tidewater Oil Company, J. Paul Getty, retired in 1971. He died in 1976 from . . . There was a postage stamp size photograph of a man' head and shoulders under which was the date 1953.

"I don't know what it means, Diana, but I'm going to find out. There's something very strange here."

She gave him a puzzled look.

"Now, come here," he said, putting his arms round her and pulling her to him, kissing her mouth. She kissed back and he felt the passion begin to rise in him.

"We need to go," she said, pulling away.

"I love you, Diana."

"There's a double bed in my new apartment," she replied with a mischievous grin. "And I hate sleeping alone. Do you suppose you could do something about that?"

"Let's go for a walk." He took her hand and led her from the apartment.

After ten minutes of walking hand-in-hand in silence along the path behind the house, he stopped her and took her by the shoulders. "There are no cameras here."

"I know."

"Say it. I need to hear it."

She pulled away and turned her back to him.

"What is it?" he asked.

She turned quickly to face him, something hard about her face. "I don't love you, David," she said. "It doesn't matter how many times you ask me to say it, I don't. I like you and I want to sleep with you, but I don't love you. So, stop asking."

"But you'll sleep with me."

"I've slept with a lot of men. It's no big deal."

Seeing the momentary flash of pain in his eyes, her voice softened. "That was cruel. David, I'm sorry. It was a long time ago after my husband went on to better and younger girls. I do like you. I like you very much but I won't let myself fall in love with you. We have just three days before you go through the Window. There is a very good chance you will die there and I'll never see you again. I'm not going to put myself in that position again to lose somebody I love."

"Your daughter."

"Yes. Her, and someone else. A man I lived with for almost two years. He was one of several men. You remind me so much of him. He wanted me. It was as obvious as *you* wanting me but because of honor and out of respect for me, he never touched me. He never even kissed me, but I think I loved him. His name was Isoroku."

"Did you tell him?"

"No."

"Maybe you should have."

For the first time since he had met her, David saw tears in her eyes. "I'm sorry, Diana. I just never seem to know when to quit. I always shoot my mouth off. I'm sorry."

"It's not your fault."

"Look, Diana, I . . ." He hesitated, looked at the ground and took a deep breath. "I . . . this may work out and it might not. The whole thing is so bizarre anyway. If something does happen to me . . . well, you've finally left Killingsworth. You're free. Go find this guy, what's his name. Isoroku. Maybe there's still a chance."

"You're giving me up already?"

"No! I'm not giving up. That's not what I—"

"I know, but there isn't any chance. Isoroku is dead."

"I'm sorry. Boy, I just keep sticking my foot in my mouth, don't I." He reached out and brushed away her tears with his fingers.

"It's all right. You didn't know."

"This was recent, wasn't it."

"A year ago."

"Would it have worked?"

"No."

"You sure?"

"Yes, I'm sure."

"Killingsworth?"

"No. It just wouldn't have worked. Even if he had lived. We came from two different worlds. He couldn't live in mine and I couldn't live in his."

Savage nodded his head in understanding. "Then let's fill up the next three days and the hell with everything else. I love you, Diana, and I'll take whatever you are willing to give me."

"There's something else you need to know, David. How he died."

"Why do I need to know that?"

"So that you will know just what your lover is."

"I *know* who you are, Diana."

"I said what, not who. I've been trained to survive. I've been taught how to kill. I intended to kill you."

"Kill me?" He was startled. "Why?"

"Because you were in my way. And as I told you, I was taking out all of my problems and frustrations on you."

"Then why didn't you?"

"I never got the chance."

"That's not true. I don't believe it. You had lots of chances."

"You know what? I don't care what you believe."

He reached out and took her by the shoulders, holding her gently but firmly. "At first, it was just your beauty, your lovely face and gorgeous body that drew me to you. But as time passed, there was more. I can't explain it. How do you explain emotions? Just suddenly, I was in love with you and there wasn't anything I could do about it. I wanted to sleep with you to consummate that love, but you were a married woman, and I couldn't."

"You're living in the dark ages, David. I could have handled it."

"Could you?"

"Yes."

"When did you know for certain you were in love with me?"

"You're a bastard, Savage. You just won't leave it alone, will you."

"No, I won't. Answer the question."

"The first time you kissed me."

"Do you love me?"

"Yes, David. I love you."

"Will you marry me?"

"I sort of have to get a divorce first, don't I?"

"Will that be a problem?"

"No. But it doesn't make much difference where we're going, does it."

"I guess not. I just want us to be married."

"We don't have the time. Come on, my darling, we need to get back. There's a lot to do."

She took him along the path and by noon, they arrived at the elevator to the underground complex. They had lunch in the dining room with the technicians and scientists working on the Window project. "I never liked chicken salad sandwiches," he said as they shared a table in the big room.

"Eat it anyway," she replied, working on a plate of pot roast with a knife and fork.

"Think they'll let me stay down here tonight with you?"

"Let's try and see."

"I don't want DeShane, or worse, your husband kicking the door in with a gun in his hand."

She laughed. "I don't think that's going to happen."

Dr. Boucree came into the dining room, saw them seated together at a table and went back out. There was a knowing grin on his face. He would eat later. There was still a lot to do.

"I seem to remember," he said, finishing the last of his sandwich, "seeing something about the Palomar Foundation was into pharmaceuticals at one time. Jade Pharmaceuticals. Do you know anything about that?"

"No."

"Come on. I want to find a computer terminal."

"Later. I have the afternoon already planned. There are a few more things we need to work on and—"

"Look, Diana, I've already put several thousand rounds through every weapon known to modern man, you've taught me all I can absorb about survival, I'm in pretty good physical condition and one or two more days of the same isn't going to accomplish anything more. Give it a rest, huh?"

"All right. An hour of calisthenics and we'll call it quits. Okay?"

"If it will make you happy."

In the gym, the hour became almost two and they were both dripping wet when they quit. They went to the showers together and stripped off their clothes then stepped into the steaming water naked. He couldn't keep his hungry eyes off of her body as she stood there with her legs spread, brushing the hair back from her face with her fingers. She became aware of his attention and said with just a hint of amusement, "You're not used to having a naked woman in front of you, are you."

"We didn't have very many naked women on Death Row."

Realizing her blunder, she attempted to correct it. "I meant your wife. She—" "She was very self-conscious about her body. A lot of women are."

"So, you never did anything like this?"

"No."

"I'm sorry, David. I've really made a mess of this. The truth is I've always been very brazen and I never had any inhibitions about nudity or sex. That's one of the reasons I survived at Hidaka-sammyaku."

"Where?"

"Never mind." She stepped to him, put both hands behind his head and kissed him as the water continued to pour over them. Feeling her body in his arms, he became hard and erect. Her breasts seemed to swell and her nipples were large and protruding.

With her hands flat against the wall, her hips thrust out, she groaned as he entered her from behind, grasping her breasts and firm nipples with both clutching hands. It was different this time, the rhythm was there but the strokes were longer, almost withdrawing completely and then plunging in deep, his pelvis slamming into her butt. With her eyes clamped shut, her mouth open to gasp in air, she felt his climax erupt in her. Men liked it that way. It wouldn't be long before he wanted to fuck her in the ass. Men wanted that, too.

Even though she didn't climax this time, his desire for her and his enjoyment of her body sent her into the heights of passion, enjoying the union as much as he. While feeling him pressed against her and still inside her, she slowly regained her composure and awareness. With a deep sigh and a move to impishness, she reached up with one hand to turn off the hot water, leaving the cold to pour over them.

"You bitch!" he shouted, withdrawing and backing away from her as the icy water cascaded down on them. "How could you do that?"

Laughing, she turned around quickly, wrapped her arms around him before he could escape and said, "feels good doesn't it."

"No, it doesn't!" he replied.

"Then come warm me up."

"Warm *you* up? You're the one who turned on the . . . I'm the one who should . . . Oh, hell."

"My new apartment is just down the hall."

"Diana, I'm not sure I can walk that far right now."

"Spent?"

"I'm not a young man, anymore. And you're more woman than most men could handle."

"Thank you. Now, you want to help me dress?"

"What?"

"You've undressed women, me included. Have you ever dressed one?"

"No."

"Time you learned."

"Why?"

"Because some women like for a man to put her clothes back on as much as she enjoyed having them taken off."

"I didn't know that."

"Come on. We'll dry off." They walked from the shower area and used soft, thick, white towels to absorb the moisture.

It was an entirely new experience for David Savage, holding the almost sheer panties in his hands in front of her as she stepped into them, then pulling them up to cover her, releasing the elastic above her hips. She would help him cradle her breasts in the bra, just letting him fumble, then finally hook it behind her back. She took both his hands in hers, placed his palms over her breasts, and showed him how to comfortably position the bra around her.

In fresh, clean jeans, shirts, socks and shoes, they walked together through the underground complex expecting looks, even comments, but they encountered no one except the Window lab guards who politely looked the other way as though they saw nobody. Diana stopped at a door and opened it. He followed her into the apartment.

Not nearly as large or elaborate as the one she shared with her husband, Diana's subterranean living quarters consisted of three rooms tastefully furnished with couch, chairs, tables, lamps and bed. One wall had floor-to-ceiling drapes creating the illusion of a window behind.

"I need to use that computer terminal," he said.

"Why?"

"Something I need to find out. What can I access from here?"

"I don't know."

"What's your husband's access code?"

"Why?"

"I need to use it, Diana. He can get into areas I can't."

"What are you looking for?"

"Pharmaceuticals."

"Why?"

"Just a hunch. Trust me."

"All right." She typed in the access code and Killingsworth's password that brought the computer on-line. "Go ahead."

He sat down in the chair before the computer console and quickly typed in, Pharmaceutical, search, Palomar, search, 1975 to 1979, search.

"You know what you're going to find, don't you."

"No, not for certain."

"But pretty sure."

"Yeah. Something just about as impossible as the Window." He looked up at her as she leaned over his shoulder. "Something as impossible as you."

"Me?"

"Do you have any idea how incredibly beautiful you are? How irresistibly sexy you are? How many men would kill to have you? To own you, to possess you? Do you?"

"You're talking nonsense."

"Am I?"

"Yes, you are. Own me? Possess me? I'm married, but Damien doesn't own me. That went out a hundred years ago."

"Maybe I just stated it wrong. I've been out of touch for awhile. Let me try again. How many men would kill to sleep with you, to have what I had just a short time ago in the shower? How many men would kill *me* because I have what they want and can't have?"

"David, I don't understand any of this."

"Yes you do. And I'm beginning to understand, too."

"Understand what?"

"That you love me."

"David, I lied. I said it because you wanted to hear it. I care for you. That's true, but I don't love you. I don't love anybody. I never have."

"You said you loved this Isoroku guy."

"That was a different kind of love."

"I love you."

"That's *your* problem."

"Why is it a problem?"

"I've told you." She threw up her arms in a helpless gesture. "Love is not something that just suddenly happens. It's something that develops over a long period of time, when two people get to know each other and they like each other and then they care about each other and *then* they fall in love. Just getting a good piece of ass isn't love."

"Is that what you are? A good piece of ass?"

"Evidently, according to you. But then, you don't have much to compare with, do you."

"Ouch. That one hurt."

"Oh, David, damn it. I didn't mean that. I didn't mean to hurt you."

"Didn't you?"

"No! I just—"

"How do I compare with Mark?"

"That's not fair, David. I never slept with Mark."

"Okay, how about Killingsworth?"

"I think I'm going to smother you with a pillow in your sleep. Now will you please tell me what you are doing with the computer?"

"Look," he replied, pointing to the screen.

In block letters, three short paragraphs appeared centered in the screen.

SOMATREM
Trade name, PROTROPIN
Genetech
SOMATROPIN
Trade name, HUMATROPE
Lilly
LEBETALOL CH
Trade name, NORMODYNE
Schering

"What does all that mean?" she asked.

"Haven't a clue."

"And how is Palomar involved? Aren't those the names of drug companies at the bottom?" She pointed to the third line of each group.

"Yeah, looks like. Maybe they developed the drugs here and sold the formula. The big question is why did they suddenly discontinue drugs and go into electronics? That's a pretty drastic step."

She shrugged her shoulders.

He printed a copy of the screen and said, "Let's go talk to our resident physician, the eminent Dr. Worthington." He grabbed her by the hand and headed for the door. "I *think* I remember where the medical office is."

They walked along the deserted hallway past door after door. Savage had the urge to stop and open one of the doors to see what was behind it, just to see if it was locked. But he kept moving. They passed several people in the hallway, all wearing white lab coats, carrying a file or a clipboard and presenting concerned looks on their faces.

Seated in his office behind his desk in his office, the physician looked up as they entered the large examining room unannounced. They were still hand-in-hand and the doctor could not suppress a slight smile. "Dr. Savage, Mrs. Killingsworth, what can I do for you?" He stood as they entered his office.

Savage handed him the short list. "This mean anything to you?"

"Right off hand, no," he replied after glancing at the page. "I've never heard of any of them. Must be some pretty exclusive stuff."

"Can you check it out for me, Doctor?"

The physician turned, pulled a thick red book off a shelf behind his chair, and sat down with the book on his desk. He checked the index. "Well, the first thing I can tell you is that these have been around for a long time, developed back in the early 70's. They're growth hormones and they affect the pituitary. That's pretty general but it's about all I can give you at a moment's notice. I could do some research on them if it's important."

"Could you give them to a person without any harmful effects?

"Yes, I think so. But why would you want to?"

"I heard Palomar was into drug research for awhile under the trade name of Jade Pharmasudicals. Could it have had anything to do with these?"

"Yes, I've heard that story, too, but it was way back before my time. May I ask why you are interested?"

"Dr. Worthington, I can't tell you. Just something that came up I'm trying to check out for my own personal information. Probably doesn't mean anything."

"Want me to do a break-down on them? What's in them and what they're for?"

"Thanks, but no, don't bother."

"All right. I have you scheduled for another physical next week."

David and Diana glanced at each other but neither spoke. It was not lost on the physician.

"That is if you can make it, of course," he added.

"Thanks, Doc." He turned to leave, urging Diana through the door ahead of him with his hand in the middle of her back.

"David." It was the first time Dr. Worthington had used his first name when addressing him. Savage stopped pushing Diana and turned back to see a concerned face and an extended hand.

"Good luck. It's been a privilege."

Savage grasped the offered hand and felt the grip. Then they were in the corridor outside and Diana said, "He knows about the Window."

"Yeah. He'd just about have to, wouldn't he."

"Two more days," she said, putting her arm around his waist.

"Two and a half," he corrected.

Nobody approached them or even seemed to notice them throughout the remainder of the afternoon. They went back to the surface to the big house. At 6:00 o'clock, dinner was served in his apartment for two, steak and lobster with melted butter, tartar sauce, baked potatoes, green beans and salad. There were tall glasses of water and small glasses of vintage red wine beside each plate. They ate, absorbed with each other, leaving the remnants of the meal and dishes on the table. With the cameras on, they undressed, went to bed and slept in each other's arms.

The next two days were a blur to them. They slept in Diana's subterranean bedroom most of the time, although electronic technology was so sophisticated now that a camera could be installed and they would never find it no matter how closely they looked. They didn't even bother.

Suddenly it was the evening before Savage was to step through the Window into the new world. Instead of dinner, the waiter brought a formal written invitation to dine with Mr. Damarjiane in the main dining room on the first floor precisely at 7 o'clock. There was no mention of Diana accompanying him.

"Diana," he questioned as he knotted his tie, "just how important am I to this project?"

"Why?" She looked at him suspiciously.

"Just answer the question. I know you've discussed it with Killingsworth."

"Well, you're not irreplaceable, if that's what you mean. I'm still here. Nevertheless, a lot of time and money had been invested in you, and our new relationship over the past few days has changed things considerably. I'd say you are *very* important."

"How much do you think I can get away with? How far can I push and not get my hand slapped?"

"David, just what are you going to do?"

"Please, answer the question."

"Short of walking out of here and telling everybody to go to hell, I'd say you've pretty much got carte blanche."

"Wanna find out?"

"How?"

"Have you still got access to your apartment on the third floor?"

"Of course."

"Go put on something elegant, something expensive and sexy and meet me back here just before seven."

"David, I wasn't invited."

"I know. Now get, or I'll take you up there and dress you myself."

"I'd like that."

He walked to the phone and picked it up.

"Yes, Dr. Savage?"

"Let me talk to DeShane."

There was a brief pause and then a faint click. "Hi, Doc. Whatcha need?"

"You got a dinner jacket?"

"A what?"

"Something formal like to wear to a State Department dinner."

"What the hell are you talking about?"

"This evening, 7 o'clock in the dining room. Be there."

"You nuts? I have specific orders not to be anywhere *near* that dining room. Straight from Mr. K himself. Nobody, and I mean *no-bod-e* goes anywhere near that room but you. My men have orders."

"Diana is coming with me."

"Don't do it, Doc."

"You are going to be there too, and Dr. Boucree."

"You trying to get yourself killed?"

"Yeah, DeShane. You're going to have to kill me to stop me. All three of us."

"Goddamn you, Savage. What are you doing?"

"Hide and watch." He broke the connection, held the button down for a few seconds and then released it.

"Yes, Doctor?"

"Connect me with Dr. Boucree in the lab."

"Yes, sir."

The phone rang fifteen times before somebody answered it in a loud, very annoyed voice. "What?"

"This is David Savage. May I speak to Dr. Boucree, please?"

"Oh, sure, Doctor. Sorry about that. Everything is real tense in here. Tomorrow's the big day and—"

"Yes, I know. I'm the main feature."

"Hey, Professor," the voice on the other end of the phone shouted out. "Doc. Savage wants to talk to you."

"Yes, Dr. Savage," Boucree said a few moments later. "Are you as excited as we are?"

"I am. Did you get your invitation?"

"Invitation? What invitation?"

"Mr. Damarjiane is having a dinner tonight. Sort of a going away party, as it were. You're supposed to be there at seven. Don't be late."

"What? I don't know anything about a dinner party."

"Diana said you would probably forget. It's semiformal. That means leave your lab coat behind."

"Oh, I just couldn't possibly—"

"Mr. Damarjiane is the host."

"He is? Oh, well, in that case, of course I'll be there. You said, seven?"

"Yes, seven."

"All right, Doctor."

Chapter Fifteen

"YOU LOOK ABSOLUTELY RADIANT, Mrs. Killingsworth," Damarjiane said as she entered the formal dining room clinging to David's arm. She had no idea what to expect. The two armed guards on each side of the dining room entranceway had given them—well, Savage, actually—a sharp Present Arms as he approached. They didn't bar Diana. DeShane must have talked to them. "Being in love agrees with you." He was seated at the head of the large walnut dinner table and though it was an obvious effort, he stood when she entered.

She wore a strapless, sleeveless, ankle-length black gown accentuating her breasts and the flare of her hips. A single strand of diamonds encircled her neck; another on her left wrist and four-inch satin-finish heels completed the simple but elegant ensemble. The cost of her outfit would keep a family of four comfortably for six months.

"Mr. DeShane. A pleasure to meet you at last. I have watched you and I have been very impressed by your work here. Please come in and join us," Damarjiane continued as the security chief appeared in the doorway wearing a white dinner jacket, black tie and slacks. He looked very uncomfortable as he stepped tentatively into the dimly lit room. The magnificent crystal chandelier above the table had been deliberately turned down to create shadows. The jacket fit him well but it was not cut to hide the gun bulging under his left arm. Killingsworth, standing beside and slightly behind his boss' chair, glowered at him.

"Sir, I didn't—"

"Oh, it's quite all right, Mr. DeShane. I quite understand. A place has been set for you."

"I'm sorry I'm late," Boucree said, rushing into the room. He wore a rumpled suit and his tie was slightly askew.

"Professor," Damarjiane said. "I'm please to personally congratulate you on your wonderful discovery. I apologize for not having done so sooner. You are seated across from Mr. DeShane."

"Oh, thank you, Mr. Damarjiane. This is a real privilege."

The table was already set for six with elegant china, silver and crystal. Two formally attired waiters stood at the far end of the room ready to begin serving when signaled.

"I chose Les Baron de Boeuf with a dry red wine for the main course. It is usually a man's meal but I do hope you will enjoy it, Mrs. Killingsworth. There is salmon and prawns in white wine sauce if you prefer."

"You knew," Diana said in surprise, then turned to Savage. "David, he knew all of us were coming."

"Really, Diana," said Killingsworth, his manner one of mild amusement.

"The phone calls," Savage informed her. "They were all monitored."

"As was the conversation in your room about how much you could get away with," Killingsworth added.

"As you knew it would be," Damarjiane added. "A very brash and possibly dangerous maneuver on the threshold of your big adventure, Doctor. You mind telling me why?"

It was slightly warm and stuffy in the room but Damarjiane wore a dark double-breasted wool suit with vest and a wide white silk tie. He looked worse than the last time Savage had seen him.

"Nothing complicated. Very simple, really. Witnesses, Mr. Damarjiane," Savage said, guiding Diana to the seat at Damarjiane's left. "You said you knew I was innocent of the murder charge against me. I want you to repeat that in the presence of witnesses."

"I see. That's the only reason?"

After only a moment's hesitation, he replied, "Yes."

"I see. If all of you would take your seats, please." When they all had sat down, Damarjiane sank into his chair, visibly tired from the exertion of standing for only a few minutes. "I had hoped this would be an intimate dinner for just the two of us, Dr. Savage. Sort of a hale and farewell and a congratulatory dinner, as it were," the old man said, addressing Savage who had taken the chair to his right. Killingsworth seated himself at the other end of the table facing his boss. "Back the way things used to be when there were castles and kings, with you and I seated at opposite ends of a long table, served by liveried servants. It would have been a grand send-off."

Damarjiane's diction was perfect, he was obviously well educated and he spoke with a distinct British accent that Savage had not noticed before so well had it been concealed. Now, it seemed, the accent no longer mattered.

A waiter appeared on each side of the table and all but Boucree were served cognac in large snifters. "A very good year, I'm told," the old man said. "Please have the first course served."

He paused, cleared his throat and appeared slightly apprehensive as though having to rephrase what he had intended to say to Savage alone. "I wanted to talk to you in private because I have some important things to tell you." He stopped as two tuxedoed waiters wearing white gloves placed bowls of white, creamy soup before each of them. They withdrew and waited outside the room to serve the main course. They and the two uniformed guards looked at each other but did not speak. "Important things that I don't wish to become common knowledge. However, that evidently is not to be, and I bow to your wishes.

"Then as to my innocence?"

"Very well. Yes. Your innocence."

"I was framed."

"Yes. In fact, you were framed, Doctor. Evidence was expertly manufactured to put the blame for the crime on you and enough political pressure was exerted to assure your conviction. You did not kill Congressman Phil Rizzo. Does that satisfy you?"

"You know that for a fact?"

"Yes, I know that for a fact."

Savage looked at Diana, at DeShane and then to Boucree. She was smiling with satisfaction, DeShane just nodded his head in understanding, and the professor didn't seem to care one way or another. Killingsworth sat impassively, tasting the cognac.

"Why?" David looked back at his host.

"Why were you framed?"

"Yes."

"I'll come to that."

"Then, who?"

"You mean the actual perpetrator?"

"Yes."

"No, Doctor, I don't know specifically who."

"How about generally?"

"I'll get to that, too." The director of the Palomar Foundation lifted his spoon and tasted the soup. He nodded in approval. As though a signal, the others placed their napkins in their laps and sipped the soup. It was a delicious creamy cheese with just a hint of onion.

"I was told that there was some difficulty in obtaining the military .45 pistol from your residence without being detected. It was the holstered handgun you wore in a number of your publicity photographs. It had your fingerprints all over it, on the magazine and on the bullets in the magazine. There was never any doubt that it was yours. Quite an accomplishment, I understand."

"I'm sure it was," Savage replied, sarcastically.

"It was needed to assure your conviction."

"It sure helped."

"Was that sufficient to establish your innocence for your . . . witnesses?"

Before Savage could reply, Damarjiane abruptly changed the subject to himself. "I have not appeared in public for many years now, nor did I intend to do so this evening, for reasons of my own."

"This isn't exactly a public appearance."

"What I meant was—"

"I know what you meant." Savage was confident now to the point of bordering on dangerous arrogance. "You haven't appeared in public since—what?—oh, how about 1976?" he inquired. "Does that sound pretty close to right?"

"Why, what a remarkable statement Doctor." Damarjiane said, actually showing mild surprise. Killingsworth wrinkled his brow in confusion. It was true that his boss had not appeared in public during the time of his employment, but a lot of older, very wealthy men became reclusive in their later years. The others looked around at each other questioningly.

Savage continued. "This company, Palomar, back in the early 70's was known as Jade Pharmaceuticals, I believe, which was into the creation and manufacture of drugs, wasn't it. Then you abruptly stopped and went into electronics in the middle 70's. Care to tell me why?"

"No, we didn't manufacture drugs; we merely created them and sold the formulas. That's all we did." Damarjiane again appeared surprised and Killingsworth exhibited a definite interest in the direction the conversation was taking.

"Your pharmaceutical lab," Savage continued, "was working on growth hormones—nobody seems to have a clue why—and you discovered something, something as radical as the Window. You told me that, remember? You said the Window was your *second* revolutionary discovery. Your first one was some kind of a wonder drug like penicillin, wasn't it. It wasn't an antibiotic, though. It was something to prolong life. And like the Window, you decided to keep it for yourself."

"So it was *your* computer inquiry," Damarjiane said, nodding his head slightly. "Yes, of course. I wondered why Mr. Killingsworth would be asking about thirty-year-old drugs. Pray continue, Doctor. I'm fascinated." There was a slight smile on his thin, pale lips and he leaned on his elbow with two fingers placed against his cheek.

"Damarjiane is—or was—the name of a sailing ship built in the 1800's. You took that name when you could no longer use your own. Why not Smith or Jones? Why something so unusual as to actually attract attention?"

"I thought the name very unique. I liked it and somebody trying to hide wouldn't use such a flamboyant appellation. I was hiding in plain sight, you might say. And, yes, you are quite right. I couldn't very well continue using my *real* name."

"Yes. I understand that now, now that I know who you are."

Everyone else's attention was firmly riveted. They had all know him for years as Damarjiane and now, another name might emerge. What name? Who could he be?

"Do you really know who I am?"

"Yes, I do."

"You only *think* you do, Doctor. However, you are quite correct in one respect. It *was* a wonder drug we discovered, but we weren't sure it would actually work over a long period of time or what the side effects would be, if any. There were all the lab tests, of course, but we needed a guinea pig for the long-term effects, a human guinea pig. Lab rats just wouldn't do if we had what we thought we had. Not just any *person* would do, either. I'm sure you understand that. If it worked, it could be eternal life, or close enough to it that the human mind couldn't tell the difference. If it didn't work, it would kill the person who took it. In spite of the danger, there were many volunteers."

"I'll bet there were."

"But only one got to take the drug. Eternal life. That was too much to offer to just anyone. Yes, you're right, of course. I took the drug and as you can see, it *does* work, with no adverse reactions. It was subsequently written off as worthless. There was a staged financial disaster that forces us to close the lab, discharge the chemists and technicians with enough severance pay and lucrative new jobs to insure their silence about this place, and that was the end of Jade Pharmaceuticals. Back then, we didn't have the extensive underground layout we have now. I had been out of the country for many years and everything was handled through Mr. Killingsworth and my executive assistant Mr. von Bülow, so there could be no connection between the pharmaceuticals and me, anyway. I was in an entirely different business."

"You're still using the drug."

"Yes. For about thirty years now."

"You're over a hundred years old."

"Oh, yes. A hundred and eighteen this year and fairly agile, I might say. Did you know the record is 130? A Negro woman who claims to remember the Civil War. Nothing to substantiate it, of course. On the new world I'll pass that."

"Maybe."

"More than maybe. Tell me, who do you think I am, Doctor Savage?"

"I worked for one of your companies for a short time."

Damarjiane nodded. "Yes, you did. I remember."

"Dr. Paul Walton, your oil geologist was a very close friend of mine and your executive assistant was more successful in his widely publicized murder trial than I was."

"Yes."

"Clause von Bülow was guilty as hell but he was acquitted. How did you manage it?"

"What makes you think I did?"

Savage just looked at him.

Damarjiane acquiesced with a barely perceptible nod. "Money. Influence. Power," he said. "The judge and the prosecuting attorney were bought. But, tell me, Doctor, how did you put it all together? No one else has."

"Maybe nobody else ever tried."

"Oh, I assure you, Doctor, they have tried. Millions have been paid, people have died and at least one or two have sold their souls to learn my identify. None did. How did *you* do it, Doctor Savage? Tell me."

"On the surface? My conclusions? The ship was the clue. It was owned by Tidewater Oil Company, a subsidiary of Getty Oil. Then there was Jade Pharmaceuticals that just faded away and then re-emerged as Jade Oil. The Palomar Foundation is no doubt funded by Jade."

"It was, in the beginning. We are completely self-sufficient now. Please, go on."

"When did you come back to California?"

Damarjiane raised his eyebrows and smiled. "Oh, I've been here off and on for twenty or so years."

"It must be difficult."

"Not so much so, anymore. I've learned how to hide."

"I'm sure Killingsworth was a big help to you."

"Yes, he was and still is."

"To help you hide your identity."

"Oh, really? You think so, Doctor? You think *he* knows?" Damarjiane came very close to actual laughter.

"You mean he doesn't?" It was Savage's turn to be surprised as he turned to look over at the lawyer who somehow managed to look embarrassed and refused to meet his eyes. "Killingsworth doesn't know who you are? Now that's hard to believe."

"Mr. Killingsworth was recruited, hired and has worked for a man named Damarjiane for sixteen years and he is a very rich man because of it. For most of those sixteen years he reported to Mr. von Bülow, not me. He is loyal and dedicated, as long as he gets paid, but he doesn't know who I really am any more than the rest of the world does."

"That just blows me away," Savage said in resignation to the truth.

"I am pleased that I can impress you." Now, with the references to Tidewater Oil and Clause von Bülow, I'm almost convinced that you really do know who I am." He interlaced his fingers together in front of him obviously enjoying the scene.

"Who is he, David?" Diana insisted. "Do you really know?"

"Yes, I know." He turned to look at the lawyer. "Killingsworth?"

"I bow to your superior knowledge, Doctor. I am indeed most interested."

"Wounds your ego a little, doesn't it."

"Not at all, Doctor. Pray proceed."

"He was *the* richest man in the world back in 1975," he said, looking from Killingsworth to Diana and then to his host. "Everybody believes you were buried at your museum in Malibu."

"Yes. It was planned that way."

Looking at the old man for a few moments then letting his eyes drift from face to face at the table, he focused on the concerned and becoming somewhat bewildered face of Damian Killingsworth then went back to Diana. "He's J. Paul Getty. One of the most successful and the most ruthless oilman of the twentieth century. His death was reported in June of 1976."

As the old man smiled, his lips and cheeks twitched in an uncontrollable muscle spasm. There was a little, he-he-he, laugh. "As Mark Twain said, the reports of my death are premature."

Killingsworth was stunned, DeShane was astounded and this time even Boucree was dutifully impressed. Diana's expression was one of puzzlement.

"You raided the company," Savage accused.

"No. I absolutely did not. It was my company. I didn't have to raid it. Everything in it was mine. The eight hundred million I took, I use to terminate the drug business, start Palomar and keep it alive, built much more of the underground complex, buy equipment, hire staff. We became profitable beyond all expectations, and this is only one of the companies I control.

"Much of the profits from our discoveries have gone into other fields. We have contracts, options, interest on loans, liens, residuals, new discoveries, more than enough to continued indefinitely. Does that satisfy your curiosity, Doctor?"

"Why Palomar? You were already a rich, successful, powerful man."

"Yes, and I was fast becoming a rich, successful and powerful *old* and *dying* man. Even the drug would not keep me alive forever. My body was deteriorating. I knew there was much more to be discovered, perhaps even a way to prolong live indefinitely but with governmental regulations, religion, morality, the miserable millions who would demand it if such a thing was discovered, I had to work in secret. I set up Palomar through Mr. Von Bülow several years before I was reported to have died, never dreaming he would subsequently attempt to kill his wife and be arrested for it. Stupid man."

"But he was acquitted."

"Lot of good *that* did him."

"He got all of his wife's money."

"Huh," snorted Getty, throwing a hand into the air in a gesture of dismissal. "A few million. I would have given him immortality." His hand dropped back into his lap and he looked down at soup bowl as though seeing it for the first time. "Where was I?"

"You were talking about things to be discovered."

"Yes. Things to be discovered." He raised his head and looked at Savage. "The discovery came much sooner than I had ever anticipated. And it worked! The pharmaceutical lab became an electronics lab, and now we have made another wondrous discovery. The world is not yet ready for either one."

"So you kept them."

"Yes. Congratulations on your detective work, Doctor. I am now more convinced than ever that you are the right man for this task. Now, I would like to say that I'm delighted that you and Diana have finally gotten together and appear to be well matched. It will make things so much easier for both of you when she follows you through the Window to the new world where we all may live forever.

DeShane still hadn't a clue what window or what new world they were talking about, but he certainly knew who J. Paul Getty was, and if he was really working for Getty and there was a drug that kept you alive, it would be worth billions. He seriously though about asking Killingsworth for a raise.

Diana knew nothing about him. She was only six years old at the time of his reported death.

"And since it seems to be of some importance to you, Doctor, a divorce has been arranged. There have been no offspring of the marriage so Mrs. Killingsworth will retake her maiden name of . . . of—"

"Monroe," Diana added quietly.

"Yes, of course. Monroe. And if you survive—and we fully expect you to—the young lady will join you and you will produce a child—which we also fully expect—we will know we have a safe, productive new world. As soon as the second Window is perfected and functioning, Dr. Boucree will be the next to go through to begin setting up a Window there."

Boucree beamed over his glass of ginger ale.

"But the main purpose of this dinner this evening and this discussion, was of a more personal nature, intended to provide you with some additional information about your conviction for murder and subsequent sentence of death by firing squad, and your escape from custody. Subjects, I had presumed, you did not wish to be common knowledge.

"Diana knows all about it," Savage replied. "I told her everything so there is no reason why she shouldn't be here. Boucree and DeShane both know too, so go ahead." He coolly sipped the brandy and carefully set the glass beside his plate. "As you wish." The old man savored the liquor and wiped his mouth with a napkin. "But they only *think* they know all about it." He paused again for effect and then continued. "The main issued behind your case, Dr. Savage, was a humanitarian one."

"Mr. Getty," Savage replied, "A man was murdered. I was framed for it. You just said so. What's all this about humanitarianism?"

"You asked me why. That is what I am attempting to explain."

"Framing me was humanitarianistic? This ought to be good."

"Be quiet, boy, and listen. This is one of the reasons I wanted us to be alone when I talked to you. Our business relationship must be based upon honesty if this project and your part in it is to succeed.

"I know you were innocent, that you were framed and should be dead now for a crime you didn't commit because I am the one who arranged it. Or rather Mr. Killingsworth did at my orders." He nodded to the lawyer and received a polite and very respectful acknowledgment. "As with von Bülow, the judge and a couple of lawyers were bought and paid for, one of which, I might add, was your counsel. He put on a brilliant defense and made just enough mistakes to get you convicted."

Savage's face went white and he suddenly felt a chill. Diana was startled. From Getty, she turned to stare coldly at her husband. Dr. Boucree sat bolt upright in his chair and for the first time appeared to be taking everything seriously. DeShane almost dropped his glass. Ashes fell from his cigarette to the polished tabletop but he didn't notice.

"Don't look so surprised, Mrs. Killingsworth." Getty momentarily turned his attention to her. "This sort of thing goes on all the time, you know. Having power and holding onto it sometimes requires methods and means unavailable to the common man. Although some of those methods and means may be deplorable, they are often necessary. You, more so than most, should understand that. I believe among the skills you acquired at Hidaka was the art of manipulation and how to kill in cold blood. What you learned there was to be an assassin." He cocked his head as though asking for agreement.

Reluctantly she gave it in the form of a slight nod.

"Now, to continue. You were a man well known throughout the world, Doctor." Getty looked back to Savage. "One of the very few, perhaps the only one of your profession, a geologist, to capture headlines and media attention. You may be surprised to learn that I followed your career with considerable interest.

"But then you became overly concerned with environmental issues to the point where you joined the Sierra Club, a radical group dedicated to preserving bugs and spiders and old dead trees. But mainly, their purpose was to prevent progress." He held up his hand, palm out. "Please don't say it. I've heard it all before. That's my opinion. May I continue?"

When Savage didn't respond, Diana said, "*I'd* like to hear it."

Getty again turned his attention to her. "Subsequently when Dr. Savage and Congressman Phil Rizzo from Louisiana joined forces and began their campaign opposing the construction of two nuclear power plants one of my companies had contracted to build under government authorization, one in Louisiana and the other in Tennessee, they became dangerous. The fact that the failure to complete those plants would have forced that company into bankruptcy is not of great importance to me, although I dislike failure in any form. The main issue at the time was that those power plants were absolutely necessary to the continued survival of the southeastern United States.

"We have fuel reserves for only a short time. At our present rate of consumption, we have coal left for about a hundred years, natural gas for about twenty or thirty, and petroleum for even less than that.

"But politicians and bureaucrats don't think in terms of more than two, four and six years at a time, the length of their term in office. What happens after that is somebody else's problem, so they are not interested in a long-term solution. Just something right now that will get them re-elected.

"Are you aware, Doctor, that with all of the governmental regulations, committee hearings, Senate debates and red tape, it takes over ten years to get a nuclear power project approved before actual construction can begin? It's true.

"The dangers of nuclear power that you and Rizzo harped on—Three Mile Island and Chernobyl—didn't exist and I could have proven it in time. The nuclear plant at San Onofre, California has been on line and operating for over thirty years without one adverse incident. Unfortunately, time was something I didn't have.

"You know, back in . . . I think it was somewhere around 1915 when I was a younger man, there was a woman I knew who was opposed to the use of electricity and she was quite vocal about it. There were a lot of them, then, but I happened to know this one personally. Her name was Emily Bauhaus and she wouldn't have electricity in her house. She publicly campaigned against it stating that using electricity would kill everybody who tried to use it.

"She was wrong, of course, as history has shown. Today, there are people who believe that using nuclear power will kill everybody. They are wrong, too.

"I am not against conservation," Getty continued, looking from face to face around the table. "But in the struggle between progress and preservation, one must lose. Look at all the black Africans, the Indo-Chinese and some of the South Sea Islanders. They have practiced conservation, living with nature, creating no pollution, and building no roads, using no factories, drilling no oil wells and using no atomic reactors. As a result, they have no medicine, no hospitals, no trade, no government and no civilization. The majority of them are still living in the Stone Age. They have not advanced any in a hundred thousand years. Is that what you would wish for humanity, the way you would want to live?" He looked at Diana, DeShane and Boucree each in turn with a cold, steady gaze.

"You are aware, Doctor," Getty returned his attention to David, "that Congressman Rizzo wasn't interested in the ecology or the good of humanity. He just used those issues to further his political career, and since you were much more of a popular public figure than he, he used you to push the attacks against nuclear power. Most of that came out at your trial.

"He was heavily invested in fossil fuels and any other inexpensive energy source would have eventually wiped out his financial empire. That came out at your trial, too. You learned of it, became enraged that he was just using you and you killed him, or so the evidence indicated. You left the gun at the scene with your fingerprints all over it. The fact of the matter is that he was a dishonest, unscrupulous man and he deserved to be killed. By placing the blame for his death on you, I got rid of both of you at the same time and eliminated the political and environmental objections to nuclear power.

"The murder of a United States Congressman and the highly publicized trial following it redirected the attention of the media and the public. It took the heat off of me and the nuclear energy issue. Much of the red tape was eliminated; the plants were built and have been operating smoothly, safely and efficiently for several years now with no danger to the public or the environment while supplying reasonably priced power to millions of people. Since they are privately owned, that power is not subject to government control, exorbitant taxation, ever-increasing costs or incompetent bureaucratic management.

"Be that as it may, you can, I'm sure, appreciate my reaction when Mr. Killingsworth informed me that you were the best man they had found—perhaps the *only* one—to complete the Window project team. I refused to even consider you, of course, given the circumstances. Subsequently, however, I decided that it was a complete waste of talent not to take advantage of what you had to offer.

"I think you can also appreciate that there was no need to tell you any of this. There is no way you could have ever found out about it. But I want to be honest and truthful with you because I need your loyalty and your expertise, and I believe you have a right to know."

"So it was you," Savage whispered, shocked, horrified, and too choked with emotion to speak aloud. The rage and hate and fury boiled inside him. "You framed me." The years in prison, his career and marriage ruined, his life destroyed, all by this one man.

"Yes, it was me. I did what I had to do. I sacrificed one for the many, a small price."

Savage was traumatized and must have gone into shock for a few seconds. Because of what he had just heard, suddenly there was an unexplainable calm within him; the hostility toward this man who had wrecked his life and put him in a cage waiting to be shot to death vanished as though it was inconsequential. Everything just shut down, he felt nothing, and he spoke with detached coldness to Getty.

"I guess there isn't anything to say now, is there. You took my life and my freedom from me and now you have given them back, maybe tomorrow to take it again when I step through this Window of yours into that alien world somewhere out there. Maybe you're just telling me this because you are afraid I might already know, that I suspected or maybe somebody might tell me tonight what you've done. Or it's just your conscience that's bothering you. I don't know. Maybe your reasons are sound and you were justified to do what you did, to sacrifice one to save the many as you put it. There are a lot of maybes. However, it's difficult to be understanding when you are the one being sacrificed. The *many* don't seem to matter."

"I'm not asking for your forgiveness or even your understanding, Savage. I'm just telling you the way it was."

"A small price, you say," Savage said as he rose from his seat with deliberate slowness, his hands dangling by his side. "My life. But it's not a small price to me."

"Please take your seat, Doctor. I'm afraid that's not all."

"What else is there?"

"After an intensive investigation, the report of your tragic death in that hotel fire has been determined to be inaccurate and it is known, or at least suspected, that you are still alive and on the loose. The authorities, casting about for somebody to blame, have heaped it all on the prison warden. What's her name?" He looked toward the lawyer.

"Bennett, sir," Killingsworth replied.

"Yes. Mrs. Bennett was dismissed from her job since she was the only one they could find to blame it on. I am informed that she has become an extremely bitter and vengeful woman using her own resources to track you down."

"You destroy everything and everyone you touch," Diana said, her voice filled with contempt. She got up quickly, walked around the table and put her hand on her lover's arm.

Ignoring her, Getty went on. "It is only a matter of time until the authorities will no doubt eventually trace you here. They have great resources. The only reason the incorrect report of your death has not been made public yet is because of embarrassment on the part of the authorities and the hope that Mrs. Bennett will continue to remain quiet for a while longer. However, there is no cause for concern. I anticipated it and we can handle it."

Savage could no longer hear him. Pulling free of Diana's hand on his arm he stood up, turned abruptly and left them—Diana, Dr. Boucree, DeShane and Killingsworth—oblivious to their searching looks, and he left Getty looking at the empty chair and chewing his lower lip, his dark-spotted hands clutched in his lap.

Diana started to follow but DeShane intercepted her, shaking his head just enough for her to see. Killingsworth took a sip of his brandy, smug in the discovery that he was working for J. Paul Getty then took another spoonful of the cream of cheese soup. His lip curled slightly. The soup was barely tepid.

Both of the guards snapped to attention as Savage burst through the doorway and headed for the hall. Seconds later DeShane followed. The waiters and the two serving cooks dressed in white shirt and trousers with white aprons and tall paper hats became alarmed as the two men surged from the dining room. The sliced, rare beef, the gravy, the potatoes, the steamed asparagus tips were all getting cold. The crisp green salad was getting warm.

Savage walked quickly through the house and out through the back door into the evening air with DeShane trailing along behind at a respectful distance. Occupied with his own thoughts, he was not aware of his pursuer or the signal that passed silently from DeShane to two of the uniformed guards at either side of the exit door.

Along an inlaid brick path wandering through the shrubs and flowerbeds, Savage strolled with his hands in his pockets, his shoulders slumped and his head bowed. Coming to the stone bench against which he had almost crushed his skull, he sank onto its cool, hard surface in total defeat. They were after him and soon he might be on death row again, awaiting the dawn and the sound of footsteps in a dark hallway. Moreover, he may well be about to die tomorrow when he stepped through the Window. He sat and he brooded.

All those years he had languished in that cell knowing he was innocent, at first expecting any day to be cleared and released, his life and career returned to him, and then finally realizing that they never would, he sought revenge against the man or men who had framed him. If he could only get out, if he could find them, he would make them pay. He thought about it, dreamed about it, plotted and planned, killed the man, the men, a thousand times in his mind. Miraculously his wife would realize he was innocent, return to him and he would have his kids back. If he just knew who had done it and why. If he could just get out he could find out who and why. That's all he needed to know. Who? Why?

Now he was out. He knew who and why, and there still wasn't a thing he could do about it. His wife wasn't coming back and he'd never see his kids again.

He was just sitting there in remorse feeling sorry for himself. That's all he was doing. Feeling sorry for himself. That was not what he had been conditioned to do. The past was past and this was the present. Getty may have put him in prison but he had also gotten him out, given him a new life and offered him an opportunity no other man had ever been given, an opportunity beyond imagination. His wife and family were gone but there was Diana, a young, beautiful woman who had given him her love, her body and who would, if he survived the new world, be his girl, his lover, his mate in the hostile environment of an alien planet. There was the probability that there might be more children on the new world. If he survived.

Hell, life was not all *that* bad after all. Who else got a second chance like this? Nobody *ever* made it off of Death Row. Alive.

Time to pay for what he had been given.

Getty *had* been honest with him. He was right again, too. There was no way could he have ever found out. Killingsworth sure wouldn't have told him and probably nobody else in the world knew. Getty was not trying to fool him or trick him, like with poor old Boucree. There was no way that Dr. Boucree, at his age, would be sent through the Window to survive in a primitive, uncivilized wilderness, and Getty was not about to lose his resident electronic genius while there was still work to be done here. Probably almost everybody knew that; everybody but Boucree.

When the authorities did come, he wouldn't be here. They could search but they would never find him. They could look at the Window—if they ever got that far—and they would see what he first saw, an elaborate three-dimensional television set. He was safe.

What was he brooding about? He had known that somebody framed him. Did it really matter who? Moreover, if he took revenge on Getty or Killingsworth, would that give him back the years he spent in prison? Would that give him back his family? He was free now and he would remain free.

He stood up, flexed his arms and raised his head to breathe in the fragrance of the flowers, the trees and the evening air. All right. It's over. That was five years ago in another life and another David Savage. Here was the opportunity man had dreamed of for a thousand years, to go to another world. What a hundred million people would give anything for, kill for, die for, he was being offered on a platter. What the hell's the matter with you, Savage? You used to be an explorer. So go explore. Take it! Take it and run with it. It's yours!

He slammed a fist into his open palm, feeling the power in his biceps and shoulders. He was a man again; a new man and he would survive. He started walking back to the house with confidence and determination in his step.

A short distance away but concealed, DeShane, watching him closely, smiled and strolled back toward the big house behind Savage. The two uniformed guards who had divided their attention between Savage and the surrounding gardens stepped back and concentrated on the darkness around them and anything it might conceal.

CHAPTER SIXTEEN

"KONNICHI WA, TOKUSHIMA-SAN," WAKAYAMA said, entering the richly furnished penthouse office and bowing in front of his boss' massive teakwood desk. Wakayama wore an expensive but conservative brown suit with matching tie and a starched white shirt. The jacket was expertly tailored to completely conceal the shoulder holster containing a German SIG, 9mm, 9 shot 225 double action automatic containing Black Talon, 147 grain hollow points. It had a muzzle velocity of 2,200 feet per second and was one of the most deadly handguns made. It rendered Dirty Harry's .44 magnum little more than a toy.

Wakayama was a trained investigator and had connections with intelligence agencies and corporate security departments throughout the world. In addition, he was a saboteur, espionage expert and a cold-blooded killer. He was not married and never would be. Like many men in his position with Japanese companies since World War II, he spoke fluent German, but unlike most others, he also spoke French and English fluently. He had been with Tokushima for eleven years and had never been paid a salary. Anything he needed he purchased and charged to the company.

If he needed cash, he obtained it from the company cashier with a voucher. There was no fund established for his retirement for it was doubtful that he would ever live long enough to retire.

"Well?" Heroshi Tokushima asked his chief of security impatiently.

"We have found Fumiko, the woman you call Diana."

There was a loud expulsion of breath, a long sigh of satisfaction. "It took you long enough." Tokushima also wore an expensive suit, white shirt and tie, as did almost all Japanese businessmen. The few women on the management and executive level in Tokyo corporations wore suits with skirts at or just below the knee and blouses buttoned high.

"The security precautions were elaborate, sir."

"Go on."

"First." He flipped open a small notebook taken from his inside jacket pocket. "Fumiko is married. Her husband is an American lawyer named Damian Killingsworth, much older than she."

"Oh." There was just a hint of disappointment in Tokushima's voice at the mention of a husband.

"She is currently living with her husband in Southern California, at an orchid farm owned and operated by the Palomar foundation."

"Palomar?"

"Hai. Fumiko's husband is a very influential and unscrupulous individual, currently the chief counsel for Palomar."

"Palomar. Then it *is* Damarjiane."

"Yes, sir. He has been spending a great deal of time there lately. Just by good fortune we have a man on the inside they know nothing about."

"At Palomar?"

"Hai."

"Very good, Wakayama. Describe it to me."

"There is a large house, well furnished, luxurious grounds and gardens and almost a hundred employees. Landing field and hangers three miles away connected by a paved road. Many other buildings on the property, mostly greenhouses. However, one building in particular purporting to be a large metal garage and storage facility for tractors, wagons and tools has very unique characteristic. People go in but they do not come out. Well-dressed men and sometimes women enter this building where there is nothing for them to see or do. Yet they often stay for hours, even days. It is the most heavily protected building on the property. No windows. One large door, one pedestrian door. Electronic, sound and camera surveillance. There are armed guards everywhere."

"Armed guards at an orchid farm?"

"Hai. And our inside man has the impression that something very big is happening there or is about to happen, sir."

"What?"

"As yet, we do not know. However, we have cultivated the acquaintance of a young woman who is a computer instructor. Her name is Marci. She gave computer lessons to a man there named Boucree, an electronics expert who worked for an American defense contractor for many years developing guidance systems for fighter aircraft. It is said he was being considered for President Reagan's Star Wars defense system before he left office and the project was canceled."

Wakayama flipped a page in his notebook. "And she also gave instructions to a man named David Savage. American newspapers and localized television have reported that a Doctor David Savage is an escapee from a prison in the eastern American province of Pennsylvania, although he was reported to have did in a fire several months ago."

"The same man?"

"In all likelihood."

"Then he did not die in the fire."

"No, sir."

"Damarjiane is hiding him?"

"It appears so, sir. And this man Savage has been seen entering and leaving the heavily guarded storage garage, often in the company of a young, beautiful woman with reddish-blond hair."

"Fumiko?"

"Hai."

"What else do we know about this man?"

"He is a geologist, explorer, adventurer, very well known in America a few years ago. He has worked for several American oil companies and is credited with at least one major oil field find."

"Why was he in prison?"

Wakayama flipped several pages in his notebook. "He murdered a prominent United States politician, a Congressman."

"Why?"

Wakayama flipped another page, scanned his notes and replied, "We don't know. I can have it researched."

"No, it's not important. What else?"

"It is believed that Fumiko is using the skills she learned at Hidaka-sammyaku to train him."

"For what?"

"That is not yet known, Tokushima-san."

"Find out."

"Hai, Tokushima-san. And there appears to be a recent romantic relationship between this Savage and Fumiko."

"Oh?" Tokushima looked up sharply. "What kind of romantic relationship?"

Wakayama spread his hands. "They're sleeping together."

"This has been verified?" He felt unexplained anger building inside him and, inexplicably, jealousy.

"Yes. Almost certainly."

"And her husband?"

"He apparently knows but does not seem to be overly concerned."

"Strange for a Westerner."

"Yes, sir."

"You said something very big may be happening there. Diana is there. An escaped convict is there. Damarjiane is there too. Over a quarter of a million American dollars in electronic equipment purchased by Palomar is probably there too. Are there orders pending for more equipment?"

"Yes."

"What?"

Wakayama turned another page in his notebook. "They ordered four lasers, LP 2309 series, two electromagnetic generators, CV 500, capable of creating an electro-gravitational field above one G, a multiversatile control board sophisticated enough to launch a Titan missile and ten thousand feet of anodized insulated cable with specified ohms. Six months later, they ordered exactly the same things again. Now, six months after the first order was filled, an order has come in from a company called Electron in Fontana, California for the exact same equipment. That order is pending."

"Find out what they're up to."

"It could get . . . expensive."

"It is worth the expense to know."

"Hai, Tokushima-san. Should we advise the American authorities that this man, Savage, is there?"

"Yes, but do so discreetly so there will be no connection with us." That done, Tokushima immediately dismissed Savage from his thoughts. "Damarjiane may have made some major electronic discovery. It would be to our advantage to be among the first to know about it."

"Hai, Tokushima-san."

"Do we have anything else?"

"There is a man at Palomar. A limousine chauffeur. His name is Mike or Mac. He is a very unhappy employee."

"Why?"

"There is an indication that he may have been involved with Fumiko before she went to Hidaka-sammyaku. Now, she is no longer interested in him. It is believe that he can be gotten to."

"Put our inside man on the storage garage. I want to know what goes on in there. Get to the chauffeur. Find out why Fumiko is training an escaped prisoner in survival techniques."

"Yes, sir."

"If necessary, could we successfully mount an assault force?"

Wakayama was shocked. "On Palomar?"

"Hai."

"To take Fumiko?" He couldn't believe what he was hearing.

"And anything else Damarjiane has of value."

"You have become obsessed with this woman."

"What if I have?"

"Gomen nassai, Tokushima-san," Wakayama said, bowing low to add emphasis to the apology. "I will research it."

"Do so."

"It could be very dangerous."

"It could be worth it."

"As you wish, sir."

"Still nothing on Damarjiane?"

"No. We know Damarjiane is an alias but we have had no success in learning his true identity. The man never appears in public, almost never meets with anyone in person, there are no photographs of him and very few people even know he exists."

"You have found no references to Damarjiane?"

"There was one."

"Well?"

"Damarjiane is the name of a sailing ship built in the 1800's."

"Odd. Find out what is going on at that orchid farm."

"Yes, sir."

CHAPTER SEVENTEEN

I T WAS AT 9:00 AM Wednesday morning, April 2nd that Dr. Boucree, Phil Dendron, a laser technician and five other members of the research staff who had been on the project from the beginning gathered in the Window lab along with Diana, her former husband and even Mr. Getty who was viewing the incredible achievement for the second time since its discovery. All of the technicians and scientists had been hired by Boucree or Killingsworth and none of them had ever met the Director of the Palomar foundation before today, and none had a clue as to his true identity. They were almost as curious about him as they were about what would happen to David Savage when he walked through the frame into whatever was beyond.

When first experimenting with the phenomenon of the Window, they had seen the dog, once shoved through the frame, take two steps, and crumple to the ground. Getting shakily back to its feet with tail dragging, the animal staggered clumsily away and was never seen again. For all anyone knew the animal could be lying dead just out of view of the Window.

DeShane was there, at Savage's insistence, being given his first look at the amazing secret he had guarded for so long. He stood to one side wide-eyed as one of the technicians explained to him in whispered tones what it was and what was about to happen. Diana hovered close, clutching David's hand. Killingsworth stood with his usual detachment beside his boss who was seated in a swivel desk chair.

David Savage wore military style camouflage dungarees with high boots laced to just below his knees. Around his waist was a web belt holding a twenty-shot Heckler & Koch semiautomatic in a leather holster. A fully automatic rifle loaded and with the safety off, hung by its sling from his left shoulder.

They had discussed and argued at length about what he should carry and wear when he stepped through the Window. An oxygen mask, body armor, even a complete self-contained spacesuit had been suggested but in the end, simplicity won out. If he was to survive there, he needed to live and breathe in that environment.

Canned and packaged foods, clothing, weapons and ammunition, a radio and TV scanner, everything they could imagine he might need had already been crated and sent through where it lay scattered on the ground in the new world. Nothing remained except for David Savage to take that one step through the Window into . . . what?

"Good luck, Doctor," Boucree said, extending his hand. "I wish I was going with you."

Savage looked at Boucree and the outstretched palm but he did not grasp it. Boucree knew that there was something more to this moment, this historic step into the unknown, and he suddenly realized that Savage knew it, too.

Almost on cue, Getty said softly, "There *is* one more thing you should know, Dr. Savage." He turned away from the Window and looked directly at Savage as he spoke. "I have waited until now to tell you for reasons which will become obvious to you immediately." He hesitated for a moment, glancing at Boucree's empty and unclasped hand sinking slowly to his side. "I told you that the authorities would not be waiting for you when you came back, nor could they come get you and bring you back. The reason is very simple. The trip is one way. Once you step through, we don't know how to bring you back. You can never return to this earth again."

"I suspected that," Savage said, his voice as soft and low as that of Getty's. "And I'm prepared for it." There was no expression on his face, no hint of emotion in his eyes as his gaze met that of the Palomar Foundation director. This time it was Getty who had to look away first.

Diana's hand slowly released his and he turned to look at her face, to penetrate her eyes with his and try to see into her mind, to lock her to him. Not a word was spoken between them as they stood face to face, only inches apart, each with their own thoughts, their memories of the intimacy between them and their feelings for each other, oblivious in that moment to everyone and everything around them. The silence in the room became almost a physical thing laying like a giant hand upon those there with its power pressing down on them. It must be the same as with a soldier going into a battle from which he knows he will never return.

Savage had left many times to go exploring, often into dangerous situations, but saying good-bye to his wife had never been like this. She never came to see him off and their good-byes at home were quick and almost emotionless. It was the same with his children, just a casual goodbye because they knew he would be back. He would like to see his kids once more, just one last time before disappearing forever. He should have asked Getty to arrange it, but it was too late now.

"You are free, Doctor, as I promised," Getty said, breaking the silence. "With a fabulous adventure ahead of you and the future of all of mankind in your hands. You are Leif Ericson, Christopher

Columbus and Neil Armstrong all rolled into one, the explorer of a whole new world. You will be more famous than any explorer in history. How I envy you."

"Yes. I'm free now," Savage replied without turning to look at the old man. "An explorer of a new world, and I'll be blind in another six months. Alone and blind on an alien planet from which I can never return and from which there will be no rescue. If I live. Is that your idea of fame and freedom?"

"We do what we have to do, Doctor. That's the way we survive."

"Good-bye, Diana," Savage said.

"No, not good-bye, David. Not good-bye, Au revoier. Until we meet again. And we will."

He turned abruptly to the Window but for a moment was frozen by her words, choked with emotion. "David, I do love you."

Afraid to respond or look back or hesitate another second in fear that he would lose his courage completely and they would have to force him through, he took a long stride forward, stepping through the Window and disappearing forever from the face of the earth.

PART TWO

CHAPTER EIGHTEEN

THERE WAS HARDLY ANY sensation at all, almost no feeling. For an instant, the tiniest fraction of a second it was as though he had jumped into a large pool of freezing water. He was very cold and could feel pressure all around him. Then as quickly as it had come, it was gone, almost before he even realized it was there. One moment David Savage was in the underground laboratory at the Palomar orchid ranch in Southern California saying his last wordless good-bye to Diana, and the next moment he was dropping two feet to the grass-covered ground in a small clearing surrounded by what appeared to be a dense forest.

The vegetation in which he was standing appeared to be normal grass and weeds as would appear on earth, varying shades of brown and green that came up to his ankles. Bushes, tall weeds, and huge trees grew all around him, underbrush and fallen tree limbs strewn about obstructed his view of what lay beyond the small clearing in which the Window had deposited him. Scattered all about were the boxes and crates of materials and supplies he would need which had preceded him through the Window. More would follow when he made a request. Anything he needed or wanted, he had only to ask.

A bright sun shown through the tree branches above and he could feel some of its warmth through the military dungarees. The leather of his boots was thick enough to stop the fangs of a snake—if there were any snakes here. The natural sounds of a forest reached his ears, sounds of the creaking and rasping of tree limbs, the window moving through the leaves and there was a call with might have been a bird or an animal of some kind, but it was too far away to be heard clearly.

A second after he hit the ground right between two large crates, he crouched, looking about him in every direction, trying to see into the thick woods, listening for anything unusual. He held the fully automatic M-16 ready in both gloved hands, his finger tight on the trigger, alert to any sudden danger.

They had argued bitterly about the laser-sighted rifle, the pistol loaded with bullets called Silvertips that exploded upon impact and the other weapons Getty, DeShane and Boucree insisted he take. Stepping into a new world fully armed and ready to kill was reminiscent of the Europeans invading North America and killing the Indians, Savage argued back. It was not right.

"We have millions of dollars and thousands of hours invested in this project and you are an intricate part of it," Getty had said. "If something happens to you, it would set us back months, even years."

"And you have your own life to protect, Doctor," Killingsworth added. "I really don't think you want to die now."

"I'm not asking you to start killing everything in sight," Getty continued, "just be prepared and as Mr. Killingsworth said, protect yourself if something does happen. You have carried weapons before on your exploration trips so this isn't anything new to you."

"Diana certainly wouldn't want to stand and watch you killed in front of her eyes simply because you refused to take precautions and protect yourself," Killingsworth added with just a hint of sarcasm in his voice.

"And if something *does* happen and I *am* attacked by someone or some*thing*, is there any-body ready to jump in and help me?"

"You know the answer to that, Doctor," Getty said dryly. Their argument won out and he went through the Window armed to the teeth and ready to kill anything in front of him. Any movement, any sharp sound, anything menacing would be met with a hail of bullets and instant death. However, nothing happened and there was nothing there to attack him.

An ache in his chest made him suddenly realize that he was holding his breath, subconsciously afraid to draw in the first lung-full of alien air. It could be deadly poison that would kill him in an instant or saturated with deadly bacteria for which he had no immunity and he would die in seconds. Or worse, he would die slowly and painfully over hours or days. Hemorrhagic fever immediately came to mind, causing profuse bleeding from every orifice of the body. A dozen other equally horrific images flashed through his mind as he stood there feeling his chest tighten and fire begin to spread through his lungs. Do it quickly. Let it out and inhale deeply. Don't fight it. Just like the gas chamber used in state executions.

They had talked a lot about dying on Death Row, those condemned men with little else on their minds. "Getting shot hurts," they said, like they'd been there and knew. "The chamber is easy. Just don't try to hold your breath, man. When you hear the pellets drop in the acid, just take that first deep breath and it's all over. You're gonna die. Get it over with."

There was no other way. Now. Do it now!

The air was warm, sweet, clean and heavy with oxygen and moisture. There was the smell of wet grass, decaying wood, fresh dirt, and a faint scent he couldn't identify. It was something he had never before encountered, a new sensation and it was titillating like a narcotic. He breathed again, forcing all the air out of his lungs then inhaled deeply. Once more. Another deep breath. Another. He was still alive. He sniffed the air as an animal might, savoring the fragrances it held.

Maybe the whole thing about an alien world somewhere in the universe was just a big joke and he really was in somebody's wooded back forty just outside of Boloxi, Mississippi. Wouldn't that be a laugh.

"Well, hello there, Farmer Jones. I just popped in for a few minutes to take care of the gophers and them old bole weevils with this here rapid firing rifle—"

Then the gravity hit him.

It was something they couldn't measure with their instruments from the other side. Like the first seconds in a fast elevator going up, it was pulling him down like a huge weight on his legs, shoulders, head and back. He weighed another twenty-five or thirty pounds, and just raising his arm took extra effort. The rifle in his hands was heavier and he knew that a bullet fired over any distance at all would drop much more rapidly, the effective range reduced significantly. He would have to readjust the sights on the weapon to compensate as much as possible.

This certainly wasn't Biloxi, Mississippi or anywhere else on Earth. There was no doubt at all about it now. He wasn't in Kansas any more, Toto.

He turned to look at the Window to reassure them that it was 'so far, so good' in the new world and panic suddenly seized him, above and beyond the gravity. He gasped aloud. There was nothing there! No Window and nothing to indicate that it had ever existed. He was alone somewhere, on another planet with no way back and no connection to the world he knew.

It seemed as though, by some sort of unimaginable magic, he had suddenly come into existence on this world, possessed of memories of a place and time that did not exist and would never exist again for him. And in thinking about it, that was probably the most descriptive and realistic explanation he could come up with.

He looked to his right then left. Nothing. He slowly turned in a complete circle. Still nothing. There was no Window. Looking back to where it should have been, just standing there staring into nothing, the shock and confusion on his face must have been obvious. Suddenly, about five feet above the ground the air began to shimmer like heat waves across black asphalt on a hot summer afternoon. Out of the shimmering waves, an object appeared in the air from nowhere, took shape, and hurtled to the ground with a thud near his feet. It was a slender metal, chrome-plated rod about a foot long, a piece of laboratory equipment selected for his weight. A large piece of paper was attached to it with plastic tape and there was writing on the paper. He knelt down and read.

Are you all right?

Reassurance from out of thin air. The Window was there and they could se him. The connection with his own world had not been broken; he just couldn't see it. He wasn't alone. He breathed a sigh of relief and looked up at where the Window should be and smiled. They were watching him. They must have seen his panic and understood his sudden felling of isolation. Somebody scribbled a note on a piece of paper and they attached it to the first object they could find to carry it through the Window. A paperweight. From his kneeling position looking up at the Window should be, he said, "I'm fine. It just takes a little getting used to, that's all."

Moments later, there was the shimmering air again and something rectangular and flat dropped to the ground in front of him. A clipboard with a paper attached had been tossed through. They were thinking now, no longer grabbing the first thing in sight to use for weight. Shortly they would have a sophisticated system for passing messages.

We can't hear you. No sound from your side. Write a note and hold it up, or use sign language.

This was something they had overlooked, or perhaps they didn't know. If they had realized it, they could have taught him sign language like deaf people use to communicate and there would have been no problem "talking" to Palomar.

Still kneeling he made a circle with his thumb and index finger that he held up for them to see while nodding his head several times. Having reassured them the best he could, he now needed to reassure himself. He took a compass from his shirt pocket and opened the case. The needle didn't move. He rotated the case and the needle moved with it. No magnetic north. The compass was worthless, but it was no big surprise. They had discussed that possibility.

He held up the compass for them to see, made a slashing motion across his throat, and dramatically tossed it away. He hoped they would understand that it wasn't broken; it just didn't work here. He would know shortly when they did or didn't send another compass.

Getting to his feet, he walked slowly to the edge of the small clearing, his rifle ready. Better find out what sort of critters live here," he said softly to himself. "And what danger I'm in." He also looked for some sign of the dog they had put through the Window months before.

Noting the location of the sun overhead, he stepped carefully into the woods and circled the clearing, keeping the jumbled array of boxes and crates in view as he walked. It only took about five or six minutes but because of the gravity, he was exhausted when he completed the circle. It was as though he was carrying a pack full of supplies on his back and wading through six inches of mud.

Returning to the clearing, he dropped to his knees and took several deep breaths. A fall of just five or six feet could break bones, his own weight crushing down on his ankles and feet could cripple him if he tripped, stumbled or stepped wrong. Here, he wouldn't just twist an ankle, he would break it.

Still on his knees, using the clipboard and the back of the paper already on it, he began to write a note with the felt-tipped pen in his shirt pocket. He thought of something. They had insisted that he take the pen. They must have known there was no sound from his side. Why didn't they tell him? No. How could they know?

Finishing the note he held it up in front of there the Window should be so they could read it.

Heavy gravity.
Tire easily.
Air seems OK.
No magnetic North.

After several minutes, he climbed back to his feet and went five yards further into the forest, circling the clearing again, carefully stepping over dead branches and around piles of brush. This took almost fifteen minutes and he almost collapsed on the ground in the small clearing, his breath coming in labored gasps. The back and under-arms of his shirt were soaked in perspiration.

He rested longer this time, his body aching and his feet sore. How was he ever going to survive here? He took a long drink from the canteen of water at his side. This must be what it's like for the astronauts after they've been on the space station in zero gravity for awhile. Nevertheless, they get used to the weight again. He would get used to it, too.

Another ten to fifteen feet in, another circle before he collapsed, rested and then did another. Using this pattern of ever widening circles, he was able to explore the area around the camp for fifty yards in just a little over three hours. He was looking for anything menacing that might attack him or harm him in some way, an animal, a poison plant, something in the grass or in the trees. But he found nothing more dangerous than the gravity.

His first few steps were slow and careful; he looked at every tree, every bush, every weed and everything in between. He looked for any sign of civilization, something manufactured or altered. He watched and listened for any sight, any sound, but the noise of his own steps cracking twigs and scraping against the brush was all he could hear.

He went back to the clearing, propped his rifle against a tree close to where he would be working moving the boxes and crates together to one side of the camp. He allowed himself a ten-minute rest then broke out an ax and a brush knife to clear the ground where he would put up the heavy, double-wall canvas tent directly in front of the Window where he and everything he did could be observed, recorded and studied. The tent would serve as his house, laboratory and home base.

How long would it take to get used to the gravity? Would he *ever* get used to it? Nobody had ever experienced anything like this before.

He took off his shirt and worked bare-backed, pulling the last rope tight, securing the makeshift structure with anchor pegs driven a foot and a half into the ground with the back of the ax. A cot to sleep on, a table assembled from plywood and plastic which took up half the space in the tent, a three drawer filing cabinet made of chemically treated, moisture resistant and fire retarding corrugated paper, and two canvas deck chairs furnished his new home. Extra clothing was packed in another moisture resistant chest at the foot of his bed. Food and anything else necessary to his survival would be sent through the Window daily, or whenever he needed it. The technicians at Palomar would work in shifts so that while he was in view of the Window he would be monitored every minute of every day by men whose only function was to sit and watch, record and report, and provide what he wanted.

The new watch he wore on his wrist was designed for the thirty-six hours of the planet's rotation as it related to the twenty-four hours of Earth's rotation and the twenty-four hour face on a military watch. Two series of numbers circled the dial. The outer-most, in black, at the top, the number 36, then 1, 2, 3, on around the face back to the 36. Add a zero to each number and you had the 360 degrees of a compass set in 10-degree increments. A watch used in conjunction with the sun became a compass if you knew how to do it. Since there was no magnetic north here, it was the best he had.

The second series of numbers, in red, starting at 24, then 1, 2, 3, around to the 24, one Earth day. He could push a button on the top left of the watch and get a digital read-out in the center of the watch face in hours, minutes and seconds. The second button on the left side gave him a digital read-out of the time on Earth, Greenwich Mean Time, coordinated with the time in Southern California.

The top, right button made the watch face glow softly to tell the time at night, and the bottom right button threw it into a mini-computer that needed an instruction book to explain all that it could do.

The watch told him he had been alternately working and resting for almost eight hours and had it not been for the physical conditioning, the tortuous training Diana had put him through, he wouldn't have lasted an hour on this hostile world trying to drag him down into the very dirt beneath his feet. The sun was getting low in the sky and it would be dark before he finished his camp. It might have been nine in the morning on Earth when he came through but it was more like mid afternoon here. He readjusted his watch to show 1500 hours Earth time. On this planet, it was 2230 hours. This was going to take some getting used to.

He set up a battery-powered floodlight and hung two more lights from the ceiling of the tent. There was a gasoline-powered generator he would hook up when he had time. He mused for a moment about asking them to send him a pizza through the Window, but he was just too tired to eat, too tired to do anything except fall onto the cot and try to sleep. If he was still alive in the morning, there would be a lot to do.

The twenty-five pound weight was now on his chest and he had trouble breathing. He tried to raise his hand and wipe away the perspiration dripping from his face, but his arm was just too heavy to lift.

It was dark when he awoke gasping for breath. The weight was still there, pushing down on him. He slowly raised his arm and looked at his watch. Two hours. He had been asleep for two hours. Just two lousy hours. He wasn't going to make it this way.

What if it started to rain? In this gravity, the raindrops might be like small hailstones. A small branch falling from a tree could kill him. How could he survive?

Suddenly, he was hungry. He hadn't eaten anything for over ten hours and he was starving. Get up. Order that pizza and have them send it through the Window. No, fix something here. Build a fire and cook something. Got to survive here. This is home now. Cook something. Would fire burn here? There might be something in the air that could prevent it. Time to find out.

Putting on his shirt and crawling off the cot, he stumbled outside and began to dig a shallow pit with the long, thick-bladed fighting knife strapped to his side. He banked it high all around with dirt and collected twigs, small branches and thicker limbs for the fire. He used the dry wood from the broken-up boxes and crates as kindling and struck a match. The kindling caught and he had his fire. It looked, burned and behaved just the way a fire would on Earth.

They offered to send him a gas grill but he rejected the idea. He had cooked many a meal on an open campfire and a mechanical grill was something he didn't need and just one more piece of equipment he didn't have room for in the small camp.

He was still more tired than hungry. Not having the strength to break out the cooking utensils and fix something to eat, he just sat cross-legged on the ground in front of his tent looking intently into the fire while ignoring the cans and plastic containers of food all around him. The M-16 rifle was across his knees and he really began to think he had been taken out of one prison only to be put into another, worse than anything men of Earth could devise. From this one, the only escape was death.

He could not begin to recount the number of days and nights, weeks and months he had spent in the North American rocky Mountains, the Eastern Appalachians, South America, North Africa and half a dozen other places around the world sitting in front of a campfire just like this. Sometimes with a guide or another geologist, but usually he was all alone on assignment from one company or another to look for oil, minerals or precious metals. He had huddled in a fur parka, in a tent near the North Slope in Alaska before the first of the big wells came in, plying his knowledge of the terrain and the probable locations of oil to earn him his living. Someday, maybe to make him rich.

But when it was all over, be he successful or not, he could always go home, back to civilization, back to the big house in Denver, a lush green lawn in summer, drifts of snow across the walk in winter, home to his family and the wife he loved. The homecomings had been terrific, the kids all around him, his wife in his arms, holding him, kissing him. Days or weeks, sometimes for months he had been gone, but he could always come home and they were there. Likely as not that evening on CNN there would be an item about Doctor David Savage returning from wherever he had been accompanied by a file clip of him in khakis with the rifle slung over his shoulder and the stupid grin on his face. People loved him.

It had been exceptionally hard for him at first and there was a lot of bitterness, but mostly it was just a lack of understanding. Sitting there in that jail cell waiting to go to trial, with no warning at all his wife had him served with divorce papers claiming extreme mental cruelty and expressing fear for her safety, claiming that she was afraid he might kill her and the children, too. Where did she get such an idea?

She never visited him, wrote to him, she never even asked if the charges against him were true. He never heard a word from her or the kids after he was arrested. Shortly after the trial started, he received a letter from his bank in Denver saying that the joint checking and savings accounts, the stocks, bonds and IRA, all amounting to almost a million and a half dollars, had been withdrawn, closed, cancelled, sold and transferred with everything going to his wife. He had nothing left even to pay his attorney. Two weeks after the spectacular trial was over and he was transferred to Death Row, he received a copy of the final divorce decree and a letter from one of his former neighbors, the only one of his friends, neighbors and colleagues to stay in touch with him. It said that his wife had married a Denver businessman, had his parental rights terminated and petitioned the court to change the name of his children from Savage to that of her new husband. Since he was a convicted felon, the court granted the petition immediately. He never saw her or his kids again.

"What's to understand, man?" the prisoner in the next cell asked him. "The chick needed to get laid, dude, she needed some bread, income, like somebody to pay the rent, yo know. She needed somebody to take care of the brats. You wasn't there and it don't look like yo done ever gonna be."

"Yeah! Lest'n you knows som'thin we don't there, old Savage man," another prisoner shouted out.

"Bread?" Savage retorted. "She got over a million dollars from me. Think that's enough bread?"

Up and down the corridor the condemned men listened to the conversation. They laughed and they added their own comments. "Yeah, well, listen heah, o'l Savage man. What's yo blaming yo o'l lady fo? So, she took yo bread. Where yo gonna spend it in here?"

Laughter. "There ain't no hope for yo ass. Yo's a dead man. Yo just ain't laid down yet." More laughter. "She just needs to get on witf her life and yo ain't no part a dat no mo. Yo dig?

"Now my o'l lady, she come to see me a couple a times after I got here, afore they put me here on the dead row, and I toll her, I say, bitch, yo gets yo fuckin ass out a'here and don't chu never come back. Yo gos out and yo finds yoself a man to take care o'yo and them kids cuz lest'n o'l Gabriel comes down here outta da sky and toots his horn right now, I ain't never gonna get out of this here place alive. And I ain't had no million bucks to give her neither. Dat's a fact."

"I guess you're a lot smarter than I am, Jimbo," Savage replied. "I would have never figured it that way."

"Sheeet. Ain't no nother way to figure it, o'l Savage man. Dat's just the way it be. And as to me be'n smart, yo got dat all wrong. If'n I was fuckin smart, I'da never got busted. I mit'a even been honest."

"Hey, Doc," still another voice from far down the corridor called. "Were you honest? Were you one of the good guys?"

"I thought I was."

"See where it got you!" More laughter from the men of Death Row.

"Killing a US Congressman, now that's really something, Doc. Me, I just wasted a couple of lousy cops."

"I didn't kill anybody. I'm innocent. I was framed."

"Course yo was, o'l Savage man. We was *all* framed. Ain't none of us guilty in here." Hoots and laughter from the condemned men waiting to die.

"How'd they take you, Savage? Was it a righteous bust?"

A year ago, he would not have known what the term, a righteous bust, meant, but he did now. "On paper," he replied. "The Feds with the locals in back-up kicked my front door in at five in the morning, swarmed into the house, scared hell out of my kids, dragged me out of bed and handcuffed me in my pajamas.

They're yelling, 'we have a search warrant, you're under arrest for murder, you have the right to remain silent, anything you say can be used against you in a court of law.' My wife's screaming her head off, the kids are crying and screaming, they come up with an old army .45 I used to carry six or seven years ago and they say it's the murder weapon. They drag me out of the house and put me into the back seat of a police car and haul me off to jail. I'm fingerprinted and put in a cell. I don't have a clue what's happening. Next day they tell me I murdered Congressman Rizzo and I'm going down for it."

"And you didn't?"

"No, Jimbo, I didn't."

"Then you just might be the last innocent man."

"Haaa. Ha. Ha. Ha!"

His head jerked up and the voices from years in the past, visions of stark cells lining the corridor all vanished. Dreaming. He had nodded off and it was all just a dream. Jimbo had gone to the gas chamber quoting from the Bible as they strapped him in, sitting there with his eyes closed and a smile on his lips as they put the hood over his head. He understood. He knew what it was all about. He played the game and he lost. He took that first deep breath and he paid the price.

Savage threw more wood on the fire and it snapped and crackled, sending up tiny sparks to burn themselves out and disappear into the night. A breeze rustled the branches of the trees. A sound in the distance, an animal voice or a trick of the wind.

Prison was far behind him now. He was free with a whole world to explore and conquer. He could never go home again. He was somewhere in the galaxy, a million, trillion miles, a hundred thousand light years from Earth and he could never go home. He had no home to go back to anyway. So make the best of it. Eat something. No. Not hungry. Get some sleep. Good idea. Tired. Think about it tomorrow.

The fire was beginning to burn low again and he cradled the rifle in his arm. Getting to his feet, he staggered into the tent and zipped the flaps closed. On the cot, he managed to get another two hours of sleep, this time dreaming of Diana. The rest helped. So did the dream. Now he needed to eat.

Turning on the lights, he peeled back the foil of what the military used to call K-rations, a thick, quick-energy chocolate bar. Looking at his watch, he saw that several hours of darkness remained so he sat at the table and opened his journal to the first page where he began to write a detailed description of what he had seen and done and experienced since stepping through the Window. First, he noted that the atmosphere did not appear to be poisonous—so far—and he had experienced no deadly bacteria—so far—then he wrote about the gravity, the crushing weight pushing down on him and the constant discomfort he felt. Next, he wrote about the quiet sounds he heard, the sunlight he saw through the forest roof, the twigs, the plants and trees that were like nothing he had ever seen before. He tried to describe the oxygen-rich air and the smell of green growing life in the forest.

Must be the oxygen, he thought. Making me remember things, like I've had too much to drink. Can't concentrate on what I'm doing. "Voices from the past," he said aloud. "And a long ways away."

As complete as he could make it—he even put in his theory of something in the air stimulating dreams and memories—he closed the journal, lay back down on the cot with the rifle beside him and closed his eyes. Getting sleep in bits and pieces wasn't good but it was better than no sleep at all. In the morning, he would set up his equipment, continue his exploration, and begin collecting samples of everything he found for analysis and classification.

Laying there in the darkness he tried to keep his mind a blank, think of nothing, remember nothing, ignore the gravity, just relax and sleep, think of Diana. No! Don't think about Diana. That would be even worse. Her touch, her kiss, the feel of her against him, her hair in his face, her mouth on his, her body . . . oh, no, don't think about that. Don't thing about anything.

After a time, he dozed again and finally he slept, but fitfully with erratic, twisted dreams of Death Row, Diana, Killingsworth and the Window all mixed together in bizarre and frightening scenes. Strange noises during the night didn't quite awaken him but they registered on his sleep-drugged mind causing him to toss and turn on the canvas cot.

What if there's no life at all out there in the vastness of endless space, on all the planets circling all the stars in all the galaxies? What if Earthman is unique in the entire universe, the only thinking intelligent being in existence anywhere? Man will spend all of eternity searching the immeasurable expanses of infinity desperately pursuing but never finding another life form like itself.

It was still dark when he woke with a start, drenched in perspiration, fumbling for the flashlight he had placed on the floor within easy reach. Something real had awakened him but he couldn't recall just what it was. A noise, a sound, a long, low, mournful moan or cry in the distance as though a lost, lonely soul was lamenting his plight. Savage had heard it before on Death Row, doomed men crying out in their sleep. Or maybe it was just a dream and there was nothing out there at all.

He *had* to get some more sleep. Tomorrow was going to be rugged.

The only books they had sent with him were scientific texts and reference journals. Nobody had anticipated that he would have enough free time on his hands or be bored enough to indulge in fiction or escape literature. So, there was nothing to read, nothing to occupy his mind and nothing to do.

He picked up his rifle and went back outside to build up the fire from the few coals that remained. The light from the fire reflected back weakly to him from the surrounding forest, flickering and dancing in the in the darkness.

With the rifle across his knees, he sat on a log slumped over the fire and with eyes closed and head drooping, dozed again. He dreamed that he was back in the Sierra Madras or in some foreign jungle—he wasn't just sure because it was all hazy—on assignment for Standard Oil looking for the right place to drill that first well, home in Denver siting on the couch with his wife beside him and his children playing at his feet, or walking hand-in-hand along the red brick pathways of the Palomar estate with Diana.

The next few hours passed with incredible dreamy slowness, but finally the first traces of dawn appeared over the treetops. His scientifically trained mind took note of it. The sun had set in that direction. He held out his arm and pointed to his right as he stood in front of the tent. It's coming up in that direction. He pointed with his left arm. So we'll call this east, and *that* is west. Counterclockwise planet rotation, the same as Earth, the first firm fact to report back to Palomar.

He looked at his watch. It showed 0200. That couldn't be right so he reset it for 0600, 9 AM on this world. He was still tired and did not feel even remotely rested because of the crushing weight on him, but slowly, laboriously, he began to prepare breakfast over the open fire. He had to eat something besides that candy bar.

Ignoring the packaged stuff, he pealed off several slices of bacon sealed in plastic wrap and laid them in the metal skillet. He cut up a whole potato and dropped the pieces into the sizzling bacon grease. He broke fresh eggs in the skilled and watched them sputter and fry and turn dark. It had been a long time since he had done that. There was probably some butter or margarine somewhere among all the things Palomar had sent, but he didn't feel like searching for it. He dipped a chunk of the hard, French bread into the bacon grease to soften it and enjoyed it more than toast.

After cleaning his dishes, he set up a large white canvas screen on a tripod facing the Window and turned on a battery-powered, overhead projector. They would be able to read and record this a lot easier than his notes on a piece of paper held up in his hand.

He quickly wrote about the planet rotation, placed the paper on the projector and let the magnified image stay on the screen for fifteen or twenty seconds. They would take half dozen photographs of it; somebody would probably write it down in shorthand and someone else would read it into a tape recorder. Then he projected the pages of his journal, one by one, onto the screen. They, too, would be recorded.

Another team or perhaps several teams would be assembled somewhere, perhaps at Palomar or probably elsewhere, to review, evaluate and attempt to decipher the information he was going to send them. There would be a chemist, a botanist, a geologist, top men and women, experts in almost every field of science, well paid and sworn to secrecy, to analyze every word, theory, fact and concept they received. The most sophisticated computers in the world would be at their disposal accessing information, comparing data, extrapolating and concluding. Any question he asked would be answered by the best minds using the library accesses throughout the world.

Morning brightened and became day. Using a spade and shovel, he dug deep holes at the edge of the clearing and buried several of the waterproof cases of materials and supplies. Putting them underground would afford him more room in his limited campsite and they would be there whenever he needed them, harder to steal if there was anybody around to steal anything.

Sitting at his table, he turned on the battery-powered AM/FM radio and slowly moved across the dial from 1 KC to a thousand MHz. Nothing. Not a sound, not a hiss, no carrier wave, not even static. There was nothing there.

On the TV set, he went from channel one through channel 400. Again, nothing. No sound, no picture, no nothing. Later he would break out the high frequency stuff, up to a million megahertz, a billion cycles per second, then onto single side band. If there *was* anything out there, radio, television, radar, microwave, sonar, he would find it.

He asked them to send him four signs, each weather proof and a foot square, containing a bold letter of the alphabet. When they arrived, he took the first one and walked to the edge of the clearing toward the rising sun. Whoever made the signs had enough sense to understand what he wanted and sent along a hammer and some nails. He tacked it to a tree. It showed a large capital letter, E. On the opposite side of the clearing, he hung the second sign showing a capital, W. The other two signs indicating North and South were also hung and he turned his small clearing into a giant compass, the directions based on the passage of the sun overhead. Later he would add in the degrees from zero through 360 that he hoped would help him develop a sense of direction.

That accomplished and again taking up his rifle, he re-entered the woods to continue his every-widening circles around the camp, resting after each one. After about four hours of slow, careful searching, he had explored an area a hundred and fifty yards deep on all sides and had encountered nothing in the form of animal life. The trees, bushes and other vegetation appeared to be perfectly normal, but he was unable to identify or classify any of them. They were a completely unknown species.

Back in his camp, he spent considerable time writing in his journal and then preparing page after page of detailed information to be projected onto the screen for eyes to read and cameras to record. They had sent him a voice activated laptop but he had spent so many years making handwritten notes and preparing reports in longhand that it was just easier for him to continue doing things that way.

He sent general classifications of what he had found but without a detailed analysis. He listed his findings as a "broad-leaf tree similar to a Red Maple with heavy, rough bark, but there are no veins in the leaves and the bark is almost like a solid sheath covering the whole trunk," and "tall bushes with berries, thick stem, small leaf, deep green in color, life obviously by photochemistry, but there aren't any roots. It sort-of sits there on the top of the ground and grows. Doesn't make any sense. I can't even figure what holds it up."

At about 11:00 AM—1600 hours here—he asked Palomar for lunch and was rewarded with two rare roast beef sandwiches wrapped in aluminum foil to keep them warm and tossed through the shimmering field followed by a plastic carton of ice-cold milk. They must have had the food already prepared and were just waiting for him to ask for it. Diana had to have been behind that. She was there too, watching, anticipating his every wish.

He unpacked and set up the delicate scientific instruments he would be using in his analysis of the environment. A microscope, a gasometer and chromatography for classifying gasses in the atmosphere, a spectrograph, chemicals, test tubes and a Bunsen burner attached to a propane bottle. When he finished, half the large table was covered and he was ready to continue his exploration and sample collecting. The results of the analysis breakdown and identification of air, water, soil, light, plant and animal life would be printed out by a high-speed laser printer in technical terms he wouldn't even begin to understand. Nevertheless, he would project them onto the screen and somebody a Palomar would understand them. They knew what instruments to send him, what tests they wanted run and his incomprehension of the results was irrelevant.

The gravity didn't seem quit as bad now. It was still there but not crushing down on him as it had when he first appeared on this world. Maybe he was beginning to get used to it already and after a few days or weeks he wouldn't be bothered by it. But that remained to be seen. In the meantime, he would struggle along, doing the best he could.

The gravity was determined to be 1.16G, atmospheric pressure of 16.5 PSI, equivalent to about 500 to 1000 feet below sea level on Earth, barometric pressure at 30.91 inches. On Earth, pressure that high would insure good weather. However, he wasn't on Earth.

The atmospheric breakdown began to print out. He watched the numbers come up:

> Nitrogen (N_2) 73.05
> Oxygen (O_2) 24.75
> Argon (Ar) 00.90
> Carbon dioxide (CO_2) 00.25
> Unknown 00.51
> Neon (Ne) 00.12
> Unknown 00.0019
> Hydrogen (H_2) 00.00005
> Methane (CH_4) 00.0009
> Ozone (O_3) 00.000007
> Unknown 00.0002
> Unknown 00.000002
> Known toxins 00.00

Carbon dioxide was low, oxygen was high, nitrogen was low. Plants lived on carbon dioxide and gave off oxygen. Animals breathed oxygen and gave off carbon dioxide. No carbon monoxide, no identifiable dangerous gasses. Everything else was just about the same as Earth except the methane. Methane was given off by dead and decomposing plants and animals, and the figure shown was more than four times that of earth. Color reflections appeared to be the same, he wrote in his journal. Yellow is yellow, blue is blue. No exceptions so far.

Almost everything absorbed and reflected light. Grass, the leaves of many plants and trees absorbed the entire range of the visual light spectrum except green which they reflected. Therefore, the eye, receiving reflected light, only saw the color green. Snow, some limestone and the peddles of certain flowers absorbed no light at all, reflecting all of it and the eye saw white. Black is the absence of color, the entire visual light spectrum being completely absorbed and nothing reflected.

He got up, stretched, rubbed the back of his neck, and flexed his shoulders. He looked at his watch. Three o'clock; 2230 hours here. He had been feeding information into the machines and sending the results to Palomar since just after dawn, just sitting in a chair and doing almost nothing physical. Still, he was exhausted. The pressure and the gravity.

Send me something to make me sleep, he wrote on a lined pad. But without a drug hangover. He projected it onto the screen.

A few minutes later a small weighted clear plastic envelope materialized in the air and dropped to the ground. Savage picked it up. Not recommended, the note inside the envelope said. Effects and side effects unknown there. It was signed, Worthington.

SEND IT!

He wrote the words in huge letters and projected the demand onto the screen. A few more minutes passed and another weighted plastic envelope fell to the ground. It contained two white capsules. If these don't kill you, I'll send more, Worthington had written.

He wrote a reply and projected it onto the screen. Too late in the day to start off on an expedition, too tired to do anything else and too bewildered to make rational decisions. These pills better work.

Closing the tent flaps, insuring that all the instruments were shut off, he undressed. Using a large wet, chemically treated cloth he cleaned himself as best he could from head to foot before collapsing naked onto the cot with the M-16 beside him

Damn stuff better work were his last thoughts before he sank into a deep, drug-induced, dreamless sleep that lasted twelve hours.

CHAPTER NINETEEN

H E AWOKE REFRESHED AND rested, turned on the lights and dressed. With several hours of darkness still remaining, he left the tent, started a fire, heated water for coffee and began fixing breakfast. By the time he finished, assembled and packed his equipment and supplies, the sun was beginning to come up. He looked at his watch. A little after nine. Just about right on. He had survived a second night on the new world.

Using the sun as his only point of reference, he set off in an easterly direction, attempting to maintain a straight course to determine the extent of the forest, hoping it would not continue indefinitely. A pack on his back held food, water, a roll of toilet paper, a camcorder, a still camera and a number of containers for samples he intended to take for later examination. The M-16, extra ammunition, a hatchet and a thick-bladed hunting knife hanging from his belt completed his equipment. This added another fifty pounds to his weight and he knew he would have to stop and rest often. The leather combat boots would protect his feet from almost anything and the camouflage clothing would help him blend in with the forest should he encounter anything from which he needed to hide.

Parts of the forest were thick and choked with underbrush and deadfalls making progress slow and tiring. Each time he stopped to rest—and those times were frequent—he mentally thanked Diana for all those miles she had made him run and all the exercises through which she had put him.

With the rifle slung over his shoulder, he used his knife and hatchet to cut low hanging branches, and to slash marks in the trees blazing a trail he could follow back to the camp. Getting lost would only insure his death from starvation, and he did not intend to die now.

There was every shade of green he could imagine and the leaves of some trees spread out in shapes that could only be described as unearthly. The tree bark was different colors of brown and black and went from bamboo smooth to huge slabs of bark sticking out in all directions. Size, too, was strange. There would be huge monsters the size of sequoias along side maples and poplars.

After four hours, he estimated that he had traveled only five miles through the wilderness with no break in the forest and no contact with any type of animal life. There was almost no air movement in form of wind or breeze so there was correspondingly very little leaf movement. There weren't even any insects he could notice. But with the noise he was making crashing through the woods, anything alive could hear him coming a long way off and would hide.

Seated with his back against a tree, he drank some water from his canteen and ate a granola bar wrapped in green foil. The temperature was only in the low seventies but once again his clothing was soaked in perspiration from the exertion of just moving.

"I'm going to need some salt tablets if I keep sweating like this. A lot more clothes, too. Maybe I can get them to send me a washing machine." He put the canteen away and climbed to his feet. "Only problem with a washer and dryer is, where do I plug 'em in?" He chuckled to himself and started off again. "Wonder if they put an extension cord through the Window, would it transmit electricity? We need to try that."

Four more hours and four more rest stops. Making the same general progress, he may have covered another five miles. At this rate, it was going to take a week to go anywhere at all. He was about ready to give up and begin the return trip to his camp before he collapsed in utter exhaustion. He would have to fix a meal, one granola bar wasn't gonna do it. If he started back now he would be 16 hours on the trail—if you could call this a trail—and covered some twenty hard miles on the round trip. Tomorrow he would try another direction. South maybe, as best he could determine from the position of the sun and his own creation of the giant compass. There just *had* to be a better way to tell directions on this world.

Go on a little further, find a better place to build a fire where the dead leaves, fallen branches and dry undergrowth weren't such a hazard. Don't want to set the woods on fire.

Shouldering his pack and taking up his rifle, he walked on around trees and bushes, fought off low hanging limbs and looked for a little clearing where he could rest again and eat before starting back.

Just up ahead the trees began to thin and he saw what appeared to be an opening in the woods, just what he had been looking for. It was the first open area he had encountered in the dense forest of strange, unidentifiable trees and bushes, weeds and grass, so he plunged on to investigate. Drenched in perspiration and again beginning to stagger with each step under the heavy gravity, determination alone kept him going.

There were even fewer trees now and he quickly realized that it was not just a clearing ahead; he had finally come to the edge of the forest. He pushed his way through the last bit of undergrowth, climbed a gentle ridge and stopped, looking out at the scene before him. Spread out in front of him was a rugged valley many miles wide with gentle slopes leading down to a river at the bottom far in the distance. Low trees, bushes, some huge rocks and outcroppings of granite dotted the scene while an elongated grove of taller trees stretched from the river up the far side to a plateau on the opposite slope more miles away. Knee-high grass covered the ground and waved gently in the first breeze he had felt.

Close to the river on both sides, the vegetation was thicker and taller, and there were a lot more trees, some resembling cottonwoods on Earth. There were no structures, no roads, no people, no animals, no signs of life. Nothing, anywhere. He was absolutely alone on a world which might be exactly like Earth in the Cenozoic era, Tertiary period, sixty million years ago when small bands of scraggly little primates first ventured out of the thick, dark jungle because of fear of predators or in search of food. On the flat, lush plains of Africa, they eventually adapted and learned to walk erect to finally become men.

The human mind cannot conceive of a time span of fifty or sixty million years. Indeed, most find difficulty grasping a thousand years or even a hundred that is longer than they will live. Some cannot go beyond fifty years or even ten, and a few live from year to year and some day-to-day, grasping nothing beyond.

If this was indeed what he had found, a young world just beginning, what would be the impact of suddenly bringing thousands, maybe tens of thousands of Earth people here to live, build and multiply? Was Mr. Getty right and this would be the salvation of humanity, the continuation and perpetuation of the human species and the creation of a new world and a better civilization of man?

"Or was Diana right," he said, thinking out loud, "and such a migration of people chosen by the Palomar Foundation to populate a virgin world would pollute, rape and eventually destroy it as they were destroying Earth?" Was he to be the last word, the final authority on whether or not they came? Was he to be the savior of mankind or the destroyer of a new world?

Clearing an area two feet square, he dug a pit and banked it. Gathering twigs and branches, he built a fire and prepared to wait for it to burn down to coals. While waiting he took out the camcorder, set it for wide-angle and recorded the valley spread out before him. Panning slowly from right to left, he got in as much of the spectacular scene as possible. This would be something for the people at Palomar to see.

Then he took out a notebook and began listing information the film would not show, such as distance, height, depth, and degree of slope. All of these things were estimated but over the years, he had gotten pretty accurate at it.

The clear blue sky was completely cloudless as far as his eye could see. No haze, no pollution, no exhaust fumes, no factory smoke. He wanted to examine the stream, the rate of flow, the gravel, the sediment, the soil around and leading to it. But there was time. He needed to eat and rest. Another day or two to become more accustomed to the gravity, and he needed to replenish his supplies, bring additional instruments and equipment to conduct his examinations.

Opening a sealed package of dehydrated beef stew, he dumped it into his mess kit skillet, added water from his canteen and put it on the coals to heat. And that was another priority he needed to address, a way to support himself here. He could not expect to be supplied through the Window forever and it would certainly be impossible when—if—more people came. There *had* to be something on this planet to eat. He just had to find it.

As he ate, he constantly searched the valley and the hills beyond for movement, some kind of animal, any life at all. Disappointed after half an hour, he covered the fire pit and prepared to return to his camp. When he got back, he would ask Palomar for stronger contact lenses.

Back in the forest again, he began following his blaze marks to the campsite. He had much to ponder as he searched his soul and his conscience for answers while he collected more samples for classification and analysis. Better to be busy and immersed in the work for which he was trained than to sit around philosophizing and start feeling sorry for himself again. Or worse yet, get too wrapped up in his own new-found self-importance.

His sample containers were quickly filled as he selected bits and pieces he did not recognize as being the same ones surrounding his camp and thereby available for collection and study at anytime. And only once did he get lost and have to retrace his steps to find the trail he had marked.

He was forced to rest more often on the return trip and it appeared to be mid-afternoon when he finally stumbled into his camp exhausted and hungry again. He had intended to approach with stealth in the event someone or some*thing* had invaded it while he was gone, but he suddenly emerged into the small clearing without any recognition of where he was. That would change, he knew, as he became more familiar with the area surrounding the camp and more accustomed to the gravity. For now, however, the damage was done, he was there and that was that. Nothing seemed to have been disturbed and there was nobody and nothing there.

Not wanting more of the dehydrated food and too tired to fix it anyway, his thoughts were of more roast beef sandwiches and ice cold milk. Dropping his pack and rifle, he hastily scribbled a note and held it up to the Window. Only a few minutes later, the sandwiches and milk appeared, dropping to the ground at his feet. Attached to the container of milk was a note asking, did you find anything?

There wasn't much he could say about the valley he had found and he didn't want to inspire false hope in a discovery that might prove to be nothing of importance. So as he ate and rested, feeling the pain in his shoulders and back from the pack, he wrote several pages describing his trek through the forest and briefly mentioned the valley. He indicated the samples he had brought back and the analysis he intended to conduct in breaking them down into their basic components. He also mentioned the electrical cord. Putting the pages on the projector, he made his report to Palomar then asked for a TV monitor so he could show the tape he had made of the valley. From the other side, they would record it off the screen.

With the tent-flaps wide, he settled again at the table to begin a study of the items that he had brought back in the plastic containers. There was an ache in the back of his neck and he was hungry again. Looking at his watch, he was surprised to discover that he had been at the task for almost three solid hours. The sun was behind the trees and it appeared to be early evening, but his watch said 1330. He readjusted it again for 1800, 6 o'clock.

Four pages in his journal had been filled and two dozen sheets covered with large block letters lay on the table close to his hand. Chemical formulas, numbers and symbols, aminos, chlorophyll and toxins, nutrients and fiber as best as he could break the stuff down. He was not a chemist and his knowledge was limited.

Although the flaps of the tent were tied open and both lanterns were lit, his eyes burned from the close work. Tomorrow he would move much of the equipment outside and work in the daylight. They could send a smaller table through the Window, broken down in sections like the large one, and he could set it up in front of the tent and work in the open air. If it rained, he could move everything back inside. It was time he set up the generator and got the electric lights working although he wasn't looking forward to the sound of a gasoline motor banging away.

He put the pages he had completed on the screen to be read and copied at Palomar, requested the additional table and ended the report with three handwritten words on a separate sheet. *How about dinner?*

Twenty minutes later, the air shimmered and several plastic containers fell to the ground. He assembled a thick charbroiled steak, two baked potatoes, and two kinds of vegetables in his metal mess pan and poured thick, brown gravy over all of it.

The meal was accompanied by a bottle of vintage wine from Mr. Damarjiane's private stock—this surprised him—which he dumped into his canteen cup and drank as he ate. Exploration trips in Saudi Arabia or the South American jungles had never been like this.

A plastic packet of papers fell through the Window along with three crates, one almost two feet square. The papers included instructions as to what they wanted him to do and the first crate contained an enlarging Polaroid type camera attached to a microscope, both thickly padded with Styrofoam so that the drop to the ground wouldn't jar anything loose. They wanted pictures of the microscopic examinations of the vegetable life, even the dirt. They would photograph them from their side, enlarge them even more and study the microscopic structure. There was even a remark about his electrical cord idea. They were afraid to try it in fear that the flow of electricity might in some way affect the Window.

The second crate, smaller than the first, contained a Geiger counter. He switched it on and immediately the instrument began chattering and clicking wildly while the needle swung across the dial and hit the peg. Either this place was hot and he would be dead from radioactive poisoning shortly, the Geiger counter was defective, or things just didn't work the same way here as they did on earth. He hoped for the third option.

The last crate contained the TV monitor that he set up in front of the big screen so it could be seen through the Window. Using a patch cord, he attached the camcorder to the monitor and showed them the valley.

The shadows lengthened and night set in. Exhausted from the long day's activities, his stomach filled and the wine dulling his mind, he closed the flaps of the tent, undressed and fell onto his cot. Without the sleeping pills, he was asleep in minutes.

CHAPTER TWENTY

I T WAS STILL DARK when he awakened but the night was mostly gone. He had slept for fourteen hours, his body rejuvenating itself, preparing for another day. No dreams this time, no nightmares of Death Row and being stood up against a rock wall to be shot. No low, mournful howling to disturb his sleep and even the gravity bother him somewhat less. Best of all, he had lived to wake up to another day.

He dressed, rebuilt the fire in front of his tent and fixed his own breakfast again. They were watching him and he could have asked for anything he wanted to eat, but the eggs and sausage he prepared in the metal skillet over an open fire were better than anything they could have sent him. He ate slowly, forking the food directly from the pan and waiting for the first light to break through the treetops.

The outer dial on his watch said 0830 when the sun first appeared. Maybe he was beginning to get it right, finally. His new contact lenses, pair of glasses of the same prescription, and the second table were sent through. He intended setting up the microscope and camera to begin the analysis of the samples he had brought back to camp but his heart was not in it and his mind was not on it. This could take several days and he was anxious to return to the valley he had found. The analyses could wait. Palomar probably would not agree to it so he didn't tell them.

Inside the tent near the back where they could not see him, he stuffed a change of clothes and enough food for several days into his pack along with binoculars and the same equipment he had taken previously. Matches, water, toilet paper, a 100-foot rope, a machete and his weapons completed the load. He would continue the analysis the rest of today but tomorrow morning at dawn he would head back to the valley.

That evening he moved everything inside, zipped the tent flaps closed and tried to get as much rest and sleep as he could. In the morning he ate, wrote a brief note telling Palomar that he would be gone for three or four days and set off through the woods before they could reply and order him not to go.

His sense of direction seemed to be improving. Occasionally he looked back to see the blaze marks on the trees he had left on the first trip. He moved through the forest with more ease and was forced to stop and rest less often. He emerged on the rim of the valley overlooking the river only a few yards from where he had come out the last time.

Establishing a temporary camp, he built a fire and fixed himself another package of the dehydrated stew soaked in water from his canteen. While it was heating on the hot coals, he surveyed the valley floor with the binoculars. Once or twice in the far distance, he thought he caught a hint of movement but he was never able to bring anything into focus through the glasses. Perhaps just the wind moving the trees or whipping up a puff of dust. He started a fresh page in his notebook, sketched and wrote down everything he saw in the event something happened to the camcorder.

Insuring that the fire was completely out and presented no danger, he cleaned his dirty dishes, picked up his equipment and moved carefully down the slope to the river, looking in all directions as he walked. He looked for holes in the ground and trails through the grass, he listened for sounds that might indicate animal life, and he thought he might at any minute see some form of early man step from behind a bush and regard him with wide-eyed curiosity. Just what would Ramapithecus or Neanderthal Man have done had a twentieth century man carrying an M-16 come strolling through their land of one million BC?

Approaching cautiously and finally kneeling down beside a wider area of the stream where it moved more slowly, he tested the clear, rippling water with tiny amounts of chemicals and found it contained only two elements he could not immediately identify. It appeared safe to drink and tasted much more refreshing than the lukewarm contents of his canteen that he emptied into the dirt. This part of the river would be a natural watering hole for animal life and he looked around carefully for any tracks, droppings or signs.

A few tall, greenish brown plants with large flowered yellow and black heads and dark green, saw-tooth leaves closely resembling very thick-stemmed sunflowers stood bowed and appeared withering several feet from the bank on the opposite side of the stream. They had a number of thumb-sized surface roots reaching out two or three feet before disappearing into the ground. They were all that was there. No tracks. No signs. That was odd.

He moved upstream, walking carefully along the banks of the river, his rifle slung over his shoulder but his hand always near the Heavy HK automatic in the holster on his belt. The river widened, moving more slowly, narrowed and flowed swiftly within its banks, twisted and meandered at random through the broad valley. The going was easy and he covered what he estimated to be six or seven miles before he finally dropped his pack and sat down on a stone outcropping to rest only a foot from the edge of the stream and beside a stand of the tall plants he had encountered earlier. These, however, appeared healthy, rising some six to seven feet into the air on their stems, many thicker than a man's forearm. He would sever a piece of one of the leaves to take back for examination.

A gentle breeze flowed around him and he sniffed the air like an animal, savoring the variety of scents and fragrances it carried. Rich, clean and invigorating, he could sell this stuff for a fortune if there was some way to get it back to Earth.

There was hardly any sound, no more than that made by a serpent slithering over a rock and the touch on the on the back of his neck was as gentle as a whisper. Without thinking, he would have slapped at it, a pesky insect annoying him, momentarily forgetting that he had encountered no insects. But he heard the warning in time. Later, sitting beside the fire at his temporary camp attempting to recall and analyze the incident, he found that he could not even begin to describe it. It was a voice that was not a voice, a sound or maybe a thought, even an emotion, an impulse that wasn't really there but which clearly and positively warned him of eminent danger. It came only a second before the attack.

Letting the rifle fall to the ground, he suddenly launched himself forward and dove headfirst over the bank into the river. The current caught him and carried him several yards downstream tumbling and spitting in the deep, swiftly moving stream before he managed to fight his way to the shore and drag himself out of the water. Gasping for breath, he lay on the bank trying to realize and understand what he had just done.

From a calm, relaxed position, seated comfortably on a rock with the rifle across his knees, he had suddenly and without apparent cause thrown himself fully clothed into the river and nearly drowned. This was not the act of a rational man. Neither was hearing voices that weren't there.

He crawled onto the shore and lay leaning on one arm with thoughts of insanity going through his mind. There must have been a reason for what he did, there had to be. He had certainly not gone instantly insane and tried to drown himself.

There had been danger. He was threatened. He had sensed it. He heard it, or *thought* he had heard it. Some sound or something in his mind. He had been sitting there sniffing the air. Maybe there was something in it, some airborne narcotic or hallucinogen that affected his mind and his reason.

Turning slowly, he looked back upstream to where he had been sitting before his wild plunge into the water. His rifle and pack lay where he had left them, but to his astonishment, hovering over them were several of the plants he had been seated beside. Their thick stems were curved over and the large, flowered heads bent down, almost touching his pack. They moved! The things were animated. He watched in horrified fascination as one after another of the huge plants bent slowly toward the pack as though inspecting it, and then straightened up.

They were large enough and their spiny leaves long enough so if they were strong enough they could grab and hold him while they fed. Carnivorous plants! Perhaps they were akin to the Dionaea muscipula, the Venus' Flytrap growing in the southeastern part of the United States. But more closely related to the huge Rafflesia arnoldii of southwestern Sumatra and Borneo, discovered by Sir Thomas Raffels and Dr. Joseph Arnold in 1818 and the inspiration for the 1963 science fiction movie, *Day Of The Triffids*. The plants were mobile and they fed on fresh, living meat. He had been their intended meal.

No wonder there were no tracks or animal signs at the natural watering hole he had found further downstream. The plants he had seen there appeared withered and sickly. They were starving. There *was* animal life here and they had learned to avoid the plants and the places where they gathered.

The plants—there were more than a dozen of them—had formed somewhat of a circle around the pack and that meant they could move. They were not anchored to the ground as were most plants. He thought about the bushes with no roots he had found near his camp. Were they related to these? Were they carnivorous, too? Could they move around like these did?

The only question now was just how quickly they could change positions and locations. How fast could they move? Did they simply wait for unsuspecting prey to venture in among them, or did they scurry swiftly across the ground to encircle, trap and fall upon the victim, slashing, killing and eating? The thought almost made him sick.

To retrieve his equipment he would have to duck in among them to grab it before they got him, or he would have to lure them away from it somehow. However, using himself as bait did not immediately agree with him. The edges of those saw-tooth leaves could well be poisonous or they could exude some kind of paralyzing toxin to incapacitate the victim while the plant fed.

The options on retrieving his rifle and pack were suddenly taken from him as the tall, colorful plants swung their large heads toward him and began to creep slowly in his direction. They spread out in a closely spaced line and picked up sped as they moved toward him. With their multiple root/tentacles acting somewhat like tank treads, they easily made their way over rocks, fallen tree limbs, whatever was in their path and quickly began forming a half circle in front of him with the river to his back. More leaves unfolded from each side of the stem, some of them over three feet long and ten inches wide. The upper part of the stem and the flowered heads waved slowly back and forth as though from the wind, but there wasn't any wind. Just a slight breeze, barely strong enough to affect a blade of grass or move a leaf. He would have to go back in the water and swim for it or attempt to break through the line.

He drew the Koch from its holster and took careful aim at one of the flowered heads. The heavy slug would blast a hole in it the size of his fist and the noise might frighten away the rest. If they could hear. Did plants hear? Some people believed they could and talked to them just like another person. His finger tightened on the trigger.

Before the hammer was half way back, another thought came to him. In all the years that followed, he was never really sure if the idea had been his own or like the inexplicable warning that drove him suddenly into the river, it was planted in his mind by a force, an intelligence beyond his comprehension. Or maybe it was just his common sense taking over, reason returning after the shock of the river and the moving plants.

You can't kill a plant with a gun! You cut it down.

Nodding slightly as though agreeing with himself, he lowered the hammer on the HK, replaced it in the holster and slowly got to his knees. The machete was still strapped to his pack so he pulled the long hunting knife with its twelve-inch blade from the sheath on his belt. He climbed to his feet and faced the plants. He had to find out what these things could, would do and if he could fight them. If not, he would be forced to abandon his food and equipment. If they could enter the water he would no longer be safe even there.

Going to a half-crouch, the knife held in a loose grip in front of him, he took a step forward in the fighting stance Diana had taught him. A quick slash at the leaves and then a deep thrust into the stem just under the flowered head followed by another slash to sever the flower from the stalk. Take them one at a time. It might work. But there were a dozen of them so he planed for a hasty retreat and a quick dive into the river if the attack failed. He took another careful, shuffling step forward toward the closest plant. The polished blade flashed in the sunlight.

Two of the broad, saw-tooth leaves of the plant moved toward him in slow motion as though to grab or encircle him. Quickly he slashed at them, severing six inches of leaf from the end of one. Another plant moved closer, extending its grasping leaves. In a flashing arc of the blade, he cut into those. A thick liquid began to ooze from the severed edges and drip to the ground.

The plants began to move back. He watched with amazement as, one by one, they slowly crept over the rocky surface of the riverbank until they were out of range of any lunging attack that he might make. There they stopped as though regarding him and awaiting his next move.

He stepped toward them again, his knife ready to slash and stab. They moved away once more. It was more than an action/reaction move. The plants seemed to be aware that he was capable of inflicting injury upon them and intended to do so. Intelligence! Could they know what the knife was and what he could do with it? Had the damage he inflicted on the two plants somehow been transmitted to the others? If so, how? There was no audible sound.

Were they more animal than plant? Did that flowered head house a brain capable of thought, the stem hold a nervous system? Or was it just the simple fact that their victims never fought back?

Mobile, intelligent plants with some form of communication among themselves, perhaps a sound beyond his ability to hear or a smell he couldn't detect. That would account for their knowledge of the knife and what it could do, if that was indeed the case. Maybe they had encountered something like a sharp blade before and remembered it, or perhaps the same warning he had received might now be warning them. What if they were telepathic? The implications were staggering.

These mobile, meat-eating plants might even be the predominate life form on this world. That would be something for the Palomar Foundation to think about. Send through the scientists, the businessmen, the financial wizards of Earth and have them gobbled up by a bunch of plants. Diana would be amused by that.

"Well, if you guys aren't going to do anything else, I'll be on my way," he said aloud. Keeping his knife ready, he walked slowly along the bank toward his pack and rifle. The row of plants parted to allow him through and, maintaining a respectful distance, trailed along behind him. He returned the knife to its scabbard, dug through his pack and got them documented with the camcorder.

Even with the knife now out of sight, the plants remained back. He wondered what would have happened had he put a bullet through the stem or the head. Would they eventually die or would it be like shoving a pin through the stem of a rose; no effect?

With his canteen refilled from the river, ever mindful of the swaying stalks behind him, he picked up the rifle and shouldered his pack to continue the trip along the river. The plants did not follow.

The ground began to rise, slowly at first and then sharply above the river, and in an hour he was climbing slowly, picking his way up the face of a severe ridge step by laborious step, the sharp edges of the rocks cutting through his gloves into his hands and into the soles of his boots. The gravity was a constant factor again. The river had cut deeper into the rock and was moving faster, making a soft roaring sound as it tumbled down the ridge.

Another exhausting hour brought him to the top of the ridge where he threw down his pack to collapse gasping for breath, then to spread disinfectant salve over the cuts in his hands and knees.

Scrub bushes and some clumps of grass grew from the cracks and crevices in the rock and in the far distance he thought he could see another stand of trees. The rock dropped off sharply a short distance to his right and he walked slowly to the edge for a look, his legs aching from the climb.

A deep canyon a thousand feet wide with perpendicular walls going down, down, to narrow at the bottom into a roaring, raging, white-capped river far below. A narrow opening in the solid wall allowed some of the water to escape and form its own little stream, the one he had been following, while the main channel of white water surged on through the canyon and out of sight in the distance. The noise was deafening.

His aching muscles forgotten, he was excited again and looked for a way down into the gorge to examine the rocks, to measure the velocity of the water. That much water had to be glacier-fed or from an enormous snow pack and it had to go somewhere, perhaps an ocean. A sea would be the place for an abundance of life, a place for animal life to begin, to grow, to develop, if the planet was old enough. With his notebook and pencil he sketched the gorge trying to keep everything in perspective and including estimated distances. Then he made a moving record with the camcorder.

If the riverbed was igneous rock, the cutting rate of the river would be about an inch per thousand years. If it was limestone or another softer rock, the rate would be a lot higher. But from the looks of it, there was very little soft rock here. Judging the depth of the canyon by eye, guessing at the speed of the rushing water, he calculated the cutting rate in his head and estimated that this river had been gouging, cutting and slicing its way through the rock for about forty million years.

The one rope he had brought was not sufficient. Without ropes and a lot of additional equipment, there was no way, from where he was, he could reach the bottom in order to actually measure the speed of the surging water, so he sat down, rummaged through his pack and found a thick package of beef jerky. He chewed on the meat and washed it down with water from his canteen, felt the sun bright and hot on his face and finally laid back with his arms behind his head to let his muscles relax. He dozed with the roar of the river gorge behind him.

David Savage had never been lonely. He didn't know the meaning of the word. Born and raised as an only child on a huge, remote farm in Indiana, he walked the vast fields of his father's property and explored the small groves of trees left standing around them. He built his fires and camped for days at a time beside the wild steam that ran through their place, sometimes alone, sometimes with two or three friends from school who shared his love of the wide-open spaces and primitive living.

His father was a wealthy man and could afford to send his only son to college. "Study agriculture," his father told him, "and finance. That's where the money is. Then come back here and we'll expand the farm, buy more land, plant more crops. When I'm gone, you'll be rich! Oh, I wish I'da had this opportunity when I was your age, son."

But it wasn't agriculture or crops that interested young David Savage; it was the river that ran through the southern part of the farm supplying water for both the livestock and irrigation. He wanted to know how long it had been there, *why* it was there, why there were different kinds of rocks in the riverbed and why there were none at all in some places.

Early on, he and his friends constructed simple rafts upon which they floated down the river. Later when they were older they built more sophisticated boats in which they traveled miles along the waterway. Using a farm pickup truck, they would haul the boats back and do it all over again. Even in the winter when farm chores demanded less of their time, they would negotiate the frigid waters amid ice-covered tree limbs and tall, dead weeds glistening like jewels in the cold winter sunlight. So, when he finally went to college, geology became his passion.

He had absolutely no desire to return to the farm and be a farmer. He wanted to explore the world. Because of this, he and his father became estranged, the elder Savage embittered that his son in whom he had invested so much had turned his back on the land and life as a farmer. Much later when he became famous because of his oil field discoveries and his 'Indiana Jones' characterization, the bitterness left him and he was proud of his boy although disappointed that he had not returned to the farm where father and son could work the soil together.

It was already late afternoon and he wanted to try to gain the stand of trees in the distance before it got dark. He shouldered his pack and set off at a quick pace.

Almost an hour passed before he entered the woods. He was again tired and hungry. He set up another temporary camp, built a fire and tore open a sealed, foil package containing what the manufacturer claimed to be a complete dehydrated roast beef dinner. Dumping it into the pan along with a packet of dried corn, he poured water over it and waited until it began to look like a meal. When the fire burned down to coals he put it on to heat, savoring the aroma of the meat and potatoes swimming in thick, brown gravy. He ate everything, swabbing the pan with pieces of thick, hard, French bread that had been vacuum-sealed in plastic.

Searching the area around his camp for any sign of the plants or some indication that they had been here, he encountered thick, dry underbrush everywhere. Even a silent, sure-footed cat would have trouble getting through that tangle without making enough noise to wake him.

Building up the fire and hugging the rifle to his chest, he lay down close to the flames and covered himself with a thin, camouflage sheet that held his body heat in and protected him from rain or severe cold. Science had advanced a great deal while he languished in his dark prison cell.

Images of the plants came to him and with them the warning he had received only seconds before they overwhelmed him. There had been no sound—he was quite sure of that—so it must have been telepathic, almost but not quite, subliminal. But what kind of life form was capable of that?

Dawn was just breaking when he awakened. He had slept the entire night, nothing had molested him in his sleep and he was still alive. Once gain, dreams or nightmares of the past had not haunted him. He looked at his watch which read, 0850.

"I wonder if that's daylight savings time or Eastern Standard time?" he joked aloud. "But, then, who cares."

His hands were still sore but there was no sign of infection, and they were healing. Either the salve worked or there were no harmful bacteria here.

Setting a match to kindling, he carefully put on larger pieces of wood, got the fire going and poured a package of coffee into his canteen cup. Filling it with water, he set it at the edge of the open flame and waited for it to heat. Using the last of his water, he prepared a dehydrated mixture of eggs and sausage. When the flames had died down and the coals still glowed red, he put the food on to heat while he sipped the coffee. It smelled good and wasn't really that bad, for instant.

The smell of the coffee brought back memories of a grizzled old man he had met in the Canadian Rockies once while on one of his exploration trips in search for oil. Kneeling down on one knee on a gravel creek-bed, he looked up to see the man standing there with a rifle across his arm just on the other side of the shallow river, watching him. There was no hostility toward Savage, but there wasn't any welcome, either.

"Morning," Savage had said. "Am I trespassing?"

The man just shook his had slowly back and forth.

"I'm a Geologist, looking for oil shale. I've got a client that thinks there might be oil deposits under here."

The man nodded his head just once.

"You think so?"

The man shrugged.

"Mind if I look?"

"Nope. Go ahead," the older man said. "Ain't my land."

"You live around here?"

"A ways off."

"I've got a camp a couple miles up there," Savage continued, jerking a thumb over his shoulder. "You're welcome to join me for lunch if you'll tell me how far up this stream goes before it joins the main river."

"Bout five miles or so," he replied.

"Can I walk it?"

"Yep."

"Care to join me? I might get lost."

"Doubt it," the man replied.

"Well, I'd like the company if you can stand it."

"How long you been here?"

"You're asking? I figure you probably knew the first day I got here."

"Can't say as I did."

"Okay. About three days."

"Find anything?"

"Just gravel. This belong to anybody?"

"Not that I know of."

"My name's David Savage."

"Pleased to meet you."

Something clicked between the two of them during the few minutes they talked and the old man accepted the invitation to lunch, then invited himself to spent the rest of the day and the evening with the young geologist at his base camp. They talked through the evening and late into the night.

The man told him he rose to the rank of Staff Sergeant in the Marine Corps and slowly began to become fed up with the way politics were headed in the United States. He resigned after fifteen years, took his retirement pay in a lump sum and moved to an isolated cabin in the Canadian wilderness to live alone for the rest of his life. Divorced—his wife had left him and took the kids while he was doing the first Bush fiasco in the Gulf and then the second Bush debacle in Iraq—he had nobody. Familiar story Savage would think later.

"How long have you lived up here?" Savage asked.

"Going on five years now."

"Alone?"

"T'ain't so bad. You get used to it. Kinda miss having somebody to talk to sometimes, though. Had me a dog for awhile. Used to talk to him. Cat got'em about a year ago. Dragged him off somewhere. I looked but I never found him."

They built up the fire and Savage offered an extra blanket he carried. At first light, the older man was awake and began building up the fire to make coffee. He did it the way his First Sergeant had taught him years before. "Real gumbo," he called it. "It'll open your eyes in the morning"

A double handful of coffee grounds thrown into a quart of water and let it boil over the fire for five minutes. Strain it though a handkerchief or through your teeth. If it didn't scald your lips and you didn't get a mouth full of grounds, you could drink it. If didn't taste very good but it would clean carbon out of a rifle barrel or rust off a knife blade better than any solvent ever invented. And it certainly *did* open your eyes. Never mind what it did to your stomach.

They parted company that day shortly before noon. The old hermit, ex Marine declined to accompany him upstream. They never met again. He couldn't remember the man's name but he certainly remembered that coffee.

As his breakfast cooked, he took off his socks and massaged his feet. There would be a lot more walking today, down the cliff, through the valley of the intelligent plants, through the forest and back to his camp. He would have liked to have explored the stand of woods in which he was camped, but there was just too much information he needed to transmit to Palomar. And, there was additional equipment he had to have to continue his exploration. He wanted to go down into that gorge.

Breakfast was as good as his dinner had been. He felt rejuvenated and excited as he scrubbed his cooking pan with a dry compound they had sent with him for that purpose. Sand would have worked just as well but there wasn't any here.

Finishing the last of the coffee, repacking his gear, adjusting his glasses and putting on his gloves he made his way back down the ridge to where he could fill his canteen from the stream. The woods, the valley, the gorge, it would take months to explorer everything thoroughly and he still had three more directions from his camp to check out. When he got back he would ask for and add four more signs, NE, SE, SW. and Northwest.

His hands didn't bother him as much now but he resolved to ask Palomar for a better pair of gloves. The sharp rock edges he had encountered indicated a lack of weathering but that could be explained in a number of ways rather than just the absence of rain and wind to wear them down. It could be new rock from an earthquake or a slide within the last hundred or so years, or maybe there just wasn't any wind-blown sand or driving rains to grind off the edges and this rock was the same as it had been thousands of years ago.

The plants were still there when he reached the floor of the valley and they began to move toward him at his approach. There were more of them now, twenty or thirty, completely blocking his path along the riverbank. Several of them were over eight feet tall and the stem was thicker than a man's forearm. The sunflower head was a foot and a half across and the leaves around the head were white, not yellow. The center looked like tanned leather with horizontal slits in it.

How had they known he was coming? Could they see him, hear him, smell him? Could they detect the vibrations in the ground as he walked? If they attacked him, he could fight off that many with his knife. With one finger at the edge of the trigger guard of the M-16, he snapped the safety off.

You can't kill a plant with a gun.

There it was again! His idea, his thought, or somebody else's?

But with an M-16 on full automatic you can mow the lawn, trim the hedge or cut anything in two with the hail of bullets pouring from it. Did the plants know that? Who says you can't kill a plant with a gun?

He backed up several steps then turned to walk rapidly back the way he had come. There was a place a short distance away where he could cross the river and continue along the other side. If the plants couldn't enter the water, he was safe.

With so many of them here, this must be a place where something, some form of animal life upon which they fed came to drink. What came here? What did they feed upon? He wanted to see and record it.

Crossing the stream with his rifle held over his head like a combat Marine, he staggered out on the other side and walked on. All the flowered heads were turned toward him as he passed by safely on the other side but none of the plants attempted to enter the water

The stream broadened and slowed. He came to the drinking area he had first assumed to be a watering hole. The stunted, withered plants did not move nor did they appear as though they could. He would ask Palomar for a couple chunks of raw meat and toss it to them. If they were still alive, it would be interesting to see how they ingested it. Who knows maybe he would make a friend. What was it Mark Twain said? *If you pick up a starving dog and make him prosperous, he will not bite you. That is the principal difference between a dog and a man.* Wonder if that applied to plants, too?

In pursuit of scientific research, he wanted to establish that you *could* kill a plant with a gun. He raised the M-16 to his shoulder and snapped off the safety. Taking aim at one of the drooping flowered heads, he touched the trigger, took up the—" slack that activated the laser, and held the weapon steady, intending to fire one quick shot and watch the results. A red dot appeared on the stalk. That's where the high-velocity .222 round would hit.

He did not shoot. What was the point? Killing even a plant for absolutely no reason was against everything he had ever believe in and he wouldn't start now. He would kill for food—he had—and to protected himself—he had done that, too—and maybe even in revenge for some terrible wrong, but he would not kill just for the sake of killing. If the plants were an intelligent life form, it might even be murder.

He lowered the gun and put it on safe.

Tromping up the hill and finding his first camp, he walked on by toward the Window. "Didn't have any trouble finding that camp," he said aloud.

He was talking to himself a lot, now. Did he do that before when he was out exploring? He didn't remember. Was it a thing with men who spent a lot of time alone to talk aloud to themselves? Or was it just the insane ones who did that?

Well, if he was insane, he could have never in his worst nightmares conceived of something like this. One man, alone and isolated on a alien world somewhere in the universe light years or light centuries from Earth, the only human being on the whole planet. How about that for insanity. Even Poe in all his macabre story settings never envisioned something like this.

Entering the woods, he set off taking a slightly different course from his blaze marks to test his fledgling sense of direction. Dangerous move. What if he got lost? Could he eventually find his way back to his camp or back to the valley of the plants? What if he ran out of food and water? Stop worrying. Just follow the sun and keep moving.

With his pack on the ground, his back against a tree and the rifle across his knees, he looked at his watch. It said, 2900 hours, about 6:00 PM Earth time. He looked up at the sunlight filtering through the trees, took the watch off and stuffed it into his pocket.

"Who cares, anyway," he said aloud. "I don't have a bus to catch."

Three more times he stopped to rest. It was almost dark when he finally arrived at his permanent camp. It looked good to him, familiar, almost like home. He stumbled into the clearing and glanced with amusement at the big letter **N** hanging from a tree to his right. Yeah, that was north.

Maybe.

Several packets of plastic-encased papers along with two small packing crates lay on the ground under where the Window hung. He ignored them and fell to fixing dinner. He was tired and would have preferred dinner served to him but he did not want to continue to depend upon the Window for survival. Half way around the world—if he ever made it that far—he certainly wasn't going to have dinner served to him out of a hole in the air.

He might have to move his camp to some place close to a source of water. Palomar wouldn't like that because he would be out of sight of the Window. He could establish another camp beside a stream somewhere. Palomar wouldn't like that, either, and he wasn't looking forward to lugging all that equipment any great distance. For now anyway, he would let Palomar supply the water.

Although still tired but with a full stomach, he put a large pot of water on the fire to heat then sat at his table and began logging the events and discoveries in his journal while they were still fresh in his mind. It was completely dark now and the cot began to look very inviting. Tomorrow he would read through the material they had sent and make notes to hold up in front of the Window. And there was still the microphotography to complete that he had abandoned to return to the valley.

He closed the journal, took off his glasses and rubbed his tired eyes. Stripping off his clothes, he padded on bare feet to the pot of hot water. If any of the female technicians were watching they would get an eye full, but what the hell. It was no time for modesty.

He washed himself thoroughly, threw his clothes into the pot and washed them, too. So much for the washing machine idea. He draped them over low-hanging limbs to dry. Futile gesture.

He could just ask for new, clean ones and they would be sent. Trouble was, just like the food, he couldn't get them half way around the world.

There were clothes made of paper, claimed by the manufacturer to be as durable and tough as cloth, water resistant, flame retardant and disposable—no washing—but Savage didn't want them. Perhaps later, he promised, when things became more familiar and he knew what he was dealing with, he would give them a try.

Re-entering the tent, he zipped the flaps closed and collapsed on the cot. The vivid memories of the gorge, the raging river and the plants filled his mind and so completely occupied his thoughts that he dropped into a deep sleep almost immediately.

He only woke up once during the night, aware of the gravity and the extra weight, but went right back to sleep. In the morning he dressed in clean clothes, fixed and ate breakfast then began going through the material from Palomar. They asked how he was holding up in the heavy gravity, did he feel sick at all, were there any signs of disease or infection, how were his eyes? They asked for complete details about the valley and what he had found. And there was a letter from Diana. He tore open the sealed envelope hurriedly.

My dearest David. It has been only a short time but I miss you more than you can imagine. It's eerie standing here watching you through the Window. It's like seeing a movie on a big screen. You walk around, you do things and it is as though you don't know we're watching. A couple of times you've walked right into the screen—ha, I mean the Window—you got closer and closer and then just vanished. You are so close and yet so inaccessible it takes all my willpower to keep from rushing through to be with you. It is terrible sleeping alone now.

DeShane and even Killingsworth—surprise!—have been very understanding and supportive of me, and knowing I will be joining you in a few months makes it easier to bear.

The divorce has been filed and will be final by the time I am scheduled to meet you on the new world. Please be careful, David. Take care of yourself. I don't want anything to happen to you now. I love you.

Diana.

He folded the letter and put it in his shirt pocket, then he opened one of the packing cases. It was a video tape player he could attach to the TV monitor. The other case contained tapes. Looking through them, he saw Geology, biology, astronomy, meteorology and botany. They weren't going to let him quit studying just because he was on another world.

Also included were a half a dozen feature length movies just for entertainment.

The stronger gravity indicated this planet was bigger than Earth with a circumference of considerably more than 25,000 equatorial miles. The distance from the sun was probably greater, too, but he had no way of measuring it with the instruments available to him, nor did he have the scientific knowledge to do it.

Writing on the lined pad, he answered their questions and then described his trip, the valley and the gorge. He told them about the plants but omitted that they appeared to be intelligent and they could move, saying only that, like the bushes he had found earlier, they did not seem to be attached to the ground as normal plants were. Thinking that a bunch of plants walking around and talking to each other out there might be a bit too much for them to believe, he didn't want them to consider that he might have begun to hallucinate in the oxygen-rich, alien atmosphere.

Taking short breaks from the tedious plant analysis and his journal entries, he went into the woods with his axe and cut firewood from the deadfalls he found there, stacking the wood near the fire pit. When darkness fell, he ate and prepared for bed. Another day, another dollar, less taxes.

The following day was much the same, the analysis, projecting the photographs and his notes, resting from the grueling trip and allowing his aching, abused muscles to repair themselves and stop hurting. It seemed as thought he was becoming accustomed to the gravity a lot faster than he should have. Tomorrow he would request the equipment he needed, ropes and mountain climbing gear. He would return to the gorge to continue his exploration, pausing for another look at the plants. He intended to take several pounds of meat to the plants down stream that appeared to be dying. What happened when he threw those pieces of raw meat on the ground in front of the plants would be an academy award winning performance. He would have the camera all set up to capture it on tape.

He wanted additional equipment that was capable of taking one frame of the videotape and enlarging the picture. That would mean developing equipment and a battery-powered enlarger. He would soon be running out of room in the tent. Maybe a second one, an equipment room, and keep this for his living quarters.

He cooked and ate dinner, turned in early while it was still daylight and completely forgot to turn on the floodlight. He zipped the tent closed, took out his contact lenses, undressed and fell asleep immediately.

CHAPTER TWENTY-ONE

H E WAS UNSURE WHAT had awakened him. It was still dark outside. He reached for the watch he had taken from his pocket when he washed his clothes. Lighting up the dial he saw that it was 0430.

He lay there half-dozing, thinking about the gorge, the plants and the microanalysis he had done on the samples. He had only an elementary education in biology but he understood the basic universal absolutes in all living things and he wasn't finding them here.

Suddenly he was wide-awake. There it was again! That sound which had brought him from a deep sleep in the middle of the night. He grabbed his glasses and put them on. A short, loud, sharp noise again broke the stillness and sent him scrambling from the cot with his rifle and a flashlight.

There was a scratching sound on the flaps of his tent! Then a soft thump from outside. Something was trying to get in! He resisted an almost overpowering urge to send a burst of automatic rifle fire through the tent flaps. Instead, he stood there in the darkness in his underwear and waited, holding his breath.

Again, there was the scratching sound accompanied this time by a low whimper. Savage snapped on the flashlight and saw the tent flaps move and flutter as the scratching and thumping continued.

Had somebody else come through the Window? Could it be Diana, unwilling to wait any longer to follow him?

"Who's out there?" he called, more to break the tension within him than to get an answer.

What if it was a creature from this world? The plants. Had they somehow followed him and were now at his door seeking a meal, or was it something even more menacing? Some monster from the Twilight Zone.

There was that sound again, low and rumbling, somewhat like the bark of a dog, a very *big* dog. The scratching was more furious now, the attack on the tent door shaking the entire structure.

Laying the flashlight on the table so that its beam lit up the doorway and substituting the Koch for the rifle, he walked slowly to the door and reached out to unzip the flaps. Whatever it was might be able to rip through the thick canvas in a short time, he couldn't keep it out and he didn't want his door in shreds. Time to face the enemy, if it was indeed an enemy.

The H&K ready in his hand with the hammer back, he pulled the tent flap open and grabbed the flashlight so its beam would shine on whatever was outside. This was the moment of truth. He could be dead in a second, before he could fire the automatic. Moreover, there was no guarantee that the weapon would even be effective against whatever was out there.

Would a gun work on this world? When he pulled the trigger, would it fire? Were the natural laws different here? Should have thought of that before now.

There was just a flash, a glimpse of something moving beyond the tent flaps and the sounds of scurried activity in the grass and weeds. Whatever it was retreated quickly away from the door and to the side of the tent where it stopped a short distance away but still in the clearing.

Barefoot and in his shorts he stepped cautiously outside and swung the flashlight beam from side to side. The floodlight wasn't on. He hadn't turned it on. The sound of the motor and the smell of the exhaust resulting from running the generator were offensive to him. He didn't need the light anyway. Palomar had not seen anything in the dark, but they would be watching and his light in the middle of the night would alert them to start their cameras and record perhaps the first form of alien animal life ever seen by man.

There was nothing in front of the tent, nothing that could be seen through the Window. Aiming the maglight at the far tide of the clearing, he saw it, behind where the invisible Window hung in the air. Caught in the circle of light, standing close to the edge of the woods was something vaguely resembling a dog, a huge German Shepherd. The size of the animal was almost unbelievable. It must have weighted close to three hundred pounds and stood waist high to a tall man. Its coat was glossy, rich and deep brown with patches of gray-white that seemed to glow and ripple in the beam of the torch held in Savage's hand.

With ears erect, mouth open slightly and fierce, glowing green eyes looking just past the light to the man behind it, the animal stood poised between fight and flight. Paws larger than the spread of a man's hand dug into the ground and all four legs trembled with tension. Great canine teeth grew down over the lower jaw somewhat resembling the tusks of the prehistoric saber-toothed tiger, but not quite as long.

An alien life form! He was finally seeing it. No plant this time. An animal. He had to get the camera and photograph it before it vanished back into the woods.

But wait. He had the high-intensity light in one hand, the pistol in the other. How could he operate the camera? From the size of that thing he wasn't sure even the Koch could knock it down if it charged, but he wasn't going to lay the gun down. If it came here looking for lunch, it was going to be a painful one. He could get off at least five shots before it reached him.

Without the light, he couldn't see it. The hell with the camera and taking pictures. Just back up slowly and get the rifle. A lot more fire power.

Then another idea struck him. Squinting through his glasses, he took a few slow, careful steps toward the animal. Each step reduced the number of shots he could get off if the thing attacked, but . . . yes. Yes! There was no doubt about it. With the exception of its size and those saber-tooth tusks, this was an Earth dog. But how—?

Of course! It had to be the dog they had taken from Diana. They didn't experiment on it or cut it up as DeShane had suggested. They sent it through the Window! Boucree had told him they put a dog through in their early days of testing to see if it could survive.

But what about the long fang-like teeth? No dog he had ever seen had teeth like that. Was it something they did to the animal before they sent it through the Window? Was it Diana's dog at all?

Better find out. Friend or foe, it was here and it didn't act as though it was going to go away anytime soon. He took a few more steps closer to the animal, his bare feet punished by the rocks, tough weeds and dead branches.

Diana's dog was very intelligent, friendly and trained to respond to command he had been told during the few, brief times she was able to discuss the dog without flaring up in anger, her eyes suddenly aglow with smoldering hatred. It was a very obedient animal and the only friend she really had other than Mark.

It was worth a try. He had nothing to lose. Another couple of steps and he was so close that one shot was about all he could manage before it would be on him. "Come here, boy!" he said firmly. "Come here."

For several seconds the animal did not move. "Come!" Savage commanded again, patting his bare leg with the barrel of the automatic.

Cocking its huge head to one side and prancing its front feet up and down, the animal slowly took a tentative step forward, its tail whipping back and forth.

"You *are* Diana's dog!" he exclaimed with delight, stooping down to place the weapon on the ground. "Come here, boy. Come on." He stood up and held out his free hand saying again, "Come here, boy. I'm not going to hurt you."

The animal took another step, then another, walking slowly to him, nose sniffing his outstretched hand, breath coming fast and hot against his flesh. For several moments the huge creature sniffed and poked with its nose. Then suddenly, it was up and on him. Huge paws slammed against his chest knocking him over backwards, the light flying from his hand. A rough tongue scrubbed over his face knocking his glasses off. With the curved tusks only inches from his throat and the heavy body pinning him firmly to the ground, the dog whimpered and barked and again lashed him with its tongue.

Savage laughed and grabbed handfuls of long silky fur, rolling and wrestling with the animal in an attempt to free himself from its weight. The dog let him up and then knocked him down again, evidently unaware of its own size and power. Huge teeth locked around his wrist in a grip from which he easily pulled his arm. Jaws capable of closing with crushing force let him go, then grabbed again in a gentle, playful hold. Prancing to the side, the dog let him up and then took him down once again, placing a huge paw full of inch-long claws on his chest. A dog's claws were like a human's fingernails. They weren't edged or retractable like a cat's and they weren't used to kill, but these could have ripped his chest open in an instant. Green eyes seeming to glow from within regarded him in the darkness.

"Son of a bitch! They told me you were big," Savage said once the wrestling had stopped and the settled down to regard each other in the moonlight, "but I never imagined anything like this. You're the biggest dog I've ever seen."

Flushed with excitement and knowing he could not get back to sleep now, he found his glasses and put them on. Finding his gun and flashlight, he said, "Wait here," and returned to the tent where he dressed and build up the fire, noting with interest that the animal stayed where he was, out of view from the Window. Did the dog really know it was there? Could he see it or somehow sense it? Did he know, could he understand that they were being watched from the other side?

Emerging from the tent, he started the motor and turned on the floodlights. Knowing they were looking at him now, he stood in front of the tent, shrugged his shoulders and held his hands out in a confused gesture. That should convince them nothing had happened and he just had another bad dream.

He appeared to wander away from the tent, out of view of the Window and to where the dog waited. The big animal seemed to be afraid of the noise of the motor and more nervous in the light. And that's the way Savage felt getting a good look at the huge canine in the bright, artificial light. "Sure wish you could talk," he said, sitting down on the ground in front of the huge animal now towering over him. "But it's nice to just have company. All these months since they put you through the Window you've been here alone," he said, "waiting for your master. I wonder how many times you've returned to this spot looking for her, not understanding where you are or how you got here. And instead of her, you get me. But I guess you'd be happy with anybody right now." He reached up and touched the animal's huge head. "I really don't taste very good so if you're considering having me for lunch, forget it. Gotta be something better out there. I can get you some hamburger or even a steak if you want. What the hell do dogs eat? Dog food, of course. What else?

"My kids had a dog. It was a little fluffy, dust mop that yapped all the time and I tried to just ignore it, but they like it.

"Diana never told me your name so I don't know what to call you. Guess I'll just have to call you Dog for the time being. You like that? Hello, Dog," he said, laughing.

With Dog again came thoughts and memories of Diana, the months they had spent together and the much too brief time they had shared love in the final days before he stepped through the Window. "I miss her, too, Dog," he said, "and three more months is a long time to wait. But with you here, it will be easier."

The dog laid its muzzle on a huge outstretched paw and regarded the man with sad but intelligent eyes. It was almost as though the animal understood him, or at least understood his mood and shared this rare moment of unaccustomed loneliness, the need for a companion.

"I never understood that feeling before, Dog. I always wondered why people didn't want to be alone, always needing other people around them. I guess they thought I was pretty strange. But, then, nobody has ever been completely alone on a whole world before. Huh?

"And you survived. That means there is no slow acting poison or delayed action bacteria in the atmosphere. There's food and water. So I'm going to survive too. That's good to know."

Dawn was breaking above the trees and Dog became more anxious and nervous. Before it was fully light, he got to his feet and walked slowly into the woods. Calling accomplished nothing and Savage was left alone to fix his breakfast and to contemplate his next message to Palomar.

That the animal they put through the Window months before had survived and appeared to be well and healthy was exactly the news Palomar wanted to hear. It conclusively established that an Earth life form could live here. He was required to report it.

So what would happen if he didn't? He would wait a few days and continue to observe the animal, be absolutely certain it was Diana's dog and not some indigenous life form. No reason to be premature and possibly give them false information. There was plenty of time.

Diana had been so dead-set against populating the new world with Earth people of Mr. Getty's choosing, and one look at the huge dog would convince them that Earth life could indeed survive here. They might not wait six more months, but start sending people through immediately. They might figure out how to build another Window soon and with it a larger one so they could send through dozens or hundreds at a time along with machinery and vehicles and weapons of mass destruction.

He wanted to tell Diana that her pet was still alive and surviving admirable, but there was no way without alerting everybody else, too. So, as with the moving plants, he elected not to mention the dog for awhile, waiting to see what would happen.

He fixed breakfast while ignoring another packet sealed in plastic appearing in the air shortly after he began eating. They would be wanting to know what happened last night, why the light, why he was out running around in his underwear, what had he been doing? Would they believe it was something as simple as going to the bathroom? The tent sure didn't have indoor plumbing.

They'd have to believe anything he told them. He had a nightmare, thought he heard a noise, went to investigate, found nothing and then went off into the woods to relieve himself. Sounded good.

First, he had intelligent plants and now a dog the size of a horse with fangs like a tiger. What would he find next?

When he finished eating and cleaning his dishes, he picked up the packet. A brief typewritten note asked if everything was all right? What happened last night?

The remainder of the papers consisted of reports, more detailed analyses on his preliminary examination of the vegetation and soil samples, and a request to complete the rest of them. There were indications of photosynthesis in the microscopic pictures he had shown them and they wanted more for continued study.

The biologists studying the information he had sent of the plant life wanted to know how the plants survived and where they obtained the carbon dioxide necessary to keep them alive since he had found nothing giving off carbon dioxide so far. It was there in the air, his tests had revealed that. So where did it come from?

Also included in the packet was another letter from Diana but he did not open the envelope knowing that he had work to do and her words would be distracting. Later, when it got dark and Dog returned he would sit cross-legged on the ground with the flashlight and read it aloud to his new companion. It would be very warm, soft and personal like her. Already he was distracted from his duties. Later.

The last page was from Dr. Boucree relaying instructions from Mr. Getty. Wherever he was, there in California or somewhere else in the world, he had been told of the valley and the gorge and of Savage's intent to return as soon as possible for continued study.

The letter was disappointing because it ordered him not to return to the canyon now. It would be there in the future. No animal life or signs of civilization had been found and Mr. Getty wanted more area explored and mapped as soon as possible. He wanted to know of any dangers, any food sources and major water supplies. Were there any areas that could be used as farmland, had he discovered any metal bearing ore? Were there any signs of excavation, anything that might have been constructed by some form of intelligence? Find an ocean or a body of water large enough to supply a city. When found, was the ocean salt or fresh water?

He was instructed to finish with his samples and prepare to leave as soon as possible, plan to be gone for at least a week, cover a wide area. The last order was that he not forget again to turn on the floodlight. Damarjiane wanted him under observation at all times, for his own safety and protection and the safety of the camp.

"Like somebody is going to come rescue me. Sure, I believe that, and I don't like being in a fishbowl. I need *some* privacy," he mumbled out loud. He should tell them.

Working diligently on the remainder of the samples, he stopped only long enough for lunch. Then wrote his findings in his journal and prepared his notes and photographs for Palomar. Each entry was numbered, as were the pictures, most with coordinating references. When they read paragraph number twenty-three, there was a corresponding photograph number twenty-three to substantiate it. There was so much information to pass on that it took him an hour standing at the overhead projector displaying the material on the screen. When he was finished the ground at his feet was thick with Polaroid shots and pages from the lined tablet. He gathered them all together and put them into one of the filing cabinets.

His back and neck hurt, not to mention his eyes from all the hours of leaning over the table. Being outside helped and he was glad for the extra table and the daylight, but he was tired of the methodical, boring, plodding, listing of data, most of which he didn't understand. Maybe Mr. Getty was right. Go explore new areas.

He requested a new rifle, a Springfield .270 with a five shot magazine and a Weaver scope. If he saw any game and intended to bring it down, the M-16 was not the weapon for it. Designed primarily to kill people by soldiers who couldn't shoot straight, the M-16 was an ideal wartime weapon but certainly not the choice of sportsmen.

Whatever happened to marksmanship? Back when front line troops used single shot and bolt action rifles, they had to be good with their weapon. Now they just held it up without looking, emptied the magazine spraying the area in front of them hoping they might hit something. No wonder that old Marine wanted out of the service and preferred to live alone.

The sun had begun to settle beyond the trees and if he was still on Earth, he estimated it would be 6:00 o'clock or maybe a little later. Were there seasons here? Would the days lengthen and shorten? How many days were in a sidereal year? He put all his equipment away, storing it carefully in the tent.

A glass of wine would go good right now so he scribbled out an order for dinner and put it on the projector. Later when things died down and there wouldn't be so many observers, he could build a fire and read Diana's second letter. Dog would come and he could read the letter again aloud.

Within twenty minutes, a complete meal arrived packaged in Styrofoam containers held together with fat rubber bands. Sitting at the table inside the tent he removed the rubber bands and opened the foam containers. He took out a charbroiled steak almost an inch thick and four inches across still sizzling. There was a steaming baked potato wrapped in aluminum foil beside it. Another container held a cold green salad with cucumbers, onions and peppers covered with Roquefort dressing, and in a third box, a full bottle of Château Lafayette Rothschild, a rare, expensive and rich red wine almost unknown to the public. There was silverware, a plate and a wineglass. Mr. Getty was sparing no expense.

Changing his mind while he ate, he took out Diana's letter and tore it open.

My dearest David,

I'm not very good a writing love letters; I've never written one before, so just bear with me.

I've though about it a lot, and you were right. I do love you, David, and I want to be with you. Not just physically but mentally and emotionally. I want us to be a part of each other. Just a few more weeks We have to wait.

Since you told us about the gravity, I've been exercising with weights strapped on my wrists and ankles so I will be prepared. Just keep loving me and we will be together soon.

I love you.

Diana.

If he survived for six months, they would conclude that the planet was safe and Diana could join him. But when the problem with his eyes became known, they considered shortening it to four months. Both he and Diana had argued for three. No final decision had been made at the time he stepped through the Window.

Now that he was here, what if they assigned Diana somebody else to train, somebody who could take up where he left off when his sight finally went? He would have done all of the scientific work they required. Somebody younger, more rugged and able to take care of Diana in a hostile environment. Maybe somebody without his scientific abilities but a man who could see, who could survive here and produce a family on this new world.

No, she would tell him if they tried to do that, unless her letters were censored. What if they allowed her to write only what he wanted to hear, what they wanted him to hear? Killingsworth could tell her what to say, or even Boucree. They both wanted the project to succeed although for different reasons.

No, that was stupid. Diana would never be a part of anything like that. They couldn't make her write anything she didn't want to, or prevent her from writing what she *did* want.

By the time he finished eating and reading the letter it was night. He heard something outside. It could be another package tumbling through the Window and falling to the ground, or it could be Dog returning.

He stuffed the letter into his pocket, took his flashlight and walked outside pretending to turn on the floodlight. But when he was beyond view of the Window he went to the place where he had encountered Dog the night before.

Swinging the light from side to side, he went almost the edge of the clearing without seeing the animal. Just as he turned and started back did he notice the big canine watching him silently from a particularly tall stand of grass and weeds. With his coloring, and standing perfectly still, he was almost invisible. Savage somehow got the impression that Dog had allowed himself to be seen, otherwise he would not have been.

"Hello, friend," Savage said aloud, beginning to feel the effects of the wine. "Can I order you something? A steak maybe, real rare. Would you like that?"

Dog just looked at him.

"Wouldn't hurt. If you don't eat it, I can throw it on the fire and maybe eat it myself. I've got quite an appetite these days. What do you think?"

The dog didn't move and the eyes hadn't changed but just for an instant Dog's tongue flicked out to lick its chops.

"Good enough," he said. "You got it. Wait right here."

His handwritten note asked for a raw steak at least two inches thick which he could cook himself. He thought about adding reasons for asking but dismissed the idea. There was no real reason to justify his request and they could think whatever they wanted. Just give him what he asked for.

While waiting he switched on the floodlight and refilled his glass from the wine bottle. When the steak arrived sealed in a plastic bag, he casually walked off into the dark beyond the Window with the bag in his hands. They would ask him to explain that and maybe he could come up with an acceptable reason, but right now he just didn't care and he wasn't going to worry about it.

A short time later Dog was licking his muzzle with a huge, thick tongue and Savage was digging Diana's letters out of his shirt pocket. "You sure made fast work of that hunk of steak. Pretty good, huh? Yeah, I liked it, too. Now listen. Diana's talking to us."

He sat flat on the ground, leveled a place in the dirt to set the glass and read both letters aloud in the light of the torch. Dog lay quiet and attentive, almost as though he actually understood what Savage was saying. "I know they are written to me, Dog, but if she knew you were here she would write to you, too. She really liked you, you know. And you knew her before I did."

He drained the wineglass as he talked and set it heavily on the ground. "You know what? I think I'm smashed. A couple of glasses of wine and I'm sitting here talking to a dog like you know what I'm saying."

The animal cocked his head and studied him with those glowing green eyes.

"And I gotta stop ordering food from over there. But, damn, it's good. Haven't run into a 7-11 here lately or any place to order wine and steak. Whaduthink, Dog?" He held his glass up in salute.

"And what I think is I had better try to get some sleep. If I'm going to move out of here tomorrow, I can't do it red-eyed and hung over. Feel free to stick around. Just don't get in the light where they can see you." He reached out his hand, stroked the broad head between the ears and climbed heavily to his feet.

Going back to the tent, he closed the flaps, took off his boots, undressed and was asleep almost instantly. The night passed and he awoke just before dawn. He looked out but Dog was nowhere to be seen in the floodlight.

Dressed in clean clothes, he fixed his own breakfast and took his time packing the gear he would take on the trip. He would need enough for several days but it couldn't be too heavy or he would spend most of his time resting. Clothes, extra socks, a large sketch pad to supplement his notebook, the camcorder, binoculars and his glasses. The contact lenses didn't irritate his eyes anymore but it felt good to take them out at times and just use the glasses. No, he would not allow himself to think about his eyes and how much time he had left.

A flashlight, the thermal blanket folded into a small square, food and the mess kit, his zippered case of chemicals and instruments for testing and analysis, and a dozen sample containers completed his pack. On the top he securely tied a small, self-supporting one-man tent with lightweight aluminum support poles. Two canteens of water, his knife, the pistol and a small first aid kit would be carried on his belt.

As he sat at the outside table packing the gear, he looked again for Dog. He thought about those long, curved tusk-like teeth extending down from the upper jaw. They appeared to be almost needle sharp although he didn't care to test them. Where had they come from? Why and how did Dog develop them? They certainly weren't natural, at least not on any dog he had ever seen. And even more curiously, why had he not been frightened of them when he first saw them? Curious about them, yes. Amazed, certainly. But he had not been afraid of that huge fanged monster, even when it jumped on him that first time and knocked him down. That was strange indeed.

Zipping the tent flaps closed, he turned the table onto its edge in front of the door to further bar the entrance, attached the hatchet to the outside of his pack and took up the rifle. Talking a last look around, he turned and plunged into the woods with the sun at his back.

Chapter Twenty-Two

H E HAD NOT GONE a hundred yards into the forest when Dog appeared silently at his side as though patiently waiting for him to leave the camp and join him. In the daylight, the animal seemed to be even bigger than he had appeared in the darkness, and the saber teeth glistened white and moist. They extended down almost four inches and in addition to the sharp points, they appeared to taper to a knife-edge on the inside, somewhat like a lion's claws. Perhaps when they got to know each other better Dog would let him examine them more closely, but for now he intended to keep his hands and face a good distance away.

"I kinda hoped you'd be here," he said. "Interested in doing some exploring with me? Maybe I can teach you to be a Seeing Eye dog when my sight finally goes."

There would be no need to mark a trail this time. Dog had been here a long time and obviously knew his way around. Should they get lost, the animal would be the best guide in the world to lead him back to camp. "I wanted to go back to the gorge and take some a buncha meat to the plants," he told

Dog, "but they wouldn't let me. I couldn't figure out a reason to justify all that meat without telling them why. Maybe a little later, we can do it."

For the first couple of miles the going seemed easier although not because the forest was less dense or the underbrush less tangled. He didn't tire as quickly and at times, Dog seemed to maneuver him toward an easier passage. In a small clearing where the sun penetrated brightly he discovered a stand of bushes bearing bright red berries about the size of his fingertip. He collected several and put them into one of the sample containers.

Throughout the morning they moved steadily through the forest with him having to stop and rest only twice. Dog suffered these breaks with solemn patience while the man regained his strength. They paused just long enough for lunch when the sun was almost directly overhead and Savage gave Dog one of the huge, thick T-bone steaks he had requested just before he left camp. They may have wondered about his again asking for fresh meat to take on a long trek, but they didn't question it. The steaks just appeared, wrapped in aluminum foil and sealed in plastic bags.

Dog ate it all, including the bone that he crunched and crushed with his powerful fanged jaws. He appeared to doze while Savage fixed the fire, warmed his concentrated food and thought seriously about keeping the other steak for himself. Slow cooked over an open fire and medium rare it would sure beat the packaged stuff all to hell. Besides, Dog had survived this long without his help and he didn't get that big and healthy by going hungry. Other than men, bears and some birds, dogs were the only true omnivores, eating both meat and plants and able to survive on either. He just about had himself convinced to keep it by the time he covered the fire and broke camp.

Moving with less effort than before, more miles fell behind as he traveled slowly through the forest listening and looking around as he went. Without concern for getting lost or being attacked, the awe and wonder of being on another world fading into obscurity and the gravity no longer a significant problem with which to contend, he began hearing things and catching movement out of the corner of his eye he hadn't noticed before. Insects, small birds, scurrying ground animals? He wasn't sure. Once he though he caught the sound of fluttering wings off in the trees somewhere, but he saw nothing.

No tall, flowered plants from the river valley appeared to bar his path. Maybe they couldn't come this far through the woods. Maybe they needed the open area to move around. No predator made to attack him and no game of any kind offered itself as a target for the rifle.

Nightfall found him still in the dense wood. He had been traveling for almost eighteen hours and should have collapsed long ago under the severe gravity. True, he felt tired, his legs ached, his shoulders were sore from the pack and his back hurt, but he was not exhausted anywhere near to the point of dropping. Amazing how fast he was becoming acclimated.

He set up the small self-supporting tent that had no ropes and required no pegs. Dinner for him was again from the dehydrated food packs and Dog ate the last steak. So much for *that* decision.

"Well," he said to his companion as he cleaned the mess kit, "we've been at it all day and there's been nothing eventful. I sure wish you could tell me how far this forest goes and what's beyond it."

Dog lay down full length and watched the man.

"Wouldn't have minded having you along on some of my other trips back on Earth, either," he continued as he unlaced and took off his boots. "But I'm not sure how you would take to airplanes and you wouldn't like being in a cage in the baggage compartment. But maybe you wouldn't have to." He chuckled softly. "One look at those teeth and they'd probably put you in first class or let you fly copilot."

Insuring that there was nothing close to the fire to catch if a spark flew out, he left it burning and crawled into the tent with the huge animal laying in front of the tent flaps. His rifle was beside him with the H & K under his folded trousers he used as a pillow, but he felt little need for them with Dog just outside. Nothing in its right mind would try to attack that monster.

He left the tent flaps open and lay philosophizing while watching the fire. This place was so much like Earth it put a strain on the imagination, not to mention credibility. What were the odds of finding another world like terra? Off the scale, that's what. Men of the natural sciences who understood the results and the effects of mass, distance from the sun, gravity, atmospheric pressure, planet rotation, orbit, all of those things that made the earth and the life on it what it was; they all agreed that the likelihood of finding another world similar to Earth was far less than finding two identical snowflakes.

But here he was. On a world found by accident and accessible to Earth by a means inconceivable to the rational, intelligent mind. It simply could not be. Yet, it was.

The fire was long dead, the sky was just beginning to glow through the trees and Dog was nowhere in sight when Savage opened his eyes, not realizing for a moment that he had been asleep for many hours. He yawned, stretched, dressed, put on his glasses and crawled from the tent. Using the wood left over from last night's fire, he rebuilt and ignited it. One dehydrated breakfast coming right up.

He wasn't sure when Dog came back. He was cleaning his mess gear when he looked up and there sat his companion a few feet away, silently regarding him with intelligent eyes.

With his gear packed and the rifle in his hands, he moved off toward the west with Dog remaining close to him most of the time but occasionally venturing off on his own for an hour or two, sometimes longer. But he always came back and Savage would glance down to see him padding along beside him.

How that big animal could move through the woods so quietly was a mystery. Although an experienced and skilled woodsman himself, his boots would occasionally fall on a dry twig or he would break a limb pushing his way through. Dog, with paws almost as big as dinner plates, never seemed to make a sound. Cats moved like that, carefully, softly and silently. But dogs thrashed around jumping and barking and knocking things down. That's what he thought, anyway.

There was no doubt that Dog had become completely accustomed to the gravity and it did not affect him in the least. That was encouraging, not to feel that extra weight all the time. He wondered how long it would be before *he* didn't notice it at all.

"Haven't got anything for you this time, Dog," he said, several hours later as he fixed lunch. "You're going to have to go to the store yourself. Unless you want some of this stuff." He held out the saucepan containing a dehydrated meal mixed with water. Dog didn't even sniff. He just looked away and yawned.

"Yeah, I don't blame you, but it's better than nothing, unless you got something better. Wanna share? I'm game." He got no takers.

Dense woods, thick underbrush, more miles and finally dinner over another fire. More sounds, more noises, more glimpses at movement along the forest floor and through the branches above. Dog could see them. Why couldn't he?

For three days he traveled without a break in the wooded surroundings. More bushes yielded larger and almost black berries, the weight of them causing the branches to droop. There was enough fruit here in this one small area to make a hundred pies or fifty quarts of jam.

He picked a small handful of the berries and held them out to the animal. Dog ate them in one gulp, swallowing them almost whole and obviously not liking the taste.

"If you can eat them, I guess I can," he remarked, plopping one into his mouth and biting down slowly. There was a slightly sour taste, akin to but not as strong as a lemon. Tangy but not altogether unpleasant. He didn't suddenly go into convulsions and die on the spot, so he picked more and ate them until he was satisfied. A few more went into a sample container.

"Well, they didn't kill me and now I won't starve. One more objective accomplished. So, onward and upward, there old Dog," he commanded theatrically. "I've got promises to keep and miles to go before I sleep," he quoted, remembering lines of the Robert Frost poem. "And miles to go before I sleep.

"Whose woods these are . . . well, I guess they are mine. Sure haven't run into anybody else laying claim. Have you, Dog?"

Once again he began to think that this forest would go on for a thousand miles and he would never find its end. When the United States was first explored one gigantic forest covered the whole eastern half of the country. Walking through it from the coast to reach the Mississippi would have taken months, maybe years. And he had only five days. Then he would have to turn and start back unless he found a food source other than the berries.

"Damn it, Dog, talk to me. How have you survived all this time? You've gotta know where the groceries are."

Just before noon on the fourth day he caught a fragrance in the air. It was the unmistakable smell of flowers. He stopped and sniffed the air, slowly turning in a complete circle. "Can't tell where it's coming from but it sure is nice. Wanna show me, Dog?"

After only a moment's hesitation and as though the animal understood every word, the big canine headed off through the trees to the left. Clutching his rifle and following along behind, Savage slowly shook his head. "Scary," he whispered. "I know *people* who can't communicate that well."

The smell became stronger and it was much lighter up ahead. The trees thinned and he walked into a long, narrow grass-covered meadow stretching for about a quarter of a mile in each direction. Thick along the far side where they could catch the morning sun was a solid wall of broadleaf plants extending up twenty or so feet on thick stalks bearing thousands upon thousands of vivid, cone-shaped, multicolored flowers among the leaves. They traversed almost the entire length of the clearing on that one side.

"Wow!" Savage exclaimed. "Now *that's* something you don't see every day." He laid the barrel of the rifle over his shoulder and started off briskly toward the wall of flowers.

Dog suddenly moved in front of him, barring his way. Savage attempted to step around the animal and continue on but again his path was blocked. "Hey! What's going on? I just want to check it out."

Regardless of what he did, whichever way he went, Dog blocked his progress into the clearing.

"You're trying to tell me something, aren't you. You don't want me to go into that clearing. Why?"

Dog was looking at him, tail moving back and forth very slowly.

"Okay. There's danger over there, right? Is that it? Something dangerous?"

The tail wagged faster.

The small of the flowers was becoming overwhelming and he began to feel slightly light-headed. "Something's not right here. The flowers? It's the flowers. The fragrance. The fragrance is poison. Poison gas? The scent from those flowers is deadly. Right? Yeah, I got it, pal. Let's get the hell out of here."

Dog's nose was twitching and he began snorting loudly as though trying to sneeze. He swiped a huge paw across the end of his muzzle, turned and retreated into the woods leaving Savage to follow at a run with eyes watering and a shortness of breath threatening to asphyxiate him. Clutching his rifle, the pack slamming against his back with each long running step, he

WINDOW IN THE WORLD

kept up the pace behind dog until they were well away from the fragrance of those deadly flowers.

Finally stopping, intending only to catch his breath, Savage collapsed with his back to a tree and sucked in air. Dog came back to him and sat on his haunches a short distance away.

"Thanks, pal. You saved my ass back there." He pulled out his canteen, took a drink and poured some over his face, eyes and nose. "Come here, Dog," he said. "This'll help." He dumped water over the animal's face and in its nose. Dog sneezed, shook his massive head and shorted. Again, there was a swipe across the muzzle with a paw.

Cleared of the poison air, the canine sank to the ground on his stomach and regarded the man with those deep green eyes.

"You knew about those flowers, didn't you, Dog. I would have walked right in there hadn't a been for you. But, you know, I didn't see any dead critters laying around. I wonder if the flowers kill them and then something else immune to the poison comes along to feed. And they give something back, whatever it might be, to benefit the flowers. Symbiosis. And I almost became a part of the food chain, lower level."

He put his canteen away and climbed slowly to his feet, readjusting the pack so it was more comfortable. Dog rose and was ready to continue the journey.

"I wonder," Savage said as they started off in a different direction, "if maybe there might be some of those sunflower guys from the valley lurking back there behind that wall of flowers. It would be a perfect set-up. One plant helping another. Survival, whatever it takes. I better be more careful. But how does a guy figure that the smell of flowers is going to do him in?"

Dog didn't answer.

The afternoon of the fifth day finally brought them to a thinning of the trees and then the edge of the forest which opened onto a flat, rolling plain stretching to the horizon. With the exception of a solitary tree here and there—and from this distance they looked a little like Dutch Elms—nothing broke the flowing landscape of grass waiving in the breeze. It extended farther than he could see with his binoculars.

It could have been Nebraska, Kansas or even Wyoming back in the fourteenth century of undiscovered America where huge herds of animals grazed on tender shoots growing among the tall stalks of thick, hearty grass. The animals were, in turn, hunted by the scattered descends of ancient Mongols who fled across the winter ice bridge of the Bering Strait to Alaska then down through Canada to North America where they multiplied then separated into individual tribes. The animals of central North America at that time numbered in the millions, food enough to feed them forever. But then the slaughter began, for sport. The passenger pigeon, the buffalo, the elk, bear, cougar and the eagles. The animal called Man sure made his presence known.

He saw that there would be very few if any real landmarks on this sea of grass. Little he could follow back to this spot where he emerged from the trees, and then to his camp additional miles away. His sense of direction was not enough. Was Dog's ability to find his way sufficient to guide them for hundreds of miles across strange country and then back again? Had dog ever been this far before? The sun would help some but only in giving general directions. He needed something more precise.

The grass came up a little past his knees and it was uniform in height as far as he could see. It resembled the vast wheat and oat fields of the Great Plains that stretched on and on for countless miles. Under it here was a thick mat of dead, slowly decomposing grass. It lived, it grew, it died back and began anew. It was seasonal and it needed water, rain. There were clouds in the distance so it *did* rain here. This land, plowed, disked, planted and cultivated could provide food for countless numbers of Earth people. Corn, tomatoes, asparagus, beans, barley, anything and everything they could ever possibly need.

Eden.

It was still daylight and he could just make out the edge of the forest in the distance behind him when he stopped to make camp. He chose a site near one of the solitary trees to set up his tent and gather what few twigs and dead branches he could find for a fire. Dinner would have to be a brief affair because the sparse fuel he had managed to find wouldn't last very long.

He dug up several soil samples from widely scattered spots and sealed them in the plastic containers. Back at his camp, he would run a complete analysis on the dirt which would tell him the nutrients, the enzymes, the nitrogen and pretty close to just what and how much the land would support. The rest would be figured back on Earth from the information he gave them.

The planet's single moon rose in full phase. Larger and maybe even closer than Earth's satellite, it cast a brilliant, almost spectacular light over the landscape of waving grass and lonely sentinels.

Was a single, isolated tree lonely? Or was it just a figure of speech, a descriptive term?

As he fixed and ate dinner he watched the flowing orb move rapidly across the dark sky lending heavily to his theory that it was closer than Earth's moon. In an hour or two it would reach its zenith and begin to sink. With this, his first unobstructed look, he couldn't tell if it was in apogee or perigee. He hoped it was in apogee because if it got any closer it would be bumping into mountaintops, if there were any mountains here to have tops.

Was it like Earth's satellite, airless and dead or could it be a world like this one rich with life? With the materials he had and considering the present labor force—one man and one dog—he could build a spaceship and go check it out. Yeah, in about eight or nine hundred years.

As he continued to watch, stars began to appear in the crystal-clear night sky. Occasionally using his binoculars, he scanned the heavens looking for a star pattern easily recognizable, such as Cancer in the Northern Hemisphere near Leo and Gemini.

All around the world on his exploration trips he had only to look to the skis and spot a familiar constellation and he knew roughly where he was. Now all he needed was just one familiar constellation among the millions and billions of stars covering the sky like tiny blazing diamonds.

There were none. The sky and the star patterns were completely alien to him. Even with the computer-generated images of what known constellations would look like from a different place in the galaxy, he could identify nothing. Not since his first experience with the stronger gravity had there been such undeniable proof that he was on another world somewhere out in the endless reaches of space. And he could never again return home to Earth.

Dog came to him and for the first time put a huge paw in the man's lap as though to offer sympathy and comfort. Somehow it seemed that the big animal actually sensed his anguish and, yes, his fear, and offered understanding and support. Savage reached out and stroked the massive head and locked his fingers into the thick fur.

I went through it too, at first, Dog seemed to be saying. I was afraid. I didn't know where I was. I understand what you are feeling. I learned to live with it. So will you.

But, of course, these were just words of consolation Savage imagined. Dogs can't talk and the animal wasn't saying anything. It was all in his mind. But nevertheless, it was actually comforting and he answered as though Dog had actually spoken.

"I've got a handle on it now, boy," he said aloud. "Just a few rough moments there. Thanks for the words of understanding."

Dog got to his feet, nuzzled the man's face with a wet nose and then walked off a few paces where he flopped to the ground, his eyes on the man.

"Quite a dog, you are," Savage mused. "You know, it's absolutely amazing the way you seem to know what's going on in my head. If I didn't know better, I'd . . . Naaaa."

There wasn't much left of the fire and the whole eastern sky was thick with bright pinpoints of light. He broke out his sketchbook, pencil, a flashlight and began to plot the stars he could see above him. Some were much brighter and he used them as key reference points, intending to chart their progress across the sky in sketch after sketch, page after page as the night wore on. The following night he would do it again to check his work.

One of his closer friends and a not too distant neighbor in Denver—back before the sensational trial—was an astronomer who had spent most of his life studying the heavens. If he was here now he might have some ideas, some insight on where they were. The opportunity to study the stars from another world had come up from time to time in their conversations over a glass of brandy on the rare occasions when they both were home, and he was sad that space travel would not be within his lifetime. He would never have the chance to view the heavens from another world.

Palomar could contact him. Mr. Getty through Killingsworth could make the offer. Would he come? Would he jump through the Window, give up friends, home and family to go to another world somewhere in some unknown part of space where he would live and die alone? Would the professor even consider that?

In a heartbeat.

Keep that in mind, Savage thought. First, however, he needed to survive.

With the movement of the sun during the day and the star patterns at night charted in his sketchbook, he would eventually be able to figure out where he was in relationship to his camp. He wouldn't worry about getting lost anymore. Even without Dog to guide him, he could find his way back to the Window.

Since the planet rotated on its axis, the stars, of course, were circumpolar. That was elementary astronomy. Now, if he could just find the pole star, or if there wasn't one, a small group of stationary stars making up the Celestial Pole around which the rest revolved, he would have a starting place. From the path of the sun across the sky, the flight of the moon at night and now the star patterns moving around the Pole, he could determine which hemisphere he was in, how long a year would be, the length of the seasons—if the planet's axis changed position with respect to the sun and there *were* different seasons—True North and then the other three directions he needed to know, and maybe, eventually, just how big this planet was. If the axis tilted away from the sun, part of the planet would get cold. He needed to know if he was on that part and when it would happen.

His eyes were hurting. He needed to take out the contacts, quit looking at the sky and get some sleep. The fire was out and he would burn up his flashlight batteries in a hurry if he kept this up. He had obviously lost all track of time and had been at it for hours. Must be something like two or three in the morning. There wasn't a sound to be heard. That was amazing. In the wide spaces around him, there wasn't a sound.

He didn't even want to think about the fact that he had managed to stretch two canteens of water over five days and now he was out. He used the last drops to fix his meal. He had to find water. If he didn't in the next few days, he would begin to dehydrate and then die of thirst.

Morning began without breakfast. He packed and shouldered his gear and started off, pulling out and chewing on the tall grass stems for the moisture they contained. It helped but it would be enough to keep him going for very long. He had to find water.

At noon he ate a granola bar and thought about a long, cold drink of water. There was nothing he could see ahead of him to indicate a break in the prairie. No depression, no valley or gully where there might be a stream, no low area where a pond or even a stagnant pool could collect. Nightfall would find him hungry and thirsty. The sea of grass went on and on.

With the exception of a slight rise or dip, the otherwise flat plane extended with no end in sight. Savage had seen no animal life of any kind, nothing flying, nothing crawling. This was like an Indiana flatland with an old cornfield overgrown with weeds and grass. Walking through it would kick up pheasants and grouse, doves and wild pigeons. Quail would explode into the air with their loud whirring-flapping sound, scaring the hell out of everybody until one of the old-timers got off a shot and brought it down.

Where was the game? It had to be here, somewhere. Dog was well fed without the steaks from Palomar, so meat must be available somewhere. Water, too. So, where was it?

It was late in the day, he was tired and had replaced the contacts with his glasses. It was warm, bordering on being muggy. Was it going to rain tonight? It had not rained since he had been here. What would that be like?

Dropping his pack and collapsing in the grass, he licked his dry lips with an equally dry tongue. Dog came to him and he grasped the animal behind the ears. "You've got to show me, Dog," he said, laying exhausted in the grass. "I can't find it by my self. I can't even find the key to the ecosystem of this place. I don't know where anything is, so you've got to show it to me. I need water and I need to find food. You don't hunt in the daytime so whatever it is must come out at night. You've got to show me."

Dog looked at him sympathetically and let his tongue hand over his lower teeth. "Later tonight, when I'm rested and it gets dark we'll go together, okay?" He lay back with his head on his pack and his hand atop a gigantic paw. His eyes closed and he was asleep in minutes, his intentions to chart the stars again completely forgotten.

Was it movement or sound that awakened him? He opened his eyes and raised his head to see Dog moving silently away from him, ears pitched forward to catch the slightest sound. In a moment the animal had vanished into the tall grass.

Alert and on his feet, he ran after the canine. There had been no time to grab the rifle laying beside his pack, but the pistol, snug in its holster, slapped his leg as he ran.

In the bright moonlight of the late night, Dog glanced back, not seeing but hearing the man pounding along behind, then continued on at a fast pace slicing through the grass. Savage once again silently thanked Diana for all those miles and all the hours she had made him run up and down the hills.

For five minutes, almost ten, he followed Dog through the grass of the prairie, the moon lighting his way and keeping the animal's wake in sight. Gasping for breath and approaching absolute exhaustion, he could not run another step further. He had to stop.

Then, suddenly, Dog was gone, disappearing down into the grass, flat on his stomach and motionless. Following the example Savage dove headlong into the grass and froze, waiting for something to happen. His glasses almost fell from his face but he didn't move to readjust them.

He hadn't thought about the headlong dive into the grass. It was just a reaction, something he *knew* he must do. An *instinctive* reaction, but what instinct? Nothing in his life had prepared him for this. He had never been in the military service and had no instinctive reaction to danger. What did he know that he didn't *know* he knew? How was that again?

Was it something like that warning he had gotten when the plants were about to attack? If so, why hadn't he been warned about the smell of the flowers. Well, he had, in a way. Dog had warned him but certainly not in the same manner.

The wait was a short one but he finally got his breath back again. Breathing slowly and steadily through his nose, he raised himself on his elbows to see a flurry of motion. Re-adjusting his glasses, he watched Dog explode out of the grass. He was up and running flat out at full speed. Like a flash of brown and sliver lightening the huge canine streaked through the moonlit grass to the attack at almost sixty miles an hour. My god, he could catch a cheetah on the run.

On his feet and attempting to follow, Savage had taken only a few running steps when he felt the ground tremble beneath him and he saw a black shape loom up directly in front of him. Up and up the thing rose. Six feet, seven, eight feet above the ground. White claws six inches long flashed in the moonlight and the huge, fur-covered shape took a lumbering step toward him.

Skidding to a halt, he dragged the Koch from its holster and thumbed back the hammer. His hands were shaking so badly that he had to use both to hold and aim the weapon. Goddamn, that thing was big, whatever it was. Only ten feet away, it was coming closer fast. Eight feet! He had finally found indigenous animal life and it acted hungry.

The explosion was almost deafening. The recoil smacked his hand almost breaking his grasp on the weapon. The bullet struck. The eight-foot monster stopped, lurched back slightly with clawed paws waving like a huge grizzly bear. But it did not fall. Savage fired again, his hands shaking less now. A third shot and the slug forced the dark shape back again.

Pointing carefully now he cradled the Koch in one hand, aimed with the other and put four more shots into the furry body in front of him. The hot ejected shell casings flew off to his right, the spinning, polished brass catching and reflecting the moonlight for only a split second before dropping into the grass.

A bullet kills by traumatic shock. Take an ounce of lead, move it at a thousand feet per second and it's like getting hit with a ten pound sledgehammer going 680 miles an hour. The explosive charge in the point of the bullet didn't make much of a bang, just enough to fragment the slug and increase the impact, increase the trauma.

He breathed a sigh of relief as the creature slowly toppled and fell heavily onto the ground in front of him. Moments passed but it lay motionless. Holding the pistol ready, step by careful step he walked forward until he could kick at it with the toe of his boot.

Ready to crank off the remaining rounds, he looked down at what he had just killed. A fur-bearing animal.

The fur was covered with dirt and there was a large, gaping hole in the ground several feet behind where the monster lay. No wonder he hadn't been able to find any animal life here. It lived underground. He had walked over it for miles not know it was there, only a short distance beneath his feet all this time.

Dog had been momentarily startled by the gunshots and had left his meal to investigate, but find the man safe and in no danger, returned to finish eating. It was a dog-size, furry thing into which he sunk his saber-tooth fangs. Smaller with shorter claws but otherwise it resembled in every way the monster killed by the high-velocity slugs.

Savage looked more closely at the huge, frightening thing on the ground. The claws were not retractable and the nose or snout was blunt, leather-like and almost square. There were no claws on the hind feet.

Looking from the hole in the ground back to the dead animal he began to realize what it was, that it had not attacked him at all. It had risen up, attracted to the vibrations of his footsteps on the ground, and had swung its claws wildly, aimlessly, in defense, but it could not see. It had no eyes.

The long claws were used for digging, not killing, and its mouth contained only grinding teeth for roots, soft bulbs and grass. Its newborn, venturing dangerously onto the surface to snip off and eat the fresh grass were the pray Dog attacked and killed. The huge creature sought only to protect them.

A warm-blooded, air-breathing, subsurface, harmless and almost defenseless mammal, a huge, timid mole suddenly breaking through the surface to guard its young against some enemy it couldn't see and couldn't understand lay dead in the grass, struck down by a weapon from another world. Suddenly tears stung his eyes and then poured unchecked down his face into his beard as he looked at the lifeless body of the harmless creature he had killed. What sort of black angel was he? The first Earthman, the first destroyer. With all of the tens of thousands of years of technical knowledge Earth had to offer, with instant travel through distance, time and space, with power almost unlimited, he had managed to kill a mole.

Dog hunted for food, to survive, but man killed out of fear and ignorance and, yes, just for fun. And it was not only the animals they killed. They killed each other by the thousands, by the millions. This is what the hoards from Earth would bring to this peaceful, unsuspecting world.

Shaken and ashamed, the gun still loosely clutched in his hand, his hunger forgotten, he made his way back to the makeshift camp. He packed his gear, covered the remains of the fire and began the trip back to the Window in the dark, leaving Dog behind to catch up when he chose. The moon was still bright and would remain so for another few hours. He could see well enough so there was no need to wait for morning.

He would tell Palomar that he was sick, that he had contracted a disease and was going to die. That would stop the invasion. Or he could tell them that he had found no food, no life at all except the plants and man could not survive here unless continually supplied by the Window, an impossible task. He would not have this world destroyed as humans were destroying the earth.

But did he have that right? Could he play God and condemn tens of millions in the name of conservation? And what about Diana? He did not want to live out the rest of his life here on and dying. Worse yet, someone else might be sent through for a second opinion. Palomar had put too much time and money into this project to accept his word alone and just lay down and quit.

The deterioration of the optic nerves was continuing and soon he would be unable to see. A blind man alone on a whole world. Better he use that pistol on himself and get it over with.

A sudden and severe rainstorm lashed across the plain, moving with incredible speed to catch and drench him to the skin before he could stop and set up his tent. His fear of raindrops hitting him like hail pellets wasn't as bad as he had envisioned. They hit harder than raindrops back on Earth but he was in no danger of even being bruised by them. Water poured from his head down the back of his neck, soaked into his pants and trickled down into his boots saturating his socks. It was a hard, pounding rain that fell in torrents, blocking out everything around him.

Quickly he removed the caps from both canteens, fashioned crude funnels from the thick paper of his sketchbook and began catching the precious water. Holding the canteens between his knees and pinching the sketchbook paper together with his fingers, he watched the liquid stream in. It would be enough to get him back to his base camp. As the rain poured down upon him, it also poured into his canteens.

He stripped off his wet clothes and stood naked in the downpour, taking his first shower since arriving here. The rain on his skin had a strange prickling, slightly stinging sensation. More like a pleasant tingle really. It was cold, refreshing and stimulating. Then it ceased as suddenly as it had started, moving on across the land. He had been caught in rainstorms before so he thought little of it.

Back in the late Sixties, Union Oil of California entertained the idea that there could be a huge petroleum field under the rain forest in Sough America. They hired him to investigate and he spent six weeks there, exploring, testing, looking for some indication of subterranean oil deposits, but all he got was wet. From a clear, cloudless sky, thunderheads would quickly role in, the water would pour from the sky and he would be drenched in minutes, miles from his camp.

He didn't find any oil and he got rained on a lot, something he just accepted as part of the job, what they were paying him to do. So, what was one more rain storm.

He put up his tent, laid out his wet clothing and soggy boots to dry during the remainder of the night, dried off the rifle and reloaded the magazine in the Koch. Finally, he curled up for a few hours sleep before dawn. He still had several days travel ahead of him and rest was what he needed now, rest and a little sleep, not much, just a little.

The sun was up and Dog was there waiting when he crawled from the shelter, still naked, to survey the plain. It was still early morning but the sea of grass appeared to have been already dried by the heat of the sun, at least the top part of it was. His clothes were still damp so he put on dry ones from the pack and chewed on beef jerky as he assembled his gear. One long swallow of water from an almost full canteen tasted very good to him. And most important, it didn't kill him.

His boots were still wet so he tied the laces together and hung them around his pack. The ground was soft and he doubted that there was any broken glass or bottle caps here he could accidentally step on. Wearing a pair of thick socks, he set off in the direction of the woods and the Window.

CHAPTER TWENTY-THREE

E LEVEN DAYS HAD PASSED by the time he finally arrived back at the Window. Passing by the elongated meadow containing the fragrant and deadly flowers, he gave it a wide berth and continued on. Perhaps at some future time he could order a gas mask from Palomar and enter the poisoned air to investigate his theory of the flowers and the moving plants working together. Sure! After he had explored the gorge, investigated the plants, walked the planes and looked for water. That wouldn't take more than, oh, say four or five years. *Then* he could check out the meadow of the deadly flowers.

The socks had worn through rapidly but he had not put his boots back on, finding that he no longer needed or even wanted them, his bare feet toughening very quickly to the ground even without the socks. He had often gone the entire summer without shoes as a boy back on the farm in Indiana and in some of the tropic zones he had worn just sandals or nothing at all, so it was not anything new to him. Even in the forest with sharp sticks, rocks and thorn bushes, he managed with little discomfort and no damage to his feet other than a small rock cut that healed surprisingly fast.

Timing his arrival during the long hours of darkness, he hoped to slip in unobserved, have all the data and information coordinated and his report ready before they started bombarding him with questions. Dog vanished as they approached the clearing.

The table was still in front of the door and nothing appeared to have been disturbed in his absence. Moving it aside, he entering the tent and turned on the battery-operated lights. Unbuckling the straps, he dropped his pack, put his rifle and gunbelt on the cot and began unpacking the samples he had collected. He worked through the remainder of the night filling out his journal and writing additional pages of explanation and description to be viewed and photographed through the Window. He would also show them the star charts he had made. Using the computers at their disposal, they might be able to determine from the pattern of stars just where he was, if he was still in the Milky Way Galaxy at all. Maybe the Window had sent him to the Great Spiral Nebula in Andromeda or to a galaxy so far away it couldn't even be seen from Earth with the most powerful telescopes.

He had read somewhere that with the Hubble telescope circling the earth, astronomers could see 10.5 billion light years. The distance light travels in just one year is six quadrillion miles. That's six followed by 24 zeros, or $10^{24.}$ Now, multiply that by 10 billion. Yeah, go ahead and try. Maybe they really could see him; probably wouldn't recognize him at that distance, though.

Briefly, he told them about the deadly scented flowers and the moles but not the circumstances surrounding his discovery of the animals. He described the berries and that he had eaten some with no harmful effects. Needless to say, he mentioned nothing about his traveling companion.

Sometime during the night he heard a soft thud outside and knew something had come through the Window. Somebody had noticed and they were aware that he was back. He ignored them and continued working.

Shortly after dawn he put on clean clothes, built a fire, cooked breakfast and contemplated an idea he was formulating, a plan for his return to the plain. There was another thump beneath the Window. Louder this time, something heavier, much heavier. They were becoming impatient. He thought of something sarcastic to say but didn't. Instead, he wrote out, *Been up all night preparing report. Tired. Please wait.* He went outside and put it on the projector.

That should stave them off for a short while. He prepared a short list of things he wanted, cleaned his mess kit and padded on bare feet back to the Window where he picked up the packets of papers collecting on the ground. Obviously, he was not the only one who had been up all night writing.

Then he laughed. Laying on the ground with a piece of paper tied around it was a brick. Someone had actually gone outside, pried loose a brick and threw it at him to get his attention. What nonsense. He didn't even look at the paper fastened to it.

He took the packets into the tent and got his notes and drawings. It was a cloudy, overcast morning that allowed him to project the material onto the screen and have it seen through the Window. In bright sunlight, the overhead projector would not have worked well.

Page-by-page and sheet-by-sheet it took half an hour to present everything including the list of things he wanted. Then he returned to the tent to examine what they had sent him. Included were several letters from Diana. These, later that night and out of sight of the Window, he would read aloud to Dog in the light of a flashlight.

Once again he reflected on the attention, the intelligence and the understanding displayed by the big animal during their trek through the woods and across the plain. It was almost as though the dog knew what Savage was saying, even what he was thinking, sometimes before he said it. All the while, those fierce green eyes were watching him intently.

Did dogs have green eyes?

The question suddenly popped into his mind. He had never heard of a dog with green eyes, particularly green eyes as penetrating and almost iridescent as those trained on him. Cats had green eyes so he supposed that it was possible. He knew very little about dogs.

Picking up the battery-powered electric razor from among the voluminous supplies and equipment they had sent with him, he ran his hand through the quarter-inch growth of beard on his face, shrugged and tossed the instrument back into its box. His hair too, was growing longer but who was here to care?

One of the thick packets contained computer created images of several of the constellations, Orion, Gemini, Ursa Minor—the little dipper—Leo and Pegasus, with five different views of how they might look from different locations in the galaxy. It was a small part of the program he had studied before he came through the Window. He was to take them with him when he returned to the plain and try to identify something. There were orders from Mr. Getty, the same as before. Go! Scout the country. Explore everything! Report everything!

Another packet of papers was from Dr. Worthington inquiring about the state of his health. How did he feel generally? How was he coping with the gravity? Was he eating and drinking regularly? Did he feel ill at all? Did he have regular bowel movements? When he got to the bowel movement part, he tossed the questionnaire aside with a shake of his head. There were also two pages and two plastic envelopes from the ophthalmologist, Dr. Gunville. One of the envelopes contained disposable contact lenses, the other about two dozen small pills. Absent surgical repair, an antibiotic he had formulated might retard and possibly arrest completely the degeneration of the optic nerve, Gunville offered. Great! He already knew he was going blind. He didn't need to be reminded of it. He tossed those aside, too.

He had been on the trip for only three weeks, Getty had said, and that wasn't near enough time to do all the exploring they wanted. Take two months, three months, whatever was necessary.

Wait a minute!

Savage looked up from the papers and charts scattered across the top of the table. Getty mentioned that he had been gone three weeks. Seven days times three equals twenty-one days. He was certain that it had been only eleven days. He had kept careful records on it. Quickly he scanned his notes and confirmed that he had been gone only eleven days. With the extra twelve hours on this world, *his* day was a day and a half on Earth. That would be seventeen days. Where did the other four days come from?

He hadn't miscalculated and he hadn't just lost a day or two somewhere. There was something different about time on this world. Well, who said a minute has to be sixty seconds long. Maybe it was eighty, and, maybe there are ninety minutes in an hour. There were certainly thirty-six hours in a day. That was for sure.

Since everything was so encouraging and he was doing so well, he asked for Diana to be sent through the Window to accompany him back to the plain. However, as he had suspected, the request was denied, claiming it was still too soon for her. They had to be *absolutely* certain that human life could survive there longer than just a few weeks or months and one life was enough to risk. When he returned from the plain again, another month or two later, they would definitely reconsider. If he was still alive, fit and healthy, she would be sent to join him. Was that acceptable?

What choice did he have? He had nothing to bargain with. As to Getty's instructions to go exploring, he accepted them willingly, anxious now to go back to the plain and find what lay beyond the grass. He wanted to find a lake, another river like the one in the canyon, and most important of all, he wanted to find an ocean. That would be his goal, from a major river to an ocean.

He began packing his gear carefully, including the items for which he had specifically asked. Two blocks of rock salt, each the size of a cigarette pack, a pair of moccasins to replace the boots and a short, powerful recurved hunting bow accompanied by two dozen fiberglass arrows fitted with three-bladed razorheads made from stainless steel in a soft leather quiver to be hung on his back. The sound of a gunshot, he had told them, would carry over a long distance and possibly frighten away the very life forms for which he was searching. It was all bullshit but it must have sounded reasonable to them because the archery equipment was delivered. They nonetheless insisted he take guns in addition to the bow, just in case. He agreed but out of sight in the tent, he cleaned, oiled and carefully packaged the rifles and pistol away to be left with the other Earth paraphernalia he no longer needed or wanted. The long-bladed hunting knife was the only other weapon he would take. All of the reports he had gotten, any unread, and the computer star charts went into the filing cabinet along with the pills and the disposable contacts the eye doctor had sent.

He packed his glasses, enough of the dehydrated food to last a month, a couple rolls of toilet paper, filled two canteens with pure, bottled water sent through the Window and used the rest to bathe himself. He remembered to include soap in his pack this time.

Clean now and very tired, he closed the tent flaps, stripped off his clothes and dropped onto the cot. Switching off the lights and laying back, he closed his eyes and slept soundly for the next four hours.

Just four hours of sleep and he awoke hungry and completely rested. Turning on one of the lights and slipping into his trousers he hastily wrote a note, went outside and put it onto the overhead projector.

Two twenty-six ounce steaks, one rare, one raw—he would cook that one later—baked potato, broccoli with cheese sauce, chef's salad with green peppers, mushrooms and onions, a quart of milk and a loaf of garlic bread. That's what he wanted.

He sat on the ground in front of the tent looking as intimidating and menacing as he could, waiting impatiently for the food. Dog would love that raw steak.

Maybe they could put some cows through the window, if they could figure out how to get them down that narrow elevator shaft. Just four of them and in a few years he would have a whole herd. They'd do great on the plain with all that grass, and he and Dog would have steaks forever.

Maybe there were cows here already, or something like them. He hadn't explored enough of the planet to know. Give it another month or two. Forget it. He didn't know how to make steaks out of cows anyway.

The food arrived in the same type of Styrofoam containers, landing with a plop on the ground. He picked everything up and took it beyond view of the Window.

"Dog?" he inquired quietly.

Almost immediately, the animal was there in front of him, appearing from the darkness of the woods.

"Manna from heaven, old dog," he said, tossing the chunk of meat to the canine. "Should have asked for china plates and real silver," he continued, opening the containers and digging into the food with his fingers. "Never picked up a filet mignon with my hands and gnawed on it before. Pretty bad manners. You mind?"

Dog was preoccupied and didn't answer.

"We need to get going at first light," he continued, licking his fingers and dropping the containers to the ground. "I've got everything we need packed. They're not giving us much time."

He crushed the Styrofoam containers and buried them in the ground, using his knife to dig a hole. With dampness, heat and cold, insects and enzymes, deterioration and monocular decay, it would take almost six hundred years for the synthetic, plastic boxes to break down and finally return to a natural state. He remembered one of the questions on a test he had taken for an environmental class he had in college. How long does it take a piece of glass to break down and return to a natural state? It hadn't been covered in the lecture material so everybody just guessed. Nobody got it right. The answer was, never. Once made, glass is immortal.

"We've got two months, maybe three at the most. I could probably get more but Diana will be coming through the Window to us. We've got to be back in time and ready for her. So, let's get to it."

Supplemented by fresh meat he now knew to exist on the plain, and with rainwater to collect, drink and refill his canteens, he could survive for many months without support from the Window. He wanted to turn south once he reached the plain in the event this planet had winter months with cold and snow and if he was in an area where it would hit. They had said nothing about snow falling over the long months they had watched through the Window, but there was probably a lot they hadn't told him for reasons of their own.

As dawn broke he secured the camp and hoisted the pack onto his shoulders. It was heavy but not as heavy as it would have been a few weeks ago. He was overcoming the gravity, actually becoming stronger because of it. Dog sat waiting for him twenty yards in the wood and they set off together once again.

They had covered almost thirty miles when darkness fell nineteen hours later. Taking in the lunch break and his rest stops he was moving through the often brush-choked forest at better than a mile and a half an hour, a remarkable pace considering that an average man walking along a clear, level pathway with no obstructions progressed at four miles an hour. His sense of direction was improving, too. He could tell if he ventured toward the south or inadvertently strayed north. Returning to due west was no problem for him.

Above everything else, the most rewarding accomplishment of the journey was that he was seeing and hearing the forest life. Once he spotted an animal with a long tail somewhat like a fox racing through the brush. A smaller creature was jumping from limb to limb overhead and a flock of flying things scattered at his passing. Squawks, calls, snarls and other sounds he couldn't begin to identify reached his ears for the first time. There was an abundance of life here.

Shortly before dark he made camp in a small clearing, tossing out the sticks and dead brush, and set up his tent. Keeping the fire low he fixed dinner, eating two helpings. His appetite was certainly improving.

After cleaning the cookware, in the flickering light of the fire, he read Diana's letters. She described the weights on her wrists, ankles and around her waist to prepare her for the gravity. Little by little she would increase the weight until she could join him without the discomfort he had been forced to endure. Three more months was so long to wait. Could he come back to the Window sooner? She had Mr. Getty's promise that she could come through the Window as soon as he returned and they knew he was alright. She loved him and counted the days until they would be together.

He regretted that there was no way he could communicate with her privately as she did with him. He certainly was not going to stand in front of the Window and display his private thoughts not knowing who else was watching. He hoped she would understand.

He did not enter the small tent but instead leaned with his back against a tree watching the fire slowly die. Taking out his contact lenses, he rested and dozed a little but he did not sleep. Dog left and was gone for several hours, evidently confident that the man was safe. The night was long and he was anxious to be up and going at the very first sign of light. An hour before dawn he finally fell asleep but awakened immediately when Dog returned.

They traveled from dawn to dusk the next day, stopping only twice for Savage to fix lunch for himself and to rest in the afternoon. They encountered nothing unusual and mile after mile fell behind them until darkness finally forced a halt once again. The morning of the third day he left the tent and the hatchet behind, needing neither and not wanting to continue carrying them.

Noon on the fourth day amid a downpour through which they continued to walk brought them to the edge of the forest and out onto the plain. The woods smelled heavily of dampness, mildew and rot, wet wood and soggy foliage. The forest floor was spongy and soft. The plain smelled better and the ground was firm under their feet.

The following day found them at the site where he had shot the mole and the memory haunted him. He abandoned his almost empty canteens there, finding that moisture was sufficient in the roots of the grass. Water was just a few inches below the surface if he dug for it and didn't mind it a little muddy. Dog began bringing in small animals he had caught and killed, sharing the meat with the man. A flying mammal vaguely resembling a cross between a bat and a squirrel fell to one of his arrows and he cooked the meat on a spit over the fire kindled by spinning a sharpened stick rapidly in his hands. This he shared with Dog but Dog wasn't all that happy with cooked meat and he let the man know it. Tubers dug from the swampy hollows tasted a little like potatoes and thorny bushes concealed by the grass yielded buds resembling grains of corn when heated in hot ashes. Berries were found on other bushes near the numerous wet areas.

The pack with its concentrated food packages and cooking gear was left behind a week later. Food was abundant now that he knew where to look for it. The game birds were there too. Feathered flying things resembling birds nesting in the tall grass and not moving until almost stepped on. Dog could sniff them out and once discovered, they were fast as they exploded from the nest and streaked into the air, but Savage was fast too. His arrows seldom missed.

Shedding his shirt and discarding it in the afternoon heat, cutting his trousers off well above the knee and reverting to his barefoot state, he and his companion turned south toward what he thought might be mountains in the far distance. The lightweight, camouflage thermal blanket he folded long-ways into a narrow strip inside of which he carried the blocks of salt, glasses and his zippered case of chemicals. Tying it together at the ends with a cord, he hung it from his shoulder. Bow, arrows and knife, binoculars around his neck, he needed nothing else. Soon the binoculars would probably go, too. He didn't use them very much anymore.

CHAPTER TWENTY-FOUR

A MONTH PASSED AS DAVID Savage and the dog he called Dog zigzagged their way south and west across the flat surface of the new world. It became warmer; the star patterns overhead became familiar although none of them were constellations as seen from Earth. There were three bright, blue-red stars forming a perfect triangle that was the Celestial Pole. He called them Draco for the dragon that curled it's tail around Earth's North Star.

They found the edge of the great plain that slowly became a desert stretching off ahead of them to the west. They saw the towering, white-capped mountain range that lay far beyond it. Turning south they waded across small cold streams and swam wide warm rivers, they bathed and played in ponds and huge lakes surrounded by thick lush green foliage and tall, stately trees with leaves in a multitude of shapes, sizes and colors. There were wide, deep valleys and narrow, shallow ravines all covered by growing things. With the exception of rocks and boulders, there wasn't a spot of bare ground to be found. In places, there were faint signs of game trails that interfered with the symmetry of the landscape, but nowhere was there any evidence of the presence of civilization.

Animal life beyond description surrounded them and from the waters, they took gilled creatures that might have been fish on Earth in some madman's dream of them. A triple-winged dragonfly the size of an eagle rose above one small pond and hovered, regarding them momentarily in his flight with multiple, purple eyes and then droned on.

They encounter a number of the large carnivorous plants standing alone or in small bunches of two or three, usually near water, waiting for something to come to drink. These he gave a wide berth although Dog showed no fear of them. He wanted to know how the animal would react to the creatures. Now, he knew. However, among all that he had discovered, nowhere did he find any higher intelligent life.

On one occasion, they came upon a strip of bare ground as wide as a city block extending off into the distance in both directions. There wasn't a blade of grass, a shoot, a twig or anything visible above the dirt. It was as though some giant Caterpillar scraper-blade had ripped up the sod and took it somewhere. Upon close examination, however, Savage saw that the ground had not been disturbed, only the plant life upon it was missing. He and Dog set off in an attempt to learn the cause of this strange phenomenon, but after several miles they found nothing except the weeds and prairie grass beginning to encroach and fill in the bare stirrup. Reversing direction and paralleling the unnatural scalping of the turf for almost thirty miles, they detected faint movement in the distance.

As they approached, Savage was amazed. A thick raft of tightly interwoven plants six centimeters thick inched its way along on the same root-like tentacle feet as the sunflowers, carrying within its leaves and winding stems billions upon billions of tiny, fat, legless, grass-eating insects that devoured everything they encountered.

The insect waste was a natural fertilizer for the plants that they could absorb through their leaves.

The grass carpet moved forward, carrying the otherwise immobile insects with it and each fed the other. Again, the perfect symbiosis.

He drew his bow and planted an arrow in the path of the moving carpet and watched as the small plants flowed around the hard, seasoned shaft, splitting apart and then joining together again. The insect's sharp, powerful mandibles nibbled at the arrow in passing but had no immediate effects. By the time the hundred yard-long symbiotic carpet passed however, the shaft would probably be gone.

There was a rudimentary intelligence here, but no way to know if it was with the plants, the insects guiding the plants or a combination of both becoming one.

Dog found no interest in the moving carpet so they left it and moved on.

He measured the erosion of the mountains and examined the sediment in the streams with his chemicals, he calculated the velocity of the water and the cutting-rate of the rivers, estimated how much material they could carry in suspension and how much they dropped along the way. As the riverbeds built up with pebbles and sediment, they cut wider channels, sometimes even altering course and cutting an entirely new channel.

Using his chemicals and instruments in the small zippered case, he identified sulfur, copper, zinc, iron, magnesium and gold in various locations in the mountain area and on the plain adjacent to it. There were also several elements he couldn't identify since they didn't exist on earth. A whole team of chemists would find years of work here.

A cave leading deep into the interior of the mountains could be explored later when he had more time and its secrets would be added to his ever increasing storehouse of knowledge.

"Some people used to believe," he told Dog as they left the opening and turned away from the mountains, "that spirits lived in caves and when you died your soul went to live in the caves under the mountains with the spirits of the land. Wonder if we could find any spirits?"

The contact lenses began to irritate his eyes so he took to wearing his glasses on occasion when he needed to see in the distance. Didn't matter much which he used since he was going blind anyway. Just a matter of time. So he used the contacts and the glasses less and less as days went by and for some unexplainable reason he could still see pretty good. It was almost as though his eyesight was actually improving. With new techniques in laser surgery they could correct the curvature of the cornea and eliminate the need for glasses. But he hadn't had any corrective surgery. So maybe the gravity or the atmospheric pressure of this world or something in the air was just different enough to cause the cornea to alter its shape slightly and direct the light onto the retina exactly where it should be. Sure, and maybe only God made little green apples and they really didn't grow on trees after all.

Whatever the reason, he was happy to toss the glasses away and forget about them. He could see.

Approaching one narrow, shallow stream at the base of the mountains, both he and Dog wrinkled their noses at the smell coming from the water. There were filmy patches floating on the surface that reflected blue, orange, and black and tan in the sunlight. He didn't need his chemicals for this. Just dip a finger into the water and taste. Crude oil.

Dead dinosaurs from a hundred million years ago? Parallel universe?

Fat chance. Ok, so how do you explain the oil?

They followed the water upstream for several miles to where it led across a flat, dead area covering half a square mile. The smell was overpowering now. Oil seeped from the ground and lay in huge black pools trickling into the stream to be carried away and eventually deposited and dissipated along the route. Petroleum so plentiful you wouldn't even have to drill for it. Wouldn't the oil people kill for that.

Maybe some of the dead dinosaurs from a hundred million years ago were still here. Seeking out limestone deposits, the geologist looked for fossils that would give him a clue about plant and animal life those millions of years ago, and the metamorphic rock that told of the great heat and pressure brought together when the crust itself was forming and cooling.

The planet was old, its surface crust supporting some type of life for more than six hundred million years; the Precambrian era. It was old enough to have developed intelligent life several times over, notwithstanding his failure to find any evidence of it. Nor were there signs of any kind of a civilization, nothing constructed, manufactured or made, no tools or arrowheads, no charcoal and no remnants of any kind of productive life force anywhere that he could find. He had not found an ocean or any huge body of water of an kind, although there had to be one. All that river water had to go somewhere.

They searched and finally found a pass by way of connecting canyons through serpentine passages that wound its way through the mountains. In only three days of steady walking, stopping occasionally to examine some unusual rock formation or a plant they had not seen before, they covered 140 miles and emerged on the far side of the towering range. Ahead of them lay yet another plain. This one however appeared to be more arid, the grass stunted and brown, and there wasn't a tree that he could see anywhere.

Another half-day of travel brought them to the edge of a great chasm two or three times wider than the Grand Canyon. Looking down, they could not see the bottom that was hidden in the depths of darkness.

"Water sure didn't do this," he said to Dog. "Has to be a plate shift. This thing runs the entire length of the continent and it could go down fifteen or twenty miles. We didn't have anything like this on Earth. Boy, would I like to go down there. I don't see a way, though, do you? Those walls look pretty sheer.

"I'll bet you don't even know what a plate shift is, do you, Dog. Well, I'm going to tell you, anyway. I've got to use all those years of education and study for something. Now, pay attention."

Dog laid down full-length, front paws extended. He looked away.

"I said, pay attention. Do you know what this would cost you if you had attended any one of my lectures at the university?"

Dog yawned.

"Now," he said, sitting down beside his companion, "the crust of an Earth-type planet is only about 150 miles thick. It floats on a sea of magma—that's molten rock to you uneducated canine types—and the heat and pressure causes expansion and contraction. It's not a solid crust, just several big chunks called plates. Enough pressure and these plates are forced together and upward. Sometimes they just keep going upward. In the space of a few hundred million years, you have a mountain range. Those plates pressing together also cause earthquakes.

"And if the plates pull apart, you have something like that." He pointed to the deep rife in the ground. "When that thing eventually closes, and it will, you'll have something like the San Andreas Fault and earth tremors all over the place. Maybe I should say land tremors since we're not on Earth anymore."

Unable to go any further because of the chasm, they continued their pilgrimage turning to the south once again, traversing the narrow strip of land between the mountains and the bottomless canyon. They might have to go another thousand miles, continue on for another year or more. Or perhaps just beyond the next valley, or over the next hill, past that mountain right there, might lay their objective. They could the alabaster city gleaming in the sunlight with towers and spires reaching up to touch the clouds, or miles of well-preserved ruins giving silent testimony to a civilization long dead and forgotten. It had to be here, somewhere.

What he had seen, however, gave all the appearances of a primitive world without any intelligent life. It was a place where humans could exist, live and thrive, with forests stretching for countless miles providing wood for building, metal ore in abundance in the mountains to smelt and mold into iron and steel to construct cities, and space for millions of people from Earth. Clean, unpolluted air and water, rich and fertile soil where crops would grow in abundance, grass for grazing huge herds of cattle and no fatal disease to sicken and kill. Mr. J. Paul Getty had his world. Mankind would survive here.

He made his decision. Tomorrow, they would go back.

Ahead in a deep valley choked with thick trees and undergrowth, his sharp eyes caught movement. A large graceful, hornless quadruped resembling a deer or Impala, but with thicker legs bounded into the open beside a rocky stream, heading for the denser foliage on the opposite side. He had seen a lot of them lately in this area and knew they were delicious cooked slowly over the fire or even raw still hot from the kill.

He quickly nocked an arrow and pulled his bow to full draw, waiting for the animal to turn from its path and expose a flank, but he got no shot. It had abruptly changed direction and headed upstream, three-toed hooves splashing in the shallow water, offering him no target.

"This canyon may dead-end," he communicated to Dog, releasing the pull on the bow. "Let's follow him."

At a fast pace along the edge of the stream, they raced in pursuit of the deer-like animal. Dog quickly took the lead and rounding a bend in the riverbed, he expected to see the creature just ahead, but there was nothing in sight except another valley extending unto the distance. He slowed to a trot and then to a fast walk waiting for the man to catch up. He sniffed the air. The prey was still there.

The valley was wide and flat ahead, strewn with boulders and dotted with little stands of trees growing ten or fifteen to a group. Dark green and light tan grass and thick brushes, some with thick leaves, some with different colored berries, grew waist high, not tall enough to conceal the prey. They would easily find it and make the kill for the very center of the valley was completely bare of vegetation. Dog smacked his jaws anticipating the meal they would have.

At the bend of the river and the entrance to the second valley, Savage was standing still and rigid, his feet ankle deep in the water, his bow hanging loosely from one hand. "Oh, my, God," he whispered aloud, his body trembling and the breath caught in his throat. The bow fell from his fingers into the stream and he took a stumbling step forward, completely unaware of its fall. Had his bare foot not fallen on it, he would have abandoned the bow without a thought.

Dog swung his head back toward Savage, puzzled at first by the stiff, stumbling pace and the straight-ahead, fixed stare of this man he had come to know so well. Then he caught the overpowering emotion flowing from him, fear, excitement and awe. The dog looked back and surveyed the wide valley looking for something he had missed before but neither his eyes, his keen nose or sharp ears could find anything that would have such an effect on the tall creature. He curled his lips and growled deep within his throat, ready to fight, attack or defend if only he could locate something at which to strike. His eyes searched frantically, they darted along the canyon walls behind the man to the far end of the wide valley ahead. They looked at and then away from the huge object in the center of the valley for it meant nothing to Dog.

Savage stumbled forward as though in a daze, his feet finding their way forward through the water, over the rocks where he pushed through the grass and shrubs into the very center of the valley where the vegetation stopped. He came to a halt on the bare ground and looked, just stared in disbelieving amazement at it. It was something unnatural, something alien, something that had been made.

Vaguely resembling a version of the huge outdoor amphitheaters built by the Doric order of ancient Greece, this was significantly different in that the huge slabs of rock yards wide and many feet thick weighing a hundred tons lay upon other slabs of rock set vertically as support posts. The slabs of rock made a perfect circle two hundred feet across and immediately reminded Savage vaguely of something he had seen before, one of Earth's big mysteries; Stonehenge. Unlike the massive ruin on the Salisbury Plain in England however, this structure was in perfect condition. Also unlike Earth's Stonehenge, this structure was colossal, layered in three tiers raising some sixty feet in the air and capped by a series of curved stone slabs locked together at the top to form an open-beam ceiling. Within the open beams at the top of the chamber was a glowing, whirling maelstrom of light and dark currents punctuated by brilliant flashes of lightning in a multitude of colors each lasting less than a second.

Circling the entire structure were what appeared to be square stones set into the ground so that only the surface could be seen. They were at a precise distance from the main structure and an exact distance apart. As he watched fascinated, a stone would glow brightly for a second and then fade. A short time later—he didn't attempt to determine the length of time—the next stone would glow and fade. Then the next until the circle had been completed. Unconsciously he estimated it would take several hours for the circle to be completed.

None of what he saw showed the slightest indication of surface weathering although he guessed it had stood there for thousands, maybe even millions of years. Speculation held that Earth's Stonehenge was constructed somewhere between 2000 and 1700 BC, probably by a group called Druids, but nobody really knew for sure. They certainly didn't know how it was constructed, so how could they know who?

His initial shock and disbelief was replaced with excitement as he walked forward between the glowing stones to place his hand on one of the uprights and scratched with a thumbnail. It was almost perfectly smooth and the hardest igneous rock he had ever encountered. There was a solid rock floor of coal-black stone in the center of the structure.

Stepping into the circle he looked up to where he had seen the lightning flashes in the maelstrom but there was nothing there. He looked through the open-beams to the sky above. Looking around he observed that there was a silver strip of what appeared to be highly polished metal or even a glass mirror ten to twelve inches wide on the inside of each of the uprights running from the ground to the flat slabs at the top. It was set flush with the surface of the rock face so that it was not possible to determine the thickness or how it was attached. He tried to scratch it with his knife but the blade made no impression. It could be metal, plastic, glass or even porcelain, but it was definitely not natural. As had the entire structure, it had been constructed by an intelligent force. He had finally found his evidence of civilization.

Looking again toward the ceiling he saw at the top of the first tier which was about ten feet high, what appeared to be the beginning of a wall but it extended down only about twelve inches, somewhat like a cornice. Spaced evenly all the way around it were symbols slightly raised from the background in relief. There were hundreds of them.

There weren't just hundreds of them, there were thousands. Every few seconds the symbols rippled and changed, some disappeared and different ones appeared in their place. There could be tens of thousands of them. The second, third and fourth tiers, far above his reach, were also covered with the symbols

He reached up and tentatively touched one on the first tier that looked like ✳ with a fingertip. It felt like marble, very smooth and polished like stone but cold like metal. He covered it with his palm and felt just the tiniest tingle of what might have been a mild electric shock. He jerked his hand away.

On the south side of the cornice, the rippling, changing symbols stopped for a short space and there was something that appeared to be words in some indecipherable language. Beyond them the symbols continued on completing the circle. The words—if they indeed were words—appeared in letters that looked a little like Greek and a little like Russian but he doubted that they were either.

ΔΙΡΕΧΤΙΟΝΣ   ΦΟΡ ΥΣΕ

Τουχη ανδ ηολδ τηε σψμβολ φορ ψουρ δεστινατιον.

Like Stonehenge, the structure could have been built by primitives and even the symbols could be prehistoric pictures like cave drawings, but the writing was way beyond that. It indicated a highly advanced civilization. If he could find more of the writing, maybe he could learn to translate it, figure out what it meant, but this was the first indication of intelligence he had encountered so he didn't have much to draw on.

Making camp some distance away, he returned again and again to the stone structure, to stare at it, to attempt to interpret its purpose, to gaze at first in wonder and then with ever growing apprehension at the polished strips on the uprights and the strange symbols around the tiers. He touched several more of the symbols and received the same electric tingle causing him to pull his hand away quickly. He wondered where the power was coming from. Deep in the ground or from . . . from somewhere else.

He shared what food he had with Dog and tried to explain in words and thoughts and gestures the significance of the thing they had discovered and the strange phenomenon of nothing growing anywhere near the circle of stones, much as an adult would instruct a child. He told him about Stonehenge on Earth and speculated about its creation and destruction. Primitive men wearing robes and worshipping the moon could no more have lifted hundred-ton stones thirty feet in the air than they could have put on a pair of wings and flew. If they *had* a pair of wings. What destroyed Stonehenge? A massive earthquake? Lightening? Cosmic Vandals? Questions no one would ever be able to answer. And what if Earth's Stonehenge hadn't been completed when it was destroyed? This structure was three stories high. What if the one on Earth was intended to be just as high with the maelstrom at the top?

Dog grasped none of it but was content with the man understood it and it presented no danger to them. He settled down with the man's hand on his paw to rest for a few hours as night approached. Hunting was better at night. They could see the game but for some reason or other the creatures they hunted did not seem to be able to see them. Curious. Dog had never thought about that before.

They spent two days in the valley, a great deal of which of the time Savage stood and stared at the flashing maelstrom in the dome but could learn no more than he had the first day. The mirror strips continued to remain a mystery, obviously there for a reason as inconceivable as the circle of stones itself.

Anxiously and yet at the same time reluctant, he left the camp and the stone structure and walked back up the valley along the stream to begin the long journey to his base camp beside the Window because he could learn no more here. There was, or had been at one time, highly advanced intelligent life on this world because somebody had built that thing. But exactly where they were, traces of where they had been or where they had gone was still a mystery, one he might never solve.

Using the sun and the stars along with his unfailing sense of direction and Dog's uncanny abilities, he retraced his steps through valley, over ridges, across rivers and plains and through forests toward the Window. With the big dog at his side, he ran, he hunted, and he ran some more, but he no longer explored or searched or stopped to examine something unusual. He just ran.

Complete mind-numbing exhaustion was his goal now, run until he could run no more and fall to the ground gasping for breath, or sit and wait for Dog to catch up for he could actually outdistance the big canine now. Rough and tumble fights that flattened yards of grass, knocked down small trees and uprooted bushes followed almost every meal and though playful and harmless in their frolicking mock battles, they fought hard and dropped to the ground spent, to rest before continuing on.

It was a wonderful and exciting time for Dog, to run and play and fight and romp without fear of hurting this tall creature who won in their fighting, clawing, kicking and biting battles more often than he lost. Dog love the man and would kill for him, die for him if he ordered it and he tried to understand the confused thoughts in the man's mind. Everything that had happened seemed to be normal, a natural progression which he accepted without question because it was. But for David Savage, nothing was normal any more.

Little-by-little, hour-by-hour, week-by-week over the years in the Pennsylvania State Prison, he had learned to accept that he was an innocent but condemned man about to be executed. He *did* accept it. Then he had been miraculously freed, his life saved and through the wonders of science he had been transported to another world somewhere in the far reaches of space. There he had found a structure perhaps older than time itself and he was doubtless the only living human being on the entire world. He slowly learned to accept Dog, an animal that could not possibly exist, given its size and weight and intellectual understanding. All of this he was able to comprehend and still retain his sanity.

What he could *not* accept, however, was his own reflection seen in the polished, mirrored strips on the inner surface of the upright support stones. *That* was the cause of his flight and the mind-numbing result of exhaustion.

He had looked at himself in the polished mirror for the first time since coming to this world. What he saw was incomprehensible.

He was still David Savage but now he stood almost eight feet tall and guessed his weight at close to four hundred pounds. His hair was light blond, almost white, and it hung in long, thick tangles down past his shoulders. His mustache and heavy beard, also light blond, grew on his face and fell to brush against the thick muscles rippling through his massive chest. His arms and biceps bulged and his back and shoulders were corded with muscle under a deep brown and flawless skin. In his present form, given Earth standards, with the exception of his face he looked no more than twenty years old.

He had not been consciously aware over the weeks and months on this planet that he could run for ten hours and feel no sign of fatigue. He could grab Dog by the fur of his neck and under his belly, lift him high above his head with no effort and throw the huge animal ten feet through the air without exerting himself. He could pull the new hunting bow carved from a solid piece of ironwood and hold it at full draw for as long as he wanted without feeling the two hundred and fifty pound pull.

He could understand when Dog spoke to him, clear and intelligent communication in his mind between two thinking beings. Dog understood him, too. He didn't even have to speak aloud. He didn't bark. Just think of something and the other knew.

"I think it's going to rain again tonight, Dog."

"Yes. I can smell it."

"I'll throw the blanket over you."

"Good. My fur itches when it's wet."

"I don't have that problem."

"You don't have any fur. You'd freeze if it gets cold."

"Do you think it will get cold?"

"How would I know?"

"You've been here longer than I have."

"I still don't know if it gets cold, like home."

"Home?"

"Where I was before I came here."

"Yes, I was there, too."

"Maybe you'll grow some fur."

"Well, it could be. I don't know."

Like Dog, he suddenly realized, he didn't sleep anymore. He needed to rest occasionally, close and rest his eyes, but he didn't sleep. There was no longer any need to sink into that unconscious, mindless state so necessary for Earthmen to rejuvenate their bodies in order to survive.

He ate his meat raw now, fresh from the kill, more often than he cooked it, tearing the flesh from the bones like any wild carnivore. It had all happened so very slowly, so gradually over such a long period of time, so long and so slowly that he didn't even notice. Days turned into weeks, then weeks into months. A muscular forearm became *more* muscular, his body became thicker, harder and more powerful to overcome the gravity. Two hours of running without tiring became three with no fatigue, then four hours. His hair and beard grew out dark only to become quickly bleached white by the sun. He did not interpret the animal sounds Dog made into intelligible words but rather he caught and understood the thought patterns behind the sounds. This, too, he did without being consciously aware of it.

There was no longer in any fear of going blind. His vision was perfect. He could also see perfectly in the dark. He didn't need light to see. He had no idea how he could do that. He could sense emotions like fear, hunger, rage and the powerful urge to recreate in the creatures around him. As easily and clearly as he could smell them or see them, he detected and identified their electrical brain-wave patterns and came to know each and every one individually. He knew that shortly he would be able to communicate with them as he did with Dog and that might well effect their roles as hunter and hunted. Could he kill and eat one after having an intimate conversation with it?

He had become a powerful, telepathic, sleepless giant capable of anything, and he hadn't even noticed it happening. That alone was enough to tax his sanity. It was however, his face looking back at him in the polished metal that he couldn't handle.

It could have been the radiation from the alien sun, some unknown element in the air he breathed, a toxic chemical in the rain that fell and soaked his body, or in the water he drank, an element in the food he ate. Whatever it was, David Savage was no longer human.

Like Dog, his eyes were a fierce, piercing and glowing emerald green. Also like Dog, long, thick, curved razor-edged fangs grew down from his upper jaw to end in needle points even with his chin like those of a saber tooth tiger.

CHAPTER TWENTY-FIVE

O N AND ON HE ran with Dog at his side, for two long months he ran, drawing ever closer to the Window, his only link with Earth, the woman he loved and the human companionship he desperately craved.

But this world would soon cease to exist as he knew it now, as the Window poured forth dozens, thousands, tens of thousands of people to spread across the land, to cut down, plow up and spoil, to build factories and cities, roads and highways, to dam the rivers and drain the lakes. They would bring tools, weapons and materials, they would make love and reproduce, they would make war and they would kill. It would be Earth all over again regardless of Getty's plans for a better society of people.

What of the inhabitants of this world? Had they reached a level so high that they no longer needed to farm the ground, to build cities or construct things? Were they invisible and so powerful that they could destroy every Earthman who came through the Window with a single thought from an all-powerful mind? Or were they the simple plants and animals he saw all around him everyday?

And not to be forgotten was that force, that intelligent presence just beyond his level of consciousness that had first warned him about the plants. He had become more aware of it during the last few months although it was still a ghost, a whisper he could not grasp onto. It was there, yet it wasn't. Had he been a religious man, he could have put a name to it.

Had the people of this world reached their peak a hundred million years ago and left the planet to go on to others, the huge circle of stones being left here unused, unneeded and forgotten? Or had there been no people at all? Had alien explorers stopped here for a time when the planet was young, built it for some reason; used it and left it?

And, could it be that somewhere on this world yet undiscovered by him, there were primitive manlike creatures just beginning upon civilization who would be enslaved or killed by the invading horde of Earthmen? Could he allow that?

This was the world Diana had dreamed of and wanted, the prefect world. It was Paradise, the mythical, Biblical Garden of Eden. Once here, however, could she stand by helplessly and watch it slowly destroyed by the invading hoards of men of Earth?

One look at him and the huge dog in their present form, standing in front of the Window would be enough to start the stampede through the opening to paradise, and once started, it would never stop. One look at him and they would abandon the idea of sending Diana to him for another six months of testing for survival while they waited patiently, growing older, sicker and near to death. They would come, they would pay a fortune to come, they would fight to come, and they would kill each other to be first through the Window in the World.

With Diana beside him and eventually a family to raise, he would be happy and content here with little need of others. But how could he convince Getty to send her through without showing himself to them?

Expecting to meet the man she had given herself to, the man she would live with, who's children she would bear, what would she think when she first saw him, the huge, fanged monster he had become? She would be terrified. He didn't know what he had become, but he knew that he was no longer even remotely human, and no woman would want to be anywhere near him.

Finally reaching the edge of the plain, he plunged into the wood—*his* woods as he had thought of them on his first trip—in almost same spot he had emerged months before. His sense of direction and location was almost perfect now. A glance at the sun or the stars in the night sky fixed his position better than any instrument. Or was it something else, some sense more primitive or more advanced than anything known to twentieth century man?

The fragrance of the deadly flowers no longer disturbed him as he passed. He merely stopped breathing for fifteen minutes until he was far beyond the little narrow meadow and the smell of the flowers.

If he could stop breathing for a quarter hour, could he stop breathing altogether? He no longer needed to sleep. Could he stop eating? Had something on this world so changed his basic metabolism that it not only altered his appearance but his life necessities too? Perhaps in time he would learn the answers to these questions. If he had that much time.

It was still dark as he moved through the last of the trees only a few dozen yards from his camp and the Window. He traveled at night now as easily as in the daytime, his strange glowing eyes gathering in the star and moonlight, penetrating the darkness and seeing with perfect vision.

Instruments and lenses had been manufactured to see in the dark, to collect faint and distant light to reveal images unseen by the human eyed. The Startron Scope was not only a powerful telephoto lens, it allowed the user to see object in almost total darkness, although the images were observed in glowing green color. Savage did not see in green.

Stopping, hesitating to walk that last few yards into the clearing, he knelt with his knees planted in the ground, his huge bulk sinking them into the soft soil. He took Dog's huge head in his hands and looked into those deep, green eyes; eyes like his.

"What am I going to do, Dog?" he asked, speaking aloud for the first time in months, pleading for understanding and help. "I don't want to live here by myself."

His voice was a harsh croak from long disuse, but after only a few words, the habit and ability of talking returned to him. What he hadn't considered was the size of his jaw and the long fangs completely changed his pronunciation of certain words and the sound of his voice to the point where he didn't recognize himself.

"I'm here," Dog said.

"I can't bring millions of Earth people here, have them change into young Gods and then eventually destroy this world as they are destroying the Earth. You would not understand, my friend, but human Earth creatures do not learn from the harsh lessons of history. We continue to make the same fatal mistakes over and over. You've got to tell me, Dog. What am I going to do?"

"The solution seems simple to me, tall creature. If you do not want them here, do not allow them to come.

"I don't know how to stop them."

"I believe you will find a way."

"Will you help me?"

"Of course."

CHAPTER TWENTY-SIX

THE SHARP CRACKLING SOUND of a branch braking came from the direction of his camp and the Window and instantly brought Savage to his feet while Dog crouched low, growling softly deep in his throat. More sounds. Something large was thrashing through the underbrush, coming toward them from the camp. Dog was ordered to circle and come in from behind while he stepped behind a tree, his hand close to the twelve-inch fighting knife at his waist.

Dawn had only just begun to break and it was still very dark on the weald floor with only a few feeble shafts of light penetrating the thick forest covering, but his eyes easily penetrated the gloom to see a figure stumbling toward him in a drunken stagger. It was man-like and it wore clothing. It came closer and he saw that it *was* a man, an Earthman. Palomar had sent someone else through the Window.

It was more his thoughts, his mind-picture than his physical being that Savage recognized. It was Doctor Boucree's young assistant with the amusing name, the chief lab tech, Phil O. Dendron.

Savage emerged from behind the tree and walked quickly to him, silently ordering Dog to keep watch. As he approached, Dendron stumbled and sank to his hands and knees, his breath coming in rasping gasps. He looked up and cried out as Savage leaned over him. Falling over backwards, he held out an arm and hand as though to ward off the creature hovering over him.

"Dendron. Phil, it's me, Savage. What are you doing here?"

"Savage? It is really you? How can it be? You look—"

"It's me."

"Oh, thank goodness. We thought you . . . we thought you were dead," he whispered, his voice labored. "It's been . . . been over a year and you . . . you never came back."

"What? A year? No, that can't be right. It's been only four or five months."

At that moment the sun broke through the tree boughs and lit up the area around them with its bright glow. Phil Dendron looked up at Savage in the light.

"Holy Mother of God!" he managed to stammer as he tried to crawl back, heels digging into the ground, shoving himself away from the huge, muscled, almost naked and fierce-looking creature with the monster face hovering over him. "What . . . what are you?"

"I'm Savage. Believe me, Dendron, I am. It's some kind of a physical change caused by radiation, I think. I don't know for sure. I really am David Savage. I *was* David Savage. I won't hurt you, Phil. Just tell me why you're here. Why did you come through the Window?"

Phil Dendron coughed and clutched at his chest. His mouth and chin were covered with blood and the short-sleeve plaid shirt was wet with a dark stain that continued to spread under his hand.

"You're hurt," Savage said, dropping down beside him and raising Dendron's head with his hand. "Tell me what happened?"

"It's all . . . it's all gone to hell, Savage. It's complete chaos back there. You'd been gone so long . . . so long . . . everybody figured you were dead." He coughed again and there was more blood from his mouth.

"Maybe you had better not talk now, Phil."

"Got to. No time. They were planning to send somebody else through the window and Mrs. Killingsworth, she . . . she was throwing all kinds of fits and making . . . making threats to come through the Window to find you. They didn't want her to go so they finally barred her . . . barred her from the lab and the last couple of . . . couple of months, they wouldn't even let her into the underground complex at all."

"Diana? What about her? Tell me. Is she all right?"

"I think so." He coughed again. "And then . . . and then, about four or five weeks ago, the professor told us a couple of Federal Marshals and . . . and some woman named Bennett showed up. Said she knew about you, that you were an escaped convict from some prison. She demanded to see Mr. Killingsworth. He said they ran her off but . . . but a week later she was back with a bunch of LA Count Sheriff's Deputies. They . . . they wanted to search the place claming that you were hiding there."

"Bennett?" Savage questioned. "Warden Bennett? How did she know about Palomar and where it was?"

"I don't know."

"Well, Killingsworth can handle that."

"No. That's not the . . . not the problem. It's all over. The Window, everything."

"I don't understand."

"I . . . I went into the professor's lab and found several strange men there with Mr. Killingsworth. They were dressed in business suits, one of them had a camera and he was . . . was taking pictures of the Window. Boucree was screaming at them to get out, then he charged right at them. One pulled out a gun and shot him right in the chest. Then Killingsworth fell to the floor. I . . . I guess they killed him, too.

"The Palomar guards . . . guards stormed in from outside and there was . . . there was all kinds of shooting. I got hit and staggered forward, I guess falling through the window. That's all I know."

"Oh, Christ! Who were they?"

"I don't know." He paused and started coughing again.

"Will more come through after you?"

"I don't know."

"We've got to get you back to the Window," Savage said. Effortlessly he scooped the man up in his arms.

"No, Savage," Dendron said, coughing blood. "Stay away from there. Don't let them see you."

"But Diana, they'll let her come through now if they know I'm alive."

"No. No, they won't. Everything's changed. If they find out what . . . what you've become, they'll never let her through. Put me down, Savage."

"But when they see that you're hurt, they'll send help, a doctor or something."

"No, they won't . . . won't give me any help. You don't know what it's like there now. Put me down."

Savage placed him gently onto the ground and knelt beside him. "Tonight after it gets dark, I'll take you to the Window where they can see you and you can tell them—"

"Hell, Savage, I'm . . . I'm not even going to . . . gonna make it another hour. I've got at least two bullets in me and I'm bleeding . . . bleeding to death."

"No, Phil, there's . . . there's something about this place, this world, something here that gives life. I don't think you *can* die here."

"Maybe *you* can't, but I'm finished. I've had it." He coughed again, the blood filling his lungs. "You've . . . you've got to make up your mind . . . your mind what you're gonna do. I can't help you. I can't even help myself."

"I've *got* to do something. I can't just let you die."

"Too late, Savage. It's too late. It's all on you, now. Do . . . do what's right."

"Phil? Don't—"

"Do what's right, Savage."

Phil Dendron's eyes closed and for a few brief seconds he was back in college studying electronics among the pretty coeds. Then his head fell limply to the side, he felt cold and the college faded along with his life.

Dog approached silently and regarded the man with understanding eyes. He sat on his haunches and panted, his tongue hanging over his teeth. Savage reached out and once again took the animal's massive head between his huge hands, staring into those cold, green eyes.

"It's begun, Dog. Everything I feared would happen. It's started. The people from Earth are coming. What am I going to do, Dog? What am I going to do?"

CHAPTER TWENTY-SEVEN

I NDECISIVE, CONFUSED AND DISTRAUGHT, he sat for much of the morning beside the dead man. Twice he began digging into the forest floor with his knife; a grave for Dr. Phil Dendron. But he never finished—what was the purpose?—and twice he started back for the plain intending to abandon the Window and the Earth with it, but both times he returned to the cold form of the lab assistant to recall his last words; "Do what is right."

How could he do what was right? He didn't know what was right or wrong anymore.

When darkness finally settled over the forest, he gently lifted what remained of Phil Dendron and carried his body to the Window. He dragged the dead man along the ground the last few feet so it would appear from the other side that he had crawled back to where he now lay. Leaving him there, Savage walked into the woods with Dog to wait and watch.

The table was still in place in front of the tent door and it appeared that nothing had been touched in his long absence. Several sealed plastic packets of papers and documents lay on the ground. They were covered with dust and were rain splattered, and on a few there were traces of red where Dendron had first fallen.

"Will he be alive again?" Dog asked.

"No. They killed him."

"He was killed for food?"

"No."

"Then why?"

"Yes. Why indeed."

"I love you, tall creature, and I share your mind, but there is much about your kind I do not understand."

"Me too, my friend. There is much about my kind I don't understand, either."

The remainder of the night passed without incident as did all of the following day. Nobody came through the Window but Savage continued to wait in his place of concealment, afraid to leave even for food or water.

Dendron had said it was more than a year. Could time be so different here that a few months added up to a year on Earth? Or had he been so involved in the exploration that he just completely lost all track of how long he had been here? His physical change, the creature he had become—could that have something to do with it?

Another day and another night passed. Dog grew more and more restless as he lay in the underbrush by the big man's side, but Savage would not let him leave.

On the morning of the third day, the air shimmered and a figure suddenly appeared in midair, dropped to the ground in a half-crouch and rapidly looked all around. He was dressed in camouflage dungarees and paratrooper boots, wore thick leather gloves and had an oxygen mask over his face attached to a small canister on his belt. He carried a Russian-made Kalashnikov AK-47 automatic rifle in his hands. If the sudden increase in gravity bothered him, he gave no indication of it other than to grasp his weapon more firmly and bend his knees.

Hovering close to the ground, the man scrambled quickly in a crab-like crawl to Dendron's body and felt the cold flesh of his neck with the back of his wrist above the glove. He turned toward the Window, hesitated a few seconds as though startled, then made a quick slicing motion across his throat with an index finger. After the initial reaction of surprise, the man did not seem concerned that there was no sign of the doorway through which he had just entered this world.

The tent came next. Throwing the table aside with one hand he hurriedly unzipped the flaps and stepped inside, his weapon ready. Seconds later he emerged and looked around again. In front of the Window, he slowly shook his head back and forth several times.

He was a short but powerfully built man, his eyes having the hard look of a professional soldier, a man paid a lot of money to do what few dared. Not one of DeShane's security force but a hired mercenary trained to fight and ready to kill anything that moved. He looked around again and then seeming to decide, he stood erect, pointed with his index finger and stepped off in rapid strides to the east, in the direction of the valley and the gorge Savage had discovered and reported to Palomar. Out of sight of the Window he swung his gun, using the barrel as a club in an attempt to clear a path through the thick stand of tall, colorful plants with large, flowered heads growing just a few feet into the forest from the clearing.

The gun, his belt buckle, his watch and the canister at his side were the only things the plants didn't eat, and it happened so fast that Savage was unable to save him. The wide saw-tooth leaves encircled him, the flowered heads dropped on him and the mercenary was gone without a sound.

The carnivorous plants might have followed his path, his scent or his spore all the way from the river when he had explored the valley and the gorge, and it had taken them this long to make the journey in search for food. Or maybe they had been here all this time, indigenous to the whole world, just waiting for food. The mercenary had blundered right into them.

There were more of them coming, dozens of them, inching their way from the woods, closer and closer to the clearing as Savage watched then creep forward on their tentacle roots. Their flowered heads were spread wide and he could sense hunger emanating from them.

For some reason, they were not aware of his presence or that of Dog as they gathered in the clearing where the body of Phil O. Dendron, once MA, Ph.D., electronics expert, lay. He was surrounded, lifted in thick, flexible leaves and consumed in full view of the Window. They touched the table and the tent, they bent low over the old fire pit; they filled the clearing.

Savage and the dog named Dog waited, waited for something else to happen. Waited for someone else to appear in the air from the Window and drop to the ground to be attacked, killed and eaten by the hungry plants.

Repulsed by what he had witnessed and powerless to stop it, Savage took Dog by the scruff of the neck and dragged him away from the clearing, deeper into the woods. He did not understand why the plants had not sensed and attacked him, but they hadn't and he wasn't of a mind to try to reason it out now. He had witnessed enough death.

He would return to the plain of flowing grass and rushing rivers, continue to search for intelligent life, knowing that the Window was now guarded and anyone coming through would be threatened. It was no longer a threat to him.

"Go!" he commanded Dog. "I want no part of this."

"But she will come," was the reply. "You have said so."

"No. I can't think about that now."

"Others will come."

"No."

"They will."

"The plants will deal with them."

"Can they?"

As he moved quickly and silently through the forest, he realized Dog was right and he understood that Paul Getty would never give up. He and his staff would find a way to fight and defeat the plants and anything else that got in his way of owning a whole world. And he was now a part of that world Getty wanted, as much a part of it as the plants and the other forms of life he had found here. He was no longer an Earthman, no longer a human. He above all should be there to defend this world, *his* world, from invasion of aliens for as long as he could, a lone sentinel against the power of Earth.

Once again he turned back to the Window but this time with a purpose and a cause. "You were right, old Dog."

"I was? I don't know. I see things differently than you, tall creature. I don't always understand everything you think."

"Am I so strange to you, Dog?"

"No, Ταλλ Χρεατυρε, you are not anymore. Just hard to understand."

"Was that my name, that sound you just made?"

"Yes, and my name isn't Dog. It is, Λασσιε."

"I can't say that," Savage replied, trying to convert the sound and the symbols into something pronounceable. "It sounds something like aoie. But I know that's not what you're saying."

"No."

"That's not dog language."

"No."

"Somehow it sounds familiar but I can't place it."

"Is it important?"

"No. It isn't."

"I need water. My tongue is dry."

"One more day. That's all."

"I will go for water."

"I need you here. Give me one more day."

"Then you shall have it, Ταλλ Χρεατυρε."

They settled down to wait just out of view of the portal through time and space. The plants also moved back a short distance but concentrated their numbers near where the window would deposit someone, as though they somehow knew that something would appear in the clearing, something they could eat. That would require intelligence and Savage had already begun to believe that they were thinking creatures.

It was a short wait this time. Early the following morning just after the sun came up, the air shimmered and another form appeared, dropping heavily and clumsily to the ground, staggered by the weight of two large tanks on the figure's back, attached to a short barrel by a hose. A flame-thrower! The only weapon capable of killing the plants and setting fire to the woods at the same time, destroying the forest. Helmeted and covered from head to foot in a silver, fire—retardant suit, this invader from Earth presented the means and the intent to destroy everything in its path to reopen the Window for Palomar. They were becoming desperate.

Fixing an arrow to his bow, Savage slowly took aim at the figure slowly looking all around. He was waiting for a heart shot and an instant kill before the assassin could use the devastating weapon. The mere twitch of a gloved finger on the trigger could send a stream of flame forty feet long into the forest.

"David!" a voice called out, muffled under the helmet. "David, are you here? If you are, for God's sake, answer me. David?"

The plants began to surge forward on their tentacle legs, attracted by the movement and the sound of the voice, a woman's voice.

"David. David, it's Diana. I've come through to destroy the plants. Are you here?"

Crouching beside Savage and recognizing her voice although not her name, Dog suddenly leaped to his feet, barking in a thunderous roar that reverberated through the trees. The plants slowly swiveled their flowered heads toward the sound.

Breaking free of Savage's restraining hand, the huge animal bounded through the brush, intending to enter the clearing and attack the plants. "She's here!" Dog said in Savage's mind. "You said she would come."

"Stop!" The powerful mental command rang in Dog's mind and he skidded to a halt just before breaking from the cover of the trees and bushes.

"Diana!" Savage shouted, lowering his bow and rushing forward to grab Dog by the scruff of the neck. "Drop the tanks and run. Run to your left past the tent and into the woods. Use your knife. The plants are afraid of a sharp blade. They know what it is."

"David? David. Is that you? Oh, thank God! You're here."

"Run, Diana! I'll distract them. Hurry. Go!"

"I can stop them with the flame thrower. I'm not afraid of them."

"No! Don't. They're intelligent life. Don't kill them."

"But they—"

"No, Diana." The words were mental this time, an authority, an order she could not refuse. "Do not kill them."

Releasing dog and continuing to use his mental commands, he sent the animal around behind the plants to growl and bark and prance through the brush and, hopefully, to further confuse them.

"There will be others coming through behind me, David. They're just waiting to see what happens to me."

"I'll take care of them. Just run now!"

"I can't! There's something . . . something pulling me down . . . something holding me. I can't move."

She began to sink to her knees.

"It's the gravity, Diana. It's a lot stronger than Earth. Remember, I told you about it. Fight it. Drop the tanks, Diana. Run. You can do it. Get up and run, just like you made me do it!"

"Help me."

"You have to do it for yourself. Go!"

Quickly she unbuckled the straps of the flame-thrower tanks, shucked them from her shoulders and let them fall to the ground. Tearing the helmet from her head and flinging it away, she climbed to her feet and staggered into the woods with her long hair flying about her head. A double-edged fighting knife was clutched in her hand.

"Keep going," he commanded, "we'll catch up with you."

Crashing through the underbrush, tripping, stumbling, falling, regaining her feet, she fought her way further and further from the clearing, the camp and the Window. When she could no longer run, she crawled. Finally, breathless and soaked in perspiration from the suit she wore and dragged down by the gravity, she fell to the ground, crawled to a large tree against which she leaned her back. Minutes went by during which time she managed to strip off the fireman's suit exposing the jeans and khaki-colored, short-sleeved shirt she had on underneath, than lay panting, the breath ragged in her throat, waiting, waiting for David to find her. The minutes slowly turned into an hour and still she was alone, hopelessly lost on an alien world.

Watching through the Window the men of Palomar would have seen her drop the flame-thrower and run. They wouldn't know why she had run instead of attacking the plants so in anger and frustration they would order her back-up, two professional soldiers, mercenaries who where to follow her through the Window should she be unsuccessful against the plants. Two more would be sent after them if necessary to secure the area around the camp.

She had to go back and find out, but she was completely disoriented and had no idea in which direction the camp lay. Her only hope was David Savage.

Another hour passed and her frustrations grew. The sun moved slowly across the sky casting ever-changing patterns of light and shadow around her. The forest was so thick and there was not a sound. Not a bird call, not a twig braking or a leaf rustling in the breeze. It was unnatural. It was downright eerie. But she was on an alien world. Maybe there weren't any sounds here. No, that wasn't reasonable.

She dragged herself to her feet and paced. She walked in circles and she kicked at the underbrush. She rested and walked again, the circles she made widening each time. She fought the gravity, the fatigue and she resolved to find her directions and the way back to the camp. David might have tried to defend the camp and the mercenaries caught him, or worse, killed him. She had to know what happened.

The long, unearlthy day dragged on, the gravity pulled her down. Exhausted, she dozed fitfully sitting upright, once again with her back against a tree.

"There's food over here," Savage's voice reached her from the dense woods and thick underbrush. "Just walk a few steps this way and you'll find it. It's some of the dehydrated stuff they sent through for me."

"David!" she exclaimed, scrambling to her feet. "Where are you? My God, I was so worried. The others who followed me through the Window—"

"Yes. I know. Don't be concerned. All is well."

"What happened?"

"The plants got them. They're waiting now for any more that might try to come through."

"The flame-thrower," she called back, "they know it will work against the plants."

"The plants are just behind the window ready to attack the instant anyone appears. They won't have a chance to use the weapon."

"David, where are you? Why don't you come out where I can see you?"

"Everything you need is right here. Just come this way."

"David? I can't walk. The gravity, it's pulling me down."

"Yes, you can. You can walk. Just a few steps. Then crawl if you can't walk."

"Help me, David."

"I can't. You have to do it on your own. This is your home now and you must live and function here. You can make it."

She staggered slowly toward the sound of his voice, quickly discovered boxes of food, clothes, matches and water in a tiny clearing. The sun was low in the sky. Late afternoon. She must have slept for several hours before he awakened her.

"David, where are you? Your voice sounds different. What's happened to you?"

There was no answer.

"David?"

Maybe he went back to the Window again for some reason, she thought and after a few minutes of standing there looking around seeing and hearing nothing, shaken but hungry, still exhausted despite the sleep, and getting no response from Savage, she began to prepare her small campsite.

The led weights she had worn around her ankles, waist and wrists, slowly increasing that weight week by week had improved her strength. Then she began wearing a thirty-pound weight on her back. Knowing, from Savage's reports that the gravity was stronger, she tried to prepare for it, walking, running eating and sleeping in those weights. She was ready but they wouldn't let her go through the Window.

"Wait," she was told, "just a couple more weeks. Maybe Savage will come back."

Then, something she had not even dreamed of had happened and all of her training and conditioning were for nothing. Now, she *had* to wait before taking that dangerous step through the Window to a world from which she could never return. Another six months at least.

She attempted as best she could to maintain her weight training and to keep herself in good physical condition but

Dr. Worthington was very strict in what he would allow her to do and how strenuously he would let her exercise, everything considered.

Now, for reasons she couldn't even begin to imagine, the man she had grown to love, the man she had come here to find was hiding from her. She sat on the ground and ate tasteless food warmed over an open fire. Memories of other meals over open fires in the mountains of a remote Japanese island. Time after time she called out for him, trying to look into the thick, deep woods, but there was no reply and she could see nothing beyond the small clearing.

It was beginning to get dark and with no sense of direction on this alien world, lost as she was from the Window, she dared not venture into the forest to search for him. Exhausted and confused, she finally fell into a tearful, restless sleep curled beside the fire, her chest rising and falling in labored breathing.

It was still dark when she awoke but the fire had been built up sometime during the night, there was additional dry wood stacked nearby and a fully loaded M-16 assault rifle lay beside her. She grabbed it, pulled back the bolt to see if a shell had been chambered, then held it steady as she tried to look beyond the firelight.

"David, where are you? I know you're here. I can feel your presence. Why are you doing this?" The frustration in her voice was apparent as she called out to the dark woods around her. "Where are you? What has happened to you?"

"I don't know, exactly." The voice came from behind where she was startling. She spun quickly, pointing the rifle, but there was only darkness there.

"There is something about this planet, this world. Maybe it's the air, the radiation from the sun, or a chemical in the rain, I don't know. Whatever it is, it has changed me. My mind is different. I don't think the same way anymore and I sense things that shouldn't be there. Maybe my brain has physically changed too, like my body. When Dendron first saw me, he was afraid of me, like I'm some kind of a monster. It was like when I first saw your dog, I thought he was a monster, too."

My dog? You mean, Lassie? Lassie is alive?"

"Lassie? You named your dog Lassie?" There was a trace of laughter in the voice that reached her from the darkness. "I don't believe it."

"I told you that was my name," the thought message from Dog informed him.

"Lassie doesn't sound like aoie," Savage responded.

"It does in the language I learned. I learned it so we could talk."

"From where did you learn it?"

"I don't know."

"Do dogs have a language?"

We do. Well, sort of a language. But as I think about it now, there wasn't much definitive communication among us. We just yelled at each other. Something happened to me after I got to this place."

"Yes, something happened to me, too."

"Yes, I called him Lassie," Diana was saying aloud. "Damian hated that name. He hated the TV series about Lassie, too. He used to tell me how stupid it was. I just did it to antagonize him. Oh, Lassie, come here. Let me see you. Come on. Let me see you." She lowered the weapon to lay across her knees as she knelt and held out her hand.

"You don't want to, Diana. Not yet, anyway."

"Why?"

"Tell me what happened at Palomar. Dendron said that a bunch of people got into the lab and shot him."

"Phil Dendron? He's here?" She looked around quickly before realizing how ridiculous it was.

"He was badly hurt, Diana, when he came through the Window."

"Where is he?"

"He died, Diana. I left his body for the plants. I thought it might stop anybody else from coming through."

"How horrible."

"He was dead, so it didn't make any difference. He didn't mind. Did you see them?"

"What?"

"The plants."

"No. They told me about them, after the mercenary had sent through just disappeared. I didn't know about Phil. Oh, I'm so sorry. He was such a nice kid."

"Somebody knew what happened to him. They were watching."

"I don't know, David. They haven't let me in the lab since—" She needed another way to tell him. This was right. "For the last couple of months. I didn't know anything until the other day. Damian said the police were here looking for you. Then he and Dr. Boucree got into a bitter argument about something. Damian wouldn't tell me, just said there might be a problem and Dr. Dendron might have to take over the project. That worried him.

"Then early in the morning about a week ago this bunch of mercenaries, some of them dressed in black camouflage, broke into the house. They were superbly trained and the raid well planned. They took out all the guards around and inside the house. Damian and I were in the lower hallway and we were taken hostage so they could use him to get into the lab. They shot him full of drugs to make him more cooperative and threatened to hill him if he didn't help them. Some of them were Japanese. I recognized the language."

"How could something like that happen? I thought security was very tight there."

"Mark, that little creep. He sold out, helped get them onto the estate and told them how to get into the underground complex.

DeShane tried to stop them and they shot him right there in the house."

"So DeShane's dead, too. Then what happened?"

"Damian told me about it later. Confused, pliable from the drugs and frightened by the threats, he got them into the complex past the guards on some pretext or other. I don't know. Then Dr. Boucree went berserk when he saw strangers in his lab taking pictures. He must have tried to get the camera away from them. They panicked and shot him. The security guards killed them and then locked the elevator at the bottom so nobody else could get in. It took a direct order from Mr. Getty to send it back up."

"What happened to you?"

"They put me in a car and took me to the landing field where they had a plane waiting."

"They were going to take you with them?"

"Yes. I'm sure that was part of the original plan."

"Why?"

"The day before I left Japan, I met a man. His name was Heroshi Tokushima. I'm sure he was behind the raid. He is a very rich and powerful man, and accustomed to getting anything he wants by any means possible. I believe they intended to smuggle me into Japan and keep me there for Tokushima."

"How is that possible? There are laws—"

"Things are very different there and, of course, there are drugs. They could get me addicted to narcotics, any number of ways to control me once they got me to Japan."

"How did you get away?"

"That's the ironic part. I escaped mainly because of Mark. He thought I would be going with him. Maybe that's what he had been told, but when they tried to put me on the plane, he realized what they were doing and he went nuts. He attacked them and I got loose. I got one with a kick to the knee that put him down and another with my elbow into the side of his face. Then this security guard, one of DeShane's men, his name was Dennis Adcock, I found out later, just appeared out of nowhere, drew his gun and opened fire hitting two of them. He was just there, crouching, legs spread, holding the gun in both hands and cranking off round after round. The rest jumped into the plane and escaped."

"What a disaster."

"Yes, but it wasn't supposed to be, I don't think. Initially it was reconnaissance's mission, not a search and destroy raid. Find out what was in the lab and kidnap me. It just went wrong and got way out of hand."

"So, what happened next?"

"Well, after the raid the police and the FBI moved in trying to get inside with search warrants and court orders. They were looking for you. Then they learned about the attack and maybe even something about the Window. But I don't think they know the lab is underground or how to get into it.

"The raid panicked everybody. Boucree was dead and Phil was missing. Everybody figured he went through the Window since there was nowhere else to go. They didn't tell me he was dead. The place was crawling with cops, Killingsworth or maybe even Mr. Getty got desperate and everything changed. They couldn't wait any longer for you to appear and yet they wouldn't let me go through so, they hired mercenaries. Hard, cold, professional men trained to fight and kill. Men that were expendable."

"Trained to kill without emotion, just like you were, Diana, in the harsh camp at Hidaka-sammyaku." It was a voice in her head, a thought in her mind, a memory of the past. Nothing more. Just a recollection of an event, a time in her life. Before she had time to grasp it and examine it, Savage was talking about something else.

"Phil, he said something about Warden Bennett being there, looking for me. Do you know anything about that?"

"What?"

"Warden Bennett."

"No, I don't know anybody named Bennett. Damian said there was just so much money involved and the project was so important, eventually somebody would find out. I guess they did."

"Bennett was the warden at the prison they got me out of. I guess she was just trying to redeem herself."

"I don't know anything about that. I was more concerned with getting through the Window to find you."

"Why did Getty finally let you come after the plants got the mercenary?"

"The flame-thrower was my idea. They were all afraid. Killingsworth, Getty, even the mercenaries. I don't blame them after what you just told me. I was afraid, too. I didn't know if you were still alive, what had happened to you. You were gone so long."

"How did they get the mercenaries to follow you through the Window?"

"I don't know for sure. Money, probably. I do know they were told that there was a tunnel behind the Window leading to the woods just behind the estate and what they were seeing was a magnified, telescopic image of the far end. They had no idea at all what was really happening or where they were being sent, and they sure didn't know they were going to another world from which they could never return."

"You were very brave to step through the Window not knowing what was here."

"I love you, David. I would go anywhere, risk anything to be with you. Don't you know that? I had to know if you were still alive."

"Obviously, I am."

"What are we going to do now?"

"I don't know."

"If the police get into the lab and the government finds about the Window and what it can do, how are we going to stop them from coming through?"

"I don't know that either."

"We've got to do something, David. We can't just let it happen."

Silence from the woods.

"David? David? Don't go away again. Answer me. David, don't do this to me. All you've done is ask questions. I want to know about you. What you've been doing this whole year here. What's happened to you? Where do you live? Is there anyone else here? David, please answer me!"

Getting no reply and not knowing what else to say, she fell silent and looked into the dancing flames of the fire, waiting for him to speak again. She didn't understand these periods of silence. It was very rude of him. Then, again, maybe he had gone. Left her again.

It was several minutes before she heard his deep voice, once again from a different location. He was slowly circling the camp so silently she couldn't hear his movements. "I found something, Diana. Hidden back up in a valley a long way from here. It's been there for a long time."

"What?"

"I don't know. A structure of some kind. Somebody built it so there is—or there was—intelligent life on this planet. I don't know what happened to them. Maybe they're still here and I just haven't found them yet. I can't explain it; I just sense it.

"So when it gets light, I want you to walk to the west, away from the morning sun. You'll find a vast plain. You can live there. There's food and water, and I'll always be close if you should need me."

"David, please come in. I need you now. I don't care what you think you've become. I've waited a whole year to be with you. Don't desert me now."

"I'll never leave you, Diana. I'll always be with you."

"David? Why are you hiding from me? Why won't you come in?" Softly, she began to cry.

After a time, she put more wood on the fire to light up the area around her. Sitting cross-legged with the rifle in her lap she continued to gaze into the fire, slowly becoming drowsy and falling to sleep where she sat. In the warmth of the blazing logs, she lay back and slept again.

The sky was light when she awoke. There was a slight chill in the air. She built up the fire and set about fixing breakfast of powered eggs, a small tin of canned ham and dehydrated orange juice. There was just barely enough water in the plastic container to reconstitute the food to normal. Along with a jacket slightly too large for her, a backpack for her gear had appeared sometime while she slept and she filled it with the packaged food while breaking camp. There was a canteen filled with fresh water and a complete first aid kit, both of which she attached to her belt. Somewhere out there in the trees, just beyond where she could see, watching her, was the man she had left the earth forever to be with but who now hid from her for reasons she couldn't even begin to comprehend. He had spoken of a structure and alien, intelligent life. Or had she been dreaming there by the fire and he had not spoken to her at all.

She covered the fire, packed her gear, slung the rifle over her shoulder and looked west, away from the rising sun. There, at the edge of the little clearing, a small chip had been cut from a tree. She walked toward it. A short distance away another blaze mark appeared and further on, still another. Through the long morning she followed the trail made for her, pausing only long enough to fix lunch and rest. Nightfall, she hoped, would bring him back to her and there would be more conversation between them, even if it was a dream. She had something very important to tell him.

As darkness finally approached, she stumbled exhausted into a small grassy hollow appearing suddenly before her in the dense woods and underbrush through which she fought her way. In the center, she found a little self-supporting tent already set up with firewood stacked beside a fire pit freshly dug. He had been there, anticipating, knowing where she would be. Dropping her pack she collapsed and lay resting from her long ordeal.

She built her fire, fixed and ate dinner, mixing the food concentrates in the folding skillet, and then lay down by the fire waiting for him to make his presence known to her. She was still amazed by the fact that he knew exactly where she would stop to spend the night.

"The divorce is final. I'm not married to Damian anymore. I wish we could have gotten married, David. You said you wanted to marry me. Do you still want to?"

She hugged her knees and tried to put the pull of gravity out of her mind. She would get used to it. She had to. This was her world now.

"We have a son, David," she said into the empty darkness around her. He was born almost four months ago. Dr. Worthington delivered him. I named him David Monroe Savage. I think he looks a little like you."

She was quiet for a long time, waiting for an answer. But only silence followed her remark.

"David, did you hear me? You have a son. Can't you say something?"

Still, nothing but silence around her.

"Don't you care?"

Silence. Once again she felt herself on the verge of tears.

"DeShane isn't dead," she continued, controlling her emotions and her voice, not knowing which way to look in the darkness surrounding her. "He was seriously wounded but he's recovering. He wants to come through the Window, too. He'll bring our son with him."

There was no reply, only the stillness and blackness of the forest beyond the firelight.

"The last I heard, Mr. Getty was still planning to come through the Window as soon as he's sure it's safe," she went on, hoping to draw him into conversation. "But now, I don't know with all the police and the turmoil there. I don't think they can get into the lab. I guess Damian will stay there. I can't imagine him want to come here to this primitive place."

More minutes passed in the same silence.

"David, will you tell me what's happened to you? Please. Why won't you let me see you? You said you've changed. Is it some kind of disease? Are you disfigured? Is that why you won't let me see you?"

Silence.

"I think I can handle it. If it's radiation or something like that, I've seen pictures. I can live with it. If it's a disease, we'll cope with it. David?"

Silence.

"Can you tell me how you've changed?"

"No. Not really." His voice came from the darkness, very close but just out of sight. "But you'll find out in time and you won't like what you see."

"Oh, David, you're here. I thought you were, but you didn't answer . . . your voice, it's a lot deeper, more powerful, different, somehow. I . . . I can't understand some of the words you say, it's like, you can't pronounce them," she said, looking around, trying to identify where he was, her heart beating faster at the sound of his words. "I almost didn't recognize it was you the first time you spoke."

"A lot of things are different here, Diana."

"Did you hear me when I told you we have a son? Don't you want to see him?"

"Yes, I heard you, and yes, I want very much to see him. But I don't think it will ever be possible."

"Why? Why would you say that?"

"I know, Diana. I just know. Please don't ask me how."

"I *am* asking. How do you know?"

When she got no answer she asked another question. "When do I get to see you? I gave up my child to come here and find you. David, we're going to spend the rest of our lives together here. No matter what you think you have become, it won't make much difference in the long run. Will it?"

"No. I suppose not." His voice was very soft and just a little sad as he spoke. "And you have a right to know, I guess, but just one shock at a time is enough. It might be hard to accept."

"Well, at least let me try."

"All right. Go to her, Λασσιε."

Diana sat up quickly, instantly alert, straining her eyes to penetrate the darkness beyond the small circle of firelight. Her heart was pounding in her chest as before.

Slowly into the firelight came a hulk, a huge shape almost the size of a Shetland pony with large, iridescent green eyes fixed upon her in a piercing gaze. Silver streaks flashed through the long, thick, sleek and glistening fur like static electricity, and gigantic paws made no sound on the forest floor as the animal warily approached her.

"My god," she whispered as she climbed slowly to her feet and took an involuntary step backward. "You . . . you're huge!"

The dog stopped a few feet from her and sat down on muscular haunches, waiting for her to find the courage to step forward and reach out a tentative hand.

"Are you Lassie?" She took small steps forward and held out her hand.

A short sniff of the extended fingers and Dog looked up into her face as she touched the broad head. There was intelligence in those deep green eyes and Diana trembled slightly as she withdrew her hand. "You remember me, don't you?"

Dog answered her but she didn't hear. So he lifted a huge paw and held it out to her, a simple trick she had taught him and one she would understand. After only a moment's hesitation, she took the paw in her hand, held it briefly, feeling its roughness then let it drop.

"I'm afraid of you. You know that, don't you. You don't look like Lassie anymore. You don't even look much like a dog."

Dog slowly got to his feet, walked a few steps away and lay on the ground facing her.

"You understand me too."

"Yes, he understands what you are saying, Diana," Savage's voice came to her from the trees. "And he can talk to you if you will listen."

"Oh, David, this is so fantastic. He's so big, and those huge teeth, they're like the prehistoric fangs of a Saber-tooth tiger. But a tiger is feline, dogs are canine. It doesn't make any sense."

"You are on another world, Diana. Nothing makes sense here."

"Ohhh."

"He will stay with you and guide you for the next few days, until you reach the plain. There are some things I have to do now but I'll meet you there. Get some sleep. It's a long trip."

"Oh, David, don't go. Please let me see you, just once."

"His name is Λασσιε but you can call him, Dog. He will tell you what to do. Don't be afraid. I'll be back."

Attempting to keep his attention and prevent him from leaving again, she rushed on. "It was Mark who sabotaged the plane." She listened for a minute and then went on. "DeShane found out about it and told me. He was trying to kill Damian so I would be free to marry him. It was he who tried to kill you, too. He thought you and I had already become lovers and he was crazy with jealousy. I didn't know it had gone that far, honest I didn't."

The big canine swung his massive head toward the dark woods, pointed ears erect and stared into the blackness for several seconds. Then, lowering his jaw onto his paws, he lay watching her and she knew David Savage was no longer there.

Preparing for bed and knowing their brief conversation was over, she took off her shoes and crawled into the tent with a lightweight thermal blanket over her. She knew she would not sleep, but she must rest to face tomorrow's trek. The forest was thick and traveling would be difficult and tiring.

Within the cramped confines of the tent, stripped down to her underwear she laid her head pillowed on her arm with the rifle beside her. Unaware that her troubled mind and jumbled thoughts were now being totally controlled, she was at peace and asleep in minutes.

CHAPTER TWENTY-EIGHT

I T RAINED VERY HARD during the night soaking everything, but she didn't hear it. She didn't feel the pull of the gravity, either. She slept more soundly than she had in months, until almost dawn when she emerged from the tent to find a fire burning brightly in the pit and Dog a short distance away watching her. She fixed herself a dehydrated breakfast and offered part of it to her dog, Lassie. She laughed when he looked away casually from the proffered skillet—turning up his nose, as it were—but then became deadly serious when she realized that he was behaving exactly like another *person* would. Not like an animal.

She broke camp early, loaded her gear and continued on west. With Dog just ahead and sometimes close beside her, she traveled toward the plain where David had promised to meet her. Continuing to marvel at the size and power of her animal companion, awed by his understanding of her wishes to stop, rest, slow down or linger over some strange, alien plant or bush, she slowly but steadily put mile after mile behind her. Rather than calling him Lassie, Dog was more—comfortable? Was that the word? David had called him something she couldn't even begin to pronounce but he said to call him Dog. That seemed to be his name so, she would call him Dog, too.

Savage did not come to her that night although she called out to him repeatedly. Finally Dog approached her and put a massive paw on her knee as she sat on the ground. He looked into her face with those glowing, intelligent eyes and she knew that David Savage was not there. He was nowhere even close, but he was somehow aware of her. With that came another revelation.

How did she know that? Did Dog tell her? Could an animal communicate by some means nobody knew about? David had said he would talk to her if she would listen. A little more afraid now, she fixed her meal and prepared to spend another night.

There was no fire and no wood when she awoke. He had not been there during the night. Had it not been for Dog, she might have begun to doubt that he had ever been there at all. It was a hallucination brought on by something in the air that was becoming easier and easier to accept. Except for Dog.

It took them seven days to reach the edge of the forest, walking around the deadfalls, through gullies, over the ridges and hills, skirting thickets filled with thorns and brambles that barred their way. The blaze marks were no longer there but she didn't need them, now. She had Dog. Along the way, she had smelled flowers, a wonderful aroma of thousands of blooms inviting her to come smell and look. For some reason, however, Dog would not let her turn in the direction of the delightful odor wafting along on the breeze. Standing in her way each time she turned toward the source of the smell, the animal succeeded in making her finally give up and continue on toward the west. She would ask David about that.

She couldn't handle the fifteen-hour days and had to stop and rest many times. Once, at noon and once in the early afternoon, she just quit and set up her camp. The night were even worse, stretching for twenty hours wherein she sat beside her fire or lay awake in the tent listening for his voice to come to her from the Forrest.

Although she was slowly becoming more accustomed to it, the gravity and the backpack pulled her down and tired her out. Thinking herself to be in pretty good physical condition after the birth of her son, she criticized herself for her weakness. It was the same as in Hidaka-sammyaku where she was faced with a harsh environment. She had survived that, and she would survive this. She wondered how David, without the weight training and not knowing about the gravity, had been able to survive those first few ways so successfully.

Why wouldn't he show himself? What about his eyes? With everything that had happened, she had completely forgotten about his sight. Maybe that was it. He was blind and stumbling around in the woods, afraid to let her see.

She had told him that she could live with his deformity, disease, radiation, blindness, whatever it was. She would live with it. She had no choice. As far as she knew, they were the only two human beings on the planet. She could live with that.

He had not answered any of Palomar's questions about the radiation level here. So they had put their own Geiger counter through the Window, watching in horror as the needle swung immediately to the red, danger level. Could it be lethal radiation? Was David dying and didn't want her to know?

Dog didn't seem to show any effects of radiation poisoning, though. Other than his size, he was still her Lassie. Well, his size, the tusks, the intelligence and about a dozen other things.

It was almost noon of the seventh day when she finally broke through the last of the trees and underbrush and first viewed the endless expanse of waving grass and rolling knolls of the seemingly limitless plain. As she stood there looking, she felt that it must have been the same with the first American explorers who left the eastern forests to gaze out over Iowa, Kansas and Nebraska, Oklahoma and Texas. Bowie, Daniel Boone, Lewis and Clark and a thousand others who had never before seen such vast wide-open spaces.

In the open for the first time, the huge, bright sun poured down its heat on her head and shoulders. Dropping the heavy backpack, she sat on the ground to rest, then found a spot in which to make camp, determined to stay right here until David appeared. He had said, go to the plain. Well, she was here and she wasn't going any further.

She set up the tent only a few yards from the edge of the forest and she dug the fire pit deep in the soft ground. She was hungry but had little taste for the dehydrated food. She needed to hunt for something to eat and she was almost out of water. Her body had not yet adjusted to the long days and nights so she was almost asleep on her feet at midday and wide awake in the middle of the night.

Returning from the tree-line, she was carrying an armload of wood to her camp to build her fire when she noticed that Dog was gone. One minute he was lying on the ground watching her. The next, he wasn't there. She looked for him and she called out but he didn't come. Sounds familiar. She spent the remainder of the afternoon alone fixing her camp for the night with the M-16 slung over her shoulder.

It was early evening as she sat beside the fire pit just waiting, watching the sun go slowly down and light up the clouds with crimson and gold, just like on Earth. She was absent-mindedly shaving a branch with her knife, more for something to occupy the time than anything else, as she prepared kindling to start her morning fire. She had not laid out anything to fix to eat. She just waited. Another long stroke of the sharp blade added one more sliver to the growing pile between her knees.

There was no sound, nothing she had heard that would cause her to look up from whittling on the stick. It could have been movement, some motion at the corner of her eye that attracted her attention, but in retrospect, she didn't think so. From deep within her own thoughts of worry, despair and concern for the man she had come here to find, she raised her head to see Dog emerge from the woods almost directly in front of her. Walking a short distance behind him there was something, something very big.

Forgotten, the stick and the knife dropped from her hands as she climbed slowly to her feet only to be paralyzed by what she saw approaching her with slow steps. Towering over her with wild tangles of white hair and beard about his head and face, massive shoulders above a broad, rippling chest of bulging muscles, the near naked figure stopped only a few feet away. The huge thing was ageless, not young, not old and certainly not human.

Burning green eyes bore into hers with a look that was both wild and primitive yet intelligent beyond anything she could imagine or understand. The bottom part of his face, under the beard, was square and corded with powerful muscles. From his mouth, she saw long canine teeth, sharp fangs curving down from his upper jaw just like the killing teeth of the animal at his side.

A quiver of three-foot arrows with thick shafts and fletched with ten-inch guide feathers protruded over the creature's right shoulder, a massive recurved bow was clutched in its—his—left hand and the twelve-inch hunting/fighting knife hung from a cord around his waist. He wore only a brief loincloth above dark, thick, muscular thighs, massive as tree trunks to support the four hundred pound bulk of the giant, tusked creature standing before her.

"This is what I have become, Diana," the mouth-full of sharp teeth and fangs said to her. "You wanted to see, and now you have."

"Oh . . . my . . . God!" She tried to take a step backward and almost stumbled. Regaining her balance she said, "Are you David?"

"No. I once was. I don't know what I am now."

A huge right hand reached down to casually stroke the head of Dog, the gigantic omnivorous monster who sat beside him watching her with the same intelligent, glowing green eyes.

"I'm not human anymore, Diana. I'm something alien to Earth and to the people I once knew. I've become a creature created by this world, formed and changed and shaped to survive here. I'm retrograde evolution speeded up a million times and I will continue to change into whatever I'm supposed to be.

"Knowing how I appear to you, I admire your courage just to stand and look at me, this thing that I am, while you remember the man I once was. I can see the fear of me in your mind."

"You . . . you know what is in my mind, what I'm thinking?"

"Yes."

"How can you do that?"

"I don't know, but I can. Your thoughts, your feelings, your emotions are as clear to me as if you had spoken of them to me. It's part of what I have become, what I am now. And I am no longer speaking to you. There is no sound. The words you hear are in your mind."

"My God! You're telepathic."

"I just wanted you to see me, Diana and to know what I am. Now look behind me, then turn and look behind *you*."

Emerging from the woods, moving slowly but steadily over and around the uneven ground, the fallen branches and the thick undergrowth were a dozen of the tall, carnivorous plants, their long tentacle-like roots carrying them forward. Stopping ten feet away they formed a half circle around him and Dog and then stood motionless, their flowered heads all turned in his direction. Looking over her shoulder, she saw another dozen or more coming through the tall grass of the plain. In the far distance there were still more.

"The plants!" she exclaimed

"They won't harm you, Diana. They understand who and what you are, and you will be safe. Don't attempt to hurt them. There is no need. I will show you how to find food and water, which direction to follow, and you will survive. We'll go now and we won't bother you again, but we'll always be close by to help—"

"David," she said, summoning all of her courage and taking a step forward. "David, don't go away. Stay with me. Don't leave me alone here. I won't be afraid of you anymore." She took another step toward him.

"Fear is not something you can control that easily, Diana. Right now, you are calling up every bit of your courage just to approach me, attempting to overcome your fright." His mouth did not move but the words to continued to sound in her conscious mind, much more clearly than when he had spoken them aloud. "And I perceive that you *will* overcome it, in time. But I discern also that you continue to think of me as someone you once knew, not what I am now."

"You still *are* someone I know, David, no matter what you look like now. You are the man I fell in love with, the man I love now. You are our son's father. Oh, don't you see, David, you've become everything I have ever imagined, everything a man could ever be for me. You're Hercules and Tarzan, the king of the world and every woman's dream of a man to possess her. Can't you see that?"

Her pace quickened and she walked quickly to him, looking up into his bearded face, reaching out and up to grasp his towering form about the bulging biceps of his powerful arms. It was as though she had taken hold of steel bars. Standing on her toes, she reached up even further and with trembling fingers touched his face and the long, curved, pointed fangs.

"Yes, I'm still afraid of you now, but I'll overcome it just like I did with Dog. I'm not afraid of him anymore. In time, I'll change too, David. I'll become what you are now, what Dog is. When our son comes through the Window, he too will change and be like us."

He let the bow fall to the ground and grasped her around the waist with huge, muscle-corded hands, lifting her effortlessly into the air, raising her face level with his. "Diana—" The words formed in her mind and the fanged mouth opened.

"No, David, you are not going to get away from me again. I won't let you. I know you now. I have seen you before. You are the man creature from my secret dreams who saved my life at Hidaka-sammyaku."

"How can that be?"

"I don't know, but it was you I saw there. I'm certain of it. Now we are here and this is our world, yours and mine and we'll be together for as long as we both shall live in this Garden of Eden."

Dog reared on his haunches, standing as tall as the man, and placed a massive, clawed paw on his shoulder. The huge tusked head level with theirs, the glowing green eyes looking one to the other with a knowledge beyond human understanding.

The plants stood, listened, and understood.

Diana reached, strained to wrap her arms around his neck and entwine her fingers in his long tangled hair. Leaning forward, she touched his mouth with her soft, hot kiss, feeling his lips and savoring the flavor. She felt the tremendous strength of his huge body and the limitless power of his mind searching hers, aware of the animal beside them and the plants around them feeling and sharing all of it with their unique ability.

Something began to very subtly change in her mind, in her personality and her very being. She was completely unaware of it and would probably never be consciously aware that it had happened.

Her soul, the very essence of her being, her training as the deadly Ninja who would kill without a regret and who feared nothing, even death, slowly faded away. The aggressive, dominating, win at all costs woman who talked and fought like a man was slowly being replaced by a one who was agreeable and almost subservient, the absolutely perfect mate and wife.

Then, for the first time since she came through the Window, in the depths of her subconscious mind and then in her conscious thoughts, only for a fleeting instant, she sensed and was aware of the awesome presence of the alien intelligence that inhabited this world and surrounded them all. It was at that precise moment a hundred million light years distant in space, fifty thousand centuries away in time, somewhere in a different universe on another atomic level, in an underground laboratory on a continent in the Western Hemisphere of a small planet called Earth, there was a small flash of light. A bright spark arced across a dusty circuit to heat and then melt a tiny wire buried in a maze of electronic equipment and break that circuit. The Window in The World, the portal through space, distance and time, shimmered, flickered, faded and then winked out of existence forever.

THE END

EPILOGUE

WHEN THE POLICE AND government agents finally obtained entry to the underground laboratories at Palomar, what they found was two empty metal frames set into bare rock walls, a mass of electronic equipment, the purpose for which, they were told, was research and experimentation with three-dimensional television. They found no fugitive escaped murderer and had no justification to confiscate the equipment. All of the scientific notes and experimental procedures were copied however and sent to MIT for study. After two years of trials and spending many thousands of dollars, it was abandoned as too costly to perfect and of little commercial value.

Damian Killingsworth, only slightly wounded in the initial assault, used his legal knowledge to avoid any involvement in David Savage's escape and J. Paul Getty's vast wealth and power allowed him to move the foundation to Argentina where his attempts, without Dr. Boucree, to create another Window were unsuccessful. He eventually died at the age of 155, unknown and unlamented, amid the Earth's pollution and overpopulation from which he had sought so desperately to escape.

Warden Bennett was taken into custody for her own protection and committed to an institution in an attempt to cure her drug addition and her insane obsession with finding David Savage. Only two months into her treatment, she died of a brain aneurysm brought on by her past excessive use of drugs and alcohol.

DeShane recovered from his wounds, accompanied the project from Southern California to central Argentina where he remained chief of security for Palomar for another twenty years. Lavishing his attention on Diana's orphaned child as, strangely enough, did John Paul Getty, one referring to himself as Uncle and the other Granddad. Years after the boy was sent away to boarding school, DeShane felt genuine remorse when the old man died and the project was terminated.

The huge fanged creatures of the planet beyond the Window, on the world they had named Eden, continued to evolve over the many centuries of their vast life span into still another and different intelligent life form. They and their many children eventually discovered the secrets of the Stonehenge structure in the valley by the stream, learning that it was an intricate, sophisticated, powerful and highly technical matter transmitter capable of instantly sending objects to anywhere in any of the atomic universes. It was a highly advanced and more powerful version of the Window. It was also a relay station, catching and retransmitting signals and transporting life forms throughout the universes, through space, time and dimensions to places and worlds in the past and in the future. For reasons they never learned, the device worked only in the absence of the light from the sun and on certain cycles of the moon from apogee to perigee.

For the hundredth time, he stood in the moonlight within the Stonehenge enclosure and examined with his new eyes the tens of thousands of symbols, finally discovering the one he had looked at before but somehow had not seen. He had overlooked it completely, probably because it was so familiar that it just didn't register in his mind, but when he finally did discover it, it was breathtaking because he recognized it immediately.

Only a short time thereafter, he also found that he could read the mysterious writing etched into the row of symbols.

ΔΙΡΕΧΤΙΟΝΣ   ΦΟΡ ΥΣΕ

Τουχη ανδ ηολδ τηε σψμβολ ρεπρεσεντινγ ψουρ δεστινατιον.

What the writing said, was:

DIRECTIONS FOR USE

Touch and hold the symbol representing your intended destination.

During the next twenty-six thousand years that David and Diana lived on Eden and roamed the planets and the star systems of their universes and the countless universes from the microscopic to the gigantic using the transmitter, the Doorway or the Window— the terms were interchangeable—created by another race from another time in another dimension, they encountered many forms of life, some intelligent, but none in advance of themselves. But most of what they found were primitive, animal-like and only on the verge of becoming reasoning, thinking beings. And, to their disappointment, never in all of their travels through all of the universes did they find the inventors of the Doorway, nor did they find creatures they had once known as Man except on the remote planet Earth that David had occasion to visit only three times.

The first time was in the Earth year 1859 in the high mountains of Tibet where the Window sent them and they appeared to a small group of villagers. He asked what year it was but they couldn't understand him. So terrified were the villagers of the giant shapes suddenly appearing amid the wind-blown snow, they could remember only one sound from the fanged mouths. That the one word was year and that's what the simple mountain villagers called them, pronouncing it as best they could in their own language, Yeti.

Again, in 1920 near the small town of Prince George in British Columbia, David Savage was seen near a logging camp where he approached a bunch of men just sitting down at outdoor benches and tables to have their dinner. Again, he asked what year it was.

They panicked. Overturning benches and food plates, all of them ran, later describing him as a "wild, hairy creature of the woods." In Canadian, the term was Sasquatch. The Indians just called him the Bigfoot.

One last time David Savage touched the symbol, felt the tingle in his hand, activated the window/doorway and visited the Earth. He appeared in the Hidaka-sammyaku Mountains of Hokkaido, Japan where he rescued from starvation and certain death a beautiful young woman who called herself Fumiko Fuchida.

The intelligent, carnivorous plants of Eden also evolved over the millennia becoming more mobile and more diverse in their diet. Some of their saw-tooth leaves became round, slender appendages ending in short, multiple tentacles capable of closing, grasping, holding and wielding. Eventually developing a simple form of audible communication, they retained only a portion of their ability to converse telepathically. Banding together in larger and larger groups, they became the dominant life form on the planet. They hunted, planted, gathered, built structures, created roads and cities and became civilized. In time, they constructed vehicles in which they flew into space to explore other worlds. They found the structure in the remote, almost inaccessible valley by the stream and marveled at its construction. They never, however, learned the purpose of the window or how to use it. It was as much of a mystery to them as Stonehenge is to 20th century Earthmen.

His housing and education in Switzerland and Germany and later at Yale and then later still at MIT, his clothes, his cars and all his expenses paid by a mysterious organization known as the Palomar Foundation—even the name was now only a distant childhood memory—Doctor David Monroe Savage excelled in his profession to become a world renowned physicist and mathematician. Although a tall, handsome man attractive to women tasting often of their charms, he remained a much sought-after bachelor devoting his energies to his profession.

On his fortieth birthday, he received a small package in the mail containing twenty-five old fashioned computer disks. The return address was that of a predominant Washington, D.C. law firm. When he called to inquire about it, he was told that the package had been left with the firm for safe keeping almost twenty years ago with instructions to deliver it on this date. Along with the disks, there was a brief, handwritten note. It said simply, "Dr. Savage, I had the pleasure of knowing your mother. She would have wanted you to have these." It was signed, Damian Killingsworth, Attorney at Law.

The disks contained scientific secrets beyond anything he had ever imagined and after years of experimentation using the information contained upon them, with three lasers and a control board he was eventually able to recreate and operate a version of the Window in the World. It earned him additional fame, a financial fortune and a Nobel Prize, and it rendered the space exploration telescope obsolete. Although through the Window he had created he could see other worlds, nothing could pass through to them.

He spent the remaining years of his life searching through space and time and dimensions with the marvelous invention, cataloging many life forms and hundreds of planets which eventually spaceships might visit, providing the world with scientific knowledge that would send Earthmen to the stars, but he never discovered the wonderful world called Eden or the parents he never knew. For tragically, they and Eden were no longer there for him to find.

Long before he was born, toward the end of World War Two, United States President Franklin Roosevelt appointed Dr. J. Robert Oppenheimer and a German mathematician named Albert Einstein to help unlock the secret power of the atom first conceived by Nazi scientists. With almost inconceivable irony, one of the very few outside of the government scientists who knew about and participated in the project was millionaire oilman, J. Paul Getty.

On the morning of July 16, 1945, in the desert at White Sands, New Mexico, a date significant in Earth history and also in time on a parallel universe in another dimension, a nuclear fission device was detonated atop a tall tower. In the instant of that terrible, hellish explosion, David and Diana Savage, their children, all of the life, the civilizations and the advanced intelligence of all the worlds and the stars and galaxies in the whole subatomic universe to which the Window had sent them, existing entirely within the nucleus of one U-235 atom, vanished in a horrible, instantaneous, micro-second conflagration of raging, writhing atomic fire.

> "All things by immortal power, near or far,
> Hiddenly to each other linked are,
> That thou canst not stir a flower
> Without troubling of a star."
>
> Francis Thompson
> 1859-1907